Hostage

"Do we, do we have coffee made, or, uh, something for dessert?" I felt my initial panic in the car returning.

"Coffee later," Bernie Cascone said, his hand on my shoulder, one finger tucked into the hemmed neckline of my silk shirt. "I'll have to leave for the airport in less than an hour. Let's have dessert right now." The words had rushed out of him, breathy and hoarse, almost.

I felt my resolve to remain platonic with the detective deconstructing. I turned in his arms as effortlessly as if sliding from backstroke to crawl in deep water. I faced him, rested my hands on his biceps. Nice, hard. A slight stain of red sauce on his chin, his brown eyes glowing like hot coals caught at me. So very human. And alive. I reached up around his neck and he engulfed me.

"Should we, can we, mmm, close the deal?" I heard his manly voice vibrate through my skull.

I tried to push the word out, *no*, and realized all the while I was nodding, *yes*, against the press of his lips on my forehead, cheeks, and chin. We half-danced, half-flew toward the other end of the apartment, still entwined.

Just before he began unbuttoning my blouse in the dimly lit bedroom he gazed down at me with a guilty expression only half-hidden by the warmth of passion on his face.

"Have to tell you something," he said. "I lied."

"What? Danny wasn't on the plane after all?"

"Shut up," he said. "That topic is off limits. No, this is worse."

Just when I got nervous, he told me the truth.

"I didn't make the *Osso Buco*. My mother-in-law did, and packed it for me to take home. She keeps saying I should meet someone nice. I think I just did."

The bubble of laughter I felt welling up never got loose. But as it rose and ballooned, it managed to bury my fear, my tension, the last crumbs of my reluctance. As he pressed me down gently on the bed, his lips on mine kept the bubble trapped and jitterbugging inside me for a long, long time.

What They Are Saying About

Hostage

Eleanor Sullo's above average who-done-it, *The Menopause Murders: Hostage,* has enough twisting intrigue and bold suspense that you won't be able to put this book down. Her unique multi-character presentation is sometimes hard to follow, when all six main characters are written in first person, however, I found this exceptionally well crafted suspense, told in an entertaining tongue-in-cheek humor, well worth the effort. By all means treat yourself. Get this book. It will keep you laughing and rooting for this group of ladies as they brave their fears, and boldly strive to protect one another against the injustices of the world.

Six menopausal ladies, and long time friends, wearing gaudy accessories, set out to create a club called "The Women Of Fire." Before they can even get their new organization off the ground someone has the audacity to kill the gardener...and slap this group of older ladies around...very ungentlemanly. But who knew enough about Ada's wealth to try to frighten her into handing over all her money? And why? Yet, things get even stranger than just a bumbling robber when these girls start unearthing all the clues to who is really behind this nefarious plot. These six long-time friends are a force to be reckoned with when it comes to dealing with the men in their lives.

I truly enjoyed this highly suspenseful plot. It will keep you guessing all the way to the very last page.

JoEllen Conger
Conger Book Reviews

Wings

Menopause Murders
HOSTAGE

by

Eleanor Sullo

A Wings ePress, Inc.

Encore L'Amour Novel

For Lydia,
Happy writing!
Ellie
Eleanor Sullo Wings
Sept. 2010

Wings ePress, Inc.

Edited by: Christie Kraemer
Copy Edited by: Rosalie Franklin
Senior Editor: Christie Kraemer
Executive Editor: Marilyn Kapp
Cover Artist: Pat Evans

All rights reserved

Wings ePress Books
http://www.wings-press.com

Copyright © 2009 by Eleanor S. Sullo
ISBN 978-1-59705-510-9

Published In the United States Of America

February 2010

Wings ePress Inc.
403 Wallace Court
Richmond, KY 40475

Dedication

For Yvette, a woman of strength and joy, who
left us too soon.

A *Glossary of* Menopause Murder *Characters*

Hannah—The attractive, streaky-blonde journalist has been scared to death of flying since her husband died in a plane crash thirty years ago. Although smart, sassy and sophisticated, she lost her job because of this crippling fear, and faces older age with a dread of loneliness. Finally listening to her emotions, she's shaking the pain of her past by counseling grieving children, and allowing herself to face, instead of merely dazzling accomplishments, a future of relationships, and a sexy new lover.

Lucia—The warm, loving and charismatic "Mama" of the group, dark eyed and frizzy haired Lu feels everybody's pain and tries to "fix" them all. But as a reincarnated Demeter, chained to the forge, her nurturing Neapolitan heart sometimes feels too big for her small life. If she could "redo" her past and open her own restaurant, the stage of her life may stretch to hold her and her brilliant cheffing skills—but only her beloved Tony is at her side.

Ada—Rich and powerful, owner of a travel agency, used to having men cave at her command but bitterly betrayed by some of them in the past and present, she uses her class and overwhelming wealth to shore up her less-moneyed friends and sometimes buy her way in life. Yet as the fashionable, silvery-gray haired inspiring "queen" of the group, Ada realizes the tragedies that strike seem to make her the most vulnerable of all. Can she wean herself from old crippling attitudes and become unselfish and independent after all?

Dorie—Skipping her way through life, this impetuous charmer's wacky logic and malapropisms often hit the mark. An accomplished artist, she's impetuous, impulsive, intuitive, and hungry for love, and, after leaving an abusive relationship, the tall and beautiful, platinum blonde Goldie Hawn-look-alike is determined to become a mature and respected companion.

Meg—Small and gray-haired Meg is plain, stern, slightly stodgy, but beneath her plainness shines a quirky sense of humor and a luminosity both as a friend and a retired forensic scientist. Her sad expression betrays the scars of her youth spent in war-torn Bosnia and her unhappy childlessness, but she knows she can't hide behind her intellect forever.

Theo—Spunky and committed, some would say "bossy" Theo, a newly wed step-mom, is as dependable and respected as the former Mother Superior she was for three decades. She inspires the spiritual vitality of the group. Too bad everyone but herself counts on ultra-serious, highly moral, classic-looking, 'groomed-to-a-T' Theo for her wisdom. And too bad she can't break from her old scrupulosity and throw caution to the wind, once in a while.

"Change of life is the time when you meet yourself at the crossroads and you decide whether to be honest or not before you die."

Katherine Butler Hathaway

Prologue

His hand, on the gun in the Armani jacket pocket, trembled as he stepped onto the lawn.

On this mild spring morning, the metal grip and snub-nosed barrel felt surprisingly cold. Alright, so he'd never actually shot it. But today even the sight of a weapon should make a loud statement, and solve his problem.

His ongoing, tiresome, demeaning little problem.

The birds chirped, a regular choir, and as he rounded the corner, the low-slanting sun nearly blinded him. His knees shook as he stepped forward.

The bushes moved, and he saw the old man's back as he worked in the foliage, heard the thwack of the clippers. The clippers paused, and the worker turned, a quick glance over his shoulder.

Enough. Enough dilly-dallying. Move.

Time to make his point and get out of here. He sucked in air, held it, yanked the gun from his pocket, twisted his hand around the barrel and raised it high so the old guy would see it. Maybe pee his pants.

But the man in the bushes did more than that; his whole body twitched, his hat fell to the side as he started to rise, thrusting himself backward defensively. Or preparing to strike.

The man with the gun gasped. He jerked forward, slammed the butt of the Smith and Wesson onto the balding head throwing the figure to the ground.

That ought to adjust an attitude or two.

"You old bastard," he muttered, "going to ignore me now?" But the old fellow didn't answer. Not listening. Not even moving. The attacker bent and placed two moist fingers on the carotid artery and nearly threw up.

Nothing.

Wait. This wasn't the plan. Just meant to scare him off. *Not—Christ!—kill him.*

Around him, the feathered choir had resigned, the air turned chilly. A car engine whined in the distance, coming closer up the hill. A jet out of Bradley gained altitude with a commanding roar. Bradley…Yes, had to hurry.

The weapon pressed like a hundred pound brick in his hand, screaming, accusing. What the hell had he done? What could he do now?

He breathed, steeled himself and wiped off the gun on the edge of the Armani. Then remembered Part B of his plan.

Alright, okay. I'm covered after all.

A crooked smile creased his face as he dropped the revolver onto the grass.

He'd almost forgotten his ace in the hole.

One

Hannah

I have to confess murder was definitely on my mind that day, and anybody watching me wipe the flood of perspiration from my face and neck would have been suspicious. Sure, it was embarrassing going beet red and folding tissues up under my bangs and behind my ears to absorb the sudden floods that were driving me to distraction. *Or to drink,* I mused, taking another sizable sip of my icy cold Riesling.

Because murder and mayhem were front and center on my mind, despite the discomforting sheen of menopausal sweat all over me, I had to commandeer the table where I could see the front door and the entire restaurant floor. Pino's is the number-one luncheon venue on LaBelle Road in Fantasy-land, where I live, a perfect community of old money and fervid-come-latelies. My journalistic imaginings told me somebody here was always doing something with someone that bore further investigation. Notice those secret looks between couples at corner tables; hear the muffling of their voices among the spiffy businessmen when the server came near.

Somebody was riding the road to Gomorrah out there, and while I waited for my three errant friends, I narrowed my eyes over my wine glass and prayed to figure out who and what. My desperation was understandable. Times were tough, and I needed the money. If I didn't get to California in three weeks, I'd miss my chance for at least a year-and-a-half to see my new, one-and-only grandchild. And newborn babies grow a lot in a year-and-a-half.

I had to get there fast, before my son's little family took off for an assignment in Japan, but airplanes were out of the question. A train, or Greyhound, maybe? Still, cross-country tickets cost, and I was broke. I hadn't sold a freelance piece in weeks; which was why I needed a hot story, right now, today, that would make my old Courant editor salivate. Sex, maybe, or murder. Both very salable.

I pictured myself sailing out of here on Monday's Accela, and when I did, a huge lump started jiggling in my throat. I couldn't leave the Brennan boy, the Selvig twins, and all those other kids who counted on me at the Mary-Martha Center for too long, so I not only had to put the trip together fast, I had to get back even faster. We had a big workshop planned for the Grief Center in two weeks, and those kids needed me there.

"Aunt Hannah," they'd say, "you made us promise we'd come, then you didn't. You stayed home."

The lump went deeper. *Admit it*, I thought in a freaking moment of sun-bright honesty that made me cringe, I needed them as much as they needed me. Those lovable, fragile kids.

I washed down my worrisome lump with white wine and studied the room again. I mean, someone had to be guilty of something.

My gaze moved over them like a security camera, relentless, sweeping the room, while giving up on soggy tissues and going for the corner of the nice, thick, linen napkin. One quick swoop around the neck under my hair, one down either side of my blistering cheeks. I exchanged waves and Mona Lisa smiles with a pair of whispering older women across the way, high level gals at Town Hall, heads bent together, though their eyeballs seemed locked in my direction. I squirmed, hoping my retro-safari suit didn't show its age, then watched a group of four familiar-looking businessmen enter, nod my way, take their seats and wait for the server to leave them before they exchanged muted conversation.

Something being conspired there, for sure. Maybe next weekend's golf game, after all.

Most noticeable and conspicuous of all was the middle-aged couple in the corner who turned their backs to the room when I nonchalantly pinned them with my gaze. I didn't recognize either one, but I had a sense there was more than sweet, uncomplicated romance going on over those glasses of red wine and petite filets.

Adultery? Intrigue?

Had to be a story in here somewhere. Something juicy I could sell for the price of a quick train ticket to California, something like corruption, lust or greed involving well-known personages. Of course, murder would be the best. Imagine, a murder I discovered and for which I had the inside track. One that would sell my free-lance piece to the papers as quickly as my semi-annual manicure took to dry.

I got so twisted by the possibilities, by the time my friends arrived I was actually praying for a murder, but hoping it wouldn't cause the injured party pain, and that he or she deserved it and didn't leave behind any kids. Otherwise I'd get to meet and fall in love with those kids at the Grief Center later and cry my eyes out, not in front of them, of course, but at the end of every day when our "groups" were over.

Cold, Hannah. That's what you are, wishing for a death: cold.

I mentally slapped myself and that quickly cleared the hot flash, sending shivers down my back. I tried to erase my previous wish for slaughter, but I knew my future prospects in heaven had definitely been compromised. Then I glanced out the window and saw two of my friends being blown my way in a stiff April breeze. A great distraction from my own evil meanderings.

I wondered why Ada, the guest of honor, wasn't hurrying down the street along with them.

Ada was never late. The rest of us were; she wasn't. So was this sudden variation on our theme a sort of divine punishment for my cruel and unusual hopes about the customers of Pino's? *Nah,* I thought, perking up as the wind slammed the door behind Dorie and Lucia.

You just can't count on people anymore.

Two

Ada

I swung the Town Car in through the extra wide garage doors with practiced ease, wondering where Raul was working. His truck was there at the side of the garage, but no sign of my gardener anywhere. What was wrong with him lately? He wasn't himself; mopey, withdrawn. Usually he bubbled over with ideas for my gardens, chatted about this or that he'd planted at his other clients' and anticipated chores that needed doing.

Huh! Money worries? Kid problems? I parked and extracted my packages from the back seat, sniffing the air, wondering if Raul was out back, burning those branches he'd pruned weeks ago. But all I could smell was the fragrance of the fresh strawberries I'd bought at Healthy Foods.

When I discovered the breezeway door wide open, I felt my cheeks flame with shame.

"Oh, shoot, I'm not over the mid-life madness after all," I muttered aloud. "I've forgotten to close and lock the door again. Happy old age to me."

At the peak of menopause I had needed tranquilizers, anti-depressants, occasional therapy and daily doses of

7

high quality chocolate to overcome my forgetfulness. It was that awful sense of increased mental flab—confusion, forgetting important details, crying over anything that went the least bit wrong—that had made me turn over the Travel Agency to Theo's management when my friend came home from 30 years in the convent. That and the fact my second husband's sexual transgressions had kept me in a constant state of self-doubt and self-recriminations for almost two years.

Until his early demise six months ago spared me a further downward decline.

I placed the box of strawberries on the counter and bent to sniff their sweet perfume. California of course, not local, but what the hey? Still delicious. I wondered if I could convince my weekly cleaning woman Chantal to render them into something serious, like shortcake, Charlotte Ruse or jam.

I turned and stared at the door I'd found unlocked and felt a quivering in my gut. How could I have...

No, dammit, I had not left the door unlocked. I specifically remembered turning the key.

Didn't I?

And where was Jethro, my cat, who always came running to rub against my legs and snag my stockings or slacks when I returned home? I'd better hurry up and find him before I had to leave for the great lunch my friends had planned for me.

I called his name. "Jethro. Here, kitty."

Silence. Too much of it.

Was something else wrong besides the open door?

I stood stock still, my brain scrambling to identify any possible differences in the house: sights, sounds, smells. There must be a logical answer, a reason.

Then why the prickles up my neck, the catch in my throat? Had I come home to something way worse than an old bubbe's blunder?

Three

Hannah

"You're late, ladies," I waved at two of the three empty seats. "But sit. Ada's not here yet anyway. Never mind the time—if you have good news, I can sure use it. So, what, Dorine? Did Bruce Jenkins like your art work?"

As always, Dorie, as the resident artiste, fluttered into her chair in a heap of flowing chiffon, luscious velvet and gold spangles. Though tall, she seemed to crumple into something small and cuddly when she sat, her upswept hair of platinum with hints of silver drifting down around her long, aristocratic face.

"He was be-smooched, especially by the pot scrubbers." Dorie tried not to giggle.

I gave her a scolding-mother stare, but Dorie had a huge propensity for forgiveness and didn't change expressions.

"What on earth does that mean?" I asked. "He liked it? He's going to use it? What pot-scrubbers?"

Lucia took over in her no-nonsense way, smoothing down her sensible taupe pantsuit jacket while she made a grab for the menu. It was never too early for Lu to order. She, too, caught my impatient glance.

"In all honesty, Han, it's one of the best things Dorie's ever done. A huge collage of fabric, paint and paper forming a gorgeous bejeweled Everywoman emerging from the sea, all pink and purple, aqua and emerald. Fabulous."

"But she had no boobs at all, so Lu suggested these bright pink pot scrubbers I had at my sink." Again Dorie tried to suppress her laughter. "Not that I've ever used them on pots. I just thought they were pretty, so I bought them. A perfect use for them. And the best thing about collages is anything goes."

Lu poked her. "They sure worked for you in your art. Wonderfully."

"Sounds like the perfect touch," I said. "Domestic but sexy."

Lu told me I'd better go by and see it. "Right in the front window of his trendy little lingerie shop, with a card crediting Dorine and giving her website. Now what's good today?" Lucia made serious efforts to settle her ample backside in the chair and focus on the pasta specials.

I eyeballed Dorine. "But bottom line, honey, did he pay you?"

She patted her old tapestry bag with affection. "He did, so I'm treating today."

"Something from the bar?" the bored waiter asked, more intent on a passing male Adonis outside the window.

"I'll have what she's having," Lucia said, pointing to my depleted wine glass. "And, no, you're not treating,

Dor, it's Dutch treat, except for us paying for Ada's birthday lunch. In fact, we should be treating you, too."

"Ma'am?" The waiter jiggled his pencil and eyed Dorine.

"Yeah, seeing as you're the kid in our group. Anyhow, congratulations, Dor." I picked up my menu to get things rolling. "I think I'll have…"

"Oh, no," Dorie insisted, "let's wait for Ada."

The waiter tapped pad with pencil and persisted with Dorie. "You want a beverage, Ma'am?"

"She'll have the Riesling." My number two lifetime goal was to help avoid public involvement with Dorine's wandering mind and abbreviated attention span. Only ridding ourselves of abusive husbands like Dorie's ex, or philandering ones like our friend Ada's deceased, earned first place.

"Oh, perfect." She smiled up at the waiter and settled her shoulders as she pinned back some straying locks.

"Dorie, dear," Lucia said, settling back with her menu, "pick out your food and be ready when he comes back. I'm starving. Ada can catch up with us when she gets through counting her billions."

I studied the specials. "Let's hope she's diversified. The market's been pretty far down. I'd hate to see Ada go into a funk over the financial situation just when she's started to get out of her depression."

Dorie's mind was elsewhere. "I like your hair, Hannah. It's gorgeous. You had it foiled, huh?" Being an artist, details of composition and color caused a high degree of forgetfulness in our friend. Despite the fact she had yet to pass through her own personal summer.

"Twice a year whether I need it or not," I said, tucking back some of the lightly sprayed streaky blond locks behind my ears. "And this time I definitely needed it. I don't mind a touch of silver frosting, but without help from a bottle, the whole damned cake was going gray."

Dorie persisted. "It's perfect. I'd like to paint you someday, looking just like you do now, your big gray eyes with that animal-caught-in-the-headlights look, your mouth tense but ready to smile."

I had to smile, despite my desperation over traveling west to meet my new and only grandchild and uncovering a local crime spree to do so. In fact almost I giggled. "You're too much."

"No," Dorie said, offended, "really. Bright, inviolable. Is that the word? Don't you see her that way, Lu?"

Lucia clucked and fiddled with the menu. "Maybe. The 'do' is gorgeous. Now, you, Dorie," she reasoned, "since you're younger than Hannah—"

"Only by two or three years." This time I knew I sounded inviolable, whatever Dorie might mean by it.

"Five," Dorine declared.

Lu was undeterred. "So you can afford to let your hair go natural. But us, we're…"

Dorie fought back. "Oh, Lu, you always look fresh out of the bandbox. Was that the saying my granddad used to use?"

"Dunno. Maybe you mean a, a…"

"Bandbox," Dorie went on. "What is that, exactly?"

I waited for the waiter to drop off the wines, and take our orders, then called the meeting to some kind of order. "Look, here's my problem. I'm trying to figure out how to manufacture a few hundred for a train ride west to see baby grandson before they leave for Japan, and you're talking about bands or boxes or something."

"Can't they come visit you before they go?" asked practical-minded Lucia.

"They're just as broke as I am."

"You should never have taken early retirement," Lu scolded. "You could have taken drugs or something and made yourself fly to Afghanistan like they wanted."

I shook my head in the face of my friends' judgment and brushed away that conversation in a hurry. "Now look, Ada's going to be here any second. So let's talk about her plan. Are we going to support her idea of this kookie club? It sounds pretty self-indulgent if you ask me. No goal but fun?"

"Fun's not against the law, Han," Lucia reminded me. "I mean, we have to support her, right?" She lowered her voice. "She's had a rough year. But she's doing better since she stopped taking the antidepressants and consuming all those soy products. I think it's healthy that she wants to do something fun."

"I know, I know. I suppose her birthday's a great day to start. Where is she, though?" I drummed my fingers on the table, watching the cars pass down LaBelle Street.

"Besides, those awful menopause symptoms she's put up with for years!" Dorie took her first sip of wine. "I'm all for Ada's plan. She's always been there for me. And besides, it sounds like fun."

Lucia inclined her head in approval. "She's coming out of her depression to put this plan together."

"Okay, I give up. We'll support her." I let go a huge sigh. It had been years since fun had been my major goal. Maybe sophomore year in college.

"I'm hungry," Lu said. "Why is she so late?"

"Dunno." I glanced at the couple in the corner, the businessmen getting louder as their martinis went to low tide, and shrugged. "But if I'm going to get to the West coast, you guys have to help me come up with a story my editor will drool over. What's going on in town? Where's the action? And…"

"Who's doing whom," Lucia added, gulping down her wine. "Tony never gives me details, but in his line of work he says he encounters lots of lascivious carriage around town. Try that."

"Sure, and just where do you suggest I get that information?" We all sat back, made way for the food service and grew quiet.

As the server arranged our plates Dorie had an answer. "Let's try Bruce at the lingerie shop. I mean, if someone's playing hanky-panky they're probably buying tons of new lingerie. Brucie would know who."

I nearly choked on my first bite of salad, and let the subject drop. Maybe Ada would have a better idea, if she ever caught up with us.

But that day she never showed for lunch, and we were baffled. After all, it was her birthday luncheon, but neither her house phone nor her cell gave us anything but voice mail. Finally, under pressure from Lucia, we pursued our meals and made short shrift of our coffee. An hour later we left the restaurant and stepped out into the April sunshine. The breeze had calmed, and we wandered toward the parking lot past the adorable shops wondering what to do about our missing friend.

"Hope she didn't have an accident," Mama Lucia fretted.

I countered with the idea Ada was depressed again and hiding from us.

"Or hurt because we haven't been so quick to jump on that club idea," Dorie admitted. Lucia hustled to keep up, but her lunch seemed to handicap her.

I checked my reflection in the glass front of a store and glanced away with irritation. A freaking 30-year old suit, my best spring outfit. Well, at least it still fit, even if the contents had settled during handling. I grinned to myself. *What handling?* That was the joke.

Dorie was over-caffeinated. "I thought it was a pretty good idea myself. We could all afford to make new friends," she chirped, "and do more fun things. I mean, we individually do these charity things, like the bereaved support group for you, Hannah, and you, Lu, with your visits to Nonna and your soup kitchen work, and besides, wouldn't it be great to include Theo, Ada's new manager, and help her make some new acquaintances?"

Lucia struggled to catch up. "But you? But you're always busy with a commission or a new creative piece..."

Dorie was breathless, babbling as we trooped along LaBelle Road, pausing only to window-shop. "I'd make the time. Besides I work irregular hours."

"Theo's a good idea," Lu agreed as they stopped in front of the area's best consignment store. "She's been out of circulation so long she doesn't have many friends in the real world. Other than Ada and me, from school days, her e-Synchrony husband, and now, you guys."

"Yet even so, a year out of the convent she loses fifty pounds, meets a guy on the Internet, marries, becomes a happy step-mom, and rises to manage the Travel Agency and run the grief center." Dorie was wide-eyed retelling Theo's story. "Impressive."

"I thought you didn't like her, Dorie. You were miffed the day you met her at Ada's." Hannah frowned.

"I do admire her, but she's pretty bossy. I'm trying automatically to stop obeying anyone who gives me an order. Done that too long. You have to admit Theo's like that, sometimes."

"She was mother superior for 20 years, for God's sake," Lu agreed. "If that's all it is, I suppose she'll get over it. She's not going to push her new husband around, you can be sure of that."

"Yeah," I agreed. "Wilson Rutledge is too powerful in his own right."

Dorie added another name distractedly. "Your friend Meg Dautrey, too, Hannah. She's been retired a week and hasn't even gone shopping with us yet! We should invite her to join our group." She paused, her face brightened by her own idea.

Suddenly Dorie waved her chiffon encased arm toward the shop front. "Hey, speaking of shopping. Look! The red shoes in Frou-Frou's window. And that gorgeous boa. Let's all buy something fun and go to Ada's. She's probably sitting there in a funk writing checks to charity when she wishes we were all joining in with her great plan."

"And becoming her royal subjects!" Lu exclaimed, following the others as they turned up the brick walk to the shop. "That's what she really wants, you know. The one who starts this sort of club is the Queen Mother of it, and the rest are her subjects."

I howled. "Oh, Lu, give it up. There'll be no rules like that for our gang."

Lucia was adamant. "You think? But you don't know her as well as I do. Ada loves stuff like that. She was student council president all four years in high school, and head of her sorority in college—which is the only reason I got in two years later!"

Dorie added her three cents. "Ada's an old softie. She just loves having her friends around. She'd do anything for us."

"Right. Dorie is absolutely right." I gripped the doorknob of the quaint little one-window shop, while Lu drew back, scowling, her full lips in a pout, her chin lifted a notch. I grinned back at her. "Come on, silly. Ada told me she sees it as a Sisterhood of the Crones. We'd be confirmed rebels against the stereotypical image of older women, like lots of those other groups are. She thought one fun thing we could do is to wear one eccentric accessory to our meetings, or when we go out together—a sort of symbol of our individuality. It doesn't have to be a crown or a certain color or anything."

Lu nodded, agreeable at last. "She said we just need to be our age, but not act our age. Those are the only stipulations."

"I love it," Dorie trilled. "Bet we could all find something like that in this consignment shop. I always loved playing dress-up. Omigosh, I could wear my old leopard skin pants. Where else can I wear them?" We laughed as the doorbell chimed, and the cool air of the interior rushed at us with its own unique flavor of bygone days and a hint of mothballs.

"When we get out of here I'll phone Meg. Maybe she can meet us at Ada's, even though she couldn't meet for lunch. Honestly, that woman can be such a killjoy." For some unconsciously bizarre reason, I headed for the vintage military gear.

"Can't blame Meg, when she's had nothing but dead bodies for company the last 12 or 15 years." Dorie sighed, gazed around and immediately dove for the pink boa in the store window, dripping with sequined feathers. "Ooh, better than leopard skin!"

I was sure they heard her squeak with delight up to the Avenue.

Still standing with her back to the door, Lu sniffed and tugged down her jacket. "Well, then, if we're going over to Ada's we ought to pick up a birthday cake for her at the Viennese. Even though she made us swear not to buy presents, it's the least we can do." The others gave her a thumbs up. Lu cleared her throat and fanned the air around her head, warding off, I just knew, a sudden flash of heat.

I promised her cake and ice cream and she relaxed. A moment later she was hounding us.

"Listen, everyone. I've always been too conservative to wear red. But I'm thinking scarlet and gorgeous would be perfect for these, ahem, fiery times."

I watched Lucia edge past Dorine with new energy. Maybe the Carabonara had finally made it past her gut.

If I could only stop worrying about Ada, this might actually be fun. I glanced at my Timex and drummed my fingers on its face.

Damn, it wasn't like Ada to be missing or even a little bit late. That was usually Dorine's game, or, in desperate times, mine.

She had better have one incredibly fascinating and indisputable excuse.

Four

Ada

My sensory check kept me momentarily motionless. I scanned the polished granite counters, ceramic floors, cherry cabinets. Nothing out of place, nothing disturbed. Chantal had the day off, and I had washed and put away my own breakfast dishes.

I peered through the windows over the sink—no sign of Raul, and not a breath of smoke in the air. So he wasn't burning branches. From the living room came the chatter of my macaw Ramon, a kind of buzzing rant, no words, just a sort of confused hum I'd never heard before.

I placed my palms on the counter and took a deep breath. The cool granite was calming, pleasingly familiar against my skin. Silly of me. There was nothing wrong here. I felt the tickle of a laugh burbling up in my throat, decided I was being paranoid, then spun around to take a quick walk through the house.

And fell back against the counter, off-balance, and with a scream half-caught in my throat.

A man.

His form filled the doorway of the dining room, tall, awkward, in ill-fitting clothes and with a face so twisted it must have been—yes, a mask. The thoughts leapfrogged through my brain—my friends were playing a birthday joke on me. They were probably all in the next room ready to burst into hysterics.

The stranger broke into a cocky grin and I knew I had it pegged. When he began to unbutton his dark jacket I gulped hard; he was a rather unpleasant looking male stripper, who was going to start dancing right there in my kitchen to embarrass me. His hand jerked downward into a pocket. "Don't you dare!" I screamed.

I raised both palms to warn him off, understanding it all except for the flash of metal in his fingers.

Five

Hannah

Dorie craned her long and elegant neck, studying the trees and shrubbery as we pulled up in Lucia's SUV. "I don't see the gardener anywhere. He must be finished for the day."

"Unh, unh," I mused, scanning the impressive estate of our dear friend, Ada. "His truck's still here, and he hasn't swept the grass from the driveway. That's usually the last thing he does."

The gardener's little pickup was indeed pulled around beside the garage, and Ada's Lincoln was in its stall. We parked behind the Town Car and giggled our way toward the front door, then decided surprise was better effected from the breezeway entrance and headed back there, shushing each other and nearly falling over ourselves; particularly Lucia, tottering in her red spiked shoes.

In the garage we squeezed around Ada's car, the driver's door still ajar and the alarm pinging, the breezeway unlocked. Dorie led the way, tiptoeing around the attractive wicker furniture, noting a shopping bag from Page-Ammen's lying discarded and tumbling out its contents on a chair, then through the kitchen door, which was also wide open.

The fragrance of fresh strawberries filled the room.

Dorie peeked into the house, and settled the pink boa around her neck. I tried not to laugh at the sight of her, and arranged my recycled green beret lightly on my new "do." Lu, still a bit unsteady, toddled along in her heels, barely balancing the cake box. Weren't we a sight? Ada would be thrilled with our invasion, ready to celebrate her birthday and her new club.

"It's the best present we could bring her," Dorie whispered.

Lu and I followed, breathless with excitement.

"Wait'll she gets a load of these—" Lucia murmured, glancing down at her red Manolo Blahniks.

We all spotted Ada at the same moment, sitting up straight on the sofa, her profile imperious, framed by the arch of the central hallway. On the other side of the room Ramon, her macaw, was making his usual racket. "Hello, very good. Hello," he said over and over. Ada cherished that bird, let it fly free half the time.

"She has company, or the bird would be loose," I whispered.

Surprisingly Ada had heard us from twenty-five feet away. Without turning in our direction she blinked, and shot one hand up in a loose fist against her high cheekbone, thumb flexed, index and middle finger pointing to the sky.

"A just-a-minute gesture," Dorie hissed.

"Or cocked like a gun," I retorted with an intake of breath.

"Ta da!" Lu called out as our little trio burst into the living room, ready to collapse around Ada in a group hug.

But leaning around the others to catch our friend's reaction and watching Ada's face, all I could think of was the time Dorie had celebrated her divorce by tossing her ex's oil portrait into the fireplace, and his features had dissolved in the flames.

"Ada?" I said through inhaled breath as we rushed toward her en masse.

"Ada. Ada," Ramon parroted.

"Shit!" boomed a male voice from across the expansive beige room. "Put up your hands and don't move. Don't even think about it!"

We screamed almost in harmony, until the man with the gun shouted at us to close it down. Even Ramon shut up.

Six

Ada

I watched his big, gangly hands aim the shaking silvery gun in our general direction as my friends shrieked. At my current level of barely maintained self-control, I couldn't decipher quite everything in the confusion. Was it Hannah who yelled, "For Christ's sake!" and Lucia who screeched, "Who the hell are you?" or did I have it in reverse? And what was Dorie moaning, all the while she fretted over that ridiculous piece of pink fluff she wore around her neck?

Hannah in a hat? And Lu in high heels, red ones? My God, they *all* wore something outrageous and bizarre—the club emblems I'd suggested—all for me! I breathed for the first time in what seemed forever. *Oh, oh, the dears!*

"Calm down, everyone," I demanded, forgetting it was only the men in my life who usually responded to my dictatorial tone, all the men except for the stranger with the gun. "No point losing our cool. You all look… lovely. Now. This gentleman wants something, and as soon as he understands I don't have it, I'm sure he'll leave."

I gestured to the seats on either side of me, then glanced up, eyebrow cocked, to see if my captor would permit the seating arrangement. For well over an hour he'd badgered me, trying to intimidate me, telling lies, being ridiculous. He wouldn't listen, wouldn't believe I had nothing of value, no safe. Well, it wouldn't be a *safe* safe if he knew about it, would it? He'd even taken me by the arm, so roughly I'd be black and blue tomorrow, if there was a tomorrow, making me race around the house with him, looking for whatever he wanted.

When all along it was so close it could have whopped him in the head.

So far under my silly panic I felt victorious, but as his composure melted, and he got more ballistic, I knew I was a tad more vulnerable. And I was beginning to tire.

"Not there," the gawky man growled as Lucia tried to take the seat beside me. "Here." He'd pointed to the slipper chair. "You two. Over there." He indicated the damask loveseat and I sighed in relief it was Hannah and Dorie taking that position, despite their bumping against each other as they sat, arms still raised, terror in their eyes. Best them and not Lucia, who was usually chewing something and had been known to leave food and beverage stains on my better household fabrics.

Now, however, my amply bestowed friend perched uneasily on the edge of the salmon slipper chair balancing a cake box on her lap, eyes darting from the weapon to the owner's face to her own purse. For a crazy second I wondered if dear, good-sized Lu were about to jump the man and save us all.

But no, Lucia wriggled backward and sat upright, staring now at her hands, and at the taupe Coach bag that had slid to the floor at her feet. My heart thumped. Could she have a gun in there? Wasn't her husband Tony in security or law enforcement or something? Might he not arm his woman? Of course he would. He would protect her! Hope shimmered in my breast.

Oh, dear Lucia, be careful, I thought, trying to send the message through my dark eyes to Lu's even darker ones. They'd been friends the longest, gone to Miss Porter's together. Well, I admitted, but only to myself, I had been a year ahead of Lucia. And Lu a scholarship student at that. Still, we'd hung out in the same crowds. Smoked together in the boxwood gardens. Always skirting trouble together in those days.

Now, Lu and Ada were in trouble together again. Not to mention competent Hannah and Goldie Hawnish Dorie.

I rocked in my seat, trying to focus. Surely this, this armed idiot would leave now that reinforcements had arrived.

"Sorry I missed our luncheon date," I said, trying to sound nonchalant. The others responded in a quick chorus of "That's okay's" and the gunman shifted nervously.

"Shut up!" he demanded, lurching toward Lucia and shoving the cake box onto the floor. Then he had the audacity to frisk her, for God's sake!

I watched Lu's eyes grew wide as chocolate pasczki.

"That's okay," Ramon echoed.

"Shut up," the gunman squawked, before he realized it had been the bird. He swung back to face Lucia, whose gaze remained on her purse. "What're you looking at?

Huh? You got a weapon? Anybody got a weapon?" The tall, skinny man did an awkward jiggle on shaky feet to study each one.

He had definitely unsettled another notch since my friends arrived. *Hardly a pro at home invasions,* I thought.

How embarrassing, being held hostage by an amateur!

And he just wouldn't stop squawking. "Gun, knife, huh? I mean business. If I find out any of ya' got a weapon, you're dead meat." He flailed at Lucia, who raised her arms obligingly so he could run his hands down her sides.

"Do we look like armed criminals?" Hannah asked, not even trembling.

I wished I could be so cool. When I noticed my own knees in my best white wool slacks knocking together, and my breath expelling in funny little shudders from my twitching body, I felt I was at the end of my tether. And on my birthday, of all things.

"Dead meat, dead meat," Ramon echoed.

The gunman clenched his jaw and moved to the loveseat, his crouching steps like those of a stalking animal, I thought.

Dorie swooned backward, leaning toward Hannah. Had she fainted? The man poked about Dorie's waistband with an odious smirk, one hand dipping roughly into her bosom, the other brandishing the gun inches from her nose. Dorie hugged the silly boa to her face and muttered, "No, no…"

"Nice," the invader moaned, easing closer.

"Nice," Ramon agreed. "Nice." Apparently the bird was taken with Farquar's voice and mimicking it was his routine of the day. In truth he was starting to irritate even me.

Hannah jerked upright to stop the man from mauling Dorine. "Look, we do not have any weapons. We don't know you, or what you want, but if you'd put that stupid thing away—"

The invader raised a hand as if to slap her, and I cringed as Hannah spun out of his range. Dorie pulled her knees up, burrowing her head so low behind the fuchsia feathers she probably couldn't see what was going on. Soft, wailing sounds came from her clamped lips. A prayer of some kind?

I stared, stupefied. Wasn't Dorie an agnostic? Or was it Unitarian?

Farquar leveled the gun at Hannah until her lips curved downward and she sealed them, paling suddenly, and looking nauseous.

"You shut up," he said. "I'll tell you when to talk. All of you. Clear?" He whirled back toward Lucia who steadied herself in her seat by sitting on her hands, her gaze now super-glued on the purse on the floor.

Heavens, I thought, she's surely got something in there. A weapon. Or some Mace. Something to save us. *But, oh, Lu, be careful.*

My voice came out hoarse, nearly a raspy baritone. "Please, Mister, uh, Farquar. I'll give you whatever you want. Take that menorah there, it's worth hundreds. The plasma TV, too, in the den. I paid $5,000 for it. Take the stereo. Just let my friends go…"

Before I could finish he'd lunged toward me. Breath left me in a shudder as he whacked the side of the gun against my cheek. A gasp traveled around the room and back again.

"Shut up," he barked. "I told you I want the money and the certificates. Paper and jewelry. Danny said you keep plenty in that safe."

I choked to force the words out: "My stepson would never—"

Going wild with the horrible weapon, Farquar knocked several pictures from the wall.

I pressed a hand to my bloody temple and cringed even more when a tiny Chagall original tilted on its hooks. If the bloody fool only knew, I thought, that picture of indigo sky and falling figures was worth far more than all my jewels and paper put together.

"Brrp, brrp." The bird flitted around in his cage, too unglued himself now to imitate. If only, the crazy idea careened through my head as I stared at my bloody fingers, he were a big, strong dog, he could protect me. I must get another Rottweiler. And where on earth was Raul? He should be looking out for me, a woman alone as I was. Yet I hadn't heard the mower or water hoses or his truck leaving either.

I took a deep breath, tried to steady my voice. "Danny wouldn't say that, because it's not true."

Lucia leaned forward. "Oh, no, sir. You're wrong. Ada distinctly told me she doesn't keep—"

"Shut up!" He was at Lu's side in a nano-second, and swung the butt of the gun across her face, too. It connected. Her nose gushed blood. This time we all broke out in screams. Lu grabbed for a tissue in her pocket and held it to her face, eyes even wider than before.

31

"Look, I told you," I said as clearly and calmly as I could manage, fighting the sting of pain in my cheekbone, nauseous over the blood pouring from Lu's nose. "I just came from the bank, and that money I already gave you is all I have in the house."

"Yeah, sure, two hundred bucks in a house like this? Bird seed, nothin' but bird seed."

Feebly, Ramon squawked, "Bird seed, very good. Bird seed."

It startled Farquar, who slapped the side of the cage with the gun, making it rattle. The bird fluttered, discharging green and blue pinfeathers through the bars.

I fell backward on the white sofa, covering up my gasp of horror with a hand over my mouth. I hoped the cat would stay hidden. If he dare hurt any of my pets…

The phone rang, and when he signaled them all to ignore it, Meg Dautrey's sober voice came on through the answering machine.

"Strange idea, ladies. Gathering up the menopausal misfits. Don't know why you're not answering, but I'll come by later to see what this is all about. Odd bits of clothing, huh? Have you never noticed all my clothing is totally made up of odd bits?" Meg's charmingly accented voice was clipped, bordering on sarcasm, her usual modus operandi.

Message over, the machine thunked its ending. I steeled myself, then straightened where I sat. To hell with him. I wasn't going to flinch for him or any man. I made quick eye contact with Hannah, whose look said, *Good girl, hold on, we're going to be okay, Meg will save the day if nothing else can.*

I tried to hang on, to stick out my chin. Thank God Hannah spoke quickly before I could. "Look, I have a little money. If you want money, take what's in our purses. We probably have a few hundred between us." She reached for her well-worn Gucci on the couch beside her, flipped open the flap.

He laughed, but it was more a gunshot cackle, that of an untamed bird of prey.

"You think I'd come all the way down here for a few hundred?" He spat on the antique mahogany piecrust table. *The rat,* I thought. Who was this awful creature? Where had he come from? And what did he know about Danny?

Only then did it occur to me to make note of his features, his clothes. Maybe we'd get rid of him and live, after all. A description would help the police. Okay. Tall, gangly, skinny. Face unevenly covered with a couple days' growth of beard, clothes too dark and heavy for the season, too small, too short. But a good cut, an expensive jacket, well-made jeans. Like the country club set wore.

Hand-me-downs, maybe.

The attacker grew tense under my stare. "Don't move!" he ordered me, then stared at each one of the others in turn. "If any of youse know where this broad keeps her bonds and stuff, speak up now before I start having to hurt her!"

Hannah's hands rested neatly on the bag in her lap. Dorie shivered beside her and adjusted the tilting mass of fuchsia frills around her long neck. Her closed-mouth murmurings grew louder, then diminished again.

The thief gestured at our heads with the muzzle of the gun. "What's with these broads? And the one on the phone? What'd she mean? When is she coming here?" He glared at each one in turn, then at me.

"A ladies' club," I said, barely able to speak above a whisper. My face throbbed. Despite my opposite intentions, I was starting to panic, not just tired of the games. "We're forming a club where we all wear funny things." I blotted my lower lids with my stained forefingers, totally unconcerned about the mess of smeared blood on my face. In truth, I was deeply touched my pals would come here, wearing odd little accessories to support my offbeat plans, then get into this, this dangerous charade... I drew in a sharp breath.

"They're willing to give you money. Why don't you take it?"

"Crazy. You're all loony-birds. You don't hand over the contents of your safe pretty quick, Mama Javitt, every damn one of you is going have some permanent holes, and not just in your stupid feathers!"

Ramon made a valiant effort to squawk out "Stupid feathers!" but it came out wrong, "Stoo-di-fers." He tucked his head beneath his wing as if in shame. Dorie shuddered aloud.

Lu made a little hand gesture, a circular jiggle from her wrist up, and drew Farquar's attention away from Dorie, who was sinking fast. "Mr. er, uh—"

"Farquar, he says his name is. A—" I choked on the word—"*friend* of Danny's from that Rehab place in Alaska supposedly," I tossed in, as if they were meeting at a cocktail party and the firearm were but a drink in the man's dark fist. "Mr. Farquar, this is Lucia Catamonte."

"Shut up," he barked. Ramon did better this time.

"Shut up, shut up." A green feather drifted toward the carpet.

Lucia brightened. "You seem tired, hungry, too, maybe. I could fix you lunch." She raised her derriere from the slipper chair, and livened her face with enough civility the man seemed taken aback. I saw his Adam's apple jiggle in his throat.

"Naw," he said, gazing at the scarlet sandals on the three-inch heels, and Lu's bright lipsticked grin, the matching streak of blood running from her nose to her chin. After a long second he shrugged and turned back to me, letting out his breath in a deep huff.

"Lady, I've had it with you. I want those bonds. I've got your son kidnapped in Alaska. He'll call soon to verify that, and you'll tell me where that safe is. Or he will. Or I start blasting you one by one." Dorie sucked in a loud, anguished breath. He swung around and pointed the gun decidedly, and her eyes popped open wider than Lu's. "Starting with her."

As I clamped my lips shut. Farquar tossed a lamp onto the rug and tipped over the piecrust table.

"Stop it," I said, firm but patient, as if speaking to a recalcitrant schoolboy. "Seriously, Mr. Farquar, if I had a safe, and more money, don't you think I'd give it to you to be rid of you? Do you think I want to be troubled by this nuisance of a game…"

"Game?" he growled, moving back around toward the sofa. "You think this is a game? I told you, I got your kid in Alaska!"

He yanked my head back with a tug on my short, silvery hair. There was a collective murmur of shock from visitors, just as Farquar glanced at the Louis XIV clock on the mantle. "When that phone rings the next time, you'll know I ain't kidding around. It'll be him, Danny. That'll prove I got him, no matter what he says." He clenched his teeth and stared for a second at his hands, one on the gun, one palm up at chest height.

"I ain't afraid to use this," he said. But his hand still shook, saying otherwise.

"I, I can't believe Danny would—" I started, but Hannah gave me a "Shush" from across the gulf of creamy carpet, while her crossed leg jerked in a rhythmic panic, up and down, keeping the beat. Dorie's whole body rocked now with the cadence of her moans.

Farquar didn't seem to notice. Just stared at the phone, and back to us, gritting his teeth, close to a breaking point.

My throat dried up. I struggled to breathe. Was Danny really in trouble? Or behind all this? No way. But look at my lovely room, all my beautiful things. Some destroyed already. I snuck a glance at the crooked Duncan Phyfe table, saw a leg had snapped, and worried about the Chinese porcelain lamp it had held, though I couldn't quite see it from where I was imprisoned.

I might have to give up the safe after all. Still, if Danny were in on this whole thing, surely he would have told this, this animal, where the safe was. And if Danny's life were in danger, what guarantee did I have this man would

have him released, even if I gave him everything in the
safe? All those certificates, my stocks and the bearer
bonds and all that paperwork my nephew Judd had said
would be secure here, more so than in an anonymous safe
deposit box.

Oh, Judd, if only you'd come along now. If only you
weren't so far away in Florida. Still, how would I have
notified him, him with his busy GYN practice, all those
women at his office doors needing his attention?

I began to shiver. I didn't like the way the thief kept
staring at Dorie. The woman was a basket case, had just
about gotten over the abuse her ex-husband had put her
through. If you ever do get over it…

Farquar seemed to know she was their vulnerable spot
and began to study her.

Next to Dorie, competent and pro-active Hannah was
wound as tight as a trampoline spring, ready to pop, that
jerking foot of hers winding her tighter. Ramon rocked on
the swing, head turned to the window.

I glanced to my left at Lucia, who continued to be
engrossed in her Coach bag on the floor. She had a
weapon. I just knew it. If I could distract the man long
enough, I, myself, would reach for the bag and fling it
open, use whatever it was, and take the danger away from
my friends! I must not wait a second longer.

My voice came out higher than I anticipated it would.
"Mr. Farquar?"

He glared at me under those black, droopy brows.

"About lunch. You could watch her while she fixes you
something, a beer, maybe? There's a cold roast. Let her
make you a sandwich. You could stand in the doorway

and keep an eye on us." I dragged the words up from some little corner of desperation. Farquar was actually looking toward the kitchen. Contemplating the possibilities.

No doubt he could see I was right. If only he'd give in to his thirst and hunger... I wondered where he'd come from and how he got here, when he'd last eaten. I'd never seen a car. And where had Raul been? Where was he now?

"Besides," I surprised myself by still speaking on one breath, "you'll want to be finished here soon. The gardener completes his chores by three and stops in to get paid. You won't want to be discovered..."

Farquar laughed, the hysterical bird caw again. He stood and pointed the gun at Lucia. "Go ahead. Get me some food and a beer and make it quick." He stepped in front of Dorie and pushed wisps of hair and pink feathers out of her face with the muzzle of the gun. "No smart moves, or..."

He didn't have to say it. We got it.

Lucia moved quickly, and as he followed her to the doorway, I reached my left leg out far enough to slide Lu's calfskin bag closer. I heard Hannah and Dorie suck in their breath. Never mind. Being nice to the man hadn't changed a thing. He was the only male person I'd ever known who was like iron under my gaze. I was sick of it. Now I'd show him.

As the refrigerator door swung open and jars and plates clanked against each other, I was sure Farquar was far enough behind me monitoring the kitchen. I took a ragged breath and swooped forward to grab the purse, flip off the cover and set it on my lap. Pepper spray. A gun?

My fingers rifled the contents, felt something hard and round.

Tugged it out.

At exactly the moment I felt the rush of Farquar's hot breath on the back of my neck, I yanked out an economy sized Milky Way, half unwrapped and bitten into. Chocolate!

Lu had been longing for her candy bar. I gasped, hearing, like the strike of an anvil, the click of the safety being released.

Seven

Hannah

The shot rang out just as Ada sat there studying the candy bar in her fist. Like a laser beam the bullet pierced the Milky Way from where Farquar stood directly over her, spinning it from Ada's hand in a swirling eruption of caramel and nougat goo. Ada jerked her hand back, a scream of terror forced from her throat. The bird keeled over, and Dorie wailed loudly enough for all of us.

That ought to bring Raul running.

"What the hell…" Farquar bellowed, so surprised he'd made the shot he dropped the gun like a hot quesadilla.

The bird revived and echoed, "Hell."

The gunman jerked downward to retrieve the smoking weapon from under the couch, then tried to hold it in the business position again, though his shaking hands made it difficult. Finally, with his other fist, he shoved the purse, the shattered candy bar, the whole mess, out of Ada's lap and onto the cushions of the white sofa. Between Ada's legs, a hole in the sofa cushion smoldered and stunk.

How could I just sit here and do nothing? What could I do? Too late to tackle him, while he was reaching for the gun on the floor. But the man was coming unglued. That was maybe a good sign. I began to feel a little island of calm inside, despite the bile that had risen in my throat.

He could be had; he was vulnerable.

Or maybe totally whacked out of control.

Desperate.

But not perhaps as desperate and wild-eyed as sobbing Ada.

I gulped a breath. "You all right, Ada?"

"Don't worry, when I don't want to miss her, I won't!" the shooter snapped.

"I'm… fine," Ada croaked.

"I have to go to the bathroom," Dorie whimpered.

In the doorway to the dining room, Lucia stood gaping.

"Get my food!" he bellowed at her. "Everyone else stay where you are!" Farquar ran in zigzags around the room, pointing the weapon at first one woman then another, and whacking the side of Ramon's cage to keep the bird quiet. The parrot's wings fluttered; he resorted to crouching in a corner.

The burn hole in the sofa was still smoking, and Ada's legs trembled on either side of it. When the phone rang, Farquar hurried to it, knocking over another delicate piece of decorative glass and smashing it against the piano leg.

Although Ada's feet in the Ferragamo suede casuals hadn't stopped twitching since the explosion of the firearm, at least she hadn't been wounded. Her eyes from across the room implored me to do something.

I'm useless, I thought, feeling my green beret tottering. I picture myself as some sort of warrior. But I won't get on an airplane and I can't help knock down an idiot home invader. What a laugh. No, not a laugh, a tragedy. Those kids at the Grief Center would never call me their hero again, and of course, I'd never deserved it anyhow. I shivered, tried to ignore my jitterbugging stomach. *I've got to act, disarm him—and quickly. The man's a psychological disaster, clearly unused to a gun, but his very inexperience makes him a ticking timebomb.*

Besides, Ada's going to lose it in the next few moments, if it really was Danny on the phone, in cahoots with this horror of a man.

When Farquar said, "Danny boy," and snorted a cruel laugh, Ada's eyes begin to dart quickly from the one thing to another, her lips for once clamped shut.

"Where is the godamned safe?" the man screamed into the phone. You could tell they were arguing, the person on the other end, and this madman.

Ada sank deeper into the cushions, her eyes blank, perhaps wondering how her own stepson could be helping this cruel man. She'd never known violence, had controlled most men in her life by smiling prettily. Men bent in her presence. True, I thought, she'd had her problems with Danny, the last few years, known his drugged torpor, his shrieking during the combat of withdrawal, even the cruelty of B. J.'s flaunted affairs and neglect of his son. But nothing, no one like this— creature—had ever defied her. Not in her refined, protected life.

The phone argument went on, Farquar spinning around to watch us, waving the gun in every direction.

I on the other hand, had known violence, knew the ripping apart of an ordinary life into shreds. Even outside the loss of my husband and my brother so many years ago. I'd done the police beat for years on the Courant, come close to men like Farquar with haunted eyes and unsteady hands. Sometimes even got them to talk, to open up.

"Look, everyone, let's give the man what he wants..." I said in Ada's direction. Would she even hear me?

Ada's eyes popped wide and she gave a quick shake of her head.

I felt my insides sink. The stench of smoking upholstery hit my nostrils harder and the weight of Dorie leaning into me suddenly was unbearable.

"Bathroom?" Dorie whimpered.

As Farquar slammed the phone into its cradle Ada jumped up and cried, "Let me talk. Oh no, Danny..." At that moment Lu returned, clutching an opened beer, and handed over a sandwich on a plate. When she spied the mess of the Milky Way, her purse and the smoking gunshot wound to the sofa, her hand went to her mouth.

Sorry, Ada mouthed. Lucia shook her head, set her jaw, and made her hands into fists. Her color was changing, she was growing pinker by the minute. Puce, even. I waited on tenterhooks. I knew Lu's Neapolitan temper, and hoped she'd restrain herself from doing anything too rash. I felt relief as she seemed to steel herself.

"Would you like to wash first?" she asked demurely. "You have something dark and red on your hands..."

"Shut up, get back in your seats," Farquar shouted, slamming his plate onto the piano and grabbing for a bite of his cold pork and roast pepper sandwich.

My heart sank as Lu's hand raised the bottle of beer with a gasp of fury coming from her lips. The attacker ducked and shoved her to the floor. The beer bottle struck the piano top on the way down and sprayed a shower of the liquid over the room. Ada screamed as Lu crumpled to a fetal position half beneath the baby grand. An intake of breath hissed from everyone of us. I hesitated before I moved, assessing the location of the gun, and Farquar's ragged emotions.

He was clearly sweating now. I watched him wipe his forehead with the back of his gun hand. His glance darted to Lu's unmoving figure beneath him and Ada's petite form a few feet from his gun. "Your whacky friends haven't helped you lady. Neither did your kid. I was going to let you off easy but now you get me the stuff in your safe by the time I count to three or..."

In that eclipsed hush after Farquar had given his ultimatum we heard the muffled roar of a high-powered vehicle in the driveway, the emphatic turn-off of an engine, a car door slamming. The man's eyes widened, and he inched toward the window, gun trembling.

"Va-room," Ramon said, hopping from one foot to the other, then flitting to his swing. "Va-room."

"What? A goddamned cop car. Which one of you bitches..." He switched the gun to his left hand and yanked Ada up close, spinning her around until her back was to him and he had wrapped his arm around her neck.

My God, it's Meg, I thought. *Thank God. Meg here to join the club*. Driving the Assistant State Medical Examiner's car she hadn't yet returned. The car with lights on the roof.

Ada's head wobbled on her neck, her body sank in feigned surrender. Farquar struggled to hold her up.

This, I knew, was the moment to act, this thin little crevice in the rock wall of our entrapment. I sucked in a breath, watched Farquar consider options, his glance scudding to every corner of the room, and to Lu's motionless body at his feet.

Cornered, ready to do something drastic.

I had to do it. Now.

In one jagged motion I reached into my own open and tattered Gucci bag and yanked out the silver cylinder. In the same moment as I flicked off the cap, I leaped from the seat so quickly I felt Dorie slump behind me. The armed gunman spun toward me exactly as my forefinger plunged the button on the hair spray can I'd purchased at my semi-annual hairdo day.

Direct hit, eyes doused.

"Eeeeuw!" screamed Farquar, arms flailing upward. The gun in his hand flew from his grip and, airborne, struck Ada's portrait on the far wall.

"Eeeeuw!" Ramon answered, rattling the cage.

At the same moment Lucia grabbed the crook's ankles and Ada helped her wrestle him to the ground. Lu jerked upward like a bobbing vessel, and kept him there with her three-inch stiletto heel in his back. The doorbell rang, and Dorie, roused from her faint, screamed at the top of her lungs.

It was that scream, we all agreed later, that had accomplished the deed. Farquar fought for his footing, all elbows and knees, toppling Ada onto her side. As he started moving, his glance grazed the floor for the missing weapon but Lu kicked him where he'd least want to be kicked, and he groaned and struggled upright. But the trail of four women, one in lethal high heels, one in a flaming feathered scarf and one in a goddamn green beret began pursuit, snatching at his clothes, his hair, the skin at the back of his neck. Sticking like glue.

He ran, shouting and wriggling to disengage us, through the hall and into the kitchen. We pounded his back and ripped off his jacket, screeching, until he squirmed past the counters, slid across the tile floor to the back door and threw himself out into the yard. Dorie was excited enough to start following him out the door, then snapped to and realized she was the only one in the doorway. She collapsed on the kitchen floor, tangled in her boa.

"Very nice. Goodbye," screeched Ramon, left alone in the living room.

Seeking reinforcements, Ada ran to the front door and opened it for Meg, whose habitually dour expression exploded into mirth when she saw the remnants of the current liberation exercise. We rushed to wrap our arms around her and give her a loud and mixed-up account of what had happened.

That changed her reaction fast.

Once she secured the gun from beneath Ada's portrait, dangling it from a pen, and began to really hear their garbled story, Meg's severe features assumed their usual cynical expression. But there was a fantastic analytical brain at work behind that look; I'd depended on it too many times in the past not to be impressed.

"Thank God you're still driving your cop car with the little blue light on top," Dorie gushed, draped weakly over Lucia.

"And that you're here to guide us through this mess," I said. My heart was racing. I tried to convince myself the whole escapade had been amusing, even in its terror. But then, I had always been the Queen of De-nial. When I noticed I was still shaking it dawned on me: my God, it would make a story—the one I'd hoped and prayed for, a free-lanced something I could sell to the paper's Northern Magazine, thereby earning enough to fly Kevin and his family home here for a visit. Or at least to buy a train ride for myself out west. And here I was, right on top of it.

Now if Farquar could be caught.

Meg pulled herself up to a bit more than her five feet two inches—or was it the pencil-striped skirt and matching vest she wore that made her look tall?—causing her to seem coolly efficient, as usual. "It is not a cop car, my dears. It's the assistant medical examiner's car, and I have it until the end of the month when my retirement becomes final. Now, shall we call the real police?"

Ada nodded weakly and sank onto the unshot portion of the sofa, but danced away from the charred cushion when she saw it. "It's a mess, a horrible mess. I'll have to call the cleaners in the morning!" Her previously perfect make-up was besmirched with flowing tears, blood smears, and a steady stream of well-bred blood from her temple had pooled in the corner of her left eye. "Danny, oh, my poor Danny," she wailed. "He could be in terrible danger. He never knew what Farquar was talking about— of course he's not involved in this horror. And us, we could have been shot! I should get another dog to replace Maximilian. A dog would have warned me…"

"But does Danny know Farquar?" I couldn't help but ask as I reached for my cell phone in the Gucci.

Ada shrugged. "Knows him, since he says he comes from that same drug rehab place Danny's at in Alaska. But I doubt he had anything to do with him. Someone must have told him I wanted him to call exactly at the time he called. Someone being that awful man."

Lucia pulled a packet of tissues from her pocket and handed them over, clearly knowing what was about to come. She was sensitive about things like that. I, on the other hand, hadn't a clue, until Theo had got me working with the grieving children.

Under a sudden waterfall, Ada reached for the tissues and dissolved onto the nearest dining room chair. I dialed my cell.

The trickle of laughter all around the room sounded sweet to my ears as the telephone rang at West Parkford Police.

Let poor Ada have her waterfall. She'd been through enough, having had her philandering husband die eight months ago, and apparently only recently marshalling her uncontrolled hormones to simmer down, and now missing her birthday celebration all because of a miserable creep of a man.

When the dispatcher answered something tickled me deep inside. I loved snapping the small town police into action. They deserved something more stimulating than patrolling the malls for the steady influx of shoplifters, the highways for speeders, or deciding which charity to support via their annual softball game. As crime reporter for the Courant until last year, I'd enjoyed the pleasure of following their pursuits. Good guys and gals with great intentions and not much to brighten their run-of-the-mill days.

Well, today they'd have something.

While I explained our dilemma, Meg ran around in an uncustomarily brisk fashion locking doors, checking windows, and peering into the woods behind the house. Dorie, leaning into the hallway, took time to adjust the slightly skewed portrait of Ada she'd painted for B. J., Ada's second husband years ago when they first married.

Farquar's gun had damaged the edge of the frame when it flew out of his hand. Dorie fingered the damaged wood and made a face. The expression said a lot, but I couldn't translate.

The officer on the line tried to pass me off to the non-emergency desk.

My voice grew uppity and terse. "Sergeant, the bastard's still out there somewhere, maybe in the woods right behind the house. He's dangerous, he shot at one of us and threatened all of us."

"Especially me," Dorie said.

Finally the person on the other end seemed to get it.

"Will you send a patrol car over here right now?" I held the phone away from my body. "They're on the way," I said, then turned back to the cell. "Forgive me, we're a little verklempt over here. The couch is still smoking and the owner's son could be in deep water... No, he's not drowning. No, I don't want the fire department or the rescue squad! I want police, I want detectives, for God's sake."

49

"It's under here, you know." Dorie persisted in jiggling the peachy gold and rose portrait of Ada. She'd always been so proud of that picture. Lu and Meg drew closer, and Ada just stared, eyes glazed over.

I covered the mouthpiece with my hand "What, Dorie?"

"What the man wanted, it's under Ada's portrait. I knew it and I almost told him so three times. See?" She lifted the large picture from its hooks. "The safe."

Lu let out a small scream, Ada shouted, "Oh, Dorie, thank God you didn't!" and my beret finally tilted completely off my newly styled and colored tresses onto the floor. Meg quickly replaced the picture as if the cold metal contents underneath might bite her, and Dorie pouted.

"Thank God none of us was hurt by pretending," Dorie said, her face only slightly accusing.

Ada admitted she'd been way too stubborn. "You're right, Dorie. I'm sorry, I'm really sorry, everyone. I should have given it to him. Oh, how awful. I could have gotten you all killed!" She couldn't hold back the strangled sob in her throat, and the waterfall started all over again. She studied her hands gripping the edge of the table.

"Or he might have killed you after he got what he wanted," Meg added cryptically.

Ada croaked out the words in breathy gasps. "It's just almost everything I have is in there. My papers, my will, all of Danny's inheritance. That emerald my George got me in Brazil, my diamonds from Daddy." She sniffed and held her head high. "But he didn't get it, did he, and we're all okay. Aren't we?" It was more a plea, than a word of reassurance.

"It's okay, Ada. And you did well, Dor," I whispered. "We all did. It was traumatic being held at gunpoint. No wonder we're a bundle of nerves."

Dorie gave up on her little outburst and Lucia retreated to the kitchen to secure beverages and snacks while Meg tried to keep everyone clear of the crime scene. "Be careful, Lu. Don't walk where he walked; don't touch anything he touched, like the doorknob, the walls."

"Okay," Lu called back. "I'll bring everything in there and we can serve it al fresco."

"Never mind al fresco, this is a crime scene. Stop milling around, right now," she told us. "Sit at this table and stay put."

Ramon was swinging again, and cheerily echoed her demands. "Stay put, stay put." Dorie walked toward the cage.

Meg groaned. Fibers and fluids and other gory forensic evidence could be at risk.

"People!" she shouted. Finally we got the point, but not until Meg gave Dorie a timeout for the lady's room. By the time she returned, Lucia had retrieved the birthday cake from the living room in its battered box, supplied china plates and forks and uncorked a bottle of Chateau Lafite-Rothschild, 1947, the first thing she'd grabbed from the wine cabinet. Meg poured, as hers were the only hands not shaking.

"Now," I proclaimed, "since the police are on their way, let's all relax a little and remember why we're here in the first place." I ran my fingers through my hair, dismayed at what felt like a collapsed thatched roof, considering I'd just had it cut, colored, teased, styled and frosted—foils, not a cap—for half the amount of the national debt. Once again I'd proved what I'd always suspected: you can't be who you're not.

I retrieved my beret in the living room over Meg's objections and placed it on the corner of the table.

As we waited for the police, we five friends agreed on a date for our first official club function.

Dorie declared, "We won't let that monster Farquar stop us."

"But we all want you to be Queen, Ada," Lucia said, lifting the second bottle of very old burgundy, and bending forward to pour, with only a faint bit of splashing, another round on the mahogany oval. "After all, it was your idea in the first place to celebrate the absolute end of your menopausal symptoms. That's original and bodacious in a most admirable way."

I chuckled to myself. Here was Mama Lu, all her fiery objections to Ada's status forgotten, leading them onward. They all remembered at once: "Happy birthday, Ada!" They chorused. Ada's eyes filled again.

"But I wouldn't have attempted this so-called celebration day without all of your support. You've helped me through my insomnia and night sweats, given me recipes for tofu suppers. And today you probably saved my life!" Ada had resumed her imperial calm, and now gestured with her glass at Dorie, Lucia, Meg and me in mini toasts, before she sipped. "There are all kinds of women's groups these days. As we get older we need the understanding and support of each other even more. You know, to promote positive attitudes, and original thinking for the, let's say, second half of life."

"While having lots of fun," Lucia declared between sips of wine.

Ada finally forced a small grin, though her hand on her glass was still shaking. "We don't have to have a queen. And if we do, I don't have to be it. One of you would be..."

"Oh, come on, Ada," Meg said. "Let's admit it: you're the only one of us rich enough to be called Queen Anything."

"And the only one of us who seems to be totally past menopause. Am I right?" Dorie asked.

"Thought so until today. I just may have a relapse," Ada admitted. "Though I'll have to take those wretched calcium pills for life, I imagine."

Lu snorted. "I may never need them, as heavier women like me have at least one advantage—less osteoporosis. Unless, blessed hope, I should suddenly lose weight. As for symptoms, except for my occasional bouts of confusion and one or two matters involving certain creams and gels, I think I'm just about home free, too."

Dorie grew wide-eyed. "What does she mean? What do you mean, Lucia?"

"Poor Dorie," Meg chided. "Lots to learn and plenty of time to learn it, m'dear. We'll be your menopause mentors. Meanwhile, when shall we reschedule Ada's celebration day?"

I was about to repeat the date suggested earlier when the doorbell rang. How had we missed the siren?

The group grew wary, focused once more on the hostage-taker and what we'd been through. As if in a panic, Ada asked if she could call Danny back. Meg said, "Okay, but use Hannah's cell phone. Preserve the gunman's prints on the other." I turned my cell over and Ada stepped a few feet away to call Danny while I ran to the door.

"Stay, everyone," I said, noticing the rustle of movement behind me. "I'm used to dealing with the police. 'Course, Meg is too, but she wasn't exactly a witness."

I drew the door open at the second ring, then gaped at the figure filling the doorway. With a quick jerk of a hand here, a pull-down there, I rearranged my clothes. There was a weird moment of mutual once-overs. Finally he introduced himself.

"Lieutenant Bernard Cascone." Broad-shouldered. Nasaly baritone. Nice eyes. Bad nose. A scent of spearmint and lumber.

I cleared my throat. "Hannah Doyle." I cleared it again. "Come on in." I glanced at the uniform behind Cascone, a chubby training officer I'd met once or twice and jerked my head his way. "You, too, Lieutenant Ketry."

The officer shook his head. "I'll need to check the perimeter, ma'am."

I choked back a retort. "Don't give me ma'am, Ketry. It's Doyle, Hannah Doyle."

The lieutenant nodded.

Cascone glanced back over his shoulder and said he'd join his colleague in a few. Ketry gave him a smirking grin. I ignored the whole thing and closed the door, leading the detective into the dining room, despite a wave of slight dizziness and crazy tilting of my equilibrium. Well, I was just recovering from a hostage situation, what did you expect, a vanilla smoothie?

My friends' enthusiasm made introductions a zoo, each trying to tell her piece of the story, except for Ada who was emoting over the telephone with her stepson. Emoting in a bath of continual salt water on my cell phone, come to think of it. Meg finally glared at us and we calmed down. I laid out the basics of our home invasion while the others forced themselves to be still. "The, uh, suspect hightailed up toward the woods in back, Detective," I finished, replacing my beret carefully at the appropriate tilt.

He nodded. "I'm going to join the other officer on the perimeter check, ladies. Then we'll speak with you all individually. Stay right here, please. Don't move around the crime scene too much."

Across from me, Meg sniggered. Cascone took a moment to survey our little group with an obvious touch of awe. Stared at Dorie's boa. Tilted his face at my beret. Then raised his eyebrows as he stood up.

"I'll show you the backdoor," I volunteered, jumping up so quickly I lost my hat again.

In his short-sleeved sport shirt with the slight perspiration marks under the arms the detective looked uncomfortable, especially under the glowing Swarovski chandelier. His beard had seemed to sprout and darken while he stood there, and his eyes, I was certain, grew bloodshot just glancing at our array of wine bottles and glasses.

"He ran this way," I explained as I led him to the kitchen.

"Farquar," Ada called out, her phone call finished. "That's his name."

"Or so he said. We haven't seen him since he barged out the kitchen door there and headed up the hill," I offered. "This on the floor is his jacket. We ripped it off." I pulled the door open and let him pass.

"Know if he had a car?" Cascone caught my eye and his mouth turned up the tiniest bit.

I shook my head and found myself fluffing my hair over my ears with my fingers, something Dorie claimed I did when I was nervous, or had spotted an extremely arresting male personage. I did an inner giggle at my own choice of adjectives. And observed to myself that even a 55-year-old female heart could still thump a response to male pheromones.

"Stay here, please, Ms. Doyle. You and Doctor Dautrey wait for the other detectives," he said in a voice that brooked no opposition. "You'll be a big help." He laid his hand on my arm, slowly, no rush.

I couldn't believe how light and warm his touch was, even with the cool exterior, that heavy demeanor, that brusque New York accent. My other arm jerked up of its own accord and my hand laid itself on my breast.

I inserted the toe of my boot into the doorway and made him stop. "But, but listen, the gardener should be out there. His name is Raul."

"That his truck by the garage?"

I nodded. "But no one has seen him all afternoon. Though he'd be the one to help you figure out where this thug came from."

"Thanks," he said, leaving off the "ma'am," and dwarfing me in the kitchen doorway. I tried to squeeze out. Instead he gently but firmly shoved me back inside, and yanked the door shut behind him, almost catching my fingers in the jamb.

I gritted my teeth and squeezed away some humming feelings across my shoulders. Then forced myself back to the dining room where Lucia was passing around a plate of crackers and cheese, apologizing for the quick disappearance of the Black Forest birthday cake. Ada chose a bit of brie on a sesame crisp, and bit down determinedly.

"Surely they'll find Raul out there," she said, when the first bite cleared her throat. "Maybe he saw this fellow hanging about here. But why didn't he come to my aid?"

Dorie muttered in sympathy. "Yeah, where is that Raul, anyway? He's always finished by three."

"And it's nearly four thirty," Lu announced, pouring seconds on the wine. "Oh, well, the officers will find him."

"Or not," Meg interjected.

Something clicked in lots of heads at once. I could almost hear the sound of it, and of lots of breath sucked in at once.

"Raul Mendino." Ada's face was pink with alarm. "My God, I hope nothing's happened..."

Eight

Meg

I wouldn't admit it to a soul, but this was the first day I felt alive to any degree since my last day on the job, over a week ago. If even one day in ten of retirement was going to be this stimulating, I could deal with it. My pulse beat quickened as I hustled Hannah back to her seat and laid down the law.

"Now listen, let's not act like a bunch of half-brains when the other detectives get here. They'll need to gather evidence. Stay around this table..." she gestured with wing-flapping arms "...since this is the only place the bastard didn't leave fingerprints or bits of his DNA. I know what you've been through is horrible, but we must act calmly. And for God's sake, be helpful. It's our best chance of catching this perp quickly. And staying safe ourselves."

Ada was still muttering. "Everyone, listen. I talked to Danny. Thank God, he's all right. Not kidnapped at all. Doesn't know what Farquar was talking about. Only knows someone at the facility told him I had called and he was to call me back at a certain time. That's why the phone rang when it did. He's awfully worried about me, doesn't like that fellow Farquar at all."

"Okay, so Danny's not involved," Meg said. "Good! Great! Now, no one touch the other phone, or anything else Farquar touched." Meg snapped. "Prints, you understand."

Ada rose again and sighed with relief. "Is it permissible to call my nephew Judd? I forgot all about calling him."

I knew Ada and her deceased husband's nephew had a close relationship. Both high society, both mutually protective.

Hannah lifted her flip-top cell phone from her skirt pocket and glanced at me. With the authority born of my former State position I nodded, and Hannah passed the receiver over again. Ada scurried off to the hallway and dialed her number. The others ate water crackers and an entire wedge of Roquefort and babbled about the horrifying experience while they waited, trying not to overhear.

Just as two more carloads of police pulled up in the driveway, Cascone and his partner came rushing back in.

"We got major problems," he told the women. "Send the rest of the team out back when they arrive."

"I think they're here," Hannah announced, rising.

"Excellent," Cascone said, fastening his limpid browns on her. "Your gardener fellow is, well, not here. Wasn't as fortunate as you ladies. We think it's him anyway."

When I saw Hannah cover her heart with a trembling hand, I knew it was not from the detective's slight overbite and strong, jutting chin that clearly made her go adolescent ten minutes ago.

"Are you, are you saying Raul Mendino is—dead? Murdered?" Hannah's stare might have burned two holes in the poor detective's face. But his nod was steady, final.

All around me I heard the jagged intake of breath, and in the next second, Ada, peeking around the corner after completing her call, was back on the floor, this time, out cold.

~ * ~

An hour-and-half later I figured things were enough under control that I could move on. The living room was still cordoned off, broken furniture, pottery and all, but the detectives and uniformed officers, six or seven total, had finished a preliminary sweep of the house and were buzzing around outside, sketching, examining, probing. They even had a police dog tracking up in the woods with his operator. Where Silver Fish Brook traversed the land, the animal seemed to get confused, and went around in circles. Cascone said it wasn't a good sign.

He and Ketry had taken statements from them all— individually, in Ada's den at the other end of the first floor, after it, too, had been thoroughly examined. Now I was itching to get out back and check out the body of poor Raul, whose wife and son were on their way over. They had been told they were needed, and nothing more. Ada had got permission from Detective Cascone to be the one to tell them.

Dorie wavered on her feet, and Lu said she'd take her home. "I don't think I want to be alone just now," pale, quaking Dorie muttered.

"Come home with me for spaghetti," Lucia offered. Dorie brightened. "How about you, Ada? Will you be all right? Will Judd be coming home to stay with you?"

"I told Judd everything. He was appalled, but after all... he just got to Palm Beach. It's an important conference. Something about malpractice insurance, which is plaguing all the O.B.'s right now."

I nodded decisively. "No need for him to fly home. The police have everything well in hand. I would be surprised if they haven't caught the idiot by dark."

"I just wish... I mean Judd always knows just what to do. He handles my affairs when I need him. Like when B. J. died and Danny was in no condition. Judd was just wonderful with the funeral services. And all of it." Ada folded her linen napkin into a small, flat bundle.

Hannah murmured assent. "We know what to do, too, Ada. Don't worry. I'll stay with you tonight. I haven't slept in 800-count Egyptian cotton sheets in a dog's age. Let the man have his conference in Florida another day or two."

I stood and began to clear the table. "She's right. Doctors nowadays don't have it so easy. One of us will stay with you as long as you like, dear. For now, I'm going out back before they remove the—evidence, and see what I can find out. Dorie and Lu, talk to you later."

As I slipped off and made my way to the kitchen door, I heard the others fluttering toward the front hall. Dorie still wore her feathers, and Lucia her red high heels. I wondered what sort of special item of clothing I'd get to be part of their club that wouldn't feel too ridiculous. Not feathers or high heels, that was for sure. It would have to be something no-nonsense, unobtrusive. Bad enough to go out in public with these wild and wacky women friends of mine, but to do it in costume seemed a blueprint for trouble.

I stepped out on the patio and pulled the kitchen door closed loudly enough so Cascone and his party of three or four glanced up, and back down again. One of them was stringing yellow tape. He shot me a second look.

"Doc Dautrey. How are ya'? They squeezing one last case out of you?"

I chortled. "They wish, Holmes. I'm off the job as of last Friday. Taking the vacation time I had coming before I'm off for good. I'm just… curious." I moved confidently toward the east corner of the house, hoping no one would stop me. There, around the side of the building, half-buried in the rhododendrons, lay Raul Mendino, his head turned away from the structure and his naturally olive complexion totally devoid of pink color, one leg drawn up as if he'd been moving when he fell over.

I took in a lungful of air and bent close, before Cascone could warn me off. I shivered, probably because it was getting chilly. Late afternoon in April, it would.

The detective sidled up next to me and bent over. "Gonna take a look, Doc?"

I breathed a sigh of relief. "Damn straight."

"M. E.'s not here, yet. Seems a long while to wait, case of homicide like it appears."

I let out a bitter laugh. "Fool's not here yet because he's too busy. Offered me early retirement—state budget cuts—and I took it for spite. Now let him work his ass off."

Cascone chuckled, handed me a pair of gloves and stepped back so I'd have room to move. I noted position of the body, glanced with raised eyebrows at the team member with the camera, who nodded, indicating he'd photographed the scene.

Then I bent to survey the far side of the body, eased back to the closer side, ducking out from beneath the lush rose-colored blossoms, trying not to inhale the sweet springtime scent. Didn't need anything to cloud the sensory perceptions right now. From the near side I observed Raul's waxy-looking face, caught unawares, the slow trickle of blood from the back of his head running down his cheek and chin, then pooling beneath him. Bled before he fell, I observed, ticking it off in my head.

Barely touching him, I again leaned across the body carefully, trying not to catch my hair, drab and horsetail-y as it was, or my simple pinstripe skirt and vest on the shrubbery branches that surrounded the man like a cozy sanctuary. Keep the crime scene clean.

I examined the head wound.

"Never knew what hit him," I said sourly.

"Do we know that for certain?" Cascone asked.

I shrugged my shoulders. No sign of a bullet's entry, but his right arm was beneath the body, with the metal handle of some significant tool—pruning shears?—protruding slightly beneath it. There was a separate darkening of the grass beneath Raul's chest. More blood.

The position of the shears told me he was probably pruning the rhododendrons at the time of the killing and had fallen on the implement, perhaps when struck in the head. Double whammy. I tugged the body upward slightly and bent low to verify my assumption.

Bingo. Both blades of the pruning implement were buried between his ribs. I eased his rapidly morbidifying body back down.

You don't get up again from that.

Something I had seen or thought preyed on my mind, but in the difficulty of rising, I forgot what it was. I stood upright and rubbed my gloved hands together gently. It wasn't just my arthritic knees, but my damned memory that slowed me down. I stopped, shut my eyes for one quick moment, and wondered what piece of information I'd just registered and had as quickly forgotten.

Then I gave up, and put more effort into trying to erase the memory of Raul's once smiling, gentle face, his charming, twisted English and good nature, his work-worn hands and tanned arms and neck, the few times I'd spoken with him. I thought of Ada, who had known this man for—how long? Four or five years?

My stomach threatened to flip-flop. I'd dealt with it hundreds of times, unexpected death, but this person had a name I knew, a voice I remembered. Damn.

Behind me, cops shuffled their feet and cleared their throats. I heard the engine first of one car, then another. The M.E., I thought. And Raul's family.

I backed away from the crime scene, ducked under the yellow tape and headed back into the kitchen, peeling off the gloves as I went.

Detective Cascone followed me in.

"What do you think, Doc? The blow to the head?"

I nodded. "Could be. Impact site the size and shape of the gun barrel, most likely the nine millimeter you took from the dining table. But the pruning loppers did their share, too. It'll take a detailed post mortem." From inside I heard the wail of a woman's voice, the harsh, hoarse cry of a young man's grief. I paused, wanting to recall my forgotten impression, then spun away. "I'd better go in and help with the family."

My ex-boss passed me with a nod as I slipped down the hall and moved to the powder room to lose my lunch. I was glad I hadn't had to say hello. I wasn't exactly in the mood. The one thing I'd forgotten for the moment had just hit me with rock-like impact.

Why the hell had Raul, an experienced gardener with a master's touch, been pruning the rhodies before they'd finished blooming?

~ * ~

"I told him, I told him," Isabel Mendino was moaning when I joined my friends, now huddled around the poor widow in the den. She was dazed, but shaking her teen-aged son by the shirtfront. "You have to be careful with that kind."

"Kind?" Ada asked. "What does she mean? What kind?"

Vittorio rolled his eyes. "Nothing. She means nothing. Mama, Mama. Be calm. Pray for Papa," the boy urged, trying to wrap his mother in his arms, while she battered his chest with her fists. He glanced helplessly at Ada and Hannah, eyes round and spilling over.

Kneeling at the woman's feet, Ada poured out her apologies.

"Lo siento, Isabel, *lo siento.* I'm sorry." Ada shook Raul's widow gently until the woman started up with a jerk and realized everyone was watching her, listening to her. Her mouth immediately clamped shut, and she shook her head violently, then more slowly, rocking back and forth to some primordial beat. She murmured prayers, prayers whose rhythm I recognized, if not the words.

Ada made quick introductions and I expressed my sorrow at Isabel's loss.

"You found out what my father died from, Missus Doctor?" Vittorio, the boy asked. They must have told him who I was.

I shrugged and started to speak, but the widow interrupted, tears running down her soft, slender cheeks. "He was a good man, a man who stood up for his family."

Nods all around.

"Someone killed him? Was it this man who attacked Mrs. Ada and the other ladies? Or—someone else?" Vittorio asked.

"We don't know yet," I said.

"Can we go see him now? I will look and I will know." The boy was jiggling from one foot to the other, needing escape.

Hannah, sitting beside the widow, offered the glass of water she had carried in, but the boy shook his head. Isabel, too. They all looked at me.

"He, uh, it appears he was struck by someone or something, he fell and—"

Isabel's scream cut the air and she began rocking again. "See, Vittorio? I told him, didn't I tell him? Said he would hurt him..." She made to rise from her seat but Hannah laid a gentle arm across her chest.

"Better to wait a little, Mrs. Mendino," I said. "The official doctor, the others are still with him, to find out what they can."

"...would kill him. I knew it could happen." The widow rocked and shook her head hypnotically.

Vittorio looked blankly from one woman to the other. "I'm sorry," he said. "She's not making any sense. She doesn't know what to do. My father and her... He was all she had." His arms hung limply at his sides, palms open.

Ada reached over and patted Vittorio's damp cheek. "No, Vittorio. She has you. And your sister. Don't you have a sister, is it Lydia? Your father spoke of her, and her baby. Said she moved. We must call her."

The loudest wail of all escaped Isabel's lips and she collapsed against Hannah in the corner of the sofa. As if her spine had lost its ability to hold her up, as if her own skeletal structure had turned to softened clay.

"I'll call Theo," I said as I backed away. To Vittorio's questioning glance I responded, "She's a friend of ours, a holy woman, she's, was, a nun. She counsels people. We'll have her come over and speak with you and your mother."

"Yes, to calm her down. I appreciate, Missus Doctor." The boy relaxed his hold around his mother's shoulders. "Thank you," he said softly. Then, to Ada, "Yes, Lydia moved away. Mama misses her."

Ada sniffed into her own handkerchief. "Do you want to telephone her from here? She ought to know as soon as possible. You can use the kitchen phone when Dr. Dautrey is finished."

The boy brushed the back of his hand across his face. Resolve tried to take shape on his soft, olive features, but missed the mark.

I moved to the kitchen, trembling. Maybe it wasn't so bad not to have children. Look what you put them through when you went and died.

I reminded myself to call Arthur after Vittorio made his call, and tell him I'd be late. Somehow the simple routine of our life in the little apartment on the Avenue seemed very inviting right now. This emotion was more than I could handle. I'd rather be back working at this moment with the Chief, checking the depth of Raul's puncture wound, and determining exactly whether the blunt or pointed instrument had put him out of his misery.

Dialing, I calculated the heft and weight of the last nine millimeter I'd examined.

"Hello," said Theo Rutledge on the other end.

"Twenty, twenty-five ounces, striated with a herringbone design," I muttered.

Theo's voice rose. "Megan Dautrey, what in heaven's name are you talking about?

"Sorry, Theo, I just realized even a lightweight gun could easily do it, especially in the hands of someone as rough as Farquar." But why hadn't he just shot him?

Theo sucked in her breath on the other end, and said, "Oh, Lord, help Meg—" causing Meg to grumble.

"Don't you go praying for me, woman," I said. "I'm not barmy, just thinking out loud. You said it's okay to process that way, when you heard Lucia do it."

"But Lu's not a born introvert like you are, lady. Now tell me who died and why you are getting involved in your first week of retirement when you should be off sunning yourself somewhere?"

"It's something that happened at Ada's house. Her gardener got himself killed."

"Not Raul, that gentle soul?" Theo's pitch lowered a notch.

"The very one. And his wife is having conniptions, screaming some nonsense her son and the rest of us can't understand."

Theo's voice brightened. "And you want me to come over and help out?"

"Exactly. Maybe you can get her to her priest or something. You'd know how. You'd know someone." I tilted my head to hear if the sobbing and the exclamations in the other room had subsided. They had not.

"It may be her way of processing, Meg. Let her be. And I'll be right over."

I pictured the former nun clasping the cross she wore around her neck before she'd grab her jacket and purse and cruise on over in her Lexus. I'd only known her a few months, but come to think of it, Theo Rutledge would have made a good queen, too.

Nine

Lucia

I felt the jitters kick in all over again as I parked the
SUV in the driveway behind my husband's dark sedan. I
was home, Tony was a few steps away. Despite my weak
knees and aching nose from the blow of Farquar's gun, I
could get through this; get through anything with Tony's
help. I wished I weren't that way; I pretended I wasn't,
even to myself, but the day's event had proved it: I needed
Tony.

I'd put on a good face for Dorie's sake. I knew Dorie's
shivers as we walked toward the house were from more
than the cool evening air. I swung an arm over my friend's
shoulder.

"It'll be okay, hon."

"But he's still out there, hurting people for all we
know. Killing them! And to think he struck you and your
nose bled, and Ada has that cut on her head and the hole
in her couch! You stay so calm, Lucia. I keep seeing it
replay over and over in my mind and it just wipes me out
every time."

"You'll feel better after we eat something warm and comforting," I said. We climbed up to the side door. "If I'd had mace or something useful in my purse, other than a stupid Milky Way, I'd have used it on the bastard. Thank God, Hannah had that hairspray."

I turned the key in the kitchen door and shoved it open.

Dorie mm-hmmed. "Hannah only goes to the hairdresser twice a year, she said, and she just happened to have that new can of hairspray in her purse from this morning."

I nodded. "Ada was brave, too, trying to get him with whatever she might find in my bag."

"A candy bar," Dorie half giggled. "Me, I never even raised my voice to defend myself against my ex and I just froze with that criminal guy, too. Can't believe I prayed, in Lithuanian, yet." Dorie, still jittery, danced into the kitchen, still dabbing tears.

I saw Tony coming toward us, and felt myself crumbling inside. Theo said it was natural, post-traumatic disorder stress or something, when people react this way once the crisis is over. All I could do was sob one loud sob, scoot around Dorie and throw myself against Tony's warm body.

He hugged me, then held me at arm's length with a question mark on his face.

"What the hell…"

"It was awful, Ton, this horrible guy with a gun, and I had to make him a sandwich and he gave me a bloody nose and hit Ada," I said between sobs. Beside me I sensed Dorie sinking down on a kitchen stool and starting to whimper all over again, and knew I had to get over it.

Like I did when Nonna Strega gave me hell for not coming to visit, even when I'd been there the day before! Suck it up and keep going.

"Poor Raul. Poor Ada. Poor Danny." Dorie's outburst made Tony's gape even wider.

"C'mon, you two. Tell me what happened, one step at a time."

We tried, but I broke in to mention Dorie's breastless creation and how I'd helped her finish it, and when I was getting to the part about walking into Ada's house, Dorie broke in to talk about the new club. Then I got back to the gunman and what he wanted, and how he shot my purse. I held up the plastic bag full of my purse contents and watched Tony's shock turn to horror.

"What…"

"They had to take the Gucci for evidence."

"And what else? Did he shoot anything or anybody besides your pocketbook and the couch, for God's sake?"

"Raul Mendino," Dorie said, taking short, wavery breaths.

"The gardener?"

I nodded, and made a throat slitting motion with my forefinger.

"Raul's dead? My God! Are you all right, sweetheart?"

I pointed to the bruise on the side of my nose and said I'd bled long enough to lose a pound or two and he gulped in a shot of air. Scowling, he examined the site, touching it tenderly.

"Do you want me to take you to the doctor's, sweetheart?"

It was the most solicitous I had seen him since our youngest son went off to Syracuse U and I'd cried for a day. Six months later, Empty Nest syndrome had finally begun to abate. But this...

I took a deep breath and convinced Tony all I wanted to do was start dinner.

"Why don't the three of us go down to the Parkville Diner and grab something, honey? You don't need to cook..."

"No. Cooking calms me." I smiled my appreciation for his thoughtfulness.

Tony let me edge past him to the work area of the kitchen, and watched me slip off my shoes, then whistled. "Whoa! Where'd you get the sexy shoes, honey? Thought you told me you were done with high heels?"

"They're for the club," Dorie explained, half a chuckle escaping her tight throat.

Tony glanced up at Dorie fiddling with her boa and swallowed hard. "That, too, I'm guessing? Okay, you two can tell me more about this club later. Meanwhile..." He fired questions as I rattled around the kitchen, grabbing my apron, flicking on the stove light.

"Did you call the police? Who found the body? Did they find the weapon?"

We nodded, and Dorie raved about Ada's and my dramatic tackle of the culprit when Hannah doused him in the eyes with hairspray. Tony blinked and let out a heavy sigh as he shook his head.

"Jesus, please us. Hairspray! You could have all been killed." He wiped a hand over his eyes and squeezed my shoulder. He reached around me and took my armload of pots to the stove. I could have sworn his eyes were moist.

"Who was the investigating officer?"

"Cascone," we chorused. "Cute."

"Good man, I met him at a meeting last week. Just here from New York. He knows the ropes. Don't worry, they'll find the bastard." Tony stared at his wife's puffy nose. "How was he killed, the gardener? Shot with that pistol?"

"We don't really know. Meg went out to take a look as we were leaving."

"Is Ada safe, Tony?" I asked. "Do you think they're okay over there? Should we have someone to protect her overnight?"

Tony looked at his watch again. "Let me get Cascone on the phone. If he thinks there's any danger, I'll send a man over."

I gulped my thanks. Owning your own security company could be very helpful at times, despite Tony's late work hours and devotion to the job.

"A wonderful idea, honey. Hannah's staying over, to be with Ada. I doubt our little police force can spare a man just to watch the house. "

"And until they catch him, there's no telling what that monster'll do." Dorie held her chin up with both hands balled into fists.

Tony glanced again at his wife's face and growled. "What the hell did the bastard want, that he should do that to you, Lu?" I could tell he had all he could do not to touch my face again.

I shrugged. "He was like a maniac, Ton. Kept telling Ada he knew she had a safe. She gave him money, and he did get some of her jewelry."

"But not the good stuff," Dorie piped up from the kitchen table. "He said he wanted the good stuff, the bear bonds or something. I knew where they were, too, but I didn't say a word."

I laughed. "None of us was thinking too clearly!" Now I had my loving husband's full attention, I felt better—renewed and refreshed.

"Not funny, Lucia. If anything had happened to you, I'd—" His Adam's apple jiggled in his throat.

"I know, sweetheart. I know. But really, it's nothing, I'll have a bruise on the side of my nose tomorrow, but not as bad as Ada's forehead. Now I'm going to fix some dinner. Then we'll feel better."

I pulled a bottle of olive oil from the cupboard in the big, no-nonsense kitchen and poured some into a skillet. Tony patted my backside, making Dorie squeak out a giggle.

"I'll call Cascone from the den," he said, and disappeared, leaving me to check the refrigerator for the rest of the makings of a meal.

Bending over the veggie drawer, I mused, "Tony takes such good care of me. I don't know why I ever complain about my life." To a package of ground meat I added some garlic, celery, onion and carrots. Finally I fished for salad makings and handed that pile to Dorie.

"He's a good man, Lu. No one ever said he isn't. He respects you, worries about you. You don't know what a gift that is." Dorie rinsed the salad makings and drew a paring knife from the wooden knife board over the sink.

I flashed my friend a big grin. "That's it, Dorie, you hit it on the head. I never thought of it that way. He may give me an argument about how we spend Saturday nights. He may bring home too much work from the office. And he may insist I iron his shorts, like Nonna always did. But—"

Dorie broke in with burst of belly laughter. I wondered to myself: why *was* I always on his case? Why did I complain about having to visit his mother, my personal Nonna Strega, at the Golden Age every other day? It was little enough for me to do. Besides, both boys were at college, I had a cleaning woman, no strenuous hobbies except my exercise regime and my Soup Kitchen work. A great life…

I shook my head and thought of Ada and her idea of a middle-aged Sisterhood and thought, double yes to that idea. And I'm going to be nicer to my husband, too.

I watched Dorie poke back into the refrigerator two or three times for dressing ingredients, humming now instead of trembling.

We worked in companionable silence while I made a simple Bolognese sauce and Dorie set about creating a picturesque salad of greens, slivered fennel, onions, tomatoes and kalamata olives with an artichoke vinaigrette. When we heard Tony hang up the phone, then pick it up to dial again, I started to worry the details of the rest of the night.

"I can't stand the idea of Ada's being alone. Even with Hannah there. Especially with Raul murdered outside her door."

"And Judd in Florida. He had to cancel a sitting for that portrait I'm doing of him to go to this conference. Did I tell you he took me to supper at the Country Club?"

"Really? A date, you mean? You didn't mention it."

"I think he felt bad he's always canceling on me. Such a busy guy, you know?"

I paused in my browning of the crumbled meat mixture and watched a pink flush travel up from Dorie's neck to color her cheeks. "I don't think it's right he didn't insist on coming home, do you, Dorie? She needs family right now. For God's sake, she doesn't even know if Danny is safe yet."

"Well, he *says* he is."

"But why did Farquar implicate him? Really, how come Dan called on the phone just when the man said he would? Is Dan being honest? I mean, you know he's had his problems."

I remembered well how my younger son Andrew had gotten a little too involved with Danny when they were both sophomores in high school. Smoked pot behind the school a few times, and finally got caught. Anthony, Junior, had set his brother on the right path by making him observe some bad cases up at Mass General Hospital where he was doing his internship. It had made Andrew shake just to watch the poor addicts shake.

Dorie tore more friseé and escarole into the bowl and picked up the paring knife, pounding its handle end on the cutting board for emphasis.

"Dammit, you're right! There's too many questions about this whole thing. Judd should come home. I don't see why he didn't insist. I mean, he's all Ada has, besides Danny. And if anything happens to that kid…"

"Ada's so good to Danny, too. She's tried so hard."

"What if they really are holding him prisoner somewhere? And so far away—Alaska, for heaven's sake. Oh, Lu." Dorie's long, artistic fingers paused over the construction of her salad, as though paralyzed. And the moment reminded me of Dorie's hands poised over her artwork earlier today. God, it seemed like weeks ago!

I turned up the heat and poured the jar of my home-canned tomatoes slowly into the browned mixture of meat and vegetables. While I stirred the answer came to me.

"We can't let it happen, Dorie. We've got to help Ada through this. Judd has *got* to come home."

Dorie was all nods and whimpers again. She carried the salad bowl to the table and slumped into a chair, the wooden bowl in her lap. Her fingers filtered through bits of greens and slices of Vidalia onion.

"But what can we—" She popped an olive into her mouth.

I reached in for one, too. "Call him, Dorie. You know Judd well. You've been painting him for six months, haven't you?"

Her face crunched into a frown. "Well, yes, but it's only taking so long because he never has time to sit. Don't blame me."

"I didn't mean it as a criticism, hon. Just he knows you. He'll listen if you tell him how serious this whole thing is. Maybe he thought Ada was exaggerating."

Dorie grunted. "Like that appointment we had on Monday, but his secretary called to say he was going to that convention in Palm Beach after all."

I suddenly pounced. "So you know where he is, how to reach him?"

"Well, yeah. He has his own place, a house right on the water. He keeps trying to get me to come down there for an overnight. Silly. He's much younger than me."

"You said it was barely a date."

"There were one or two other times, as well. Just dinner. But not for lack of him trying for more."

"Good, then. You're elected." I pointed my wooden spoon in my friend's direction.

Dorie sighed, set the bowl on the table and brushed bits of greenery from her delicate fingers into the bowl.

"In a way I don't like to call him, Lu. Then it might seem as if I owe him or something. Judd Javitt is so persuasive with women, everybody says so. Always leaving some young thing with a broken heart. Don't know why he's interested in me."

"You're an attractive woman, Dorie, and maybe your inner qualities have affected him. Maybe he's in love."

Dorie scoffed. "Phhtt. I saw through Judd long ago, Lu. If he's got any feeling for me, it's a different four-letter word starting with 'l'."

She fidgeted with her multi-layered garments, the pale lavender over-blouse that picked up the violet in her wide eyes, and suddenly placed her hands squarely in her lap and stared at them. I hesitated, before cajoling her further. Finally Dorie drew in a big gulp of air.

"Maybe this time I don't have a choice."

I jabbed the air with a finger, then started to fill a pot with water for the pasta. "Do it for Ada." I rattled the contents of the pot cupboard for a cover.

Dorie jumped. Just then Tony came into the room, looking haggard.

"They haven't got a lead yet on this Farquar guy. Found some of his clothes, though. A watch cap, a black turtleneck and dark CPO jacket you all ripped off him. Everything torn at the arm seams."

"Yes!" I drew my fist downward through the air, almost unsettling the pot of pasta water I was putting on the burner. "The tears are from us, we tried to keep him from running."

"I heard them rip," Dorie affirmed.Tony groaned.

"Where'd they find the tee shirt and cap, honey?"

"In the woods behind Ada's, all labels clipped out, nothing in the pockets. But no way to tell how he got away from the area—no evidence of a vehicle. And the dog lost the scent about 200 hundred yards back, where Silver Fish Brook crosses through beneath the ridge. They're surveying the neighbors now, and checking Union Station, bus depots in Hartford and New Britain. Nothing, no one, so far, answering his description."

Dorie was on her feet. "So... so... he could still be out there, near the house, still somewhere in West Parkford!"

I grimaced as I flicked on the heat. "Tony?"

My husband nodded, the look in his hazel eyes consoling me with its concern. "And I called your friend Meg Dautrey. She verified Raul was not shot. Final reports aren't in yet, on what actually caused him to die.

He suffered both a blow to the head, and a, well, pruning tool to the gut."

Dorie wailed and I exclaimed in anger, "How awful!"

He opened the wine cooler and took out a bottle of Sangiovase, uncorked it. "Don't worry. I've already called the office. They're getting someone over there for tonight, front and back. I told Cascone, he's okay with it."

We sighed with relief.

Dorie stopped to hug me with one arm as she passed. "I'll call Florida."

Ten

Dorie

"Damn, Dorine, I didn't realize how this guy terrorized you all. Aunt Ada made light of it, insisted I not come home. But of course I've been so worried about her." Judson Javitt's words caressed me like warm honey.

"So are we, Judd. This guy is a madman. That's why Tony set up security people at the house for the night. Until they catch him and we know Danny's alright."

"Rest assured on that end. I called my cousin at the rehab place and they said Dan's fine, out on a half-day leave to visit his girlfriend."

"That's wonderful. That means Danny has more privileges now, so he must be well on the road to rehabilitation."

"Yeah, but I want to hear his take on this guy from the rehab showing up at Aunt Ada's. What did he know about him coming here, anyhow? Says he's without a clue, but—"

"You sound like you don't believe him."

"Well, frankly, that boy's been trouble since way before my uncle died. First it costs a bundle to finance that habit of his, then to try and cure him of it. I hate to admit it, but…"

"Oh, Judd, say you don't suspect Danny. He wouldn't have done anything to hurt his stepmother. He knows Ada loves him. She's been so good to him."

"Maybe too good. Maybe that's part of the problem." Judd cleared his throat. "Look, Dorie, I'm not saying he did anything. Danny's a good kid at heart. But why did Farquar—was that the guy's name?—why did he say Danny was involved? It just seems like a conspiracy between those sons-of—oops, sorry. It just pisses me off. I can't stand seeing my aunt go through this. She's had a hard enough time, losing two husbands in what—five years?"

"You know, I think if you came home it would help. Ada… needs you." There was a full second of silence. I thought I could hear him exhaling smoke from one of those long Cuban cigars he carried in his lapel pocket. Funny, I didn't remember telling him Farquar's name. Ada must have mentioned it. I took a breath and plunged on. "Though, I suppose, who am I to ask?"

"No, no, really Dorie. You have every right. You're Aunt Ada's friend, and mine, too." Judd's voice got that deep, tremulous quality that made something turn over deep in my insides. I'd been trying to avoid that very sensation during the half-dozen sittings I'd had with him. And during dinner at the club last week. But Judd Javitt was a damned attractive guy.

"Look, I'll catch the nine-fifty home. It's never crowded. Though, shoot, I didn't leave my car at the airport. A friend drove me. I could rent a car at Bradley, I guess."

"Don't be silly, not at that hour," I was surprised to hear myself say. "I'll pick you up in my Bug. If you don't mind the squeeze." I pictured the sandy-haired, handsome doctor alongside me as I shifted the VW into fourth, my head tipped back in laughter. *Stop it*, I told myself. *Grow up.*

Judd told me the squeeze would have its compensations, gave me the arrival time and hung up. I gulped hard, rattling the receiver as I replaced it. It was just the day's events, I told myself. At my age I ought to be immune to purely visceral attractions. Shouldn't I?

Then again, I'd seen Hannah go mushy all over when that nice Italian detective spoke directly to her. Like she was special. Well, she is. If she could be rattled by a good-looking hunk, why not me?

During my dinner with the Catamontes, I only said Judd was flying home as soon as he could get a flight. Later, when Lu poured the last of the coffee, and we pushed back our chairs for comfort, Tony decided it was time to plan the rest of the evening. He gave Cascone another call. Still nothing on the gunman.

"Dorie, you better stay overnight," he said when he'd hung up. "I don't want you going home alone. Who knows what information this guy may have on all of you."

"I don't think he knew anything about us at all, hon," Lucia insisted. "Just Ada. He knew his way around there all right."

"Except for the safe," I interjected.

Lucia nodded gravely. "But I agree, Dorie should spend the night."

"You're sweet, both of you, but I'm committed to picking up Judd at the airport at midnight."

Lucia's cup settled with a splash and a jangle into her saucer.

Tony shook his head. "Not a good idea. Then you're driving around town at two in the morning to get yourself home."

"I'll have him drop me at home and borrow my car until morning. He can check my house when we get there, if it'll make you feel better, Tony."

Lucia dabbed at the coffee on the tablecloth and nodded. She liked the plan. She assured Tony it would work. "Besides, maybe by then they'll have caught the s.o.b."

Tony relented, if Dorie would call them herself when she got home. "No matter what the time."

I didn't dare let Tony sense the tickle of laughter I felt in my throat. Seeing Judd Javitts in the middle of the night, on this day which had so upset me, didn't seem like such a scary idea.

Sometimes I just didn't understand people.

Eleven

Hannah

An hour of tossing in those silky smooth sheets I'd coveted in Ada's guest room seemed enough penance for refusing the sleeping potion she'd offered me out of her cabinet of unlimited pharmaceutical resources. Though I did have a couple of perfectly good reasons for my wakefulness, not all of them related to the hunky middle-aged detective from the Bronx whose acquaintance I'd made and that stuck on me like night cream.

No, it was more the pepperoni, having been a hostage, and the news from across town. Once the crowds had thinned Ada and I had shared a large delivery pizza, and now she snored heartily in the room next door while I cursed my Irish gullet that continued to record the pie's spicy journey downward.

Another half-hour of twisting mercilessly in these self-same sheets also convinced me I had to let go of the day's replay racing through my mind: Raul's widow and son cut down by grief, Farquar terrorizing us with whacks and gunshots, and us retaliating with feeble hairspray, and Lu's candy bar. True, there were private security guards out front and back to keep us safe tonight, and Ada's nephew Judd had called from the Palm Beach airport to say he was on his way back to Connecticut, which meant he would be here to console Ada as pieces of today's horror were put together over the next few days. I did, after all, have to get back to my sessions with grieving kids at Theo's counseling center. This was all good, positive news. So why couldn't I sleep?

Probably it was Dorie's fault, or the fault of whoever had convinced her to travel out to Bradley to pick up the prodigal nephew at midnight, when our favorite friend of feathers and fears ought to be snug at home in her bed. Who knew, the home invader could still be on the streets of West Parkford. And even if he weren't, sticking fluffy, frilly Dorie in a very small car with the suave Lothario Judson couldn't possibly bode well. The man hit on anyone in skirts, and was still single at fifty, without ever having lost that particular gleam in his eye that started at seventeen.

From what Dorine had said, Javitts had been pushing all her right buttons over the weeks she'd been painting his charming features on canvas for the Hospital Board commission. God knew what line he'd take with her now when she needed love and consolation.

Feeling for the roll of antacids in the dark, I popped another and forced myself to chew. It was too late, and I was too tired to do anything more than hope by morning we'd have Dorie safe in her own bed, Farquar in cuffs or a prison cell, and the reason at last why Raul Mendino had to die.

I'd just slipped into my first full-fledged dream of the night—Raul's face as a death mask, smiling in the slightly apologetic way he had, and Bernie Cascone in some sort of tin man armor, taking me by the hand and trying to hide Raul from view. In the dream sequence the detective pulled me into the light, where bells began to ring and buzzers sounded. Loud, clamoring noises. Like a party, like New Year's, or the Fourth of July.

No, the ringing was the doorbell. The real, actual doorbell.

I jerked upward and leaned on an elbow to flick on the bedside lamp, burping up the last whiff of pepperoni and double cheese, and asked myself if the doorbell was ringing. It was.

I groped for the robe Ada had loaned me.

"Coming, I'm coming." I stumbled my barefoot way through the upstairs hall, found a light switch and scurried down, hoping all the while Ada might have heard the commotion and come running, too. No such luck. I always did have a tendency to underestimate the power of pharmaceuticals.

I tied the belt of the blue silk wrap more tightly as I approached the front door and acknowledged the too-rapid beating of my heart. Wait. It could be that bastard again, guy with the gun, or a new gun... Through the sheer coverings on the sidelights of the door, male forms appeared ominous beneath the single porch light they'd left on for the guards. But who would be ringing at this hour? And why...?

I heard the detective's voice first, reassuring, calm.

"West Parkford Police, ma'am. Cascone here."

I recognized with a jolt down to my toes the sinus trouble over the husky baritone, and fluffed out the hair over my ears before I turned the deadbolt. A girl had to be presentable. I glanced down at myself and chuckled. Yeah.

Hazy-eyed, shivering a bit from the shock of coming out of REM sleep, I studied the trio of men pushing in: a husky young security guard in a charcoal uniform, the selfsame Cascone with his cute overbite framed in a tight smile, and—

"Danny! Thank God you're okay. How on earth…?"

I made way for the entry of the group, but only Danny Javitt came forward, throwing his arms around me, his eyes wide, face tormented.

"Aunt Hannah! Is Mom all right?"

"Yes, yes, asleep upstairs. We never thought you'd come home, Danny. You shouldn't have left rehab."

"They let me, gave me a 24-hour leave. There was a flight from Anchorage. I just made it, thanks to my counselor Joe. Drives like a maniac. I was too worried about Mom, with Farquar coming here and scaring her, killing old Raul, and everything. Then pretending I had something to do with it! And hurting Mom and Aunt Lu. And threatening Aunt Dorie."

He held so tightly to my arms I could barely turn back to the other men.

"Is everybody okay?" Danny demanded.

"Well, yes, but you…"

Cascone cleared his throat and took a step into the foyer. "Said he lived here, Ms. Doyle, but when Stubbs here caught him fiddling at the front door—"

"I couldn't remember which key it was for the front door, it's been so long, and this guy comes out of the shadows and asks who I am, and all I could think of to say was 'Who the hell are *you*?'" Danny's chagrined glance back at the security guy made Stubbs chuckle.

"It's okay, kid. Didn't mean to scare you, but no one said you were coming. And it's almost three a.m., for crying out loud."

"Mr. Stubbs is private security put on to protect us for the night until the intruder is caught," I explained.

"So this *is* Ms. Javitt's kid?" Cascone's eyebrows lifted halfway up his forehead. I didn't know which face I was happier to look at, Danny's, or the New York import's. I must find out somehow if he was married. The detective, that is.

"Stepson, yes. This is Dan." I swung an arm around the boy who'd grown at least three inches since I'd seen him and pulled him close to my side. I could feel him shivering despite his parka. "Thanks for checking everything out, Mr. Stubbs." The security guard waved in acknowledgment and turned to go back to his post. "You, too, Detective. It's late. You ought to be getting home to your wife." I tried not to sound coy despite the finger I automatically pointed into his chest. In embarrassment I gulped, "I mean, it's late."

Cascone flicked a two-fingered salute and grinned. "Thanks. Stubbs will be posted out front the rest of the night. And his partner's out back. And I think I will meander home now. In spite of the fact I live alone."

Breath filled my lungs in a rush. My indigestion had suddenly cleared up, leaving me knitting the ends of my robe's belt through jittery fingers.

We said our goodnights, and, half-reluctantly, I locked the door behind the two men.

Danny, dumping his parka on the corner post of the handrail to the upstairs, as he always had as a kid, asked me for a full reporting of the day's events. I sat sleepily with him at the kitchen table where we shared glasses of milk and Danny scarfed a half-package of chocolate sandwich cookies, while I sketched out the events as I could still recall them at three a. m.

When I paused, Danny wiped the milk mustache from his face and shook his head at the same time. "You took an awful chance, Aunt Hannah."

"Somebody had to do something. The man was a basket case, the gun ready to fly out of his hand. And when I doused him with Glamour Freeze Number One, it did. Freeze him for a second or two."

He nodded. "He is a basket case, a nut job. I just can't figure out why he set me up to call home at a certain time, claimed I was being held captive, then went and killed Raul, and hurt Mom and tried to rob her. I haven't had anything to do with him since I moved into the place."

"He was a patient too?"

Danny nodded. "That first day when my cousin Judd brought me up there, Farquar was nosing around. I didn't like his looks, the way he tried to weasel information out of us while I was being admitted. He, like, worked in the office there, running computers or something for this other guy who helped the counselors, Stoner. Both in their so-called last stage of rehab. Diehards."

"But still on the stuff?"

He nodded, chin dropping to his chest. "You can get it if you want it bad enough. Anybody can."

"I thought he seemed jumpy. Like he needed a fix. Or wasn't used to handling a gun. Did he know your folks, that is, <u>Ada,</u> had money? A nice house? Had you ever told him anything about your dad's estate or anything, Danny?" I tried to keep my snide little feeling of suspicion out of my voice. After all, in the past this young fellow had done his share of nastiness, rifling Ada's purse for his own "fixes," selling a few pieces of his father's jewelry when Ada passed it on to him after the funeral, all, Hannah recalled, over Judd and Ada's objections.

His stepmother had hoped the sentiment attached to his dad's rings would inspire Danny to get his act together. It hadn't.

"No way. I remember Judd and the Stoner guy shooting the breeze while I filled out some forms. Farquar was all ears at Judd saying how he was a doctor and they had computerized all his records, and stuff about software not working and such. Seemed like Judd was looking for free info for his office system. Later, Farquar tried to cozy up to me, but I was in a fog those first few weeks, and I've always avoided him. Everybody knew he was still using. I think the staff realized it, too. Then about two months ago, he just disappeared."

"And this girl you go with, Dan? Did she know him?"

"No, couldn't have. She's a sweet kid. Just started working there about six weeks back, but we, like, felt attracted right away." He blushed and studied his hands. "She's a good kid, Han. Taking a course in rehab therapy. She's been encouraging me to go back to college and finally get my architecture degree. It's what I've always wanted. Just seemed so big and unmanageable to me before."

"And now you're the little engine who could?"

He grinned at the reference. "Yeah, feel like it, anyway, thanks to Janet. She worked her way through school, comes from a poor family but doesn't let it get her down. She's solid, you know, tough. Never mixed up in drugs or anything like that. And never even met Gordon. That's Farquar."

"And you didn't owe this Gordon anything? He wasn't into you?"

Danny set down his empty milk glass with a thump. "No way! I'm telling you I'm really trying this time. Not to throw away my life. You gotta believe me, Aunt Hannah. You know I would never do anything to hurt Ada. Not now, anyhow. I'm clean. She's the only mom I ever really knew. I gave her and Dad a rough enough time these past few years. But I'm over it, I'm *getting* over it, damn it."

I tapped his soft, peach-fuzzed cheek and stood up. "I'm very, very happy about that, Dan. You and Ada are going to be a family yet. She needs you."

"And let's face it," the boy said, his eyes dropping to the crumbs on the table, "I need her." He pulled himself up out of his chair and made a concerted effort to brush the crumbs into one hand. "I mean, it's bad enough about

Raul, and I feel terrible for his family. But if anything had happened to her…"

"I know, honey. Now come on, let's hit the sack. I imagine that Detective'll want to see you in the morning. And Judd'll be home from Florida, and you and your mom will have a big reunion. Then she's going to help Mrs. Mendino make the arrangements. Lots to do."

I waited while Danny rubbed his hands together over the kitchen sink. He followed me up, shutting off the lights as we passed from one room to the next and up the stairs. From the doorway of the guest room I watched him peek into Ada's bedroom, sigh, then take a deep breath and enter his own childhood room across the hall with a whispered "'Night."

A sudden question popped into my mind just as Danny's door closed: *how had he known Raul was killed? Ada never called him back to say so, had she?* It wasn't something I wanted to think about. I was too suspicious for my own good—as had been pointed out to me many times. As I turned over in the silky smooth sheets, I preferred recalling the words and facial expressions of the New York detective who apparently had no wife.

On that note, and thanks to the glass of milk, I finally slept. Whatever dreams floated past me were fleeting and fragmented, a face or two, a dance step in swirling colors, vague—a lot like my writing in recent days. I'd have to work on that, and pay better attention to those images of faces and dancing in my unconscious.

I hadn't danced in years.

Twelve

Dorie

"It's way too late for you to go home and stay alone," Judd insisted. His arm stretched across the backrest as I drove. Every so often it curled around me comfortingly as I steered with caution through the cool, windy and overcast April evening and retold the tale of the home invader.

"This must have been terrible for all of you, Dorine. Come stay in the guest room at my place, and we'll both go to my aunt's first thing in the morning. She knows I'm coming."

"But we had it all planned that I'd—"

"No, sweetie, you've been through way too much. I can see it took a lot out of you. And to stay up late to pick me up at Bradley after the day you've had is way beyond the call. I wouldn't feel right. I just couldn't let you do it."

I tried not to sigh aloud. Judd did know the right thing to say to soften up a woman like me. Keeping him at arm's length had been no problem when I was painting him in broad daylight, in his greenhouse off Mountain Ridge, lush plants and the scent of earth and orchids creating a sense of safety, and my work—and the promised commission—keeping me focused. But now, in the dashboard-lighted dimness of the car, his deep, golden voice luring me into a somebody-cares kind of ambiance, I felt my resolve slipping.

I *had* had a terrible day. Well, it had gone downhill from triumphantly delivering my latest work of art to being terrorized at the hands of that, that bully! My hand went to the "vee" of my blouse, as I recalled the awful groping of Farquar. The same dread had built in me I used to feel when Harry came home intoxicated, looking for a punching bag to vent his frustrations, someone to use to express his sexual fervor. Violence was more like it.

I sighed again, wishing I wasn't so mamby-pamby, but rather a strong, decisive woman like Ada or Hannah. Here by my side was a gorgeous, considerate man wanting to comfort me, protect me. And to stay in that glorious house on Wrenwood, just up the hill from Ada's, with the lights of the city in the distance... Probably the same Egyptian sheets Hannah had looked forward to. I bit my tongue rather than sigh again.

"Great," Judd said. His arm slipped from my shoulder as we pulled out of the center and swung the car west, past Mountain Ridge instead of toward my eastward neighborhood. "You won't be sorry. We've both had a hell of a day." With the fingers of his left hand he traced the curve along my cheek, and told me he'd find some pajamas and a toothbrush for me, no problem.

"I could go home first," I said, hoping to gain some momentum back toward the original plan. "Pick up a few things." *Yeah, like a chastity belt.* My hand fluttered the hem of my chiffon overblouse restlessly and Judd captured my fingers in his own, then rested his warm, velvety hand on the thin fabric of my skirt over my thigh.

"Dorie, you're exhausted, sweet one. We're ages from your house, but a few blocks from mine. I've got a hundred-year-old sherry that will make a terrific nightcap for us both, then it's beddy-bye until morning."

I focused on the traffic lights, mostly flashing yellow at this hour, with no required stops for the final mile. When I turned into Judd's driveway, I was surprised to see half the house lit up. Probably a high-end security system, I thought, as I switched the engine off. When I turned toward Judd his face seemed ashen white in the bright light coming from the front rooms. What had happened to the sunburn I'd admired in the airport lights?

"Oh, um…" He cleared his throat, then took my hands in his own.

"You know, Dorine, I've been a selfish idiot." He fastened my glance with his own. "You've been a sport to put up with me and my bossiness. Of course you don't want to stay at my place after the stress of today. Why should you, when you can sleep in your own comfortable bed in familiar surroundings?"

"But, but I don't m—"

"I insist," Judd Javitt told me. "I'm taking you home. Now switch with me and let me drive."

My hands cramped on the wheel. What had changed his mind, I wondered. I forced a hand up to cover my face from Judd's view. *My God, now he's seen me in the light he realizes I'm an old hag. Too old for him.*

But he already knows I'm years older.

Why would he try to lure me into his house, his guest room, his pajamas? I felt my jaw clench with a clawing disappointment. For about fifteen minutes I'd felt like a twenty-year-old under Judd's persuasive charm. Desirable. Yearned for.

And I had to admit, I'd liked it. Who could blame me? Even cynical, cool Hannah had shown signs of caving for that handsome detective that showed up at Ada's today. And Officer Cascone had seemed interested in Hannah, too. Though not as much as Judd had seemed in me. Until a minute ago.

I shook my head, to make myself stop thinking.

Now I felt like an old shoe. Running shoe, moving fast, downhill.

Suddenly Judd's cool fingers were on my neck, massaging lightly, drawing me close.

"C'mon, Dorie. You were right, I was a bully. Let me drive you home and take your car back here until morning. I'll pick you up whenever you say and we'll go to Ada's together." He leaned closer with a rustle of clothing—his perfect Palm Beach sweater and duck slacks outfit oozing manly, spicy scents—and kissed me, a little too warmly, on the cheek. I almost choked. It wasn't all that platonic a kiss. And I wasn't all that distressed by it.

On again, off again. The man was enough to drive my libido to distraction.

Thinking of the half-finished portrait in my studio, and the money I needed to recoup from the Hospital, I thought it wise to say nothing at all. I didn't need Judd Javitt as an enemy. So he was impulsive. So what?

"I'll drive," I announced. He relented.

As I turned the key and backed out of the driveway, fingers trembling on the steering wheel, I noticed how the shadows of the newly leafing trees danced across the front windows. At first I thought something had stirred behind the curtains. But of course, it couldn't be. No one was home. All the time it was just the breeze in the birches.

Maybe the whole mix-up was my fault. Maybe all I needed was a good night's sleep.

Thirteen

Hannah

In the morning, after I'd showered and found the white silk shirt and clean Jockeys Ada had laid out on the dresser, I made myself presentable and went downstairs to find my hostess's part-time cook had the coffee poured and juice decanted at my place.

"Morning, Chantal. Mrs. Javitt up yet?"

She grinned at me, and a plate of wheat toast appeared hot and crusty even before I picked up my coffee spoon.

"Yes, Ms. Doyle. She found Mr. Danny's jacket on the banister there and went running back upstairs to see if he was in. I guess he was, as there was cookie crumbs in the sink and some dirty milk glasses. Must have got in late."

"Yes, I let him in. You know about what happened?"

Chantal turned her Valkyrian form back to the stove and flicked on the gas under her cast iron frying pan.

"If I didn't, those three police cars parked in the street would've told me quick enough. They all over the backyard, 'spectin' and 'spectin'. But Ms. Javitt already told me when she called me early today, making sure I'd want to come anyhow. I heard about that poor man on the news. What a awful way to go. No warning. I know Ms.

Ada'll be mighty glad to have the boy back home. Fried or scrambled, Ms. Doyle?"

"Over easy," I said, just as Ada's joyful noises began filtering down. By the time I'd explained about Danny having to go right back to Alaska, Ada and her stepson had joined us, clamoring for coffee and eggs.

The cook took two bouncing steps over, and gave the boy a bear hug that made him wince, but with a grin as wide as Farmington valley.

"Good to see you having an appetite again, Mr. Danny. Times you weren't much for eatin'."

"Sorry about that, Chantal. You always cooked real great, too. I was a fool to let those... other things take over my mind against your great pies."

Chantal turned away again. "I'm gonna have to cook real fast today if I'm gonna get some of them things in you before you leave again. Now, fried or scrambled?"

Ada scooted into her usual chair at the table's head and gazed at the young man with definite fondness. There was little talk, but much pleasure in being together.

When they were still finishing their breakfasts, Judd Javitt let himself in looking glum, and shocked, to see his young cousin at the table.

"How did you—" he started. Then he paused to greet his aunt and Hannah Doyle.

"Judd, darling, thanks for coming home. How nice of Dorie to pick you up, too. There's so much for you to help me with, Raul's services and all."

"Yeah, Dorie and I switched cars this morning. She was a sweetheart, all right. Of course I came home to be with you."

He gave me an off-putting smirk. We'd never had much to say to one another.

"What were you ladies gathering for yesterday, anyhow?"

I jumped in. "Well, I'm sure you know it was your aunt's birthday, Judd. We came bearing gifts and cake and were met by the home invader from hell."

Judd's gaze stayed fastened on his aunt. "Of course I knew it was Aunt Ada's birthday. Took her out to the Club last night before I left for the conference. Chateaubriand for two, right, Auntie? Nothing's too good for Ada."

I felt a wave of nausea thrum through my belly, and it wasn't Chantal's cooking.

Ada smiled. "You shouldn't have come home, Judd. You've been a dear to me. You need your time away—"

"You've been through something terrible, Aunt Ada."

"But I have both of my boys here now, and it's going to be okay. Danny just had to come check on me, too."

The boy stuck out his hand to his uncle but Judd turned away to signal Chantal for a coffee. "Anyhow," Danny said with a toss of his head, "I came even though she said she was all right, because I had to see for myself. Hope no one minds, but I used that open-ended return ticket."

Hannah noticed some displeasure on Judd's face, but surely not Ada's.

"We're thrilled to see you, Daniel," Ada crooned. "Nothing could have cheered me more."

Judd studied his coffee mug. "Still, you shouldn't tamper with the work they're doing up there, young man."

"I know, I know. Don't worry, I'm booked for tonight's flight." Danny gulped down his orange juice and poured another, and I stifled the instinct to step out on the patio for a cigarette. Somehow the Javitt family fireworks seemed more stimulating than nicotine at the moment.

"Of course he's going right back," Ada explained. "Danny's so close to the end of his program. His counselor says he's doing great."

Judd Javitt slowly made an attempt to reach out across the table to tousle his cousin's sandy hair, but his arm sank heavily at his side before he reached the boy. In the coloring and the chiseled features, the Javitt genes surely made themselves known in both men. But I guessed Danny would never have his cousin's suave, country-club looks. His light hair stuck out in the wrong places, and his nose was more turned up, not classic like Judd's. Nor could I picture Dan in starched collar and tie.

"Well. Congratulations, kid. Stay clean, then, and you'll be back on track in no time. Making healthier connections, finding a girlfriend, thinking about an education." Judd paused to loosen his tie and signal for more coffee to Chantal, who was serving up another order of toast to her youngest customer.

"He's already made some strides in all those directions," I had the pleasure to announce before lifting my cup yet again, leaving Danny to explain. I never did understand my need to upstage Judd Javitt. Something about him put me on the offensive. Maybe because as a womanizing O.B.-GYN he made his living on women's bodies, yet took his pleasure off plenty of them, too, with nary a commitment in sight. Carefree, pretty self-centered.

True, he'd always been there for Ada. Taking care of her when the weepiness and other torments of menopause nearly drove her crazy.

I shouldn't snipe at him the way I did. What would Ada do without Judd?

Ada was wrapped up in her stepson, leaving Judd on the cool edges of the conversation. "Oh, Danny darling, that's such good news." Ada couldn't tear her eyes away from the boy. It was as if suddenly he had become her barque in the storm. I liked their leaning toward each other as they spoke. It was a good sign. In the past Ada had been forced to shut the boy out in order to keep the hurt at bay. She'd suffered enough. Maybe now he *could* help her.

When Danny explained about his new friend Janet, and his desire to get back into school, Judd's eyebrows lifted almost as high as Detective Cascone's had last night.

"That's good, really fine, Dan. But what about this trouble, this murder here at your house? What the hell happened with you and Farquar?"

I saw Ada slip her arm around Danny's shoulder, and the comforted way the boy relaxed into it.

"That's what I want to find out. Another reason I come home, to make it clear I didn't have anything to do with what happened yesterday. I swear. Nothing to do with that bastard... Sorry, Mom, Aunt Hannah." His eyes pooled without a second's pause. "Can't believe Raul is... dead. His poor family. Lydia and them. I'd like to stop over there. And we're going to have to go see that detective real soon, Mom, because my plane leaves at six tonight."

I rose and cleared my dishes, bumping into Chantal who was hovering to do the same. Judd, meanwhile, lifted his cup to his lips.

"No need," Ada said, smoothing out her linen napkin on the tablecloth. "I called Lieutenant Cascone already and asked if he could stop over here. That way he can talk to all of us, one at a time, of course. I told him you'd be here at some point this morning, Judd, and he said he'd like to talk with you, too."

Judd gulped the coffee, clearly forgetting how hot it was, and reacted aloud over his scorched lips. "Damn it! Ow! Uh, of course, I'd be happy to speak with him. Help him know all about Danny and the rehab place and anything else I can."

"And surely about Raul, too," I asked, my gray eyes wide hopefully wide with innocence as I backed away from the table. "Weren't you the one who got Raul to work for your aunt?"

Judd frowned, gently dabbed at his lower lip and motioned to Chantal for a glass of ice water. "Why, yes, I believe I did. Is that right, Aunt Ada? I certainly didn't know the man, just heard he was looking for work. Some patient or other might have had to lay him off at the time, and he needed another customer."

"Something like that, I guess." Ada flashed her perfect lipsticked smile first at her nephew, then at her stepson. She seemed comforted with her men around her. The opposite sex had that effect on Ada.

I almost giggled aloud, recalling the new detective had that effect on me, too.

It was the perfect moment to interrupt and explain I had to be off for some volunteer work at the Mary-Martha Center. Ada and Danny both rose to kiss me and thank me for staying over. Judd Javitt sipped his ice water, still nursing his scalded lip, and gave me a finger wave.

"Bit of butter might help that," I cooed, as I passed him by. Every time I ran into the man around town, he had a different young woman on his arm. His reputation for philandering was citywide. I'd even heard from another volunteer at the Center that Javitt's mouth was magic. I didn't ask for details.

But as I picked up my purse on the sideboard I thought how curiously satisfying it was to know his blistered lip might hamper his style for a day or two.

At the doorway I turned back for one last wave and observation of the family scene trying to knit itself together at the breakfast table: Danny lounging back in his chair and suddenly downcast, Ada too bright and loud all of a sudden, and the handsome and very eligible doctor eagerly holding forth, swollen lip and all.

Only Chantal caught my eye, and that was with a curt little shake of the head and a rolling of the eyeballs I did not miss.

It was only when I got out into the driveway, my car keys finally fished out from the bottom of my purse that I remembered my car was still in the town parking lot where I'd left it yesterday after lunch. Only Judd's chrome-bedecked white Beemer was parked in front of the garage.

Oh, yeah. That's right. Lucia had driven us all over in her big new SUV yesterday. It had been a surprisingly comfortable ride, and a blatant reminder of how tempting over-consumption could be. In my new old green beret, I had as usual lectured Lucia about the world's dwindling resources and her personal carbon footprint. It seemed like weeks ago.

Now I stood there in the spring sunshine grinning, both from thinking of my friends, and at my own foolishness. Forgetting where your car was seemed more a Dorie thing than a Hannah's. Was it caching?

The Sisterhood of Goofy Middle-age, I thought, putting a title on it. Maybe I could do a piece on the topic…

I lit up a cigarette, then paced back and forth across the driveway, while I figured out what to do.

In the open garage, one lone detective from the Force was still ferreting out evidence and dropping it into little white waxy bags. His cruiser was parked at the curb, but there was no way he'd offer me a ride. I was about to return to the front door, hating the possibility that nephew Judd might have to be the one to chauffeur me, when Bernard Cascone pulled up his unmarked car a few yards behind the Beemer and switched off the ignition. I made an effort to keep my hands away from my hair, and smiled to greet him.

"Leaving or arriving?" the Bronx-bred voice asked.

I laughed and explained my dilemma as we walked up to the entrance together. Then Cascone stopped, and put a big square hand on my arm.

"Why don't I drop you at your car before I go in, Ms. Doyle? These folks will wait. I don't think anyone here is running."

"Hannah, please," I said, shifting my bag to my shoulder and stuffing my beret into its open side pocket as we strolled back down the driveway.

"Hannah, then. Bernie here." I nodded, reaching for the door handle of the black Nissan. Cascone beat me to it.

"You always this gentlemanly?"

"Naw, only first thing in the morning." He went around to his side and as he got in I couldn't resist.

"I'll have to remember that."

He gave me a sideways grin and turned over the engine. I explained where the car was parked and asked if he'd take care of the ticket if I'd gotten one.

He laughed. "Don't think rookie detectives have privileges in that department."

"How come you're a rookie detective, Lieutenant? And formerly of NYPD? Couldn't take the heat in the city anymore?" I absorbed, more than studied, his profile. It was that of some Roman emperor I'd read about in history class eons ago.

"Naw. Whole family's here now. I was born in the city, then moved here and joined the force in '81. But a couple years later I left for Manhattan, where things seemed more upwardly mobile in the detecting department. Got my twenty in, good retirement check then made the move back to West Parkford the first of the year to be with family."

"Yeah, 'cause otherwise I'd have known you. I covered the crime desk for The Courant until recently. Knew all the detectives, and certainly the brass, in most of the area departments. But what family? You said you lived alone."

When I saw his glance linger on my crossed legs I wondered if I should pull down my skirt, which had ridden up a few inches above my knees. What the hell, we're grown-ups, I thought to myself, and didn't bother. Something wicked made me even swing my top leg to the beat of the song on the radio. Salsa, nice and peppery, helpful when the caffeine hasn't kicked in yet.

What had gotten into me? I felt a flush color my cheeks and prayed it would stop there.

Cascone might have read my mind, because he seemed to be fighting a smirk, as he made his turn toward the center of town. Once focused on the road again he got serious.

"I did say that. My wife's deceased. Cancer, a year ago. My girls live up here with their grandmother, and I wanted to be near them. Maybe have them live with me eventually. Though one's going away to school pretty quick. She's in her junior year at Conard High."

"Sorry," I breathed, "about your wife." So he knew loss, too. Loss of the one he loved, as I did. But for him it had been no doubt a slow, gradual tugging at the fibers that hold two people together. Was it different, I wondered. The dying over a long, agonizing period? Different from the crashing and burning of a life plucked away by an angry God? The familiar tolling of mournful bells somewhere inside me turned down the corners of my mouth and shut me up.

"You okay?" Cascone asked.

I hate people who are that perceptive. What business was it of his how I was? Then I thought of Raul's widow and kids, and what they were going through today.

I moved my head a notch up and down, once, so he'd know not to ask again. I gulped a little air. "So your oldest will be in college? My youngest just got out of graduate school. The perpetual student."

"Yeah, and two of the three damn schools she picks are in California, of all places."

I was grateful he ignored the age-difference implication. What was he, fifty? Not even.

He rattled on, watching the traffic. "Wants me to take her out there after high school lets out, so she can visit a campus or two. I dunno. Kids. You can never figure them. You keep yours close to home?"

I shook my head. "The youngest is in Boston still job-hunting, so we see each other, every few weeks or a month. It's not bad. But the oldest went to Berkeley, married, and stayed out there. They just had their first kid. It's driving me crazy I haven't got to see him yet. Three months old and all I've got are digital pictures!"

"Why don't you hop on a plane and give the kid a big squeeze?"

Yeah, why don't I? Because it's expensive, and I'm trying to live on a small income. Because they're leaving for Japan in a month for Kevin's new assignment and the baby'll forget me anyway. Because... "I'm scared to death of flying."

I exhaled in relief when he didn't show any shock, or glaring condescension. Most people did; they judged me—unbelievable, afraid to fly in this century?

More relief: Cascone pulled into the city lot and my Volvo was still there, no pink slip on the windshield.

I glanced back to see him studying my face like it showed a pot of gold at the end of some rainbow. I gulped, and pointed, and he coasted over to the spot.

"Perfect," I said, when he pulled up and braked at last. "Thanks a lot, Detective."

"Bernie," he said. "And we're not done."

Close up like this I could see behind the shades that a grin played with his eyes, making them crinkle beneath those heavy dark brows.

"What do you mean?" I yanked out my keys and rested my fingers on the door handle.

"I'd like to discuss the case with you. Where're you planning to have lunch?"

A frisson of pleasure tickled my tummy, and deeper, way deeper. "Where I'm spending the day, at the Counseling Center where I volunteer a few days a week, in the old Armory building. It's called the Mary-Martha Center, you know, after the two sisters in the Bible who mourned the loss of their brother?"

"Lazarus," he said.

I almost whistled in relief.

"You brown-bag it there?"

I shook my head. "There's a snack bar right next door, grilled cheese, hot dogs, chili, that sort of thing. It's my one vice on otherwise virtuous Wednesdays." I could see he'd bitten.

"Twelve o'clock?" he asked, as I slipped out onto the macadam.

"One. It's quieter then. We can talk as long as we want. Or at least until my first clients come in at 2:30."

"Better yet."

Fourteen

Ada

Detective Cascone was definitely overstaying his welcome at my house. First he had interviewed Judd for an extended amount of time, now Danny. As I helped Chantal set the table for lunch, Judd fussing behind us at the Chippendale desk, I realized we'd barely have time to eat before we met Isabel Mendino and her family for the appointment at the funeral parlor.

"You're not going to pick up the whole tab to bury the old fellow, are you, Aunt?" Judd was rifling pages, checking my account balances and clucking in disapproval. Somehow account balances didn't seem important to me right now. A terrible thing had happened in my backyard, the police were still out there looking for clues, and, yes, I felt responsible.

"Of course, dear. Isabel hasn't a penny. I gather from what she told Theo her daughter has needed quite a bit of help recently. She had a child, and isn't able to work due to some complication. Isabel and Raul exhausted their own savings."

Judd coughed, then recovered, patting his own chest. "But really, you have no legal liability here." Peering over the glasses few people ever saw him in, he fastened his gaze on me.

"Surely the old fellow had life insurance."

I straightened the soup spoons, admiring the shine of them against the Belgian linen.

"Borrowed on it, dear. And Vittorio is hoping to go on, at least to technical school, when he gets out of high school. Whether I have a legal liability or not, Judson, I *feel* responsible. You keep calling Raul 'old.' He wasn't that old, dear—only 55—a few years older than you. The man's life was cut pitifully short. It's a tragedy, and I want to help."

"I'm sorry I ever got him the job with you. Nothing but trouble ever since," Judd grumped, shuffling the papers he'd been perusing. "I made a mistake, Aunt Ada. Forgive me."

"No such thing, Judd. Why would you say that? He's been a fine and loyal employee for over four years. Ever since you recommended him. He's done a great job on the yard, even put in extra hours when I had special events here, and wouldn't charge me. Not many do that, you know."

"Well, you'd best be watching your accounts, Auntie. I see there are a lot more deposits into that trust fund you set up for Ms. Boulé and her daughter. How much are you planning to blow on that? You know the market is shaky right now—a good time to be cautious."

I exhaled loudly. "I had some excess from a CD that matured, Judd. I'll never miss it. And without that small monthly check Dorie wouldn't be able to continue painting."

"Mm. Good of her to pick me up last night. She said to tell you she'd stop by later. One of her clients wanted help hanging a new piece she did for him."

I smiled. "There, you see? She's becoming very popular with her creative work. And Judd, dear, lots of artists have to depend on some sort of sponsorship. I consider it a privilege. Look at the beautiful piece she's doing of you for the hospital."

"Still," Judd said, "you aren't the savior of the world."

"Of course I'm not." I laughed. Leave it to Judd to make me sound like a saint or an angel. "All I hope to save today is our luncheon, and the funeral arrangements for poor Raul who died under my very dining room window. I do pray that detective won't be much longer with Danny. He's probably frightening him to death."

Judd checked his watch with obvious impatience and removed his glasses. "I wouldn't worry about the boy. He's had plenty of scrapes with the law that the process must seem quite familiar."

"How can you say that, Judson? Those were boyhood scrapes. Except for the drug selling that one time. And Driving Under the Influence. But this is a murder, for heaven's sake."

Judd gave me a reassuring peck on the cheek. "What makes you vulnerable is you always think the best of people."

I made a quick comeback. "I was just thinking how you always think too highly of me, dear."

Judd scoffed. "Just telling you, not many people have your kind of faith in human nature."

"You think I'm a fool, don't you?"

He reached across and touched my cheek. "Absolutely not. It's a lovely trait. No wonder my uncle found you so endearing. I just worry…"

"Don't, dear." I felt my skin mottle to deep pink. Not for the compliment, but because Judd seemed ignorant of how little his uncle did love me after all. I blinked. "True, Danny's been a handful these last few years. Even B.J. lost hope and wouldn't give him a stitch of time or money those last couple of years. But Danny's not a killer, not like that awful Farquar."

Judd spun away and coughed again, covering his mouth before he spoke. "Well, let's hope they catch the guy, and soon. We can't afford security people night after night."

Deep down I realized Judd was only looking after me the best he could. He worried so much for my sake, considered it his job since he was the last of the Javitts, he and Danny.

Trying hard not to get too sentimental, I blinked several times, felt that nervous tic coming on, and focused my most pleasing smile on the handsome man before me. It was a difficult gesture, one that cost me, because Judson Javitt so resembled my deceased, philandering husband a bit too much, triggering memories I had chosen to dismiss—romps with the office help and employees of the Country Club—right under my nose, for God's sake.

And seeing Judd up close, knowing his own reputation for attracting the ladies, made me squirm the tiniest bit. It ran in the blood. Not, I hoped, in Danny's.

He stared at me with those blue, blue Javitt eyes, waiting for my response. I breathed deeply. "Please don't worry about it, darling. I'm sure it won't be necessary after another night or two. Tony Catamonte may not even charge me. Besides, I just saw my accountant Sol Sherman, who says despite the dip of some of my holdings, we're in decent shape. Your uncle left me plenty of Blue Chips, and Money Markets going up slightly helps. Now, doesn't Chantal's soup—that beef-barley Danny loves so much—smell just heavenly?"

I adjusted the rhododendron blooms in the crystal bowl Chantal had set out and was about to comment on the table and its beauty, when the phone rang.

Judd answered and handed it to me. "Your friend, the escapee from the Maryknolls."

"Oh, Theo! How sweet of her." I removed my left earring and pressed the receiver to my ear. "Theo, dear, how is everything? Did you see Isabel today?"

As I listened to my office manager's response, I watched Judd straighten my portrait on the hallway wall. The damage to the frame was glaring. He shot me a look that said, "Why haven't you tended to this?" I turned my back to him and concentrated. What a perfectionist Judd was.

On the telephone Theo said Lydia, Isabel's daughter, was getting into the bus station from Boston this noon. "So Isabel wondered if she and I could meet later, after the funeral director's appointment. I said fine."

"Oh, good, dear. I'm so glad her daughter came home. It will surely be a help. Did she bring her baby?" Behind me I heard Judd suddenly punching numbers into his own cell phone, and stepping out into the vestibule. He coughed again, and I worried about him. He had been sick twice this winter. Too bad he hadn't stayed in Florida where the sunshine might have helped.

Theo said yes, the daughter had brought the little one, and that was helping to distract Isabel. "Although it's important not to stuff away our grieving, as you know, Ada. Sometimes it hurts so much in the beginning, it helps to have a baby or small child to focus on. She needs the break. And by the way Lydia wants to meet you, so she'll pick up Vittorio herself tomorrow afternoon after he helps you in the gardens."

"Oh, good. I'll be so glad to meet her." I was about to ask more questions, when I realized Judd had come around in front of me and was gesturing impatiently for my attention.

"Theo, we'll talk after the meeting at Reilly's. I need to hang up now. Someone needs to speak with me."

"Fine, dear, give Danny my love. I'll see him when I drive him to the airport."

"See you then. Bye-bye."

I hung up the phone and before I could even replace my clip earring, Judd explained. "I won't be able to stay for lunch. Emergency in the delivery room."

"Delivery! But Judd, surely you had someone covering for you while you were away at that medical convention. Can't they handle it?"

117

He leaned forward and gave Ada a warm, quick hug.
"Sorry, dear one. Full moon tonight, you know. Cushman
is covering, but has one of his own gals in trouble, too.
Meanwhile, I'm here, and Dotty Romansky needs her
obstetrician. A possible Caesarean in the offing if she
doesn't deliver *very* soon. I'm off."

He was slipping his phone into his pocket and
snatching out his car keys as he moved to the front door.

"But, Judd, Danny…"

"Tell him I had to go. I'll try to stop by later. Sorry,
dear. Babies won't wait."

I watched him close the door quietly behind him, and
heard the low rumble of the BMW starting up, before I
accepted his absence. I glanced at the table set for three.
Well, then, maybe we could convince Detective Cascone
to take the extra place. Chantal would be upset to find her
soup so unappreciated.

In any event, it had been nice to have my two boys
around: Judd and Danny. Though I could hardly call Dr.
Judson Javitt a *boy* any longer. He'd be fifty soon, at the
top of his career, what with the hospital naming the new
obstetrics wing for him, thanks to B. J.'s and my
generosity. Judd did put so much into his work. But a boy
he certainly was not. There were too many frown lines on
his forehead for Judd Javitt to be called a boy. I knew it
was a tough life, always on call for his patients, never
finding the time to settle down, marry and raise his own
family. At least not yet.

And the last few years he'd had escalating insurance
premiums that took much of the profit out of his work.

Poor boy said he was absolutely scraping pennies together for vacations these days.

I ought to relieve some of his pressure. Make a cash bequest to Judd as well as to Dan this year. Fifty each, maybe. Dan would need re-settling money when he came out of rehab, have to buy a car, get started in school again. And I'd never miss the money. The trust from his father would take care of tuition, as it was intended. And there was still plenty left for my golden years.

If, that is, I'd stop getting robbed, beaten and scorched by those awful hot flashes. I raised a hand to my forehead, felt the still aching bump and went to the side window to watch the detectives grousing around in my flowerbeds and lawns.

One was apparently making a cast of a footprint, another closely examining the branches of the rhododendron for fibers and hairs, Lieutenant Cascone had explained. A third was walking back and forth in the yard up to the woods, bending over and examining every deviation in my once perfect lawn, and another pair were taking the handsome Shepherd dog through his paces again. Fool dog kept leading them back and forth from the side yard to the driveway, where Judson's car had been parked a few minutes ago. I was beginning to lose faith in the local department. I'd told them there'd been no car there when my home was invaded.

When they were finished I'd need another gardener because the grounds would be a mess.

Oh, Raul, why did you have to go and die? I miss you, old friend. Not to mention your excellent and timely work.

Damn Farquar. Who sicced him on me? And where is he now?

~ * ~

I smiled to see Theo and Hannah had come back in time to accompany Danny and me to the airport. Theo opened up the doors to her gorgeous Lexus, and Hannah helped Danny stow his backpack and a container of goodies from Chantal's kitchen in the trunk.

"This lad travels light," Theo said, watching with a grin.

"Heavier than on the way in, I'd say." Hannah winked at the boy.

He blushed. "Mom insisted I take back extra shorts and things, with summer coming, otherwise I wouldn't have anything but Chantal's pie and cookies."

"Poor boy came empty-handed, he was in such a rush," I said. I let Danny sit up front and scooted in next to Hannah. "I appreciate having you both take us to the airport. Look, it's not even dark yet, and Tony has his security people already on the job. I don't know if I'll ever get over Raul dying right there."

"You will, darlin'," Theo declared. "Oh, you'll never forget. You've had your share of losses to know that. But time will heal."

"And once they catch the nasty man who did it, you'll rest a whole lot easier," Hannah reminded me.

I agreed. "I can't understand why they haven't been able to track him yet."

"Maybe he's never left town." Theo shifted and made the turn out the driveway, heading north toward Bradley Airport.

I shivered aloud.

"Please, Theo, don't say that. I never want to see that face again. I can't bear to think he's still in the area."

"Well, he certainly didn't come anywhere near the Travel Agency looking for a way out of town," Theo giggled. "I'd have nabbed him if he had."

I pooh-poohed the joke. "He's way too furtive for that. Cascone says they've located him in the National Criminal Intelligence system, have his photo out there, and have even matched his prints."

"You'd think they'd have known about his record up at the Rehab," Danny griped. "Mom says you identified him from his picture this afternoon, right, Hannah?"

"Exactly. He's got a record, all right, for drug related crimes. Nothing violent. But he's obviously graduated beyond that."

As they rolled past my burgeoning green lawn, no one except Danny turned back to watch the last few detectives measuring and poking around in the shrubbery. It was still a sight that made him squirm.

"Damn, Mom, if that bastard so much as passes by the rehab place up in Fairbanks, I'll let him have it. He's ruined your life, and the Mendinos' most of all. It's not fair. And him trying to put me in the middle."

I leaned forward to ruffle Dan's new short haircut. I liked it clipped clean above his ears. "Sweetheart, none of us ever believed for a second you had anything to do with it. It was just so bizarre you called when he said you would."

"Because of that message the counselors gave you," Hannah cut in. "You don't think any of them are in on this whole deal, do you, Dan?"

He tossed a look over his shoulder and scowled. "I can't think who. They're mostly pretty decent people."

"But you said someone was supplying Farquar with drugs."

"Yeah, you're right. But I think it was someone on the outside. He had town privileges, like I do now. He could have met someone and got the stuff that way. I tell you, I'm getting to the bottom of it. Janet'll help. We'll question the folks on the staff."

Leaning forward, I made a flurry of gestures that ended with a not-so-gentle grip of Danny's shoulders.

"No, Danny. I don't want you endangering yourself in any way. Or your friend Janet. She's been good for you, I can see that. I don't want the two of you getting into something that might be dangerous."

Theo was quick to agree. "You may think we old ladies are being overly cautious, but Ada's right. If somebody up there put Farquar on your mom's path, that's another someone to stay away from. And you don't know who it might be. Just remember they're no friend of yours, or they wouldn't have tried to implicate you."

Danny sulked, and when he eventually nodded, it seemed forced. "I hear what you're saying. What do you think, Aunt Hannah?"

Hannah drew a deep breath and glanced from her purse to her fidgety fingers, as though she were wishing for a cigarette.

"I guess," she said at last, "they're right. Like you, I'd have a hard time not finding out who was out to get me. I'd go poking around and get myself in trouble. Or get my friend in trouble..."

"I don't want anything to happen to Janet. She's had a crappy life, alcoholic dad and all. It's time I started helping her. Taking care of someone I love, like you try to take care of me, Mom. And like Judd does. When I get out, Janet and I..."

He let the words drift off and I prayed he was going to ask if they could come and live with me for a while. But the boy grew glum, and, besides, we were pulling up to the departure lane. We talked about the flight, and who was going to meet him and drive him back, and he withdrew even more.

When we hugged goodbye I reminded him I'd always be there for him, whatever it was he wanted or needed. Danny looked off into the distance, like he was either touched or distracted. As much as I thought I knew men, and how their minds worked, I was baffled this time.

On the ride home, ensconced in the front seat next to Theo, I told my friend she ought to slow down and drive more like a nun. We all laughed, and the tension was relieved.

"Much as I want to get home to talk with Judd about Danny, I'd be more comfortable under the speed limit."

Theo slowed her luxury car down a notch.

"Thanks," I said. "I didn't like the way Dan seemed when he left. He seemed so—"

I heard Hannah clear her throat in the back seat. "Guilty?"

Theo nearly choked on the mint she was sucking. "Hannah Doyle, for heaven's sake."

I wiped the lipstick from the corners of my mouth with thumb and ring finger tips, pinky arched. I sat erect and regal on the leather upholstery, and tried not to whine.

"No, Theo, she's right," I said softly. "We have every reason to think Danny might be involved. Good grief, I've even had pause to realize he might have come home just to throw us off from suspecting him. I want so very much to believe in his innocence. Yet I realize those, uh, *substances* he's been involved with can do a number on people. I swear they've killed some of the boy's brain cells."

"I don't believe a word of it," Theo said. "He's just shattered you've had all this trouble, and from a man *he* met at the rehab facility. In that one sense, that he had to even be in such a place, he may feel responsible. God knows he loves you, Ada. You can see it in his eyes."

"Meet my friend Pollyanna," Hannah quipped from the backseat. No one laughed. "Not that I'm saying Dan is guilty of a thing. Just I wouldn't jump to any conclusions, and I'd be mighty careful of anyone and anything until the police get to the bottom of this."

"Or we do, ourselves," I said, chin up and jaw clenched. "Why do we have to wait for the slow churning wheels of justice? We're not stupid. If we all work together, we can solve this whole mystery. I'm more like you than you realize, Hannah. I want answers, too. I want to know why Farquar invaded my home, and if anyone else was involved. Why did he kill poor Raul, who probably never said a cross word to anyone in his whole life? And why pretend Dan was involved if he wasn't? It's all too bizarre."

"The police do move slowly," Theo agreed.

"And hopefully thoroughly," Hannah said.

Theo nodded. "You talked to that detective today, right?"

"Had lunch with him at the snack bar. That's when he showed me the pictures."

"What's he think? Any idea why a criminal with a drug record would finger Ada? What direction is the investigation going?" Theo released the cruise control and managed the car off the exit ramp, and back toward town.

I twisted a bit in my seat. "Honey, I didn't know you had lunch with Cascone. No wonder he wouldn't accept my invitation to lunch. How sweet. What's going on there?"

Hannah flicked away an imaginary fly. "Nothing much. He wanted to show me the pictures of Raul lying there, explore a couple of possibilities."

Theo nearly choked. "And just what possibilities were those? Illicit and personal ones?" she teased.

"Oh, Theo, cool it," Hannah snapped. "Points to do with the case."

"Like what, dear?" I insisted.

"Well, like could Farquar be looking for Dan's leftover drugs in the house?"

I jerked around. "But he never left me to go searching. Claimed all he wanted was the safe's contents, then dragged me around from room to room, insisting I show him where it was. When we got back to the living room, he seemed weary, like he couldn't figure out what to do next. He made a phone call in the living room, whispering so I couldn't hear him, then after a half-hour or so you all arrived in your wonderful new garb. Wait 'til you see Hannah's beret, Theo. For this new club we're starting."

"No, look," Hannah said, "we should inform Detective Cascone about that outgoing call—see where he was calling. Also, Meg pointed out Raul was chopping away at the rhododendrons when they hadn't finished blooming. She says everyone lets the shrub complete its blossoming before trimming away the old wood. At least that's the way her Arthur used to do it. He's quite a botanist. You know that."

"Ha!" Theo let out a rush of air. "Of course, you let them bloom in all their glory first. Even I know that. Oh, how awful—to think Raul might have been involved in some way! Being where he shouldn't have been."

"No, oh, no. Of course, we did discover from the detective the way Farquar got into the house was with Raul's key, probably stolen from his pocket after he'd been killed. Surely Raul wouldn't have had anything to do with that madman. Hannah?"

Hannah paused before answering, and I judged her grin to be based on thoughts of her handsome detective friend.

"Cascone went over to interview Isabel and her kids again today. He was sorry about doing it in the midst of their grief, but the quicker they get a lead on Farquar the sooner they'll find him." Hannah fiddled in her purse and pulled out her cigarette package. "Theo, do you mind if I smoke?" she asked suddenly.

I spoke up before the ex-Maryknoll could. "Of course she does, dear. Theo has asthma. All those years in the mountains of Bolivia and Peru."

Hannah slid the Carletons back into her purse. "Sorry, Theo, I forgot."

"No problem, Han. Here." She handed back a roll of her mints. "Yes, I was there when your detective buddy arrived, having a chat with Isabel myself. And I must admit he was very gentlemanly about it. Talked to the boy Vittorio alone, then to Isabel, who cried a lot and said little, from the sounds of it. I played with darling little Putito, Lydia's baby, while they talked. Cascone wanted to speak with the daughter, too. To Lydia, but she was rather surly."

"She's had her share of problems lately, dear. Seems her dear baby was born with some sort of disability and needs her constant care, so she can't work. Some love affair gone bad has put her in a bind, from what Raul says. Said." I rested my head on the head restraint and sighed. It had been too long a day again today, and I still had to meet Judd and Dorie at home.

Passing the "60" mark had its drawbacks, even when you had the wherewithal to stave it off as well as anyone. Harder yet to bounce back from bad days. But at least I'd not been as teary over this horror as I'd been for years as B. J.'s wife.

Theo harumphed. "Whatever her problems, Lydia ought not to be so resistant to police questioning. It makes her seem, well, suspicious. She wasn't even very nice to me, and I was only there to help her mother." Theo angled the sleek sedan onto Mountain Ridge and Hannah made an assenting noise.

"Really! Being a resistant witness is the first thing to put the cops on guard," she said. "Cascone will interview her again, I'm sure of it. Probably after the funeral." They pulled onto my block and Hannah pointed out the window. "Oh, look, Judd's Beemer."

"He took Dorie out to dinner, dear. Wasn't that nice? For all she did for him yesterday." I was smiling as they pulled up.

"Or," Hannah added in a cryptic undertone, "for all he hopes she'll do for him tomorrow."

"Hannah!" Theo burst out, barely disguising a chuckle.

"Don't worry, Theo. I understand Hannah's dislike of my nephew. Wonderful as he has always been to me, it's no secret Judd likes attractive women. For God's sake, it runs in the family. But I think Dorie's too smart to let him gain any yardage there. Besides," she said, quick to open her car door as Theo shifted into park, "she's old enough to be his—"

"Mistress," Hannah said. This time no one laughed.

Theo drove off in a hurry, saying her husband Wilson would be holding dinner for her. "I'll be at the office in the morning, Ada. Have some itineraries to get out by noon. Then I'll call you."

I thanked her, and said goodnight, while Hannah lingered by her battered Volvo, fishing in her purse for keys and Carletons.

"Want to come in, darling?"

"If you need me, Ada, I'd be glad to stay over another night. Perhaps I'll just run home for a change of clothes." She lit up her Carleton and took a deep drag.

"Thanks, dear, but Dorie is taking a turn tonight. Didn't I tell you? I do appreciate everything my friends are doing for me. Now, if somebody would only catch Farquar, and if only the funeral were over—"

"Yeah, right," Hannah said, holding her cigarette off to her side while she gave me a peck on the cheek without disturbing my make-up. "Then we can get on with our new club and have some fun."

I snatched up her wrist and frowned. "Oh, no, Hannah. I didn't mean it like that at all."

"And I didn't take it like that at all, Ada dear. Just being my usual flip self. I'm sorry—I shouldn't have teased you."

I proffered another hug and held tight to my friend's arms. "You all have been so good to me. I'm glad you have something going with this hunky New York policeman. You've needed an appreciative fellow in your life for a long time."

Hannah laughed. "Haven't we all?"

I nodded sadly.

Hannah blew her cigarette smoke off to the side. "Thank God I've always had Devlin Doyle the First, whom I wouldn't trade for Mel Gibson, Bernie Cascone or any other unit of testosterone!"

I smiled and shook my head. "Don't blame you. He's a very special man, that father of yours. Sexy, from my point of view anyway." Hannah's eyes bugged out momentarily. I went on, unfazed. "My dad and I were close, too. He raised me, as my mama was too ill to do much of anything. Still, our love for our fathers can't be compared to what I think you're starting to feel for the detective."

Hannah's eyes caught the dying light of the day in the western sky behind me, sparkling in a way I had never seen them do.

She took another drag, let it come out with her words. "God, am I that obvious?"

"Never mind that. You're a vital woman, after all."

"Did I tell you, he wants to take me out to dinner after the funeral?"

"Another plus for him, then. At least he's respectful of the dead. A man like that is hard to find." We shared a half-laugh as Hannah climbed into the Volvo and backed out of the driveway.

As I scooped up my tan Siamese, still skittery after having hid in the bushes for most of the day before, I glanced at the retreating car and sighed. Perhaps something good would come of this disaster after all. I hurried in, remembering Judson and I had a lot to discuss.

Fifteen

Dorie

If Judson Javitt eased any closer on the couch I figured I'd be able to tell if he wore boxer shorts or jockeys. The warmth of him pressed beside me was pleasant enough on this cool evening, but there was something worrisome in the man's determined pursuit.

Judd had been tracing my profile with his forefinger, sniffing my shampoo. Next thing you knew he'd be kissing me. I wasn't sure how much our age difference had to do with my discomfort. Or how much my own reawakening feelings did.

"Give me a break, Judd," I burst out at last. "Could you, y'know, lighten up? We hardly know each other." I suddenly realized what scared me the most was the fear I might cave under his touch. It had been so long that a kind and attentive man...

Judd laughed and eased away to the opposite end of the leather couch. "I'm hoping we will get to know each other real well, and soon. You do things to me," he said, stretching languorously. "Every time I sat for the painting all I could do was stare at your beautiful swan-like neck, your long slender legs, and that gorgeous—"

"Whoa!" I shot back, moving farther away. Ramon the parrot, transferred here since the living room was still set off by crime scene tape, echoed my "Whoa!"

We laughed and Ramon mimicked that, too.

I gulped. "Seriously? That's why you always had that rakish gleam in your eye when you posed for me? And I thought it was your *joie de vivre*, or your eagerness to get back to the darling babies at St. Peter's!" In my retort I heard an echo of Hannah's sarcasm and it made me grin. Maybe I was growing out of being such a total wimp.

Thank heavens for green berets and pink boas.

Judd shrugged. "You're a fascinating woman, Dorie. Hard to resist." He started to lean closer again, but I yanked a long, impressive-looking cigar out of his breast pocket and slid it under his nose. Better to occupy him with his smoking than have to keep escaping from his too-enthusiastic moves.

His eyebrows shot up, and he smirked a crooked smile my way, then busied himself unwrapping and lighting the cigar. I watched, still tense, but happy to be distracted from his hovering closeness, and from the words he'd said, words that hung like tantalizing perfume on the air. Squirming, I settled deeper into a corner of the couch, pulled up my legs beneath me and tried to relax. I liked the scent of a good cigar. It fit the animal skin throw rugs, the burgundy leather, the very masculine den B. J. had left behind. The room was softly lit, the music on the CD pleasant enough, and the glass of fine muscatel dessert wine in my hand should help make me more mellow anytime now.

Though not too mellow, if I could help it. *Come home soon, Ada, do.*

I watched the macaw dance from one foot to the other on his perch as if distressed, and had to admit even as physically comfortable as I was at the moment, inside I felt as uneasy as the skittering bird. I realized no matter how flattered I was at Javitt's interest in me, I needed to stay in charge of myself. I'm so damn easily influenced. My sexuality is so volatile, my desire for man-woman contact so close to the surface of my skin, I felt I'd burst. I'd trusted those darn incendiary feelings too easily in the past, and sometimes it got me into serious trouble.

Like causing me to marry my daughter's father in a weak moment. Moment, heck. More like endless smoke-hazed hippie days. I'd always been a sap for romance, I thought now, twirling my glass and watching Judd examine the cigar he'd lit. And every time I kicked Harry out for verbally abusing me or worse, as happened in the last few years, I ended up taking him back after penitential scenes and kisses and the nosing of my hair. I straightened a little in my seat.

"Cuban," Judd informed me. "A friend gets them for me. Might as well enjoy them now. Won't be able to afford them much longer." He looked pensive.

"Why not?" It was only politeness asking. Never having enough money was commonplace enough for me the topic didn't seem worthy of discussion.

"Damned insurance companies. Know how much they hiked my malpractice this year? Two hundred per cent. Next year even higher."

"Wow. That doesn't seem fair. How come?"

"Wow!" was Ramon's comment, too.

I set down my wineglass. Except for the momentary ecstasy on his face when he inhaled his cigar, Judd seemed distressed as he talked about the insurance problem.

His shoulders let down. "People want perfect babies. So much can go wrong in a delivery. Often does. Things beyond our control. And the legal profession has taught the public malpractice insurance will pay to ease their disappointment. To a ridiculous degree. In turn…"

"The insurers have turned up the heat on you doctors."

"Bingo. It's almost too expensive to hang out a shingle anymore. That's why I want you to come back to Palm Beach with me. I may not have it for long."

"Thought you were joking."

He shook his head. "My uncle meant for me to have the house, and Aunt Ada's agreeable, even though her name's on it, too. But I have to pay the taxes, the upkeep. Pretty soon I may have to sell it to support my medical profession." He laid the cigar in an ashtray behind him and smiled his brilliant white-toothed smile at me. "Might be our last chance, you know, to play in the sunshine."

I tried to breathe. The lingering smoke made it difficult; even the bird was making curious coughing noises. I recalled with uneasiness what Judd had said during dinner: Come down and stay with him for a few days while he finished out the conference. He'd sit for me afternoons and I could finish the portrait. He'd have time for me, too, he said. We'd swim and sun ourselves, try the Palm Beach art galleries and nightlife. Sail.

At first it had seemed such a ridiculous idea, I'd scoffed at it. Now, it seemed appealing, a help to get the portrait done and my commission fully paid at last. And to think a man like Judd was making such an offer. A holiday amid the palm trees... I got giddy just thinking of it, the giddiness quickly rousing my pleasure points.

Did he realize how vulnerable I was, I wondered, as Judd took my hands in his. His touch was cool and smooth, his hands soft as a woman's. I glanced down at his fingers, long and strong, wrapped around mine. How surprisingly tender. My mind raced: of course, he was used to touching women, knew their need for gentleness and care. Something of which I'd known little in my life.

The thought snapped me to attention: how long had it been since a man... was interested in me in that way? I let out a ragged sigh, too audibly.

Javitt leaned closer and put both arms around me so I couldn't escape without a struggle. Half-giggling, I muttered, "Help!" and was echoed by Ramon, "Help! Help!"

When our lips met, I sucked in my breath, unintentionally pinning him more securely against me. He murmured under our embrace. I felt myself going weak, breathless. Parts twitched low in my belly.

Just for a damn kiss, for heaven's sake. What would happen if he pushed it to—something more?

When we heard cars in the driveway, Judd released me and grinned. "Dorine, don't you see? We have to give this thing between us a chance."

I smoothed my clothes. Wouldn't look at him.

He chuckled.

"Okay, I'll drop it for now. Aunt Ada's back, anyhow. What a trooper, huh? To have gone through what she did, and still hauling that kid around. He continues to be a source of pain."

"But Danny's doing so much better. And she counts on you, you know."

Judd grew solemn. "I count on her. I never knew my parents. Did you realize that? Uncle B. J. was the only family I ever had, and he wasn't exactly interested in raising a snot-nosed kid. Shipped me off to prep school as soon as he could. I was 11. Before that, it was servants that took care of me, mostly. Me and, later, when B. J.'s first wife died, Danny. When my uncle married Ada, a softness came into my life. She was always there, almost like a mom to me."

I squeezed his hand. "I know. She's that way with me, too, though I'm almost her age."

"Hell," Judd said with surprise, "not hardly. You're closer to my age, I'll bet. How old…"

I clamped my lips closed and shook my head.

"Okay, okay," Judd said. "Anyhow, back in med school, Aunt Ada was always bailing me out of some trouble or other." Judd's gaze grew dark. "Now she's saddled with the kid."

At the sound of Ada's key turning in the lock, and her sharp staccato route through the hallway, we quickly rearranged our little tableau. By the time she peeked in, I had primped my hair as back into place as it ever was, and Judd was taking another deep drag of his cigar.

"Thought you two would be in here," Ada said, trying too hard to be bright when I knew she must be feeling awful, leaving Danny at the airport. "Especially since they still have the living room cordoned off."

"Danny leave okay?" I asked.

Ada nodded, and sat across from us on the recliner. "Theo drove, and Hannah came along to give us an update on the case." Despite her perfect make-up and smooth cap of silvery hair, tonight Ada looked her age. Oh, the laugh lines and eye wrinkles were minimal; everyone knew Ada was on friendly terms with the local Botox source. But beneath her eyes, and in the slight sag of her chin, she looked closer to Social Security Age tonight. Not even the trim royal blue Bill Blass pants suit could disguise it.

Judd must have noticed, too.

He rose, poured his aunt a glass of the French Muscadet and brought it to her. "Here, darling. Relax. I know it's been a tough couple of days." He kissed the top of her head and picked up his smoke again. "So what does the indomitable Hannah know that we haven't been told yet?"

Ada sighed. "Thanks, dear." She sipped the wine, pressed the cool glass to her forehead and sipped again, then waved Judd's smoke away with her be-ringed hand. When Ramon made another choking noise, she looked up, startled. "Oh, heavens, Judd. Your smoke is making the poor thing ill."

Judd took another drag, then stubbed off the ember from his cigar and let it die out.

Ada smiled at him. "Thank you."

Ramon fluttered to the bottom of his cage with great drama and gasped "Thank you, thank you," before whistling a few bars of "When the Saints Go Marching In," the tune his former owner, a jazz trombonist, had taught him.

Ada praised his efforts. Then turned back and filled Judd and me in on Farquar's identification and police record.

Judd nodded. "What did Dan say to that, about mingling with a criminal?" He parked on the couch arm, leaning toward Ada. Suddenly neglected in my corner, I smiled to myself; I liked men who were attentive to family matters. Judd was certainly that.

I added my two cents. "Don't be silly, Judd. Danny had nothing to do with that, that animal!"

Judd shrugged. "Nobody but Danny knew him, though. The kid disappointed to be going back to Alaska?"

"No, not so disappointed, I think." Ada smiled over her wine glass. "He really likes this girl he sees. Anxious to get back to her. I'm tickled about that. But he has this cockeyed notion the two of them will find out how Farquar targeted our home, killed Raul. The whole mess. I told him not to get involved, to let the police handle it."

Judd leaned forward. "He okay with that? Sometimes that boy has the craziest ideas."

"I know." Ada set down her glass and shifted in the chair so the leg rest was elevated. She leaned back and let her eyes droop. "Theo gave him a lecture, too. I hope he'll listen. If anything happened to that boy, Judd..." Ada dabbed at her eyes.

I felt her pain and worry. "If you like, we could fly out to Alaska together and keep an eye on him. Make it an early vacation. We always had such fun, you and Liza and me, when you took us away on those other summer vacations, remember?"

"Surely do. Newport, one year, and a trip to Gettysburg and the other Civil War sites. Survival trips, you called them. I sometimes feared I was enabling you to stay in that awful situation."

"Never fear that, Ada. You were, and are, always a needed supply of oxygen for Liza and me."

Judd sat more upright and gave me a nod. "I'm so glad Aunt Ada has made arrangements to help you, Dorie. But just wait a minute before you go romping off with her. I've invited you to travel in quite the opposite direction, Ms. Boulé. I think I'm first on the list."

Ada perked up. "What's this about?"

"Oh," I said, feeling my skin warm to the scalp. "Florida. Judd seems to think I should come down while he finishes up the conference. But I couldn't, not right now, after what you've been through, Ada, and all of us so nervous about that creep still out there."

Judd jumped right in. "You can't let that idiot put your life on hold, Dorine. Right, Aunt Ada? In Florida with me she could complete the damn portrait and have some vacation time, too. Maybe get to see her daughter at the university for a quick visit."

Ada's eyes widened. "Why, Judson, that's a fabulous idea. Florida this time of year is still acceptable, though just. Dorie, for Zeus' sake, you could use a break. And you'd be taking your work with you. Would it be far to visit Liza at Gainesville?"

"Not too far," I admitted, unable to keep a widening grin off my face. But I also knew Ada knew the real reason her nephew wanted me with him—personal pleasure. It was common knowledge that, beyond his professional success, Judd's attraction to pretty women brought the man as much pleasure as one person deserved. Hadn't he broken two engagements last year alone? And had an affair with a patient?

I gulped hard and felt myself shaking my head when I pictured Hannah's reaction to the whole idea. Mentally I spanked myself. Now wait. The man was a doctor, for God's sake, a kind and decent man after all. He delivered babies. Beautiful, innocent babies. Willful? Maybe. So what if he was a man who knew what he wanted and went for it. Privileged, true. And determined. I gave him that.

I glanced up into Judson's blue-eyed, smiling face. So maybe, in this life, you had to be that way. What was so awful? I'd been willy-nilly for far too long about both my career as a painter and my dysfunctional marriage. That's why now, almost over the 50's hill, I was still reaching for stars and saving soft drink cans to help pay the utilities. And, oh, what a treat a few days of living without financial worries would be.

I studied Judd's hands, lying one strong one over the other on his knee. Manicured fingers, early tan, a gorgeous onyx ring. He reached toward me again, and I had to admit I admired a successful person like Judd.

And no matter how privileged his life, now he had to worry he'd lose his vacation home on the Florida beach because his profession might be snatched away from him. Something even deeper inside than my physical hot spots softened to the man. Judd picked that very moment to bring my hand to his lips.

"Mmm," he said. "Burned my lip on hot coffee this morning. But you make it feel so much better."

He brushed those swollen lips across my fingers, then turned my hand over and kissed the meaty pad of my palm. His scent, all-male, and tinged with fragrant tobacco and a hint of bay rum, engulfed me.

Across the room Ada cleared her throat. But louder in my ears was the unsettling music from parts long silenced in my body. When I shivered, it wasn't from the cool evening air.

~ * ~

In the morning Ada and I breakfasted on the sun porch discussing what needed to be done in the garden. The Belgian waffles with strawberries and cream seemed indulgent, but Ada insisted the occasion called for them.

"Garden planning is an investment in the future, dear," she said, mulling over full color ads in the latest seed catalogues. "And strawberries even better than these will be in season in less than six weeks. Raul had already fertilized our little patch back there." She gestured toward the west end of the garden.

I chewed thoughtfully, spearing another forkful. "Yes, you're right. But now, what about that drab spot where they dug up the grass along the woods after finding Farquar's clothing?" I asked. "Some annuals there would perk it up. Mauves and purples would be nice, but not too gaudy."

"Petunias, then," Ada declared. "And I think some azaleas about to bloom could be used out front. Be cheerier for people arriving, don't you think?"

"Perfect." I'd been staring in amazement at Ada's renewed make-up, fresh-eyed smile and perfectly matched Talbot separates this morning. I felt like a bag lady next to this paragon of womanly charms. I sighed.

Chantal placed seconds on our breakfast plates and agreed with azaleas. "Those nice bright ones, Miss Ada? Fuchsia, I think they are."

"Oh, she's right." I squinted, seeing the idea in my mind "And maybe flanked with some respectable white pansies that would already be in full bloom. Great drifts of them around your white pillars out front." The others murmured agreement and Chantal returned to the kitchen.

Ada jotted something on her list. "And I'd like to have a small tree planted in Raul's honor. Isabel could throw on the last shovelful of dirt tomorrow as part of the little memorial she's planning with her children. I hope it will be warm enough outdoors."

I picked up my coffee mug and warmed my hands around it. "You're so generous, Ada. I know they'll be grateful. As I always am when I consider how I'll be paying that tuition bill with your help."

Ada turned her head to the side and waved her fingers in a never-mind gesture. "Strictly self-interest. I'll have the satisfaction someday of knowing I helped make great art available to the public."

I blushed and started on my seconds and found myself thinking of Judd Javitt's blistered but persistent lips instead of the berries. I nearly choked on the last mouthful. To keep my mind on more mundane matters, I helped Chantal clear the table as Ada drew up her lists until, around 10 a. m., all three of us watched the police personnel finally depart, their yellow plastic tape dragging along behind them, their sketchbooks, cameras, plastic and waxed paper bags full of bits and pieces of Ada's world packed up and gone.

"Now it's up to the Forensics Lab to come up with answers," Ada declared, pouring another cup of coffee from the white Lenox pitcher with the gold rim.

I nodded. "I slept so soundly I never heard them arrive this morning."

"You had a call a while ago, didn't you, dear? Chantal mentioned it."

"Two, actually. Liza called from school. She's decided to take that job in the Zoology Department at the university for the summer. And I can't afford to bring her home for even a week's respite before she starts. I know I shouldn't complain; she wouldn't even be going to school if you weren't helping us. But I do miss her."

Ada made a soothing motion with her manicured hands. "But that's wonderful news, darling. Liza had e-mailed me she'd be able to get a job anyplace when she graduates if she could put that animal tech program on her resume. Besides, once she's making some money, she'll be able to afford to come home."

"But she'll be full time and won't have days off," I wailed.

"Then Judd's idea to get you down to Florida would, as they say, kill two birds with one stone." Her smile was wry, as if she knew I'd been thinking the same thought myself.

"Exactly what your suave and handsome nephew pointed out when he called a few minutes later. Honestly, Ada, if I didn't know better, I'd swear he had set up this whole job for my little girl as a ploy to convince me to go with him."

"I'm sure he didn't, Dorie. Impressive as Judson is, he would have no influence at the University of Florida. But he is smart enough to know Gainesville is just a…"

"Little over a four-hour drive from Palm Beach," I filled in, then lightened my third coffee with a touch of cream and drank. "I think that's what he said. Of course, it would just be for the painting, Ada. The hospital wants it soon, and he never has time for uninterrupted sittings here. Everything's on schedule with the new O.B. wing except the portrait of Judd. They'll need time to frame it, insure it, all that business. And I could use final payment. It was a healthy commission, thanks to you and the hospital board."

"So you're going to make the trip?"

I thought of my few summer clothes, raggedy and out of date, but all in my inimitable funky style, with floating panels and multi-layered tops. They would do. They would have to. I sighed heavily. "But not until after the funeral."

There was a commotion out in the front hall, and Chantal ushered in Theo Rutledge and the Mendino boy.

"I am here for to clean up your yard, Missus," Vittorio explained.

"Thank you. I appreciate your coming today, with the loss of your father so fresh."

"School says I can have three days off. This work, it's good to help me get over Papa's death."

Ada's eyes filled, and I was glad to see Theo break off a piece of an unfinished waffle and dip it into the extra strawberries, then make a place for herself at the table. It lightened a very sad moment.

Theo took over the conversation. "I explained to Vittorio that you'd be hosting the reception after the funeral and you wanted the yard spiffed up. He says he learned a lot from his father, and knows how to do whatever you tell him. He's glad for the chance to help."

"Would you like something to eat first?" Ada asked.

"No, thank you, Missus Ada. I work first." The boy stood jiggling from one foot to the other.

"Then come along, son." Ada stood and guided Vittorio by the elbow to the porch exit.

"My friend and I have been talking about what needs to be done. I'll show you where the grass needs cutting and raking and leveling off again, and which branches you must gather and bag. Your father had done some pruning that day…"

Theo and I caught each other's eyes and returned to the strawberries with renewed interest.

From the porch they heard, "I'm ordering some new plants this morning. They'll be delivered later."

Ada's voice faded as she walked the young man around the corner of the house.

I exhaled heavily. "Poor kid, working where his father died. It seems cruel."

"If you knew how desperately that family needs some financial resources right now, you'd say it was a gift, not cruel," Theo snapped.

I blushed. "I didn't mean to be insensitive, Thee—just the opposite. Coffee?"

At the nod of assent, I poured a mug and Theo took a sip, black. "I know. Sorry I blew at you. You're the most sensitive person I know. And I guess of any of us, you would understand the Mendino's predicament. Here only a few years from Ecuador, with very little family around."

"Well, it's true that, since Grandpa, except for a few relatives left in France, I have no family left but my daughter, and she's down in Florida," Dorie said. "Ada's a dear to give the boy work. I'll bet she keeps him on, if he wants to. Though he's surely not as skilled as Raul."

"Yes," the ex-nun agreed, "but Ada could always get any male to do her bidding. And she's a genius in the garden herself. Before she had the Travel Agency she headed up the Garden Club for years. She'll teach him some very valuable skills, I'm sure." She pulled back her shoulder-length black hair glinting with a few strands of silver and wound it at the back of her neck.

"You surprise me, Thee," I burst out without thinking. "Ever since you came home after 30-some years as a nun you've matured. In the best sort of way. I mean, I'm sure you were always an attractive woman. But the one time I met you when you were in the convent you seemed barely put together. As though appearances didn't matter. Which is fine, it was your spirit that mattered more, right?"

Theo nodded, impishly for her.

"Now—wow!" I gestured toward the perfectly matched slacks, blazer and scarf Theo wore. "And yet you haven't changed, not really, not inside."

Theo laughed, munched another broken piece of waffle and waved a hand full of rings at me. "Oh, yes, I have. One thing about meeting and marrying Wilson is I'll never again have to worry about having a pair of pantyhose without a run. My clothes will match, and my haircut be a good one."

"Exactly," Dorie said.

"Wilson Rutledge can afford it, hon," Theo said. "And it makes me feel good about myself. Not because those are the most important things in the world to me now, but because I've noticed the way I look affects people's comfort level. If it helps them pour out their troubles and feel trusting, whatever. Who am I to complain? Whether it's counseling folks at the Mary-Martha Center, or running Ada's Travel Agency for her, I seem to get a lot more work done when my skirt matches my sweater, and my earrings jangle a bit against my cheeks."

"Oh, I get the jangling bit," Dorie laughed. "But I'll never have the money to buy clothes where you and Ada shop."

Theo laughed, just as Ada returned to the sun porch, having overheard. As she reheated her coffee from the pot, she was quick on the uptake.

"For Zeus' sake, Dorie, I for one have a decade on you. You don't need expensive clothes yet, darling. You're absolutely stunning just the way you are. After all, you have the most eligible bachelor in Parkford practically dragging you down to Florida for a little *tête à tête*."

"Dorie—you rascal. Who is it?" Theo asked.

I flicked my wrist a few times as if waving off warmth. "It's nothing really. Ada's nephew wants me to complete his portrait down in Palm Beach and I'm—"

"Judson? Not considering it, I hope!" Theo's face had developed some instant worry lines.

"Oh, stop, Theo, for heaven's sake. Don't impose your morals on poor Dorie. She's a big girl. If she wants to have a couple of weeks of fun, let her. It's not every day…"

When male throat-clearing reached us from the hallway, we all three blushed. Judd Javitt had heard it all, and came in stealthily, for effect. He came right to my chair and kissed the top of my head. I felt his lips burn through my tangle of wispy waves and I laid my hands on the table as if to hold myself up.

"Yes, Aunt Theo, do let her. So you've made up your mind, dear one?" Judd slipped into the last chair remaining at the table, waving hello to his aunt and her manager.

"I… but I'm not sure when. The funeral, of course… and I'll want to spend a few days with Liza down there while she has time off." I lifted my chin a notch, reminding myself of Ada when she was in trouble. Only I was not in trouble. I had a wonderful, caring group of friends, a huge commission that would buy groceries for half a year, and a very handsome younger man waiting patiently to romance me.

"Dorie?" Judson asked, eyes wide, a hand reaching out to mine. I met it with my fingertips, then pulled back to pour him a cup of coffee. "Thank you."

"Only for the painting, Judd."

"Bravo," said Ada.

"Sounds impulsive," Theo added, garnering a frown from Judd across the table.

The noise of the lawn tractor started outside, and Judd blanched. "For a moment," he said, "I thought..." He craned his neck to look outside.

Ada eyes filled as she set down her coffee cup. "Oh, that it was Raul? No, darling, only his son, Vittorio. He's going to clean up the yard for the gathering after the funeral."

Theo brightened. "If you don't mind, Ada, Isabel would like to scatter his ashes here. You've always been his dearest client, a real friend, and you continue to do so much for that family. Her daughter agreed. When Lydia comes by for Vittorio later she'd like to pick a spot out back for the memorial service after Mass."

"She's coming to pick up her brother?" Judd sweetened his coffee, one spoonful after another.

"She is," Ada said, "and it's a perfect idea to have the man's ashes spread where he made such a lovely garden."

"Under your tutelage," Theo murmured.

Ada sighed. "In any case, I'm honored."

The whole plan made me tear up, too. I noticed even Judd had a hard time speaking, and, as the tractor moved slowly past the sun porch, he rose without touching his mug of French roast and gave me a peck on the cheek.

"I'll be leaving for Palm today, sweetheart. Must get going. Can I help you pack?"

"Oh, no, Judd, thanks. Don't you want to be here for the funeral?"

He shook his head. "Got to get down there for a crucial afternoon meeting."

"Then I'll join you on the weekend, if that's okay. Besides, I'll have to have the painting crated properly. Don't want it spoiled before we get to the important part—your handsome face." I suddenly smiled, and the release of it was like the wings of birds lifting inside me.

I'd been too serious, too cautious and too wounded for way too long. This man made me feel like feathers on the breeze, instead of a steam iron at the bottom of a basket of laundry.

Out the window the lawn tractor chugged back into view, as Vittorio returned for more branches. As it roared closer Judd kissed me again, then put a peck on his aunt's cheek and shook hands with Theo Rutledge. "Ladies, I have to leave you if I'm going to catch my flight. You seem to be in great hands, Aunt Ada, but call if you need me. Dorine, I'll have your tickets e-mailed to you later today," he smiled. "Be good, everyone."

"What fun is that, nephew?" Ada teased.

We women shared a smile as he left.

"Good genes in those Javitt men," Theo commented, watching his backside retreat out the door into the hallway. She fanned the air around her blushing face. "Thought these hot flashes were done with. Ada, I may have to borrow some of your soy milk. What a build."

Ada laughed.

Automatically I pictured that backside in swim shorts, or less, and felt something more taunting than humor cause me to suck in my cheeks. A bubble of laughter escaped me, nevertheless, and Chantal, entering to bring a plate of waffles for Theo, grinned with a puzzled expression. She was usually the first to catch the humor; this time she'd missed it altogether.

Within the half-hour Theo and I drove off together to Lu's house, where Hannah and Meg were helping with the refreshments for the post-funeral reception. Ada stayed at home to supervise the Mendino boy and the housecleaner, who would be coming at noon. "Cleanliness is next to godliness," she always said, firmly believing she alone could supervise the process to perfection.

~ * ~

"Cheaper than catering," Lu rationalized as she welcomed Theo and me and doled out tasks. "Not that Ada would mind the expense, but it's our way of showing we care about Raul, too."

Meg and Hannah reported their heap of meatballs was ready for cooking.

Lu applauded. "Good job. I'll cook them and make the gravy later. But first, everyone, let's have a tiny snack of this extra double chocolate cake I made while I waited for you all. Couldn't fit it all in the bundt pan for the reception, so I made this little eight-inch layer, too. It's an old recipe of my mother's, but I top it with chocolate buttercream. C'mon, it'll spark your creativity in the kitchen, ladies."

The five of us swooped down on the cake with forks poised and cake plates a-flutter. We stood around the white granite island counter that was the centerpiece of Lu's kitchen muttering our approval between bites.

The beautiful range in the center of the island sparkled, as if in readiness for their efforts, and Theo and Meg perched on upholstered stools while the rest of us leaned elbows on the granite and forked the cake. For a long blissful moment, no one spoke.

Then I giggled. "Ada says she learned on the Internet that chocolate is a health food."

The scoffing around her remained muffled due to full mouths.

"I knew you'd say that," I laughed. "But seriously, it is. Loaded with high-quality poly—something and antioxidant compounds. Right, Meg?"

The resident scientist nodded. "Exactly. Polyphenols, as in fruits, vegetables, green tea, red wine and chocolate."

"My favorite food group," Hannah said between bites.

I bubbled on. "Researchers believe consuming these compounds in healthy amounts could lower the risk of developing cancer and heart disease."

"Did you memorize that, Ms. Boulé?" Theo asked.

Lu jumped in before feelings could be hurt. "I'm all for healthy amounts of chocolate," she muttered, working on her icing and grinning maniacally.

Hannah whooped a joyous cheer. "Thanks for the health food snack, Ma," she said to Lu. "I'm a little under the weather, so can I have another?"

"Not until you fill us in on the case. I hear you have an in with that cute detective."

Lucia shoveled another slice of cake onto Hannah's waiting plate, then offered glasses of milk all around.

"Only if it's skimmed," Meg said with a straight face. "I'm watching my figure."

"We are, too," Theo said, eyes round in Meg's direction. "It's like mine—hard to miss."

We all nearly collapsed in laughter.

"Update on the case," Hannah said, having washed down most of her seconds. "The police have nothing new to report, no responses on the APB. They did find Raul's key to the house on the breezeway, where the perp Farquar must have dropped it."

"After he killed poor Raul to get it, no doubt," Theo said. "And what about the jacket?"

"Handled by a dozen shops in town and many more online," Hannah informed us. "It's a popular coat, though an upscale version, and hardly seems like it was originally Farquar's."

"Why haven't they found the man yet?" Meg asked.

Hannah shrugged. "Ada thinks we should help the police by working to solve it ourselves. Says we have the brainpower and resources to do it. Especially with you around, Meg."

Meg dabbed at her mouth with a napkin and said with exaggerated mouth movement, "Read my lips: re-tired!"

"But you actually saw the body, we didn't, Meg, honey," Lucia reminded her.

"Lucky you," Meg said, frowning and jumping up to retie her black rubber apron, a take-home peripheral benefit from her recent position as post-mortem specialist at the state lab.

I got wide-eyed at the sight, and the others turned in their empty plates and glasses with an "eeuw!" look on their faces.

"What?" said Meg, wearing her no-nonsense Buddha face. "If it's good enough for people, it's good enough for the dead fish Lucia is tossing my way." She held the open package of fish up to her nose and breathed deeply.

"Not just dead fish, silly," Lu corrected. "It's the freshest of the fresh. Red snapper. Perfect for *seviche*."

"Speaking of fresh..." Hannah said, as she tied on a more ordinary apron of white cotton, imprinted with '*Carpe Diem*—Seize the Day *and* Night', "Would it be out of order to wear our new club gear to the funeral? I thought it would cheer Ada up. If it's not disrespectful."

"You mean my sexy red high heels?" Lu asked, obviously shocked.

Theo shook her head. "Not disrespectful at all for Isabel's people. I asked her yesterday if she'd wear black, and she said that to her people, the funeral mass is a celebration of life. As it's supposed to be in our culture, too. But they really try to practice it. She's wearing a bright green dress and jacket, herself."

"Settled then," Lu announced. "Those who have club gear, wear it. Now, here, Dorie. Here's the recipe for the *seviche*. Meg will cut up the filets, you juice these limes and chop the cilantro and garlic. Raul's people all eat *seviche*, they'll expect it. Hannah, you start on this cookie recipe, but triple the batch. When you're ready to form them, you can talk to us about your detective friend. While you're measuring, concentrate."

Hannah groaned. "Measuring's not my thing."

"Well, then," Lu shot back, "peel potatoes. We'll want potato salad for sure. Lots of it."

Hannah shook her head brusquely and set to measuring flour and sugar. "Thanks, but I've just reformed. I adore measuring."

"I'll do potatoes," Theo offered. "High-carb prep was a required convent course in the old days. I'm well-versed." She stood at the sink and tackled the heap of potatoes with the peeler Lu handed her. "Just don't tell Wilson. He thinks I'm domestically-challenged because I never had my own kitchen."

"That's the spirit." Lu flicked a handful of eggs into a pot for boiling and began mixing up the salad dressing.

I had already selected my favorite knife from Lu's rack, and was delicately mincing herbs. I couldn't wait to tell my news about Florida, but also dreaded it. I knew I was in for some teasing, or for serious criticism, especially, again, from Theo and probably Hannah.

Lucia, organized in her best mother-of-the-clan mode, continued doling out recipes and ingredients like they were competing in *The Iron Chef*. Or like there was no tomorrow. But unfortunately, there was. Tomorrow was the funeral for Ada's gardener, Raul, who had been murdered while he trimmed the shrubs.

There was that oddity, I knew, trimming rhodies when they were still in full, luscious bloom. But no one could convince me a sweet, simple man like Raul had done anything to deserve what he got. I shivered to recall Meg saying it was the pruning shears he held which pierced his own gut, that had killed him, ultimately. Not a bullet, after all. Of course, he first had been struck on the head with the butt of the very gun Farquar had used to scare us out of our gourds!

I brushed cilantro leaves off the seven-inch blade and applied it to the garlic, trying not to tremble at the memories.

Whatever had been going on with Raul, that Farquar had to be to blame. Though how and why, like Ada and everyone else, I could not imagine. Danny seemed to be the only link, and most of them would not believe he could be responsible for such a crime. I wanted desperately to believe in Dan's innocence, but I had been there one night, having escaped Harry's wrath while Liza was in her first year at university. Danny came home half-out of his mind, needing a fix, railing at B. J. and Ada, begging for money, then terrorizing them with a kitchen knife until I intervened and tried to talk some sense into him.

At that point, I myself had no fear left. I was so depressed over my husband's growing forms of abuse I hardly thought I mattered as a person anymore. So to step in front of poor, writhing Danny and his knife had seemed like a nothing gesture.

But it had worked. And Danny relented, fell crying in my arms as the knife clattered to the floor.

I straightened now, wakened by the scent of the potent bulbs as I smashed and diced them. During Farquar's attack, I'd felt like a cringing old scaredy cat again. Until Judson Javitt had begun to romance me…

I'd always thought of myself as a coward, but once through the divorce process, with the support of my women friends, I finally had hopes of regaining my self-confidence. Farquar hadn't helped, but Judson did. On the ride over I'd mentioned that to Theo, who'd explained it was merely post-trauma distress order. Or something like that. Now I realized that on rare occasions I had been very brave indeed.

I chopped harder, until Hannah, across from me at the opposite end of the counter, looked up and squinted in my direction.

"What?" Hannah's glance said. Hannah's face was so readable, I wondered how she could play poker with her dad's friends. I tried to ignore the look.

Damn it, yes, I had been brave that time Harry threatened me with a broken bottle. I'd taken Liza and locked us both in the bathroom, then escaped out the bathroom window and run to Ada's. The police had found him passed out drunk outside the bathroom door with a gun in his hand. Finally, I'd pulled the plug on our marriage.

Now, I reasoned, I'd been brave to accept Judd's vacation offer, to go all by myself to a perilous bachelor pad where I'd eventually have to face the decision of "to do or not to do."

"What are you grinning about, girl?" Meg asked, finishing up with her cleaver and arranging the cubed fish in a pottery bowl.

I scooped the herbs and garlic in, sliced the limes in half, then took the juicer from Meg and began twisting the halves 'round and 'round. Lu, suddenly interested, paused in her whisking of mayonnaise, paprika and mustard.

"You swallow a mouse, kiddo? What's up?"

"My vacation, I guess," I answered, feeling four pairs of eyes suddenly bore into me.

"Exactly which vacation is that, Dorine?" Lu asked. She always called me that when she was irritated with me.

"She's going to Palm Beach with Judson Javitt," Theo burst out. "I just can't believe you'd do it, Dorie. Unless you're so innocent you don't realize—"

"Hey!" Hannah stopped measuring long enough to tease Theo. "Talk about innocent. As I recall, you were still a virgin when you turned senior citizen, Madame Holy One. So who put you in charge of advice to the lovelorn?"

Theo laughed, but also turned pink, and Hannah called Dorie's bluff. "Tell me she's wrong and you aren't ever going anywhere with Lothario himself?"

I nodded weakly. Then I thought of what Ada had said, held my knife point up and stood tall again. "You better believe it. And don't any of you tell me to be ashamed of myself. Because I'm not. I'll get to visit Liza before she starts her summer job, and I'll finally finish Judd's portrait and be able to pay the utilities again. And..." I paused to pour the lime juice over the fish, loving the dramatic scent, "...and I just may get to sleep with the most handsome, *unmarried* man who's ever wanted me to, besides! Have a, what do you call it, a '*revendous*'?"

A hush fell over the room, and four voices squawked at once into ayes, nays and buts. No one wasted time correcting my admitted mispronunciation.

Hannah's voice cut through the chirping, "Dor, the man's a predator. Could even be dangerous."

"And it's not like you're engaged or anything," Theo insisted.

"So what?" Meg's cranky voice cut across the rest. "What do you mean, 'dangerous,' Hannah?"

"Hold on, everybody," Lu commanded, "Dorie's had one hell of a decade. Does anybody remember that, by any chance? Can anybody see how far this woman has come? She's supporting herself and her daughter, by God. She's still gorgeous, in a native girl gone artsy sort of way. We've got a live one here! And she may not be engaged to studdy Juddy, but they've dated, they've spent a lot of time together, and maybe it's time for her to test the waters."

I gulped back a breathy laugh. "Of the Florida coast, she means."

Lu had sidled up and given me a one-armed hug. Across the island counter, Hannah's voice changed first. "I'm sorry, Dor. Lu's right. You're old enough to make up your own mind. Maybe some of us wish we were as live as you are! A fling by the balmy waters of Biscayne Bay could be a tonic."

"Or a ticket to some serious trouble," Theo added, but not as harshly as she'd spoken earlier. "The man does have a shady reputation among women. And I've noticed the tight control he keeps over Ada's purse strings, even at the Agency. As if he had some right. Though she does listen to him. He's even the one who got Ada to hire Raul Mendino after all. But dangerous?" she paused to drop along curl of potato peel into the disposal. "I don't think so."

Meg chimed in again, growing impatient with Theo's moralizing. "If you mean dangerous like being taken hostage was dangerous, or, or as in some remote connection to Raul's murder, surely Ada would suspect something if her husband's nephew were connected to this mess. Wouldn't she?"

"Look," Hannah pressed, "I didn't mean he had anything to do with the loss of Raul. Or that idiot Farquar. Impossible. It's just he could cause you pain, Dorie. Psychological pain, if nothing else. You've had enough of that lately..."

"Maybe pleasure, too," I snapped. "I certainly haven't had enough of that in a long time."

Theo rinsed a potato and jumped in. "Hold on, everybody. I admit it, she's a grown-up." She eyed me with a chin nodding up and down, and I sighed with gratitude. Theo was our moral compass; if she approved, who could argue?

There was agreement, though some hesitant, all around. Theo tossed a few potatoes into the pot with a clatter. She flicked on a back burner. "There's something else, though. As Hannah said earlier, Ada wants us to try and figure out how this awful thing happened and not wait for the West Parkford Police. How are we going to do that? Don't we need Dorie here to help? How do we begin?"

Lucia turned down the burner on the boiling eggs and clicked on the exhaust fan before she spoke. "I for one would not eliminate Danny himself for involving Farquar. Maybe he just got Farquar to rob Ada for them to share in it; he didn't expect that fool to kill poor Raul, and Raul just happened to catch Farquar breaking into the house."

"No, no, that can't be," Theo said, dropping another potato into the pot. "He would have been found near one of the doorways then, wouldn't he? Meg, did I hear his own pruning shears did the fatal job on Raul? At a time when he shouldn't have been pruning? What do you make of that? Could someone else, Judd or, or Danny somehow, have given him the orders to prune behind Ada's back?"

"But why?" Lu cut in. "What's he guilty of, liking short shrubs?" There were titters around the counter.

"What she's saying is it's almost like Raul expected Farquar," Hannah snapped. "Maybe was in on something with him and everything went wrong. You know, like drug deals that go bad and someone pays the ultimate cost."

Lu was quick on the uptake. "Yeah, Farquar killed Raul, that's what went wrong. No, Raul planning to rob Ada or having some evil plan with that creep is just too strange to imagine."

"Speaking of strange," Hannah jumped in, "I ought to mention Cascone says Lydia Mendino is acting strangely, and won't give him the time of day or anything else. All she'll say is she moved to Boston about a year ago. But Isabel mentioned Lydia is a practical nurse."

Lu jumped in. "Yes, St. Peter's, I believe. My Anthony knew her in high school."

"Where does Judd practice, St. Peter's, Meggie? So if Lydia went to school and worked there, could she and Judd know each other? Is that how Raul got the job at Ada's?" Hannah gave a final stir to her cookie dough.

Meg was methodically mixing the *seviche*. Now with the olivewood spoon she stirred in a generous amount of red pepper flakes, salt and the few scraps of garlic I still had on my knife. Meg let her gaze linger on each of her friends around the roomy space in Lucia Catamonte's sunny, fragrant kitchen and pointed the spoon at each of them.

"Wait just a minute. I'm not giving out any further information about the case, even if I had it, which I don't. It doesn't seem right. If you bimbos are hinting Judd Javitt has anything to do with Raul's death, for Hippocrates' sake, cool it. The man's a doctor! He's into birthing, not killing. From what I've heard, he's helped Ada with everything imaginable since B. J. died, even trucking Danny off to one wilderness rehab place after another. He's got plenty of money, and could have no possible motive in setting up a robbery and murder at his aunt's home. Sorry, ladies, but if you think that hunk of an MD has some ill will toward his sweet aunt or toward Dorie, you're mistaken."

I suddenly found it hard to swallow. For some reason, I saw the image of Judd's brightly lighted house, the front windows dappled in dark, moving shadows. And I thought of his insurance premiums, gone sky high. Then I jerked myself back to reality to hear what Theo was saying.

Theo sighed. "You're absolutely correct, Meg. I saw the way the man looks at Dorie, and he's plain old smitten."

"And why wouldn't he be?" Meg asked. "She's a damned attractive woman."

"Thanks, but you're right about helping with the case. I can't do that from Palm Beach. Maybe I should reconsider. We've got to catch Farquar before he does this to someone else."

Hannah began rolling balls of macadamia nut chocolate chunk cookie dough "No, " she said. "You go ahead, and have a wonderful time. But if there's anything you need, any problem that comes up, promise you'll call us." She held my glance and grinned.

Smears of flour jotted her nose and cheeks, and I thought, how lucky I am to have such good friends.

I leaned across and brushed the flour away, hugging Hannah and crushing a ball of cookie dough between us. Hannah squealed and picked it off her apron, biting into it and popping the rest into my waiting mouth. We both laughed, and the group renewed its usual chatter

As I wiped up the counter from my chopping, I pictured myself packing for the trip. I thought of suntan lotion, and my beach cover-up—mustn't forget them. I'd do my nails in currant beige which would look great with a little tan. I held out my fingers to imagine painted nails.

"Wait, everybody," I said. "I just thought of something no one's mentioned about Farquar. When he held us hostage." There was a pause in activity, and even Lu stopped bustling around the kitchen, to listen.

"Well?" Lu said.

"Wrists," I answered, "I tend to notice people's hands and wrists. Maybe because I have trouble painting them, they're so full of expression, you know? And I thought of Farquar's wrists. That CPO jacket he was wearing was way too small on him, remember? And his wrists stuck out. I noticed those bony hands of his when, when he came—at me. And we all saw the stain on them. Could it have been dried blood?" I paused to take a breath and Lu put an arm around my shoulders.

Hannah gave the verdict. "Yes, we all saw that. He did have big hands, there was blood smeared on them, and the sleeves were short."

Meg straightened. "You people never mentioned the blood."

"Guess we were blocking it," I went on, trying not to feel again the terror of how the man had groped me. "But besides the blood you could also see his hands were dark, the backs of his hands and wrists were very tanned. Except for where a watch should have been. There was a white line, there," I pointed at my aged Bulova, "like he'd recently worn a watch but no longer did."

Across the counter Hannah puffed out air. "Jeeze, Dor. That's brilliant. A very white watch line it was, too. I remember now."

Meg let out a long, low whistle. Lu picked up on it, harmonized with it, and settled herself on a kitchen stool.

"So Farquar had been someplace sunny," Lu said.

Dorie answered quickly. "Not in Alaska at all. That's what Danny said, right? That he hadn't been around for months. They don't have much sun in Alaska through February, March and most of April." I nodded with satisfaction at my conclusion.

"But he claimed he had just come from there, and he and Danny were in on the whole thing together, isn't that what you all said?" Theo plunked the last potato into the pot, salted them and placed the lid on firmly. She gazed around the room watching heads nod up and down.

Meg, meanwhile, sniffed the tossed *seviche* and nodded with approval. "Good job, Dorie." She pressed a layer of plastic film over the marinating fish and set it in the refrigerator. "Hannah, tell Cascone maybe I ought to talk with him. I keep thinking there's something else I forgot about the crime scene, a sort of senior moment blob in the brain, and if we talk maybe it'll come back to me. And of course he ought to know about this, what Dorie said. Maybe focus his search for the guy in sunnier climes."

"Like Florida," Hannah retorted, avoiding my piercing glance as she balled up another chunk of dough.

Sixteen

Hannah

I worried about Dorie's planned trip for half the night, and found the other half compromised by my hormonally challenged condition, heat arising out of nothingness, resulting in a change of nightclothes three times. Which only contributed to my groggy late awakening, when I had planned to begin my freelance piece on the home invasion at Ada's and the murder of Raul Mendino. Suddenly I felt determined somehow to derail the upcoming Florida junket. I took my coffee to the computer to do a Google search on Judd Javitt—all part of background research for the newspaper article. Sure.

The screen I first pulled up referred to several articles in my own *Hartford Courant* of a few years back, whose content gradually came back to me. I whooped, then sat there half dressed and shoeless, dallying in the *Courant's* online archives until I found a single story about him that did *not* relate to the upcoming Obstetrics Wing that was being named for his family. The story was three years old, about a patient who'd sued for malpractice.

Obstetrical suits are common, the article pointed out, but this claim had been astronomical, and settled in the patient's favor, although Judd's only apparent crime had been arriving to the labor room a little tardy during what had been a protracted labor. Despite his seemingly best efforts, the hasty, forceps-assisted delivery most unfortunately precipitated a permanent disability in the infant.

Judd's lawyer was quoted as saying later insurance costs would rise exorbitantly for practicing obstetricians unless the legislatures put a cap on damages. Soon no one could afford to conduct such a medical practice.

"Who will deliver our babies then?' Doctor Javitt himself asked reporters on the steps of the Courthouse. 'Who can guarantee each infant will be without flaw, each delivery perfectly controlled? Only Nature, or God, can do that.' Following the judgment," the article concluded, "Dr. Javitt left the courtroom surrounded by loyal female patients offering their support."

I guffawed and thought about showing the piece to poor, vulnerable Dorie. Loyal female patients my foot. Girlfriends was more like it. Nature or God, yeah, right. The guy *did* think of himself as God. That had always been my impression. Was Judd's real concern the perfection of babies or the state of the local economy, including that of his own shares in the region's insurance megaliths?

Hartford, after all, was the Insurance Capitol of the world, and malpractice suits made minced meat of company profits. And, I thought wryly, of executives' bonuses. Judd's uncle, the infamous B. J., who had left

Ada a philanderer's widow long before he died of cardiac arrest in a compromising position at the home of a lady friend, had been one of the top execs of Standard Life and Accident, one of Hartford's biggest and best. The Javitts held massive amounts of stock.

"Whoa!" Suddenly my hands froze over the keys.

What if Judd's insurance premiums had risen drastically, threatening both his lifestyle *and* company profits, and, financially desperate, he somehow put Farquar up to robbing his aunt of treasures Judd felt were rightfully his? That scenario could make Judd, not just Farquar, a major suspect in the case. I shook my head, and exited the site with a few clicks and jiggles of the computer mouse.

It didn't make sense; I was letting my prior prejudice toward the town Lothario affect my judgment. Not thinking clearly.

Since... Judd surely knew where Ada's safe was located, and Farquar hadn't had a clue. Besides, if he really needed money, why wouldn't he directly approach his aunt? She'd been more than generous in the past to him as well as to Danny. And what possible connection could the Ecuadoran gardener have had with Judd's waning accounts?

As I showered and dressed, the questions kept popping up. Who was Judd's insurer, anyhow? Or his accountant? Would it be Sol Sherman, Ada's man?

I thought I'd give Sol a buzz. Or locate Judd's lawyer. I might find out something that could help my group of new Miss Marple associates figure out if Judd had a motive for such a horrific crime. I kept trying to forget I wished there *were* such a motive lurking somewhere, especially before Dorie went traipsing after Judd tomorrow on the weekend shuttle. I checked my watch and rushed through last minute preparations.

Maybe what Judd needed money for was not something he could explain to his aunt. Something, uh, hedonistic? With his reputation for wooing and wowing the ladies. Or even something as illicit as drugs, or gambling debts. Maybe. But how would it have involved Raul?

I zipped up my long dark skirt and fluffed my damp hair out over my ears, trying to focus. But when the phone rang as I was slapping color on my cheeks I got a bad vibe. Several, actually. Lu had often accused me of having extra sensory perception, but I was not a believer. I let it ring three times for spite, then picked up the phone with a grimace.

It was Ada, her voice quavery and hoarse.

"You've got to help me, Hannah. I'm so upset. I don't want to believe it, I refuse to, and yet—"

"Tell me what's wrong." I leaned against the wall, tightening my abs and holding my breath, while Ada blew her nose. Couldn't be anything serious. We'd all had enough of that. Maybe her cat died, maybe the flowers didn't arrive.

"It's Danny. I called him because I couldn't stop thinking of how sullen and distracted he got just before he left the other night. I wanted to keep him posted about the funeral plans and all, and thank him again for coming home."

I twitched with impatience. "Ada. What about Danny?"

A little sob prefaced her response. "He's not there, Hannah. According to Joe, his counselor, he never came back from Connecticut. He's—oh, God, and he was doing so well—he's AWOL!"

"Jesus!" Not a good sign. "Maybe he's with his girlfriend."

I could almost see Ada shaking her head. "Yes, but doing what? I asked about that Janet person, and the counselor said she hadn't shown up for work yesterday at all. Today's her day off. He sounded funny, though, like maybe he wasn't telling me everything. I'm scared to death. If Danny really was involved with that terrible Farquar, and with Raul's murder, I'll never forgive—"

"What do you want me to do?"

"Hannah, you've got to find him for me. Fly to Fairbanks; leave this morning. I'll give you my credit card. Fly up there and find Danny. Please."

My back rode down the cheap wallboard behind me as I slid to the floor. I raised my knees and buried my face against my arms. I exhaled my held breath, and a whole lot of sighs. "Ada, I can't. You know I can't. No. Now listen." I stalled for time, praying for an alternative to pop into my mind. I thought of my new detective friend. "I'll call Bernie. He'll know what to do. You know I can't fly, Ada. It tears my guts out to even think of it. As much as I long to see my grandson before they move to Japan, I won't even fly for that. Haven't since the accident! Not for 30 years. I can't, I couldn't. Forgive me."

Ada was quiet. "I know. I, I forgot. I just thought, you'd be the one who could figure it out, track him down, talk to people. I'm sorry. Maybe I'll have to…Yes, I'll fly up there right after the funeral."

"Wait!" I sprang to my feet. "Don't jump at this. Danny and his girl may just be having a romantic reunion. Maybe he's trying to find Farquar and figure out why the bastard did what he did. And Janet's helping him. That must be it."

"But that's bad, don't you see? He'll go getting himself killed!"

I felt like a heel, and made myself speak through a total drain of energy. "Please, Ada," I sighed, "let me talk to Detective Cascone first. We'll talk at the Memorial. Don't go buying tickets."

~ * ~

I slipped out of church early and went back to the house to help Chantal get the food on the tables. Then, after joining the small crowd for the brief memorial service in the backyard, where they fertilized Ada's lilacs with Raul's humble remains from a red marbleized box, I called Cascone on my cell phone.

"Shit!" he exclaimed when I told him about Danny. Then, "Sorry."

"There's more. Dorie recalled Farquar was deeply tanned. Had a white watch line—something that wouldn't have happened in Alaska, not in the season that just passed."

"You're absolutely right, Hannah. So where the hell did he come from? Listen, first I'm going to try like hell to contact Danny, either through the rehab place or with the help of the Fairbanks police. Dan wouldn't give me the girlfriend's number, when I asked him to, so if he's there..."

I perked up. "If he called here from the girlfriend's that day, wouldn't you be able to trace that? Plus, meant to tell you, Ada says Farquar made an outgoing call before we arrived, too. Maybe to Alaska"

Cascone said he could check, unless maybe the outgoing call was to a cell phone. It was his number one priority to locate Danny and the girl and see if they warranted further exploration. "I told him to stay put, said I might need him for further questioning."

The guests were filtering into the house. I wanted to tell him what I had discovered about Doctor Judd, but there was no time now. I rearranged my green beret; ready to return to the dining room to help.

"Well, he certainly doesn't seem to be available for even that right now. And, Detec—uh, Bernie?"

Was that a certain warmth I heard creep into his voice when he answered, "Yes, Hannah?"

"Meg Dautrey wants to talk with you. She's trying to recall some little detail she meant to tell you. Figures if you two talk, she'll remember what it was."

"That's great. I've wished she'd been on the case all along, instead of that hurried boss of hers who's given us so little. Nothing but a broad range of time of death, and identifying the mortal blow. Could we stop by after our dinner and speak with her tonight? Would she be open to that?"

I laughed softly. "I thought we were having dinner tomorrow night?"

"That, too," Cascone said.

A sense of warm vibrations took over my body, catching me unaware. I struggled to keep down the frog in my throat.

"Uh, okay, I'll ask Meg if we can stop by her condo. But we'll make it an early night. I'm counseling kids at the armory again tomorrow. Three teen-agers who lost a best friend in an I-84 accident and are devastated. Somewhat of an emergency."

"Always is, right?" the baritone voice on the other end asked.

"Well, it is to me, because I should be there, right now. Just like, *The Courant* asked me to cover the story of the continuing famine in Afghanistan, the hill fights between clans, and how the Taliban, even relocated elsewhere, affects women, and girls growing up over there."

"You wouldn't go?"

I shook my head, remembered he couldn't see the gesture and laughed wryly. "I told you I don't fly. And Afghanistan is a long walk."

I heard Cascone expel a heavy breath. "So that's it, why they let you go, a brilliant, savvy, attractive woman like you?"

"You got it," I said. "Though I imagine the attractive was a non-factor."

"That's what you'd think, being a brainy but nearsighted lady."

I laughed again. This man was good for me. Trying to make me like myself for a change. "Thanks," I said. "Now let me go pour coffee. I'll meet you in Chiodo's at eight, okay? That the plan?"

He grunted a non-verbal response and I could hear a smile in it. "I'll make the reservation. I'm hoping I'll have good news about the Javitt kid by then."

But he wouldn't. I just knew it.

When Dorie stepped over to help me pour coffee, I told her about Danny's absence and Dorie's frilly boa nearly fell from her shoulders. Then she looked momentarily guilty.

"What?"

"Well, it certainly doesn't look good for Danny, then, does it? I've always been afraid of that. I feel bad, but I just couldn't believe in him anymore. Even Judd says..."

I cut her off, resistant to that quote source at the moment. Lu, slicing cake at the other end of the table, toddled over in her red high heels and asked what was up. We explained, and the brunette clamped her lips shut tight and raised her feet one at a time to rub the aches away in her arches. Her long *au naturelle* eyelashes quivered against her cheeks.

"I'm sorry, but it's what I thought all along. Some deal those two cooked up when they were supposed to be getting drugs out of their systems. You know there's a huge recitivism rate with addicts, don't you?"

"There is, I s'pose," Dorie offered. "But you'd think the rehab would work. Poor Ada's tried so hard..."

Lu popped half a macadamia chocolate chunk cookie in her mouth and labored to get it swallowed before Hannah could cut in. "Mmm," she said, "you'd think. But sweet as Dan can be, I know how powerfully he was ruled by the coke, the booze. My Andrew could never get over it, how Danny lived and breathed for the next high. Maybe you can never truly control an addiction like Dan's."

Dorie groaned.

Lu shook her head and bent to better organize the plates of cookies and cake she'd carted over earlier this morning. As the first guests approached, finished with their salads and *seviches* and cold cuts, she offered cookies, her chocolate wonder creation and Chantal's special coffee cake to them.

After a few moments, a young woman approached, her large brown eyes glazed with emotion, her small chin tipped upward, her petite but curvaceous form encased in black. I realized it was Lydia Mendino, when I saw Vittorio accompanied her, dressed in a suit too large for his slender frame. Probably his dad's. I winced. I poured them coffee, then watched Ada come rushing over while Lu cut them cake slices and piled cookies beside the cake.

Ada handed the plates over to Raul's children. "Lydia, dear, these are my friends, some of those ladies who were here when, well, it all happened. Your mother met them that day, you, too, Vittorio, huh? Don't they all look wonderful in their bright new accessories? I just know they wore them today to cheer us up."

Lydia Mendino did not smile, but her expressive eyes rounded even more, as she studied each woman, nodded, and pulled an old-fashioned beige mantilla close around her face.

"We're terribly sorry, dear," Lu said, placing her arm around the young woman, but withdrawing it rather quickly when her hug was shrugged off. Vittorio nodded, and stuck out his hand.

"Thank you, Missus." He greeted Dorie and me warmly, too.

"We appreciate everything you and Missus Ada do for us," he said, his cheeks coloring as he spoke.

Lucia handed him a plate of dessert and his eyes sparkled with a grin, a boy lifted momentarily from under the pall of grief. But Lydia, Hannah noticed, kept staring around the group, from one to the other, as if she couldn't find the particular someone she sought.

"How is your mother doing, Lydia?" I asked.

Lydia sulked, picked at her cake and let her gaze catch mine for a second. "Her life ended when my father's did," she said. "It's our destiny: death." She shrugged and moved away from us, sliding her dessert plate back onto the corner of the table and lifting her head high as she found her way out of the room.

Vittorio scrambled to recover her plate and followed, making apologetic noises. "Lydia, Lydia, you forgot this," he called to his sister's retreating back.

Ada and her circle of friends stood there, stunned. Breaths came hard.

"What on earth...? It's like she's mad at all of us. As if we were responsible," Dorie wondered aloud.

Ada hurried after the boy, but he had blended into the crowd and she turned suddenly back to us, arms akimbo.

"They're all falling apart, falling apart and disappearing. All the men in my life. And now this poor girl just hates us..." Her beautifully manicured hands flew to her face and, for a moment, she rocked back and forth.

"Ada," Lu said. "It will be all right." She moved toward her friend, arms wide.

But Ada stepped backward and uncovered her face, her eyes brimming. "I don't think so, Lucia. Raul is dead, Judd is off to Florida again, Danny is missing, Lydia hates us and Vittorio is protecting her. From what? For the first time in my life, except for the days when my George was still alive, I honestly don't think it will ever be all right again."

Dorie's expressive features twisted in matching grief. "Oh, my dear, how awful. Judd shouldn't have left. You need him here. I'm so sorry. And I won't go either."

We watched Ada take a deep breath and flick her hands at us as if to dismiss the subject. "Oh, yes, you will, Dorie. It's the one joyful thing about this week. You and Judd getting together down there. You *will* go." Then she squared her shoulders and left the room to greet more guests and urge them in for refreshments.

"The woman's incredible," I whispered, blotting the perspiration on my forehead with a paper napkin. "She's like that battery that never gives up. I wish I were as strong. I wish I could go to Fairbanks for her. If I didn't melt from these damn flushes first." I motioned to Dorie to pour coffee for the incoming group and stepped away. "I need air," I said, and the sweat glistening on my face backed me up.

~ * ~

Out in the yard, under a special canopy Ada had rented for the affair, Isabel Mendino cuddled her baby grandson on her lap. Beside her, Theo sat holding a plate of goodies for the two of them to share. Pressing a third napkin to my eyes and cheeks, I caught up to Ada just as she approached Raul's widow and bent to greet the child.

"Oh, Isabel, he's adorable. Look at those curly dark locks, just like yours and Lydia's."

Isabel smiled. For the moment she seemed to relax in the delight over her little grandson, who was squirming on her lap until Ada reached for him. Suddenly interested, the six-month-old held out his arms, and Ada cuddled him on her shoulder.

She cooed at the baby and seemed comforted, herself. Never having had a child seemed to leave a hole in Ada somewhere, I always thought, for her heart was big enough for many children. I turned and expressed my condolences to Isabel.

"This can't be easy for you, Mrs. Mendino. Being here, where..." I paused to extricate foot from mouth.

Theo jumped in. "I said the same thing, Hannah, but Isabel says Raul loved this garden of all the places where he worked. So it makes her happy to see how beautiful he made it, his lilacs just blooming, the Easter lilies over there still so fragrant and white."

"And the trees budding with new life, they are like my grandson," Isabel admitted. "It makes me happy and sad at the same time. Is this possible?" She looked at Theo and the older woman wrapped an arm around her.

"Possible, and natural." Theo was cut off as the stunning, dark-eyed Lydia scooped up her baby from Ada without a word and stood holding him close.

"I want to show Putito where his grandfather died," she said. "Mama won't tell me, not Vittorio, either. If one of you ladies won't, I'll phone the police and ask them." Her look was menacing, more angry than grieving, and it set Isabel off on a new rush of tears.

I got a nod from Ada, and one from Theo, too.

"Come this way, Lydia," I urged, guiding her away from the group. "We are all still so saddened. You can't blame us for avoiding the pain."

Halfway to the side of the house where the yellow tape had finally been removed by the detectives only yesterday, I halted and took a breath. Lydia pulled up sharply next to me, the baby round-cheeked and grinning in her arms from the jostling.

I hesitated. "Are you sure it's the best thing to know the details?"

"How would you feel?" Lydia snapped. "Wouldn't you want to know where your father breathed his last breath?"

I felt my knees go weak. Sometimes the children at the Center were helped by knowing the simple facts of a parent's or sibling's death, instead of imagining worse case scenarios.

"You're right," I said. "My dad is a travel photographer. His adventures take him all over the world, and I worry from the second he leaves until he gets home. To imagine he's never coming back—I would miss him so much. He's been everything to me, mother, father, supported me with his love since my husband died 30 years ago."

I had no idea why I was spilling all this personal data to Lydia Mendino. But it seemed to strike a nerve. Lydia's eyes had filled with tears.

"Then perhaps you understand. You are the one to show me where my father died." She tugged on my arm.

I nodded and squared my shoulders, trying for Ada's kind of determination in times of trouble. Watching our footsteps in the grass instead of the bright blue sky, or the people around us, we walked on, then eased around the corner of the house and left the gathering behind.

Beside the newly clipped rhododendrons in the side yard I paused, offered to take the baby, and gestured with a nod to the ground beneath the dining room windows. Lydia's breath caught in her throat and she made a choking noise as she handed over the child. Then she fell to her knees.

"Ma...ma?" the baby cooed, with a question in his voice as he saw his mother bend forward and press her face to the grass.

I hugged him as close as I dared. I thought of another child, a bit younger, my grandson Dylan, on the other side of the country. A little boy I would not see growing through the sweet stages of childhood. I pressed my chin into the baby's silky hair and when he cooed again, held him out from me to appreciate his round-cheeked grin, the two tiny teeth just clearing his lower gums. He waved a hand in my face as if to greet me, and when he stopped I blinked to admire his amazingly blue eyes.

I stepped away, talking to the child in grown-up language as he babbled back to me. My chest tightened, filled with sorrow, for Lydia and Isabel, for this baby, and for myself, whose husband had left me a widow at 25, whose only sibling had deserted me at the same moment, and whose best link with the future was 3,000 miles away and completely out of my reach. I nearly sank to the ground myself.

Suddenly Lydia stood, disregarding her own tear-stained face, and reached for her child.

"I'm sorry," she said, dropping her gaze to the baby. "I've been impolite to all of you, especially Mrs. Javitt. I apologize. Would you tell her for me? And tell my mother I'm going home, taking her car. She can call me for a ride when she's ready."

"No need," I said. "I'll be glad to drive her and Vittorio home. And I am sorry for your loss, Lydia. I understand how hard it is for you."

"Perhaps," the woman said, shifting the baby to her other shoulder, "but I believe someday it's going to be harder still for all of you. Especially her." She gestured toward Ada, who was coming around the corner toward them, a look of concern deepening the few shallow wrinkles in her well-tended face.

When I turned back to where she'd stood, Lydia and her child were gone. It would be cruel to pursue them. I wondered briefly what Lydia had meant, then took Ada's hand and led her back to the canopied yard.

"Have you had anything to eat, my friend?"

Ada shook her head. "Has Lydia gone?"

"Yes, it's all too hard on her, she said. She apologizes if she's been unkind to you. I told her I'd drive her mother home later."

Ada nodded. "We have much in common. I lost my father when I was about her age. Did you know she and Danny were in some of the same classes in high school, even though she was a couple of years ahead of him? They were in band together. She played the clarinet, I think."

"And Dan was banging away on his drums?"

Ada smiled, but shakily. "Another thing he never got far with. As for Lydia, she got her practical nursing degree by the time Dan graduated. Such a bright, attractive girl. Now such an unhappy woman. Isabel says something happened in the birth, and she can no longer have children."

I sucked in a groan of distress.

Ada only nodded, as we walked slowly back. "I've actually known Lydia longer than I knew her father. Admired her determination and ambition."

"I didn't realize. I thought Raul had worked for you for years."

"Only after B. J. told off our last gardener, one of those surly Wagner boys, who was good at what he did, but didn't do nearly enough of it for what my former husband paid him.

"Then I was stuck without anyone for a while, until Judd mentioned one of his patients knew a nice Ecuadorian man looking for more customers. This would have been his fifth spring, making the yard so beautiful." She blotted her eyes with a hankie and took a deep and steadying breath.

"Hannah, what about Dan? What did your detective friend say?"

"He's definitely looking into it. Seriously. Said if he can't reach him through the rehab, he'll call the local police. He'll take care of it."

Ada shook her head. "I should be there. I don't want him hunted down like that. There must be a reasonable explanation."

We parted quickly when a small knot of guests approached Ada. I left to see if Chantal and the others needed a hand. My heart was heavy; I'd had enough thoughtful conversation for a while.

~ * ~

"It was quite an affair," I told Cascone later as we dined on pasta primavera and foccaccia in Hartford's Southend. I had introduced Cascone to the neighborhood, and he was thrilled to find Italian food as good as his native New York's.

"Lots of people. We had a cruiser doing surveillance in the neighborhood, but nothing or nobody that looked suspicious."

She mmm-hmm'ed with a mouthful of spicy bread dipped in olive oil. "Lots of parishioners from their church, and all his other clients, everybody Raul ever worked for, I think. They all spoke so highly of him. I don't think he had an enemy in the world. What about Danny? Any luck?"

Cascone dashed hot pepper flakes on his bread and prepared to take a bite. "You were right about the phone. Listed to one Janet Feather, of Fairbanks, Alaska. No answer. I'm having the police check the location three times a day but so far no one appears to be in. What do you think the kid is up to?"

I shrugged. "He acted strangely on the way to the airport, full of bluster and bravado about catching up with Farquar and doing him harm. But it's hard for me to think of Danny as evil, someone who would hurt another individual."

"I trust your judgment. You've known him longer than I have."

"Speaking about knowing someone a long time..." I hesitated.

"What?" the detective mumbled through his teeth as he bit off more bread.

I sipped my Cabernet and sighed. "Raul's daughter. Turns out she and Danny knew each other in high school, though she's a bit older. The woman's a basket case. I can understand, though. I lost two people I loved and depended on when I was about her age. You feel your legs are cut out from under you." My eyelids closed and I winced. "Sorry," I said, turning my gaze back to him. "You would know that, having lost your wife."

"It's all right." He washed down his foccaccia with red wine, asked who I'd lost.

I blurt it before I could chicken out. "My husband and my brother, both. My brother Joe was a flying nut. Had a new biplane, did phenomenal stunts, performed in air shows with it, and my Glenn was the calm, quiet, no-risk taking sort of guy. Me? I once jumped out of Joe's plane. Free fall. I loved the thrill, the dare. So I figured, in my own inimitable superior way Glenn ought to be more daring, more out there."

Even now, the memories thickened my voice and made me suck in too much breath at a time. I paused, sipped my wine, and looked at Bernie Cascone, patiently chewing and waiting for my next volley.

"The boldest gambles he ever took were in designing new pieces, making some table or dresser no one had ordered and might never order. He made furniture," I said, feeling the old beam of pride light up my face. "Good stuff, often by commission. He was 27. I was 25. Only I figured I was the genius in the family. Getting my journalism degree with two babies in nursery school."

Bernie reached out to cover my trembling hands with his own. I shook him off and picked up my wine. Before I drank I finished the story. "I dared him to go up with Joe. He gritted his teeth and did it. Something malfunctioned, and they crashed into Mt. Tom. Our boys were two and four."

In the silence that followed, I saw moisture well up in the deep brown eyes of the man across from me. Probably grief of his own, I thought. But before I could form another thought he had risen from his seat and pulled his chair around alongside mine. He reached an arm around my neck and pulled me toward him.

I forgot to breathe. I hoped this wouldn't be the moment of another very damp and noticeable heat flash. I wriggled to shrug him off but he wasn't leaving. He let the moment linger just long enough for me to feel comforted, to sigh, and emit a soft, embarrassed burp. I slapped a hand across my mouth.

He leaned back and his look wrapped me in warmth.

"Sorry for the emotion," I said, realizing for once the warmth wasn't the start of the old familiar detonation of sweat. "I didn't think I was still that needy. It's been so long."

He scooted stealthily back to the other side of the table, his gaze never leaving my face.

I dabbed at my eyes with the coarse cotton napkin and placed it in my lap, then idly broke off a piece of bread.

Finally I let myself look at him, full in the face, eye-to-eye. The man cared. About me.

Could that be?

"Thanks," I said, conspicuously clearing my throat. "So... when do you think we'll get our salads? I'm hungrier than I thought."

Seventeen

Meg

At the last minute my diligent husband Arthur decided he could not postpone the weekly mite treatment of his African violets to drive Dorie to the airport, so I called Theo and invited her to join us. I had long had a dread of driving alone especially after dark. There was always the nagging fear I'd be forced to stop and help at an accident scene, like the one that killed my father in Bosnia, so many years ago. I couldn't risk remembering all the feelings of that night. I refused. It was my Achilles heel, like flying was for Hannah.

Theo scooted low to slide into the back seat, clutching her middle, and when Dorie and Meg saw why, they hooted.

"Darling," Dorie cooed, "your poncho! It's wonderful."

Theo beamed, moving this way and that to show off the colorful embroidered flowers and the birds that practically sang from her exotic wrap.

"Impressive, Thee," I said as I zipped away from my driveway and headed toward the interstate. "Looks like something you inherited from your mission days."

"You'd have made a great detective, Dr. Dautrey,"
Theo declared. "Exactly right. I got to thinking about my
time in Guatemala. The women in the village where I ran
the school made these, every stitch by hand."

Dorie craned her neck. "Mmm hmm. Exquisite. You
could frame it and hang it on the wall."

"I've thought of it. But I feel so luxurious with it
hanging from my shoulders."

I eyed her in the rear-view. "I like it, Theo, it's quite
authentic, isn't it?"

Theo told them about the Guatemalan stories whose
themes were echoed in the nature scenes depicted in the
shawl. "Sorrow and joy, both, for they believe that's how
we are meant to live our lives."

I'll vouch for that, I thought. "Tell me, has Ada seen it?
This leaves only the two of us without our special gear for
the new club. Ada and me. You've all gone way beyond
anything I'd be comfortable in. Do you think I'll ever find
anything that won't look like soup or fruit on my head or
my back?"

Theo huffed. "Are you insinuating mine looks…"

I grumbled an apology. "On you it looks fantastic,
Theo Rutledge, and you know it. With your long, dark
hair, and your lovely high cheekbones, nothing could be
better than an exotic wrap full of reds and greens and
yellows. But what the dickens do you put on this salt and
pepper bubble head of mine with its wooly fringe of hair
and double chins, and not a thing about the face or the
form to redeem it?"

Dorie gasped. "Megan! How can you say that? You
have the most wonderful features, that little "v" mouth,

those wonderful slanty eyes. They'd be gorgeous set off by a, an English schoolboy cap, a scotty, something geometrical, a pillbox, maybe."

I grunted. "Sure, and call for Philip Morris, my dear."

Theo's laughter rolled forward from the back seat.

"Anyhow," Theo said, "I thought I'd start getting used to the poncho for our first royal meeting. How about it, Dorie? Will you be back in time for the big event?"

Dorie insisted she would. "Just a day or two with my Liza, then I'll get right down to painting Judd, and if he behaves"—the other women's throat-clearing did not seem to faze her—"I should be done in a week. Besides, I don't think Judd can afford any more time off from his practice. He left early on Tuesday morning, before that awful Farquar debauchery, no, debacle, isn't it? Then came back and returned to the conference, so he hasn't put in a full day since.

"I would think his friends will be tired of covering for him after another week, even if part of it was for that OB-GYN conference he's attending. Besides, there'll be a full moon early that week, a time when most OB's get very busy indeed."

"Huh." I checked my watch and eased into the passing lane. Dorie hadn't allowed much extra time for checking in at the airport, and they were pretty particular these days. I boosted the speed to five beyond the limit and cruised along thinking of lucky Dorie, off on an assignation with a charming, lively fellow like Judson Javitt. Theo and Dorie discussed the likelihood of the full moon affecting the birth rate.

That made me think of the death rate, and the very recent death of Raul Mendino. No wonder I'd spent my recent life examining cadavers; I was obsessed with death, and I freely admitted it. Having had a baby might have corrected my imbalance, but that had never happened.

I pictured the gardener as I had cursorily examined him the other day, lifting him up and back slightly by the shoulder and seeing the weapon, the long handled shears, plunged into his chest wall. The blood beneath him. The— My heart skipped a beat; that was it, the thing I kept forgetting to mention to Cascone. The blood...

Theo and Dorie were bantering back and forth, and I detected a bit of tension in Dorie's giddiness. I pulled up at the departure gate and patted her hands, clutched together in her lap.

"It's okay, sweetie," I said, in my scratchy top sergeant's voice. "You and Liza, and you and Judd, have a lovely time. If you don't get back for our big meeting, you'll be here for the second. Don't worry about a thing."

Dorie's grin mirrored the surprise she felt. "Thank you, Meg. So much. I've never—got myself in quite such a position. I don't know what will happen, what I'll... decide to do when it comes to Judd. But whatever, you've been very supportive."

Theo harumphed, got out of the car and helped Dorie with her crated painting, and her bags. When they hugged goodbye at the skycap's kiosk, Theo held the younger woman at arms' length and surveyed her, in her silky aqua pants and stripey over blouse with its floating panels of yellow and sea-mist green. I strained to hear her.

"I'm not an ogre, Dorie. I do understand you're a vibrant woman, with a zest for life. Just be careful, pay attention as you always do, and be sure before you commit. Beyond that…"

I called out an interruption from the open car window, beckoning Theo back in with a wave at the same time. "Beyond that, send postcards!" I called, causing laughter to erupt from the two embracing friends. "And you hurry up, Sister, the cops are kicking my ass out of here!"

~ * ~

"He may have been killed elsewhere and moved by someone to the site." Now that I'd passed everyone else a glass, I methodically poured my own sherry slightly above the acceptable line.

Arthur looked up in alarm from his seed catalogues and mumbled something inaudible.

"The M. E. never mentioned the possibility," Bernie Cascone said. "Why do you think so?"

I sank into my swivel rocker admiring the way Cascone kept an arm across the back of the sofa, virtually encircling Hannah in the crook of his shoulder. I wondered how attached the two of them were, glanced at Arthur and stared into my glass.

"Blood smears," I finally answered. "When I examined him from the right, I lifted him by the dorsal of the left shoulder. Remember?"

Cascone did.

"And the blood was of course pooled there heavily. You'd have photos of it, I'm sure."

"Yeah, the detective with the camera was still there, taking random shots as you poked around."

"And some blood was smeared on the grass, as though he had been moved again after he was bleeding?" Hannah asked.

I nodded. "Quite a bit. You may not have noticed, watching me from the dining room window."

"Journalistic scrutiny," Hannah admitted, blushing. "I thought it might be an angle to pursue for the story I'm doing."

Cascone sat more upright.

"So, Doctor Dautrey, you think he could have been killed elsewhere and carried there?"

I paused to run over the facts I had in my data bank. Despite the twenty years of experience and my solid reputation I didn't always trust that mind any longer, which was one reason I'd accepted the early retirement without an argument. Some days I felt myself losing touch, forgetting things I should have remembered, like dental appointments, and watering Arthur's violets when he was out of town. Even thinking of the possibility my brain was not up to its previously remarkable facility was cause for new stress in a super-competent woman like me. Hannah insisted it was delayed menopause symptoms, but how could I be sure? I sighed.

"Carried there? Probably not. Though it is a possibility. Wouldn't hurt to consider. At the very least he was perhaps dragged farther under the bushes in hopes of concealing the body longer."

Cascone was quick to respond. "That makes sense. They've checked everywhere else for possible signs of blood: inside, outside, the garage, the porches, the cars, even the woods. The dogs would have picked it up. But they lost the man's scent once he apparently waded through the damn brook."

"And who knows where he went from there," Hannah said.

"What about Raul's truck?" Meg asked.

"Clean. No fingerprints but his and members of his family, his wife, the boy."

I sipped more of my sherry and placed the glass on the side table. I noticed Arthur do the same, as he studied me, intent for once on my face.

"So if he was killed in the same spot where you found him, where would the blood smears have come from?" Arthur asked, his own scientific brain calculating and recalculating.

"Easy," Cascone said, disengaging himself from Hannah's side and rising while he drained his glass. "I think what Meg is saying is somebody moved Raul Mendino's body before she did. Not a lot. Maybe to take a look, like she did. Perhaps to be certain he was dead. Or to conceal him from the road. Although the paramedic who declared him did not move the body, I was standing right there and warned him off."

Hannah perked up suddenly. "Wait. This makes me think of something Dorie said, or was it Lu? They passed by there early that morning on their way into town and saw Raul creeping beneath the rhododendrons."

"Creeping? What on earth was he doing?" Arthur Dautrey asked.

I cut him off. "Probably nothing. I think he was already dead."

Now Hannah stood, too, and grabbed at Bernie Cascone's hand. "But Farquar didn't take Ada hostage until about 11:30. Dorie and Lu passed by around 9:30. If Raul was dead at that time, that's even earlier than the M. E. estimated."

"There was some morbidity by 5 p.m. when the M. E. got there," I reminded them. "He estimates the time of death between 10 a.m. and 11. He could have been lying there dying, bleeding out for an hour or more. Or Doc could be off by even an hour."

Hannah nearly lifted from her seat. "So, what, dead at 9 a.m.? Where the hell was Farquar all that time if he hadn't yet broken into the house?"

"Waiting for Ada?" I asked.

"Or did somebody else do the job long before Farquar showed up?" Arthur asked, with nonchalance.

Cascone pointed at him with a bold forefinger stuck out of his large fist. "Excellent! You people ought to get paid by the town," he said, "as adjunct police force. That's an angle we hadn't considered. I've got to go back and look at the photos and sketches again, Hannah. There very likely *was* someone working with Farquar. This puts a whole new spin on things."

He turned toward me, as I enjoyed the last drops of my sherry and the slow warmth that was spreading through me from it. And from the way this discussion had gone. So I could still think things through. Surprise myself. And imagine Arthur poking in.

Cascone did a just-a-minute gesture with the arm that wasn't wrapped around Hannah. "Meg, is it possible that after the pruners hit his gut Raul might have tried to rise, and the action would have smeared his blood around on the grass?"

"Highly unlikely, Detective," I mused, twirling the empty sherry glass by its stem. "The blade was buried a good three inches into Raul's body. He was not a fat man, either. Another inch or two and it would have gone all the way through his back and out I would put money on the fact he was unconscious from loss of blood almost instantly. But since he was lying on the wound, compressing the wound, so to speak, it took a while for him to finish bleeding out."

I closed my eyes for a minute, shook my head and opened them again. Should I say it? Arthur would be angry I couldn't stay away from the job. Too bad. He'd have to suck it up.

I took a noisy breath. "Okay, you might as well know. I went down to the office and poked into the report after hours yesterday. The shears slashed Raul's aorta. No way he could have risen. Somebody else moved the body before I did. It's a fact."

Arthur blustered out a few indistinct complaints. Then focused hard and spat it out. "You, you promised you were through out there, Meggie. You said you turned in your keys. Why'd you go getting involved?" He made a feeble attempt to rouse his pot-belliedfigure from his recliner but quickly gave up and watched us congratulate each other.

Hannah had stepped over to my chair and stuck out her hand. We shook. "Because she's part of the team, Arthur," she said. "As soon as she gets some fabulous new piece of clothing for our club, it's official. How can you keep such a brilliant forensic mind down? Right, Detective?" She punched the smiling detective on his sizable biceps and dragged him toward the door.

"Right, Ms. Doyle. I'm feeling pretty confident right now that…"

"That with our gang on the case, you'll solve this one soon." Hannah opened the door and tugged his hand to pull him with her.

I let loose a belly laugh. "And maybe only *with* our gang on the case. And one more thing, Detective."

Cascone stopped abruptly, turning to hear. "Go ahead. I'm not shy about asking for help."

I chortled. "I'm pretty sure you took a couple of light colored hairs from Raul's clothing. I remember seeing them stuck on his jacket."

Cascone nodded. "Safely tucked into a waxed bag at Headquarters."

"I'd like to point out that no one in Raul's family is blonde."

Hannah's eyes popped wider. "Nor Farquar, either."

My head moved slowly from side to side. "But all the Javitt men are. Though I'm not suggesting anything…"

Hannah jumped in. "Unless the Mendinos have a cocker spaniel they haven't mentioned?"

"By God!" Arthur muttered.

Cascone shook his head. "Good observation, Dr. Dautrey."

"And I just recalled some information on one of the Javitt men I need to tell you about, Detective," Hannah whispered as they stepped out into the hall.

"I'm all ears."

Echoing their chuckles, I waved good night as they found their way out of the condo. Arthur scowled, smiled, then heaved himself up and gave me a rather lingering peck on the cheek.

"Sometimes you amaze me, Magilldah," he said. "I've never said so, but your science makes me proud. It's good science. And you never miss a trick."

"Oh, I've missed a few in my lifetime, Arthur. What do you say we go up early and keep that from happening again?"

Eighteen

Lucia

I scooped up the breakfast dishes and rinsed them in a flurry under the faucet. The rattling cutlery crashed against juice glasses and china and brought Tony running.

"What's wrong, Lucia? What's the racket?"

I stamped my foot. It was a gesture I hadn't resorted to in years.

"I'm so ticked at that Danny Javitt," I said. "He must have been involved in this break-in and the attack on Raul. Because he's missing from the rehab center. Ada just called. She wants to fly to Alaska to track him down, and I worry about her going alone. I feel so damn helpless."

"Go up with her, honey, if it'll make you feel better. Though I wish you'd both let the police handle things." Tony folded the newspaper and stacked it on the kitchen desk, where he'd retrieve it later. He reached for his windbreaker and adjusted his sport shirt collar. Suit and tie were reserved for weekdays and client meetings. Casual Saturday visits to the office had become a pattern since Tony bought into the Security Company where he'd worked.

I understood, and respected his sense of responsibility. It mirrored my own.

"Tone, you know I can't go. Your mother's been acting funny lately. If I don't go to see her the next couple of days she'll get all depressed again and stop eating. Besides, I'm due at the soup kitchen Monday, and Dorie promised to call me from Florida today and…"

Tony chuckled and came close for his goodbye kiss. "That's the whole truth of it, then. You can't wait to hear how your best friend is doing on her assignation with that Javitt fellow."

I tilted my head away from its resting place on Tony's lapel. "You don't like the guy much, do you?"

Tony shook his head. "Too suave, too rich, too easy with the ladies."

"Yeah, Hannah doesn't care for him either. I mean, I know he's always on the make, even when he already has one attractive society girl on his arm. But Judd's always been a gentleman with me. And he'd do anything for Ada. Besides, he does give his time at the soup kitchen's monthly maternity clinic, and donates to every charity in town."

"Whoa," Tony said. "You don't have to defend the guy, Lu. If Dorie wants a romance with Javitt, that's her decision. And her tough luck. Besides, I like Ada, and I would never complain to her about her relatives, that's for sure."

"Well, I do. I complain about Danny all the time. He still hasn't shown up and Ada's frantic. You really think I ought to fly up there with her? What if she wants to leave today?"

"Just go. Call to tell me. I'll stop and see Ma myself on the way home. Explain you had to help a sick friend."

I rested my back against the cool edge of the stainless steel sink and nodded.

Tony reached out to grip my arms. "But talk to Cascone first. See if he's found out anything. And if you go, sweetheart, don't take any silly chances. Please. Understand me? No hairspray in anybody's face, no tackling a crook by the ankles."

"You wouldn't let me take one of your guns?" I tried to keep the edges of my mouth from twitching.

Tony caught the twinkle in my eyes and gave me a "You bad girl!" look.

I leaned in for another kiss just in case it would be a while before I saw him.

"I'll call your cell if we decide to leave. I just wish Dorie would call first."

~ * ~

I was dressed, and debating over whether to wear my new red shoes with my black suit and checked blouse for my planned lunch with Hannah while I munched on the last Krunchy Cremo donut in the box, when Dorie did call.

"He's so sweet, Lu. You just wouldn't believe it. Let me use his car, it's this cute little square sedan like some old car my Grandpa used to have. A, what do you call it, a BT Bruiser or something. I'm in it right now, driving up to Ganesville to see Liza. I started out early. Can't wait. We're going to have lunch and Judd wants me to bring her back for the night, but I don't know. I just want to be with my little girl for a bit."

"So is it heating up, the romance? Do you have your own room or what?"

Dorie's laughter was like warm breezes ruffling palm leaves, and chilled tumblers clinking together. "Ye-es. The place is huge. He's busy with the conference. He had an evening meeting the first night, and had a car pick me up at the airport, with this guy, his valet or something, Martin. I never saw Judd until yesterday morning. But Lu?"

"Yeah, Dor?"

"He smells so good, and he's so tanned, and the ocean rolls practically up on his lawn. He sat for the picture a couple of hours yesterday, then we went sailing on his boat, and I got a little sunburned. Dinner at this gorgeous marina restaurant on the Intercoastal. Afterward I was so exhausted I just went to sleep. He had to go to a late evening session."

"But when you get back, Dorine," Lu said insistently.

"Yeah?"

"Do you think it'll heat up? I mean, I'm all for you having a good time, but I worry…"

"About what, birth control? Don't be ridiculous, Lucia. I'm a big girl, you said so yourself. I've got to admit, when I'm close to him, like when we're driving, or dancing, or on the boat, like last night, I get all the right feelings. Who knows what will happen when we have the next sitting for the portrait? We get so close together. Now erase that. The one I'm worrying about is Danny. Any word on him?"

"No, Dor, and I may fly up there with Ada. She's a wreck over it. And Meg discovered Raul's body had been moved or something before she examined it. And Hannah's pursuing some angle about Judd having insurance problems."

"Oh, yeah, that part's true. But why's she doing that, Lu? She can't think he had anything to do with Farquar. That's ridiculous! He's too noble a person for that."

I grinned at the adjective. I wouldn't have picked quite that word.

"So he *is* having insurance problems?" I asked.

"Sure. All the obstetricians are."

"Who's his insurer, do you know?"

Dorie mentioned the company Judd had been damning the night he talked to her about his financial woes. I jotted a mental note, agreed to let her know if they got any word on Danny, and made her promise to give Liza a kiss for me.

When I'd hung up the phone I rinsed the donut glaze from my fingertips and scooted out the door, my new Coach bag in hand, whooping cheerfully. The company Dorie had mentioned was the one where my very own cousin worked: Gemstar. I'd pick up Hannah and invite cousin Judy to lunch. At last I had something to contribute.

Later Ada would have decided if we were going to Alaska or not. I hurried out to the SUV thinking, what a great spring morning for an adventure. I'd focus on that, instead of how I was already missing Tony and how my feet were already swelling in the new red shoes.

~ * ~

When I offered Judy a lunch at Maxine's, my cousin couldn't refuse. She promised to sneak into the office first and look up the information I needed, and, when she breezed into the glass-fronted restaurant later, she was grinning ear to ear.

"She found something, Han, look at her."

Hannah's nod was droll. "Probably gaping at the two of us, you jiggling your foot in that hot red sandal, and me topped off with a screamin' green beret. We really shouldn't be doing this without the rest of group, should we? Isn't it illegal or something?" She rearranged her beret and shook hands as I introduced them. Judy sat and stared.

"You two have a certain, I don't know, offbeat fashion look," she enthused.

I laughed. "We're part of this special organization," I started.

"Dis-organization," Hannah said. "Middle-aged women in bizarre clothing determined to have fun."

Judy's face flushed with even more excitement. "I want to join. Though I look awful in green, and I don't wear high heels anymore."

"No problem, honey," I said. "No rules. You pick out exactly what feels right for you."

Judy giggled. "I'm getting wicked ideas already."

"It has to show on the outside, you vamp." I shook my head.

"Still sounds good. Let me know next time you meet."

We ordered Judy a matching glass of Pinot Grigio and selected from the classy menu.

As the waiter stepped away, I settled my elbows on the table and went for the jugular. "Tell us what you found about Judson Javitt."

"You gals are serious, huh?" Judy's voice went hushed. "Look, I'm not really supposed to be doing this. In that sense I'm glad it's Saturday, and there weren't too many people in the office. Let's say I just happened to be looking for a file in the data base today, and I noted a certain doctor's premiums have skyrocketed more than the average bear's in each of the last two years."

Hannah and I exchanged serious glances. Hannah was first to ask, "Higher than others in his field?"

"Way. But no names, okay?" Judy clarified, accepting her glass of wine from the waiter and chugging half of it down. We nodded.

"We're not stupid," Hannah quipped. "Even though we may look a bit flaky in our club gear."

I started to rebel at the adjective, but Hannah patted my wrist and I was so stunned by the human contact from my business-like friend I chilled. "Go on, Judy."

"Well, I only checked a couple of others. It's not the field I deal in ordinarily; I'm more life and annuities. But I'd say the doctor in question is up there among the highest billed. I don't have the details; they weren't accessible, but there have been several cases settled out of court, then that big one a couple of years back I remember from the papers."

"Still," I mused, sipping her wine, "how horrendous can a malpractice policy be for a guy who inherited a bundle and lives like a prince?"

Judy shrugged. "I just know it's tripled over the last few years. He'd better be making big-time bucks, or he'll be forced to support his obstetrics habit from the family trust. Assuming he has one."

"Oh!" Hannah brightened. "He has one. But what he doesn't have is a wife, so flitting from one attractive woman to the next is something else he needs to support."

"And being in that field, he has access to plenty of vulnerable females." I shook my head at my own lethal observation.

"And married women, from what I hear." Judy drained her glass and leaned closer across the table. "They're generally safer. And don't require or even desire a marriage commitment."

Hannah shuddered. "Also, I kind of recall Ada saying Judd's trust has this stipulation that a chunk of it is not released until he marries. Which means he could be hurting dollar-wise because of the proviso. See, Lu? A slug. Like I said."

I sulked. I'd wanted different news. "I'm going to call Dorie right now." I eased away from the table.

The waiter approached and Hannah jolted upright. "But, Lucia, your Italian Wedding Soup is here. It'll get cold."

I shook my head. "This is more important." I picked up my new purse from beneath the table and insisted Judy and Hannah carry on, then hurried off to the corridor by the ladies' room.

When Dorie answered her cell phone, I breathed a sigh of relief. She was still in Gainesville. Quickly I explained where Hannah and I were, and what we had discovered about Judson Javitt. "My cousin told me his premiums have gone way up, more than other doctors' have. He must be settling lots of cases out of court. There's something funny about that, Dor."

Dorie only laughed. "What are you trying to say, Lu? He can't help that. People pick on OB's because they want perfect babies. You're not saying Judd is running out of money because of the insurance hike and that he would have, could have—"

I took a breath and crossed my fingers. "Yes, *might* have been involved with Raul's murder. Detective Cascone is pretty sure there was another person in with Farquar. I know, it sounds fantastic. Judd comes from money. But maybe not an endless stream. Maybe he was hurt in the downturn of dot-coms last year. Maybe Raul knew something that would have hurt him more, made his premiums go even higher."

There was a long pause before Dorie spoke again. "You're all going crazy," she said. "What on earth would Raul have to do with anything obstructical, or however you say it. Besides, Judd's a sweet, good-hearted man. And I think I'm falling in love." Her voice wavered, then recovered. "I think you're just jealous. So shut up, okay? All of you, just shut up!"

I hated myself for bursting Dorie's bubble. I hadn't heard my artist buddy sound so happy, and now so angry, in a long time. Maybe never, since I'd only known her from around the time her previous husband had been psychologically abusing her.

"Well, okay, Dor, maybe I'm all wet on this. Please don't be mad. You know I for one suspect Danny more than anyone of being involved with Farquar. But I just thought you ought to know."

"And maybe it's neither of the Javitt men, Lu. Maybe it has something to do with Raul or his family. Did you notice how distracted the daughter, Lydia, was at her father's funeral?"

"I did. But I think she's just grieving, hon. And still apparently upset about whatever went wrong in her delivery. They say her child has some sort of birth defect, though I couldn't see what. He's adorable."

"Still, if there was anything wrong with him, she'd be upset. Like I said, people expect to have perfect babies, Lu."

There was a long moment of silence. I felt helpless to respond. But I didn't have to. Dorie answered her own question.

"Come to think of it, she must have plenty to be upset about. Did you notice her wrists?"

I shook my head, realized Dorie couldn't see me and burst out, "No, that's your department, as I recall. What about Lydia's wrists?"

Dorie's voice got quiet. "Scars, Lu, on both wrists. Not fresh ones. But sometime in the past couple years I'd say Lydia Mendino has tried to kill herself."

"Christ, Dorie!" I stood there feeling the blood drain from my face. "Why didn't you say something before this?"

"I had other things on my mind, Lu. What's the big deal, anyway?"

I turned hastily toward the wall and lowered my voice as two chattering women entered the rest room. "Listen,

Hannah told me something this morning. Did you know that Lydia went to school with Danny Javitt?"

Dorie said she hadn't known.

"If you're right, maybe the something Lydia Mendino was upset about is based on her connection to Dan. That settles it. I'm flying up to Alaska with Ada. I'll convince her we ought to. Hannah says Cascone has the Fairbanks police on the lookout for Dan, but they're getting nowhere fast, because technically he's not wanted for anything, except skipping out on The Recovery Zone, his rehab. Now, I'm wondering."

"Maybe Cascone should question Raul's daughter again," Dorie said. "She's got problems. So maybe her father did, too. And the two of you stop trying to involve Judd, and stop worrying about me. That's an order."

"Mmm hmm." I pictured Dorie in one of her delicate chiffon creations, her wispy silver-blond hair drifting down around her face like Goldie Hawn's, and sealed my lips to keep from giggling. I couldn't imagine anyone alive ever feeling compelled to obey an order from dear, dippy Dorie.

As I made my way back to the table, I worried Judson Javitt would be equally resistant.

Nineteen

Ada

I was relieved that, because of the time difference, we had arrived in Alaska while it was still daylight. We'd spent all day flying in and out of several airports to reach Fairbanks.

"It's amazing Dan could get home as quickly as he did last week, with all the stops you have to make." Lu tried not to sound suspicious.

"Well, he barely made his connections, he said. He must have been exhausted. I wish Detective Cascone had had some luck locating him."

"Mmm. Speaking of whom, Cascone and Hannah are kind of an item, huh? They make an attractive couple, don't you think?"

I nodded. "But I hope he doesn't rush her into anything. We hardly know the man."

"We?" Lu asked. "You sound as if we could control Hannah if we wanted to."

"No, of course we can't. I know *I* certainly can't control anyone, not Hannah, my ex-husband, or even my own stepson. God knows where he is, Lu. I have to admit, I'm scared."

Lu made motherly noises and tried to change the subject. "Look at that, the sun's barely going west, and it's 6 p.m. Apparently their window of sunlight is expanding each day." She maneuvered their rental car around the city with cautious confidence, grateful for the clear road signs.

"I expect they're up to 15 hours a day by now. Danny always kept me informed about such little things. He's the one who told me about the hotel, should we ever want to come here, Judd and me, to visit him. It's three stars, you know." They had checked into what seemed like the one hotel remotely close to Ada's version of luxury, and now were headed to The Recovery Zone, per the concierge's directions.

"That I knew," Lu answered. "What I hadn't expected was they'd have a concierge."

I felt Lu's shock mirrored on my face. "But how could I stay anyplace where there isn't one?" I asked.

Lu's answer was a smirk. I sniffed, and gazed around at the half-finished look of the Fairbanks streets. "It was pretty cruel of me to send Danny so far away from home. I don't know how he stands it. And where can he be, in this wilderness? I only hope Farquar doesn't have him for real this time, and is going to hurt him."

"Ada, let's take it one step at a time. First, the rehab, then that girlfriend of his, if we can find her, then, if he doesn't turn up, we panic. Deal?"

"No, no, really, Lu, I'm all right. I won't panic. That nice Bernie Cascone said we should call Lieutenant

Harriman on the police force, and he'll be of help to us. Our West Parkford Police have already alerted him about Dan's absence."

"Good. We'll save that for the morning. Do you think we'll find a decent place for dinner?"

I knew I'd heard Lu's stomach rumble. To distract her I pointed out the University of Alaska's Fairbanks campus on either side of us. Soon we took a turn that wound a bit further onto country roads.

"As for dining, dear, don't worry about it. The concierge tipped me off to the best place in town. Linens on the table, good wine list. But he said to get there by eight. Things are not very cosmopolitan here in northern Alaska."

What seemed like moments later I spotted the left turn we were scheduled to make, and Lucia managed the compact nicely down the gravel roadway. "Three miles of this?" she asked incredulously.

"Mmm hmm," I sighed. "The boonies. Judd thought we ought to isolate Danny as much as possible, help make the drugs more inaccessible. And no friends within shouting distance to help him out."

At The Recovery Zone we were fortunate to catch Danny's counselor preparing to leave for the day.

"Mrs. Javitt! You should have telephoned you were coming in. You nearly missed me."

Full cheeks sculpted with deep dimples easily revealed the swarthy young man's Inuit background. He spoke slowly, his English blipped with a trace of a regional accent. I liked him right away.

"Well, I'm glad we caught you, Joe. I couldn't stay at home in Connecticut thinking Daniel might be in danger. Any word?" I could almost feel my worries wrinkling my features. I made an effort to stand taller and smooth my expression out.

The man shook his head. "Not so far. But Janet, his girlfriend on the staff, came back today. She was out sick with the flu, she said, too sick to call in." Joe led Lu and me into an empty lounge where a television set was blaring to bare walls. Evidently the residents had just departed for the dinner hour.

As we perched on the edges of well-worn upholstery, I introduced Lu, then went right to the point. "Does Janet know where Danny is? Where is she now?"

"Gone for the day, ma'am. Janet's a recreational therapy intern, goes to the University down the road. She's usually here only from 9:30 a.m. to 4 p.m. She mostly takes folks on field trips, hikes around the facility, brings in films and entertainers sometimes. Of course, we asked her about Danny right off, but she hasn't seen him since he flew back from home."

"And you believed her, Joe?" Lu demanded.

Joe's eyebrows shot up. "You think she'd lie to protect the kid? But why? He's doing great. The discharge plan is, *was*, for him to be out the beginning of July."

"That's why I'm so worried. If he's doing so well, why jeopardize his discharge? I think maybe he was so determined to find that Farquar person, the one who brutalized my friends and me, he wouldn't come back until he found him. And if he does find him, Daniel could be the one in trouble. The man murdered my gardener." I had swept it all out in a breath; now I sank back in my chair, my energy drained.

Joe's eyes popped wider. "Murder! I didn't know anything about a murder. I heard he held some people hostage, wanted money. Damn him. I knew Farquar was a sonofabitch. Sorry for the language. I voted against his release, but everybody else said he was in control, employable, and ought to go, to make room for someone sicker."

Lu fidgeted. "Have the police checked in with you? Are they doing anything?"

Joe smiled. "They don't do much for us. Tolerate us. Don't want our people mixing in with the town people 'cause we're a bad influence, they say. They were here once, looking for Farquar, that's all."

"What about this Janet? Did they interview her?" I asked.

Joe shrugged. "She never mentioned it to me."

"Where does she live? Do you think she'd mind if we stopped by?"

Joe stared down at his hands. "Don't think I ought to tell you that, folks. I mean, she's staff. I'm not allowed..." He stood and brushed off his shirtfront, as if preparing to leave.

Lu stood, too, and planted herself squarely in the doorway. "Look, Mr., uh..."

"Eagle Feather," Joe said, squinting to see what she had on her mind.

"Mr. Eagle Feather, please, we've come thousands of miles. Call this Janet person on the phone, ask her if we can speak with her."

Now I stood, too, my features tightening I was sure into a map of worry lines again.

"Joe, Danny trusts you. You're our only hope. If that girl has any idea where he is, she's got to help us. She's his friend, as close as you are to him, as trusted—"

I stopped short and shot Lu a look. Lu caught her meaning and Joe Eagle Feather got Lu's best glare.

"Or not," Lucia said with deliberation. "Ada, we thought Joe here was more than a counselor to Danny. More like a loyal friend. Get Lieutenant Harriman on the phone and tell him to come on over. Between the three of us, we ought to be able to convince Joe we need to find Danny fast."

The color drained from the young man's face, and his hands started to twitch. He looked everywhere but at me or Lu. I came up beside him and snatched at his bulky arm with my French manicured fingernails.

"I think my friend's right, Joe. She has intuition. You have Danny somewhere, don't you? And Janet's related to you, right? I'd heard the name before, from Dan, I think, but just figured out the connection."

Lu cut in, putting her face up close to the young man's "You two are hiding him, in case Gordon Farquar comes back to hurt him, aren't you?"

"Tell us where, Joe. Don't make us bring the police and your bosses in on this." I felt Joe's taut muscles go limp. From several inches above me, he gazed down into my eyes, and I could see he was not happy.

"Please, not another word until we're out of here," Joe said softly. Leaning close, he mouthed the next words more than spoke them aloud. "Go out to your car. I'll follow in a minute. Stop after you turn out of the driveway. I'll talk to you there."

I nodded at Lu and the two of us shook hands with Joe, pretended cheerful goodbyes, and left the building, our sensible heels clicking with firm resolve on the hardwood floors. A couple of patients glanced up at us from their tables by the dining hall door, an aide waved, and we were suddenly outside in semi-darkness.

"Keep walking," Lu said.

Inside the car we both exhaled.

"Was he behind us? If he was, he's so light on his feet…" Lu fiddled with the keys, started the engine on the second turn of the key and fastened her seatbelt.

"He's moving toward that old VW bug there, on the right," I said. "Drive down the driveway like he said, Lu. I think he knows where Danny is. I think he'll help."

"Either that," Lu muttered, her tires spitting gravel as she took the long dirt track out of The Center's lot, "or he'll take us hostage or some damn thing. Honestly, Ada, I don't know why I hang with you."

When we finally turned onto the gravel road and eased over, Joe pulled up in his Volkswagen close behind us, lights out. Lu turned off her lights, too, and rolled down the window. Joe came up beside her.

"Not one word to anybody, especially not the police," Joe warned us.

Only the faint lights from the dashboard illuminated his face, which seemed misshapen and mask-like in the shadows. I shivered.

"There are some people at the rehab *and* on the police force I'm not too sure about. When Dan called that he was coming back, I had Janet pick him up and bring him out to our parents' place, an old hunting lodge about 30 miles from the city."

"Your parents' place? So you and Janet are—?"

"She's my kid sister. It took every bit of her energy to convince Dan to stay out at the lodge, in case Farquar or some of his cronies set out to find him and really take him hostage this time. Excuse me for saying so, but they know you're loaded, Ms. Javitt, and some of these sickos are desperate for drug money. They're hatching schemes every day around here."

"Please," I said, leaning around Lucia, "take us to Daniel. I'll bring him home with me again. Get him away from any suspicious—"

Joe shook his head, shadows dancing in the slight hollows beneath his high cheekbones. "Can't do that, Ma'am. Some people might be, probably are, watching me." He glanced back toward the driveway and his eyebrows twitched. "But I'll tell you how to get there. If you wait until morning, it'll look better. You know, two Statesiders with cameras and such heading out to photograph wild life. You might want to bring him some food, though. He's got plenty of fresh water, weapons to hunt in the area. Janet's spending a few more days out there with him. I'm sure she showed him how to set traps for small animals, how to fish in the streams. But she has to show up for work or lose her job, and she doesn't have much money. He'll be on his own after today, so it's probably good you're here to hold him down."

I let out a huge breath. "No, Joe, I can't possibly wait until morning. Tell us how to get there now. Please. I can't."

Lucia squirmed. "Ada, he's right. If some bad cop or twisted counselor is watching, they'd think it strange if we went out into the wilderness tonight." She glanced down at her wool dress suit and wiggled her high-heeled clad foot in Ada's direction. "It's not exactly exploration duds we're wearing, dear. We'd lead Farquar's cronies right to him."

Joe shifted restlessly at the side of the car, thrust his head in further. "I gotta go, people. Another worker might leave the rehab soon, and I want to be outta here. For Danny's sake. I'm going to say the directions once, then jump in my bug and beat it. Listen hard."

The two women took matching deep breaths.

"Take Route 6 out of town to the east. It's also called the Chatanike Highway. Take the cutoff for Chatanike State Recreational Area. At the first unmarked fork turn right and stay right until you pass an abandoned gas station. Take your first left, and soon after, there's a gravel road uphill. Take it, and clock 3.5 miles in. You have to park there, on the stony shoulder, and walk the rest of the way in. The road's washed out."

Lu tried to interrupt to question him, but he steamrolled right over her. "Start looking for it after about three-fourths of a mile. It's a pine log cabin on the other side of a running stream. Not a deep stream. You can ford it, or almost jump across. He has no phone so I can't let him know you're coming. Just call out when you get close so

217

he won't shoot you by mistake. The boy's a nervous wreck."

"But wait!" I insisted. "Can you repeat that?"

Back in the direction of the Rehab, the hum of a motor broke the stillness of the night. Joe shook his head and scrambled into the Volkswagen. As he switched on his lights Lu switched on hers and put the car in gear. She spun gravel as she lurched ahead to the next intersection without taking a breath, and in her mirrors we watched Joe swing around and take the left turn in the opposite direction.

"Good job, Lucia. Oh, look," Staring into my side mirror, I watched the car that came out of the Rehab's driveway. "Oh, God, he's following us, not Joe. Do you think the driver noticed us parked when he came out of the drive?"

"I hope not," Lu said

"Nervous?"

"You kidding? I can barely see the road or hold the wheel of this midget car. Give me my SUV any day. Oh, Lord. I only wish I could call Tony and ask him what to do. Ada, look, we absolutely can't head out for Danny tonight. We might be followed. We wouldn't find our way in the dark, either. Let's do what Joe says."

"He could be lying, Lucia. He might be heading off there himself right now to hurt Danny before we can get there."

Lu speeded up to keep well ahead of the car lights in her mirror. "I'm sorry, hon. I'm going back to the hotel. Or even better, to that restaurant the concierge recommended. I've always wanted to see Alaska, but I'd rather see it from a vertical position and freely walking on my own than knocked out, chained or otherwise held captive."

"But—"

"No. Tomorrow we go exploring. Tonight, we're going out for dinner like two normal women a few thousand miles from home. And for God's sake, write those directions down before we forget them."

I growled, hated not being in charge. Still, I depended on my friends for so much. Although, I'd never thought of them as normal, they often had more common sense than me. Of course, Lu was right. Only Hannah of all of them might have relished the nighttime hunt.

But unless she could drive or take a train, Hannah wouldn't have made it to Alaska, at all.

"Okay, you win. In the morning we get outfitted for a trek into the wilderness. You can get some decent shoes. Maybe I'll find a bright day-glo hunting cap so I won't get shot. That would be good, wouldn't it? Danny would see us coming, and know we weren't the enemy."

I pulled out a notepad and pen and jotted down what I could remember of the directions. If Lu hadn't been so hell bent on a good meal, I could have skipped dinner altogether. I only wanted time to pass, so I could see my innocent boy again and know he was safe.

Twenty

Hannah

When Theo joined us at the window-side table at Pino's arrayed in her Guatemalan poncho, she knocked my socks off. I made a gesture as if literally yanking up my metaphorically fallen knee-highs and gaped at Theo's evanescent purple flowers and orange tropical birds.

"I know, I know, it's getting late for wool," Theo Rutledge apologized. "But won't it look great for our first Women on Fire meeting?"

"Is that what we're calling it? Perfect. You will be," I cooed, "you already are, a hot lady, a knockout, Sister Mary Francis."

Meg chortled one of her half-escaped laughs. "Told you you'd love it, Hannah."

Theo jiggled her finger at me. "Stop," she said imperiously. "You can't call me that anymore. The nun part. Let's get down to business."

"Let's order French white Burgundy all around. My treat. Daddy came home from his junket yesterday, and has already sold some beauties to National Geographic, so he insisted on bestowing on me a picture of his favorite president."

Meg groaned. "You people scare me with all your treats. Arthur and I are definitely on a limited income now, and I won't be treating anybody to much of anything, if I want to stay in my cozy Park Road condo."

Theo patted Meg's arm as I ticked off the wine on the extensive list. We ordered our food, and when the server left, she asked Meg why, if Arthur was retired from the University, he hadn't a decent pension.

"We moved around so much he never made full professor," Meg explained. "I barely got in my ten years at the Connecticut M.E.'s office."

"But you came out brimming with brilliant theories, Megan Dautrey," I said. I explained to Theo about the smudging of blood beneath Raul's body. Meanwhile, the waiter brought the bottle of chilled wine and uncorked it. I sniffed, tasted and approved, and my friends immediately brought low tide to their wine glasses.

Meg looked pleased with my comments about the case, so I hurried on.

"Cascone's looking into the definite possibility of a second person being involved. It seems Raul died too early for Farquar alone to have been responsible. Although he had stolen Raul's key and could have been in the house that long."

Theo interrupted. "The other question is, where the hell is Farquar? Why haven't the police found him in Alaska?"

Hannah shrugged. "Cascone's embarrassed. It's his first big case since returning to his rookie police job, and he's stalled. Of course, there is Dorie's theory Farquar had come from some sunny clime when he arrived in West Parkford. He was tanned—except for a watchstrap. Still, the feeling now is he didn't work alone."

Theo clapped a hand over her mouth. "A second person? Oh, God, Hannah. Could it have been Danny? I mean, how did he get here so quickly from Alaska that day? And why? Do you think he might have set up the whole thing?"

Meg shook her head. "I know I mentioned the Javitt men to Cascone when I saw the blond hair on Raul's clothing but I really can't think it's Danny, or Ada's nephew, Judd, either. You people are morbid. Why do you think it has to be so close to home?"

"We're morbid?" I teased. "Who's been incising body parts all these years, Dr. Dautrey?"

"And loving it!" Theo added. "I just think you're the Queen of De-nial, Megan."

"And here all along I thought that was my crown!" I muttered.

Theo laughed. "You'd think I'd be the naïve one, having spent thirty-six years in the convent. But I understand about evil. That some of us can't seem to help ourselves, but are created by our sorrow, and grief, and mishaps. And God knows what else." Theo's eyes glazed over as she ran her forefinger around the rim of her glass.

"You're talking about Lydia Mendino," Meg said.

Theo nodded. "I drove her to the airport with her little son. Isabel said she was too nervous to drive. She begged the girl to stay longer, but Lydia had this closed, I'm-taking-no-risks look. She's afraid of someone or something around here. Or maybe more than afraid, maybe full of hate."

"Did you get her to talk about her attempts at suicide?" I asked.

"Briefly. She admitted life has not always been kind. That it's tough to support a sick baby now she's unwell herself. I think it's the mental problems, more than anything, depression, I suppose. I asked about the father of the baby and she got this wild-eyed, guilty look."

"But she's in the medical field, a licensed nurse or something, right? Aren't nurses in demand? Couldn't she get a part-time job at least?" Meg drained her glass and swiped at her lips.

I knew our Bosnian doctor friend had little patience with those who couldn't survive life's harsher circumstances. Her early life in Eastern Europe had been a living hell—bombings, lost family members, ethnic cleansing.

Theo leaned forward. "My question exactly. She says she's afraid to leave the baby with strangers and knows practically no one in Boston. That's where she's living. I shouldn't be telling you all this, but she definitely did not see me as a therapist. And she even made the point she has no secrets, anyone can know what she told me. Kind of defiant, I'd say."

I had to harrumph. "If she doesn't care who knows the circumstances of the baby's birth, why won't she come home and let Mama take care of him? Especially now that Isabel will be so lonesome and in such pain without her husband. Seems they could comfort each other."

I refilled our glasses, then picked at my food with the tines of my fork, raking apart the elements of the mixed salad plate.

Meg took a forkful of her own chicken salad and commented on the excellence of the dressing. "You're not hungry, Hannah?"

I stabbed ineffectively at the salmon chunks, then paused to press both hands on the table.

"Saving room for the tiramisu. Now wait a minute. What hospital did Lydia Mendino get her degree from? Did you find out, Meg? She was living at home, then?"

Meg nodded. "Isabel said she attended St. Peter's."

Theo piped up, "She's Danny's age, you know, or two or three years older, so maybe four-five years ago." She spooned her soup enthusiastically, then paused to give me a what-are-you-getting-at look.

Meg got distracted by the mention of Ada and Danny.

"Any word on Dan?" she asked me.

"Yes, and no. But wait, Meggie, wait just one minute. Suppose Lydia was working at St. Peter's in some capacity that she came into contact with Judson Javitt. You have friends over there. You could ask."

"Oh, no, you don't," Meg muttered. "I'll do no such thing. Honestly, Hannah, you're determined to implicate the man."

"He just looks squirmy to me, Meg. And Lu's cousin told us how his insurance has gone up. Way up. I'm going to try and get his accountant to give me the inside scoop on the man's finances later today."

"But that's nasty, Han. He's Ada's nephew. How could you?" Meg scowled into her remaining field greens.

Theo put out her hand in a peace-making gesture between us. "Come on, you two, let's hear the news about Ada and Danny. That's where I'm thinking this whole thing is going. We know now Danny knew Lydia in school. Maybe he broke her heart. Or she, his. Maybe Raul was angry at Danny."

My burst of ribald laughter calmed them down. "I don't think Dan had the energy for romance when he was souped up on drugs and alcohol." I took a few bites of my lunch and picked up my napkin. "As for where he is now…Bulletin: Lucia called late last night. Woke me from a beautiful dream."

"About the cleft-chinned detective?" Theo taunted.

I felt myself reddening. "Maybe. Anyhow, they're determined to find the kid and his girlfriend. Settled in at the best hotel in town. And listen to this! They got secret directions from Dan's counselor how to find him out in the woods somewhere."

Meg whooshed out her surprise in a long, low expulsion of air. "So are they going to go get him and bring him home, or what?" She carved off a piece of the last roll and buttered it neatly.

"Hopefully. I guess the counselor has Danny hiding out in case Farquar shows up looking for him." I checked my watch. "They should be on their way by now."

Meg opined she hoped they're taking proper clothes for hiking around the boonies. "Who knows where they'll have to go to ferret out that wily kid."

"Why don't they get the police involved?" Theo ladled up the last of her minestrone and laid her spoon beside the empty bowl. The waiter came by, cleared away dishes and poured more wine. Gave us dessert menus.

"Well?" Theo whispered.

"Cascone gave them the name of the local police lieutenant he spoke with, and the telephone number. They promised to call should they need help. But this counselor, Joe, says to hold off. No one can be trusted."

Theo moaned. "Oh, Lordie, can you see those two in their high heels and earrings traipsing up some mountain in Alaska…"

"Chased by a bear?" Meg added and hooted. But suddenly their glances all met and their faces paled. "Or by Farquar?"

"Jeeze, Meggie, I never thought of that." I pushed away my plate and drank more wine.

Theo made tut-tutting noises. "Let's not get dramatic. They'll be fine. Lu's as sensible as they come. She'll make sure they have proper walking shoes and, and—"

"Proper hats," I burst out, a smile finally curving my lips upward. "Lu said Ada was thinking of getting herself an orange day-glo hunting cap, so when they finally get to Danny at the hunting lodge he won't mistake them for the enemy and shoot at them!"

I meant it to be funny. But an icy pall of fear spread around the table like hoarfrost. When coffee came we gulped it down, failing to decide on our next move in the local investigation. We'd even lost interest in ordering tiramisu.

As we walked close together on our way down LaBelle Drive after lunch, we passed the consignment shop where Lu, Dorie and I had acquired our first offbeat accessories. I had an idea.

"Come on, Meg. Let's get you ready for next week's meeting."

Meg's face flushed to the neckline of her black pantsuit and plain white tee shirt. "I feel silly buying something ridiculous when so many people are in danger. It seems, I don't know, disrespectful. Frivolous."

Theo scooted around her and clutched her by the shoulders. "No, Megan, you're wrong about that. Exactly when we feel helpless, and afraid, is when we put on our best face, our clown make-up, our best coat. If you ladies think dress-up is just for the fun of it, without any redeeming psychological or spiritual benefits, you're wrong. Look at Holden Caulfield in *Catcher in the Rye*. Look at Isabel Mendino. Even she's going to buy some special piece of clothing and join us for a meeting. Remember the *Red Badge of Courage?*"

I couldn't help but hoot. "Wow, woman. That says it all! What do you think, Meg?"

Without meaning to, Megan Dautrey turned toward the consignment shop and studied her figure in the window glass. She inhaled deeply. By the time she turned back to us we were practically carting her toward the door, and she was laughing.

"I think you taught high school English way too long, Sister Mary Francis, that's what I think," Meg muttered. "Taking charge of me like this. Now let's hurry this up. When we're done here I'm going over to St. Peter's and see if I can get a peek at some employment records. I know someone over there who owes me a favor."

~ * ~

That afternoon I called on Sol Sherman, an old friend of my dad's, and father of dear neighbor Sophie, and got him to admit he was Judd's accountant. But his lips were sealed about the status of Judd's affairs.

"Well, you can be sure the police will be bringing you a warrant, Sol." I tried not to bite my lower lip, the move my poker-playing friends have admitted was my give. "They'll need to take a good hard look at your paperwork. And while they're here, they'll probably stumble on a few other undotted *i's* and uncrossed *t's* in the tax records you keep for the town's biggest and best."

"Shame on you, Hannah. I know my rights," Sol assured me. "They'll have to do everything by the books. Look, I've never led Judson Javitt into anything the least bit, shall we say, colorful. Nor approved of him moving in that direction."

I chuckled. Sol and I had known each other for ages, but he also knew when I was working a story I could border on ruthless. 'Course, I couldn't purposely get Sol in a jam. He and my father had gone to school together, along with Jack Zimmer, now ailing with Parkinson's, and the three still played cards on winter evenings. As for his mom, who lived downstairs from me, she was like a Grandma I'd never known.

"I think I understand Judson's capable of making colorful moves all by himself. Look, Mr. Sherman, let's keep this amicable and maybe the police will have no need to come snooping. Just give me a sort of weather report. Would you say Judd Javitt is looking at rainy days in the future, or permanent sunshine?"

Sherman croaked out a long laugh. "Nicely put. You can tell you're Devlin's daughter. By the way, Mom appreciated that pie you brought up the other day. Says you and Devlin are the nicest people in the building. Never sees anyone else."

"She's a hot tamale. Called me to come up and taste her borscht yesterday. We try to keep an eye on her. She's gotten a little unsteady, huh? I see she's using a cane these days. I tell her to call me anytime I can run an errand or do anything for—"

Sol nodded, leaned back in his chair, raised both his arms and gave time-out with a hand gesture. "Okay, Ms. Hannah Doyle, you win—up to a point. Just between friends, there's not much sunshine in Judson's picture these days, which is why, I've heard tell, the man's spending whatever time he can in Palm Beach. He probably won't have the beach house long. Unless Ada redeems him, he's due to lose it soon."

"But his uncle left it to him, didn't he?"

"Yes, but not free and clear. He's four months behind on the mortgage, and the bank is not pleased. It's not a huge mortgage. 'Till it's paid, Ada's the primary owner. If he could get hold of even a small trust from Ada, he'd make it. But with the insurance costs rising every year…"

"So would you say the man's desperate?" I wouldn't be stalled.

Sol cleared his throat. "With all those rich, beautiful women around? I wouldn't say so. Lots of consolation in romance, they say. But he might be tempted to marry for other than love, at this point. Only gets his main trust when he marries. Though he's very wary of these young socialites he thinks will, to be polite, unman him. He wants to be his own boss, and he wants that damn house. I saw him almost cry when I explained he might lose it."

I took a deep breath. I'd call that pretty desperate. "Thanks, Sol, we may have to get back to you, but for now, that's fine. I'll tell your mom you said hello when I drop by to see her later. My dad, too."

Sol grinned.

Later I brought two beautiful ripe pears up to old Mrs. Sherman and left her a stack of recycled recent magazines. Then I shared a drink with my father, gave him Sol's regards and told him about Judson's sinking ship.

Dad jiggled the ice cubes in his scotch to water it down. "Ada will probably bail him out, though I don't know if he deserves it. Quite a playboy, isn't he, Hannah?"

I nodded, then got so uncomfortable thinking of Dorie going off with the man I changed the subject and told my father I was meeting Bernie Cascone that night at his place.

"Meeting him? What sort of meeting?"

Hannah hesitated. "He's making me *Osso Buco*. Decided there's no place in the area where we can get it as good as his mother-in-law makes. And he learned to make it from her."

"Sounds serious." Devlin Doyle filled his pipe, tamped and lit it while watched.

"Not serious, Dad. But interesting. And it's a big help knowing where the police are on finding Raul's killer."

"Are you saying, my darling daughter," Doyle asked, his curly gray eyebrows arched, "that you're using the poor man?"

I laughed. "Come on, Dad. You don't *use* a hard-boiled Bronx detective with 24 years' experience. He'll outwit me anytime. But with all my friends together, we make a pretty formidable sub-branch of the West Parkford Police. And he appreciates that. Besides, he's easy on the eyes, and he likes me." She checked her watch. "I'd hoped Lu or Ada would've called from Alaska. They should have tracked Danny down by now."

"I just hope they're not in any danger up there, honey. I'd hate for anything to happen to those two. That Ada is a fine-looking woman, heart of gold, too. And sounds like the kid needs her more than ever. As for Lu, poor Tony would be lost without her. She's over visiting her mother-in-law more'n he is. I see her when I visit Zimmer."

"They're my best friends, Dad. Them and Dorie. I'm also worried sick about her, down there in Palm Beach with Casanova."

"Well, don't feel it's all your responsibility, honey. They're all grown-ups. And you're not their mother. They've got to take care of themselves. Now, let me show you the film I developed today."

"The baby? Oh, Dad!" I hurried to my father's worktable. On his way home from Mt. St. Helen's, where he had recorded the re-forestation of the volcanic mountain for National Geographic, Dad had stopped to visit his first and only great-grandchild Dylan, something I had yet to do. I was crazy to go, and the case I was writing about, though keeping busy, might get me there eventually. Bernie Cascone was a nice distraction in the meantime.

But I practically drooled when my father displayed the twenty or so shots of the three-month old. "Oh, God, he's darling," I couldn't help but coo. "Looks so much like Mom."

Devlin Doyle nodded. "They say he's changing every day, and I could see it, too, those three days I was there. He makes more and more little baby noises all the time, punches the air with those fists, and even smiles in response to his name. Hannah, you shouldn't wait much longer. They're going to get that assignment to Japan any day, and when they do, they won't have time to fly home and show you the baby."

I closed my eyes tightly, nearly squeezing out the tears just behind the lids instead of hiding them. "Worse, Dad. They called the day you left there. They got the assignment, and are ready to book their flights. The only solution is for me to take a train. I'll call Tim up in Boston and see if he'll come with me. Maybe one of my pals will fill in for me at Mary-Martha Center. Right after the first meeting of our new women's group. If, that is, my friends are all okay and the killer's been found. Even if I don't have the story finished yet."

I flipped through the last of the pictures and grabbed up three of them to take with me.

"You got an assignment from The Courant on this, honey?"

I shook my head. "Just freelancing it, but they know I'm on it. A feature article, kind of a behind-the-scenes look at police procedures. But I can keep working on it while I'm gone."

"Then do it. If you could bring yourself to fly out, you'd be there in five hours." He drew on his pipe and the ring of smoke curled around me, making me turn my face away, despite its sweet scent.

"You know I won't do that, Daddy. Too many ghosts. Can't. But I'll see Dylan before he's another half-month old. I promise. If I have to sit in a boxcar with my knees pulled up to my chest. Or in a Greyhound bus with the lovely scent of all humanity around me for a week. I will."

It took the entire ride over to Cascone's apartment for me to battle down the continuing sting of tears. Was this why I was so interested, so obsessed, with the Mendino case? Because it gave me an escape from my own problems? Damn my inability to fly and reconnect with my family who mean so much! And maybe spending time with Bernie Cascone was nothing but an avoidance technique to make me seem whole, grown-up, an adult woman with a normal amount of passion.

Was I using him in an even worse way than my father had suggested?

Or, maybe, and the thought sent chills up my back, Cascone was using me, too, to help him get at the core of the case. Maybe he was not so interested in the person of Hannah Doyle Delay, with her fake blonde hair, her out of shape abs, and her nasty, negative, suspicious mind that kept people at arms' length. Come to think of it, why would he be?

Maybe he just cottoned to what I knew about people, the way my brain worked. I gasped.

My knuckles were white on the steering wheel.

As I pulled up at the apartment block on Woodland, and double-checked the brass numbers by the front entrance, I finally heard the absurdity of my own thoughts and found myself laughing deep down. The laughter banished the tears I'd tried not to shed over my grandbaby, but when I found the one remaining parking slot at the end of the macadam, my entire body shuddered, like it did when you were coming down with a super bad cold.

What the hell was I doing? Once I thought I'd lick the world, become a great journalist, brave the biggest wars and toughest people, do *anything* to get the scoops, even win a Pulitzer, maybe. I'd kept my maiden name, Hannah Doyle, as a professional tag.

Now I couldn't get up the courage to imagine myself involved beyond the dinner hour with a very sexy guy. Not to mention how bizarre it was he was probably six or seven years my junior. What would I say to him all evening long? What would I do if something, well, intimate, came up?

How would he react to my aging body?

Won't, I decided. I'd never have the courage for that! A fleeting picture of lonely Mrs. Sherman jetted across my mind. An old woman with nothing much to look forward to but a neighbor stopping by with fruit and an old magazine. Someday I might be that age, and alone.

Cuddling up to a piece of pie.

I locked up the car quick before I'd chickened out and run, then chugged up the incline for the front door, head bent into the breeze. There I steadied myself, tucked my hair behind my ears, took a few deep breaths and tried, as my young husband had once confessed he did during certain personal moments: to think of the ballgame. Okay, Boston, one, New York, one.

I could beat this. Maybe.

I rang the bell, responded to Cascone's invitation through the answer box to "Come on up!" and held the bottle of Cabernet out in front of me as I approached his second floor apartment. The door was open, the activity inside emitting the most sensuous of cooking aromas west of Hartford's Southend.

Cascone eased me into the apartment, took the wine and placed it on a table behind him somewhere, and pulled me toward him.

"What—?"

I tripped forward against his chest, forgot to breathe, forgot to think. I let the cascading feelings remind me how grown-up a woman I really am, and after a long, slow kiss—our first—I leaned back against the door and grinned to realize I had nothing to say that wouldn't sound obscene.

"Thanks for coming," he said, retrieving the wine bottle to cover his embarrassment. "Sorry for the bold greeting, but I've been wanting to do that for nearly a week."

"And nothing else?" I asked, wanting to slap myself upside the head for the mischief.

"Whoa," he shot back. "You're perceptive, Ms. Doyle. You figure it out."

On wobbly legs I followed him into the kitchen where fragrant tomato sauce bubbled up around some huge and melting chunks of meat on the tiny apartment range.

"I get it," I said at last, unable to quit my perennial role of smartass. "Your primary goal is to solve the case. And that's why I'm here." In the lull before he retorted I slipped out of my purple cardigan and straightened the dressy black pants and silky lavender top

He grinned at me from the kitchen table, where he was applying the corkscrew to my gift.

"Among other things driving me in the same direction."

I liked that he was blushing down to the neckline of his cream-colored silk shirt. "Smells wonderful in here." I folded my sweater over the back of a chair, hands trembling.

"Best Osso Buco you'll ever have." He passed me a wooden salad bowl filled with a variety of greens and asked me to toss it. "Fork and spoon there on the table. I've already splashed it with oil and vinegar."

I breathed, and eased into the domestic flow. At his direction I carried the bowl to the small dining table he'd set with pretty dishes and a pillar candle in the living room. Then I went back to the kitchen to watch him stir, season, and plate our main course. I couldn't help but notice Cascone was wearing dark slacks that trimmed pounds off his derriere, compared to his baggy daytime detective chinos. Not bad.

He turned toward me with both plates held aloft in some kind of victory gesture, and I gave him what I judged to be my best smile. As he passed by me the scent of his limey cologne blended with the tangy tomato and garlic of the food he bore. My insides leapt to attention, felt hard and twisty as they hadn't for ages. I exhaled through my mouth, fanning the air with my fingertips. Was that a hot flash, or passion riding up my insides? I prayed for it to abate, before the eruption was beyond my control.

Cascone didn't look up from his ministrations at the table. I was grateful. Even if nothing more came of this evening alone in Bernie's apartment, I was thrilled to know, with a certainty now, all my inner parts were still working just fine. Resurrected, I thought, after years of abandon.

He finally caught my self-satisfied, wild-eyed look and stared back down at the plates as he set them on the dining table. "What? Did I do something wrong? Damn, I forgot the parsley." He started to run back to the kitchen, and I grabbed him by the silk fabric of his shirt and yanked him back.

"Forget the damn parsley, Cascone. I'm starving."

We ate, forgetting to dim the lamps, light the candle or turn on the music he said he'd prearranged on his portable CD player. With every bite, I murmured my appreciation. It *was* the best *Osso Buco* I'd ever had; fork tender, full of luscious juices and redolent with spices and herbs and just enough salt. We ate the salad last, European style, and when I finally cleaned my salad bowl with a chunk of spongy Italian bread and dabbed my mouth with the high-quality paper napkin he'd provided with apologies, I permitted him to bring up the case.

He asked me what I'd heard from my friends up north.

"I haven't heard from Ada and Lu since last night, and frankly, I'm a little worried."

"They insisted we not get in touch with the Fairbanks police?"

I nodded. "Said someone there might be dirty. What are you thinking?"

"Could this Joe and his sister Janet be in on the whole deal? Trying to get your friends off in the wilderness for their own purposes."

"Naw." I absolutely would not allow such an evil thought to permeate the well-fed bliss I was experiencing as I finished off my second glass of Cabernet. I kicked off my shoes and inadvertently ran my foot along Bernie's ankle and didn't even blush. "If they're in on it with Farquar to get Ada's money, wouldn't sending her a ransom note to get Danny back do the trick?"

He shook his head, lips clamped shut, the appealing little overbite hidden as he wiped his own mouth clean. "Not if Farquar himself did the murder all alone. Then he can't let himself be found, ever. These women would be the very witnesses who could put him at the scene."

"As can I, and Dorie. But what about Meg's theory someone lifted the body to check on whether Raul was dead?"

"I was thinking about that, Hannah. I know you don't want to hear this. But suppose Danny is in on this whole conspiracy with Joe and Janet and Farquar. He's the only one who knows about Ada's comings and goings, when the gardener works, and that she meets with her finance guy every Tuesday."

"Wait," I said. "I talked to Sherman today. He handles Judd's money. Said Judd's in serious trouble and may lose the Palm Beach house soon. But that's off the record."

Cascone cluck-clucked at her. "I'll file that away. Thanks. But meanwhile, try this scenario: Danny knows Raul's there on Tuesday. He comes over, tries to convince Raul he's there with his buddy from rehab to surprise his aunt for the fun of it—it's her birthday, after all—and for some reason Raul thinks he's not telling the truth. He threatens Danny with the shears, and Farquar, coming along behind him, whacks Raul over the head, sending him to the ground, where the tool shreds his aorta and ends his life."

I shook my head. "Then what? Danny takes off and leaves Farquar to rob his mother?"

"Well, there was no car there, was there? Danny knew the neighborhood. He could have parked on a back street in a rental, up on the other side of the woods. He got out quick, afraid Ada would find him there, and left Farquar to do his dirty work. He could've forgotten to tell Farquar where the loot was kept."

"The phone call, Bernie. You forgot the phone call from Alaska."

The detective muttered a curse and gazed across the table. "Which you made me verify, as I recall. Okay. But let's say, for argument's sake, somehow they rigged the phone call. Patched it in somehow, with Janet and Joe's help on the other end. Danny hides out for a while, pops up fifteen hours later saying he just got into Bradley to check on Ada. Flew what, American?"

"Easy enough to check," I said, handing my cell phone to Cascone. "I'll clear the table. You call."

He was agreeable.

In the kitchen I listened to the murmur of his voice as he quizzed personnel at the airlines. I rinsed plates, loaded them into the tiny dishwasher and scooped leftover tomato sauce into a small bowl for saving in the refrigerator. The man was a genius, to be able to cook like he did. For someone who hated cooking, like myself, he'd be a catch. I found myself thinking of the nest of dark curls burrowing at the throat of Cascone's ivory-colored shirt, the arch of his eyebrows, and the feeling of his taut, warm body against mine when I'd arrived. The living room grew quiet.

Then Bernie came up behind me and put his square hands on my shoulders.

"He did fly American that night. At least his name is listed. I got the name of the two flight attendants who were on. One of them will be at the airport later boarding tonight's flight for Seattle. I'd like to show her Danny's picture." His fingers were rubbing up and down my arms, sending a variety of sensations across my back.

While I rinsed my hands under the warm water, Cascone nuzzled his chin into my neckline, sniffing my shampoo and murmuring niceties.

"Do we, do we have coffee made, or, uh, something for dessert?" I felt my initial panic in the car returning.

"Coffee later," Bernie Cascone said, his hand on my shoulder, one finger tucked into the hemmed neckline of my silk shirt. "I'll have to leave for the airport in less than an hour. Let's have dessert right now." The words had rushed out of him, breathy and hoarse, almost.

I felt my resolve to remain platonic with the detective deconstructing. I turned in his arms as effortlessly as if sliding from backstroke to crawl in deep water. I faced him, rested my hands on his biceps. Nice, hard. A slight stain of red sauce on his chin, his brown eyes glowing like hot coals caught at me. So very human. And alive. I reached up around his neck and he engulfed me.

"Should we, can we, mmm, close the deal?" I heard his manly voice vibrate through my skull.

I tried to push the word out, *no*, and realized all the while I was nodding, *yes*, against the press of his lips on my forehead, cheeks, and chin. We half-danced, half-flew toward the other end of the apartment, still entwined.

Just before he began unbuttoning my blouse in the dimly lit bedroom he gazed down at me with a guilty expression only half-hidden by the warmth of passion on his face.

"Have to tell you something," he said. "I lied."

"What? Danny wasn't on the plane after all?"

"Shut up," he said. "That topic is off limits. No, this is worse."

Just when I got nervous, he told me the truth.

"I didn't make the *Osso Buco*. My mother-in-law did, and packed it for me to take home. She keeps saying I should meet someone nice. I think I just did."

The bubble of laughter I felt welling up never got loose. But as it rose and ballooned, it managed to bury my fear, my tension, the last crumbs of my reluctance. As he pressed me down gently on the bed, his lips on mine kept the bubble trapped and jitterbugging inside me for a long, long time.

~ * ~

The slim, naturally blonde flight attendant, all of about seventeen years old, held up the picture and nodded.

"Yeah, cute kid, sweet but needed a haircut and with a look like he might have been around the block. Nervous, the whole trip. Drank coffee like it was his life's blood."

I poked Cascone's side so he'd stop staring at the blonde's ten-thousand dollar teeth.

"That's our guy, then." Bernie thanked the young woman and retrieved the photo. As we turned to go, my muttering was lost in the breeze.

Clacking away down the endless corridor to the front entrance, my heels woke up the airport mice. I wasn't wasting any time. The man in light shirt, dark slacks and a black windbreaker broke out in a sweat trying to keep up.

"What?" Bernie said. "You mad about something?'

For a reason I couldn't understand, tears pooled in my eyes again. Cascone wrapped his arm around my shoulders and made me walk to his beat. I stumbled against him twice, then got my footing and matched his pace.

"Tell me. Are we going to be a flash in the pan of pleasure, Ms. Doyle, or are we gonna be more than colleagues? What's it gonna be?"

I looked up into his overbite, spread out now in a broad, half-confident smile. Suddenly I knew what I wanted it to be. And what I had to do on my part to make it so. No matter how many young babes Bernard Cascone took the time to look at.

"Let's have it here," I said from deep in my throat, nodding at the coffee-cocktail bar on their left. "Our coffee."

He started to explain he had espresso ready to go at home, then brushed something from my cheek and nodded. As soon as he touched my skin, I felt tight bonds around my heart falling away, leaving me rudderless, confused. I stumbled after him into the dimly lit coffee shop and took the chair he offered. I looked up at him with a vague sense of not knowing him, not even knowing myself.

The damned abyss again.

When he ordered and turned back to me, his eyes so fastened on mine I thought the words *Super Glue*, and a snip of a giggle snuck from my lips. What the hell was I doing, being romanced by a guy half my age?

"Well, not half," I said aloud, admiring the heft of his shoulders and the five o'clock shadow darkening his cleft chin. His look said he had no idea what I was talking about.

"That is, I mean, I might be too distracted back at your place to want more than half a cup of coffee."

"This is good news," Cascone said. He loosened his collar with his fingers, even though it was not a buttoned-up collar. He wiped a hand across his reddened face and I saw his effort to concentrate. "Also good news about Danny being on the plane, right?"

I nodded. "If you haven't already noticed, Cascone, I'm an impatient woman. I want to solve this case..." He started to speak but I held out a stop sign hand in his direction. "...almost as much as I want to know what's going on with us. I should have been smart enough to ask you this question before I got introduced to your fancy memory foam mattress

"Bad back," he said. "Injured on the job. I—"

I held my finger up to his lips. He shushed.

"But since I wasn't smart enough about our relationship either, I've got to check out the evidence on this particular case thus far. The Bernie and Hannah case."

He nodded, eyebrows lifted as if he were afraid to speak. We got our coffees, and, while we dressed them, I couldn't help it, I kept rattling on.

"We like each other, right?"

He grinned, flashing those excellent teeth.

"We could maybe even grow to like each other more."

He nodded again, grinning and nearly choking on a mouthful of coffee this time.

"So why the hell did you bring your mother-in-law into it? Before we, you know…"

His expression said he didn't know whether or not to answer; I gave him permission to speak with waggling fingers.

There was a laugh stuck in his throat. "Honesty," he said, the word tight on his lips which barely moved.

"Explain."

"At first I wasn't going to say anything. Okay, I was trying to impress you. My kids said, 'Daddy, you're going to tell your date you didn't make it, aren't you?' Their words haunted me. Then, when we were getting close to the 'you know' part…" He struggled against a frog in his throat. "I, uh, it just suddenly reminded me, I'm sorry, I have to say it, of being with someone else I was close to. She and I could never—"

"Your wife and you?" I felt my grip on the coffee cup weakening and so I placed it firmly on the table. Inside me, tight bonds were rising up from nowhere and trying to circle my heart again. An actual chest pain stabbed my sternum and faded on either side into my breasts.

He nodded, and it took a minute for him to go on. I noticed, and liked the waiting, liked that it was hard for him.

"She and I, we had this kind of, I guess you women call it intimacy or something, where we just automatically opened up to each other. We could never, you know, go to bed without getting it off our chests, whatever 'it' was. A purchase she hadn't told me about, a girl at the office I'd flirted with. That sort of thing."

"I'm not getting the connection," I said, trying not to be irritated. I didn't appreciate this peek into Cascone's past. It seemed illicit, somehow, and made me an outsider. Maybe for the best, though. Maybe I could never be an insider with anyone, ever again. I breathed. Studied the coffee level in my cup.

Bernie stopped to drink deeply from his. Smacked his lips. "Simple. When I realized it was going to happen, us getting very, very close, I thought, I got to tell her everything. Be open. There's no future in it unless I do."

Far in the distance the loudspeaker system announced gates and departures, missing passengers, encouragements to check in. Glasses clanged at the bar behind us.

Future. *Future?* He'd said it. That word.

"So you, you were being intimate, in a way. You think there is a… future." I couldn't look at him as I spoke, fear tightening my throat at what he might say, some flip answer he might give to send me packing.

"I said 'future,' Hannah." His hand crept across the table and covered mine beside my cup before I could yank it away. "I'm no fortune teller. But maybe…" He flipped my hand palm up and ran his finger along the lines and markings there.

I relaxed and grinned up at him. That was more like it. I could handle maybes. I could manage the future when it was a gray blur of timeless happenings. What I couldn't handle right now was commitment. But I sure as hell couldn't handle him walking away either.

"Okay. So. As long as we're being honest. I'm 55 years old," I said, "unemployed, otherwise healthy, and thinking of having an ass tuck."

Cascone burst into wild laughter, drawing the attention of half the place. Before I could get chagrined, he leaned over, tipped up my chin with his big thumb, and kissed me. I stared up at him, a bit hurt.

"You said honest."

He laughed again, but swallowed it quickly.

"You think it's funny?"

The detective shook his head, paid the tab, and led me out of the coffee shop trying to control his mirth. "I think *you're* funny," he said. "Lady, you need an ass tuck about as seriously as Parton needs implants. Whatever you've got, I like. But I've only got 48 years of experience. Forgive me my immaturity."

I knew he'd said it tongue-in-cheek, and loved him for it. Right in the middle of the concourse I spun around and pulled his face down to mine. When we peeled ourselves apart I yanked my cell phone from my purse and started dialing.

"What, what are you doing?" Bernie asked.

"Shut up," I said. "Coffee break's over. We're back on the case. And I need to reach Lu and Ada and tell them what we found out, or I won't sleep a wink all night."

"I was planning on that in any case," Bernie said.

Twenty-one

Theo

I got up extra early to pray, because once I got to the Travel Agency I could get so busy, my only possible prayer for the next seven hours would be rhythmic breathing. I had coffee with Wilson, who was in a rush to check out our horses before he left for the office. Then I hurried out to meet Megan at everybody's favorite bakery and coffee shop. We barely got our hot bagels buttered or cream-cheesed and our coffees cooled enough to sip when Megan let it all hang out.

"Hannah was right. Though I still can't believe it. Lydia Mendino worked in the Delivery Room her last year at St. Peter's. After I verified dates and other details in the employment records, I called the daughter of another doctor friend who was in the same class as Lydia. She said the girl definitely worked repeatedly with Judson Javitt during that year."

I munched on my bagel and sipped the hot coffee. "That in itself is not damning, Meggie. It's not that big a hospital; you can't help but meet people."

Megan smiled her enigmatic smile that always tickled me. Like she had a huge secret she was trying hard to keep. But this time she was ready to spill it.

"My friend's daughter says Lydia fell hard for Judson." After she let the bombshell drop, Meg neatly excised a slice of her bagel and popped it into her mouth.

My eyes grew round. Suddenly I felt my well put-together look scatter. I tugged at my shirt collar and lifted my blunt cut hair from my neck. "Whooo! Go ahead, go on, woman," I demanded, resisting any more of my breakfast.

Meg let me wait while she chewed ceremoniously, then washed everything down with black coffee.

She nodded her head slowly all the while.

"What?" I urged. "Damn you. Go on."

"They had an affair." Meg leaned forward conspiratorially. "They were insane, met for rendezvous in goddamn storage closets. This girl said some of the nurses warned Lydia about Judd's history, tried to tell her to watch out, take care of herself, that he had a reputation. That he'd dump her when he found some society girl ready to play house."

I had gone speechless, holding my next bite of bagel in midair while my mouth formed a round "o." Finally I bit, chewed, swallowed and said, "That bastard. He went and did exactly that to Lydia, didn't he?"

"I'd say so. I doubt it was Lydia who broke with him."

"Then why on earth didn't Isabel tell me? She must have known."

Meg finished her bagel and studied her half-empty cup. "Could be irrelevant. Maybe they parted on mutually friendly terms."

She paused to study Theo's response. Together we muttered, "Naw."

Meg jumped in. "Seems like Isabel deserves another visit, Theodora. Want me to tag along?"

I nodded, nearly choking on the last bite I could manage. I pushed my cup away, fished out a tip for the server, and dragged Megan out the door.

"I have appointments all day. But if we go right now, we'll catch Isabel at home. She cleans a couple of houses each day. Raul's truck needed work and is in the garage, so she has to wait for a neighbor who can cart her around."

We scampered down the street to my parked Lexus. Meg sighed, climbing in.

"Long way from a Geo Prism," she noted as she sank into the soft interior.

I started to answer as I flicked on the ignition. Then the breath caught in my throat. "God, Meg, do you think Dorie's safe down there with that idiot? I never wanted her to go in the first place."

Meg shrugged. "Dunno. Got a cell phone? I had one via the State until now, so I never had to invest."

I shook my head as I nosed through the early morning traffic on the Avenue. "Unh unh. I'm on the phone enough at the agency. Cell phones destroy the clean simplicity of a semi-contemplative life."

Meg nodded. "Kind of like the effect Judd Javitt seems to have had on the women in his life, huh? No problem.

I'll call Hannah from Isabel's and tell her to get on Dorie. I want to know what she's heard from Alaska, anyhow."

We found Isabel Mendino dressed in jeans and a blue plaid blouse, ready to go to her part-time work. "It'll be my first day back after... you know."

The other two women nodded understandingly. Theo pointed to a chair by the kitchen table and Isabel sat with them.

"You have been very good friends, Miss Theo. And you too, Miss Dautrey. Doctor Dautrey, my daughter says."

Meg used the comment for an opening. "Yes, Doctor. But not the kind of Doctor Judson Javitt is. Your daughter worked with him at St. Peter's, didn't she?"

Isabel was taken off guard, nodding before she could stop herself, then turned away as if betrayed. I reached out for her arm.

"Isabel, we know all about Judd and Lydia's affair. Were you and Raul upset about that?"

Isabel stared into the face of the woman who had shown her such compassion. She didn't blink, but her eyes filled, and grew red, and at last she put a hand up to cover her mouth, as she nodded and reached for a hanky.

She said a swear word in Spanish, which I recognized and Meg did not.

"You trick me. I am not suppose to tell how he betrayed...." Tears found familiar paths down her cheeks and chin. Her face reddened. "Not nice, Mrs. Theo. To trick a widow who cannot think straight still."

Meg reached out a few cautious fingers and laid them on Isabel's hand. "We didn't mean to trick you, Isabel. We—" Isabel yanked her hand away.

"Not fair," she muttered. "You don't understand." Her voice had risen, and she seemed ready to explode, to throw them out altogether.

I stroked her arm. "Isabel, no, it's not a trick. We know he betrayed your daughter. But don't you see? This might help the police find out who killed Raul. It can't hurt Lydia. Tell us what you mean, about how Dr. Javitt betrayed her. You mean by breaking up with her?"

I sighed when there was no response but the soft, repetitious sounds of Isabel's weeping. I judged myself cruel for adding to the woman's pain. I looked helplessly at Meg, who leaned forward in her seat, arms on the table reaching toward the crying widow.

Meg tried again. "Mrs. Mendino, Isabel. The detective wants to come back and talk with you more, because you didn't tell him everything before. But if you tell us first, maybe it will be easier for you. Please, we can see Lydia was badly hurt by her association with the doctor. How, and why? What exactly did he do?"

Isabel looked up, her furrowed olive-toned face glazed with tears. Her glance flicked to the left, where the brand new five-by-seven-inch photo of her baby grandson sat on the telephone table.

Megan drew in a lung full of air. "Oh, no," was all she could say.

I nearly jumped out of my seat. "Isabel, Putito with his blue, blue eyes. He's, he's Judd Javitt's son!"

Isabel let loose the last torrent of inner rain. When we insisted she splash cold water on her face and drink a glass of it, too, she complied. Then she blew her nose half-a-dozen times, and made a fresh pot of coffee. By the time we were sipping the dark, rich brew, her anger had dissolved. We drank in near silence, letting the widow set the pace. When the phone rang, Isabel came back from it saying with disappointment her friend would not be able to take her to work today.

I put down my cup and said, "No problem. Doctor Dautrey will drive you wherever you have to go. I'll take you both back to the center where her car is, and I'll go to the travel agency. I have an appointment I mustn't be late for."

Each of us wrapped an arm around Isabel as we left. "Come," Megan said, opening the front door for the grieved woman. "After Theo lets us off we'll stop at the consignment shop and we'll both look for something to wear at Mrs. Javitt's new club. The first meeting is next week"

Isabel stared up at her as she slid into the Lexus with a look of wonder on her face. "Well, maybe not next week. I'm, I'm so ashamed of all this. I couldn't come, not now. One day, maybe yes, I'll come. Because Missus Ada asked me. She said it would help my sorrow, and Miss Theo agrees."

"That I do," I answered, turning the key in the ignition.

"But, but I thought, since my girl has been involved in this way with the nephew of Missus Ada, you would all be angry with her and with me. And with Raul, too." She sniffed back more tears.

As Meg found her place in the seat behind Isabel, her intake of breath was audible.

"Isabel, in all this talking we forgot to ask about your poor husband. How did he feel about Doctor Javitt deserting your daughter in her time of need? About the father of the child not taking responsibility?"

Isabel shrugged. "He was *inciniento*, very mad at Doctor Javitt. At first the doctor paid her bill for *doctora*. But she had to go to hospital in Boston, many doctors. My Lydia, oh God, she was hurt for life, my *pobre chica*. But I mustn't talk of it. Lydia made me promise *never* to talk of it."

The woman swung around in her seat and confronted Meg, then me. "Promise me you'll tell no one," she demanded. "She's so embarrassed, she can never come home."

We were quiet for the last few minutes of the drive back to LaBelle Road. Then I put the car in park, and gave Isabel her full attention.

"Dear woman, are you ashamed of your daughter?"

"Me, ashamed of my Lydia? No, never. How could I be?"

"Are you ashamed of the baby?"

Isabel almost shouted her answer: "Of course not, he is a beautiful, blameless child. He is our future, him and Vittorio."

"Then for his sake, and for Vittorio's and Lydia's, we have to tell others what you told us. There's no way revealing this secret can hurt Lydia. It can only help her and her baby. Maybe bring them home to you! It's Dr. Javitt who should be ashamed. Ada will be ashamed of him, too, believe me. Don't ask us not to tell, Isabel. Please."

"But—" she started.

Meg interrupted her from the back seat.

"Pull around the corner, Thee. We'll get out there. Come on, let's walk down the street a little way to my car, Isabel," she said. "I want to tell you a story. Mine. One I tell very few people. Then, perhaps, you'll understand what Theo means about shame and secrets."

They disembarked, and I, feeling a bit again like Sister Mary Francis, paused to pray before I took off. If Isabel Mendino was wrapped in her own grief, Meg was about to loosen the ties. Because, although her story wasn't told very often, Theo knew from personal experience it included the most horrific events a life could contain: war, rape, miscarriage, the death of parents, mental breakdown and worse. Someday Magilldah ought to write a book.

Twenty-two

Lucia

Ada and I were bleary-eyed when we opened the door to the sporting goods store closest to our hotel. The sun had risen at 5.30 a.m. and kept us from falling back to sleep, so we'd had a substantial lumberjack's breakfast in a diner near the hotel, and were at the door of Big Jay's Outfitters when it opened at 7 a.m. on Monday morning.

The place was huge, a "shopper's woodsy wonderland," as Ada called it, and the two of us flitted from rack to bin to table, snatching up whatever we thought we needed for the trek into the wilds, denying our fashion impulses and going for hearty and durable. We selected jeans and sweatshirts, then Ada chose an orange and black checked lumber jacket because it matched the day-glo Sherlock Holmes hunting cap she'd found in her first sweeping glance around the place.

With the ear flaps up, and tied together on the top of her head, and just a fringe of her neatly styled silvery hair poking out as a halo beneath it, she made a picture.

"Elegant," I told her with sincerity. "Too bad it'll be way too hot at home for our first Women on Fire meeting."

"For the jacket or the cap?" Ada asked, non-plussed by my sarcasm.

I shrugged.

"Don't worry, dear," Ada assured her. "No problem. I'll find something in my attic that will be perfect for the meeting. I had a great aunt who was a suffragist. I may just wear something of hers. This I can save this for next winter. I love the density and warmth of wool."

She helped me find a canvas barn coat I was comfortable in, since wool scratched my silky Mediterranean skin. "I prefer cotton and linen," I explained, flipping up the drab brown coat's corduroy collar and spinning before the full length mirror.

"So chi-chi," Ada told me. "I've seen the very one advertised in New York magazine."

"Never mind the pedigree. It's comfy enough, and weather-proof. Good for the worst days next January when I have to visit you-know-who at Golden Age," I reasoned. "It'll do." I snatched a green neckerchief from a rack and determined it would be perfect for keeping my frizzy hair tamed out in the wilds.

Then I selected a backpack we could fill up with groceries in case Danny hadn't had a decent meal up at his isolated cabin. Ada invested in high-end hiking boots and wool socks, and I in bright white Reeboks.

"I need to get into an exercise program at home, so these'll come in handy," I admitted. "I've put on a few pounds over the winter."

"But it's all in the right places, dear," Ada encouraged me. "If I didn't have that little gym at home, and some very good friends in the cosmetic surgery field, everything I own in the raw would be falling into the tops of these socks."

As we piled our selections on the counter to check out, the clerk agreed Reeboks would be okay for hiking at this time of year, provided we were not planning on more than an hour or two on fairly level terrain.

I nodded. "I should hope 'level.' Even that's optimistic for me. You can check me out, then, I'm ready."

Ada lingered a few feet away, studying the weaponry mounted on the wall behind the clerk in locked glass cases. Her fingers tapped a tattoo on the counter top with polished nails and I turned to follow her gaze.

"My God, Ada, you're not thinking of that, of getting …" Her words dropped to *sotto voce*, "…a *gun*, are you?"

Ada sighed. "Maybe just a teensy one. You never know what we'll meet out there."

I shivered. "I can't even imagine using one, having had one slapped against my nose less than a week ago."

Ada's deep brown eyes pinched nearly closed. "Let's face it, I had one fired between my legs!" She whispered, trembling at the memory. "I'm so sorry you all had to go through that just because that man was after my money. I feel responsible. I shouldn't think like him, of doing violence, or even having a firearm, should I? Being stupid, I guess."

The clerk began to check out my purchases, and I kept one eye on him as I reached out a motherly arm and drew Ada closer.

"No, you were absolutely right to think of it, dear. I shouldn't have said a thing. To be honest, scared as I am of ever having to use a firearm, I did ask Tony if he'd lend me one of his for the trip and I was a little ticked when he wouldn't even consider it. Said I wouldn't be able to carry it on board anyhow, with the new security regs."

Ada nodded. "Lucia, sometimes I don't know what I've turned into since that awful man attacked us. It helps you were thinking that way, too."

The clerk read off the amount on the cash register tape and I reached into my wallet for plastic. At the same moment I spotted another display behind the clerk. "No," I said with a jolt. "Wait! Ada, you're right about protection. Young man, I want one of those," I told the baffled clerk waiting for my credit card. "The biggest one you have."

He gave me a look that said I-don't-think-you-know-what-you're-doing, but reached behind him, lifted a key and unlocked the case. With great ceremony he forked over the largest hunting knife Ada and I had ever seen. A classic Bowie, he proclaimed. In my case, the *only* hunting knife I'd ever seen.

Gingerly, I took it from the clerk's hand. I unsheathed it, felt the heft of it in my right palm, then gripped the shiny bone handle and drove my arm up and quickly downward, as if I meant to slice the counter top in two, pausing inches above it, with what I was sure was a slightly maniacal grin on my face. Ada drew an audible, worried breath.

"It would carve a mean roast," I said, flipping it back and forth in my hand and glancing at Ada with a sort of crooked grin on my ladylike, made-up face. "I'll take it."

Ada recovered instantaneously, batted her mascaraed eyelashes at the man and piped up, with perfect equanimity, "Me, too."

The man scowled, and she immediately relented. "Okay, then, that one, the smaller one, with the pretty gems in the white handle."

~ * ~

An hour later, while Ada settled at the wheel of the rental car, I packed the groceries—a huge roasting chicken, some apples, onions and sweet potatoes, eggs, butter, cream and coffee, a bottle of red Australian Shiraz, and a chocolate cake mix—into the backpack. The French baguette was problematic, as it was too long to fit, so I pulled out my new blade, sliced the loaf in half in midair, paper packaging and all, and tucked both halves into the pack.

"There," I said with satisfaction, easing myself into the passenger seat. "The Bowie's already paid for itself. Who says we can't survive in the wilds?" I re-sheathed the knife, admired its handle, and slid it into the roomy pocket of my barn coat. Both of us had changed into our jeans and other accessories.

Ada laughed from the belly, surprising herself as we drove off looking for the route Joe Eagle Feather had given us. It had rained during the night, and the roads seemed washed clean, brilliant in the late morning sun. In our new outlander gear, Ada said she felt a little hopeful about finding Danny safe. She even looked forward to spending time with him up in the wilderness while they figured out what to do next. Of course, I would do what I always did to help—cook.

Route Six was a city road, fraught with traffic lights, a motley assortment of businesses, plenty of weary frame houses and several trailer parks, even a few new condo developments arranged to catch the sunsets where they rose up above the city skyline. After several miles those newer developments thinned out, and only an occasional gasoline station, run down motel or auto repair facility clogged the byways.

Ada's face soured when she glanced at the trip mileage recorder and determined they'd come eighteen miles already and no signs for Chatanike State Recreation Area.

"Yeah," I commiserated, "and it's hot in here. We don't need the hats right now, or the jackets for that matter. And aren't your feet hot in those heavy boots?"

Ada admitted they were, and was just about to yank off her hunting cap when the dark brown state facility sign poked up amid the weeds at the roadside.

"That's it, Lucia! Watch for the turn now."

I did watch, and watch and watch. I began to worry about the health of the groceries in the backpack, so we turned on the air-conditioning to cool things off. As we drove, I tried to use my cell phone to call Tony and Hannah, but couldn't get a signal. "Damn hills," I cussed.

"I think it's the curve of the earth. We're a long way from Connecticut."

Another eight or ten miles and we finally came to the cutoff for Chatinike. Along here, the roadway was deserted, only one other car passed coming from the opposite direction, with patches of snow still marking little valleys in the distance. After another long trek I began to mutter and beg for food, water, anything to break my current oral fast.

"There's only wine, Lu. Joe said Danny had fresh water up here, so we didn't buy any, remember?"

"Wine would be nice," I said, but admitted it would dehydrate me even more. I squirmed out of the barn coat, reached into the backpack behind us for apples, and made do. By the time we'd finished our apples we'd found and taken the unmarked fork and come upon an abandoned gas station. Out here, the land looked and felt like a state preserve. We spotted a bald eagle soaring overhead, crossed a fairly wide river on a simple wood frame bridge, and felt the open blue Alaskan sky spreading out over us.

I came out of a reverie and realized I'd seen, and we'd missed, the first left after the gas station, and convinced Ada to stop, K-turn, and go back.

At the gas station Ada pulled the car over because I promised to seriously dampen the seat of the rental if I wasn't allowed a pit stop. Out of the car, the air was more chilled, and we both hurried through nature's call behind the ramshackle building, then scrambled back in, turned down the air, and slapped on jackets and hats once again.

"It's eerie out there," Ada said, executing the turn. "So quiet and still, nothing moving but the aspen leaves and a few birds." We bumped along on the gravel, gazing around in awe.

"But wouldn't Theo just love it for a meditation spot? And Dorie? She'd set up an easel right here and paint that vista. Look, Ada, on that snowy hillside, the log cabin, smoke coming out of the chimney. How quaint."

"Gawd," Ada gulped. "Could that be Danny's cabin? Way over there on that mountain? Do we still have that far to go?"

"Could be. But it's not really a mountain, hon. More of a hill. Are you clocking the 3.5 miles in? Or was it 5.3?"

Ada slowed down, put a hand to her forehead and groaned. "I forgot to do that, Lu. It feels like it's been at least 5 miles, but I haven't seen any rocky shoulder where we should have stopped."

I muttered a prayer to St. Anthony: "Something is lost and must be found," I finished. At the same time I hoped and prayed it wasn't Dan Javitt who was lost, seriously, morally lost, and near to Gordon Farquar, because here in the wilderness, without even a cell phone that got a signal, Ada and I could be sitting ducks.

I squeezed back my negative thoughts, tried to think of Tony and his logical, clear-headed ways, and remembered to breathe. I was about to open my window for a breath of calming air when I saw it.

"There, Ada! Up ahead, along that curve, the patch of stony roadway to the right of the gravel."

"Looks like a parking spot," Ada agreed. She gradually slowed, then pulled the car over on the stones. It fit perfectly, with just enough room for another vehicle behind it. We piled out excitedly and gazed upward at the continuing gravel roadway ahead of them, broken down and half-covered with boulders, weeds and bits of grass.

"Thank heavens, Lucia. Then that could have been the cabin, the one we saw from the road back there. You can still see the smoke rising from it, but the trees here obscure the house."

I was fastening the backpack straps around my middle. I had to adjust them twice to make them long enough for my generous waistline. "Too depressing," I muttered.

Ada locked the car, snapped her more modest hunting knife to a belt loop on her jeans, and slung the touristy, inexpensive camera she'd bought around her neck.

I still struggled.

"You ready, Lucia?"

I tightened the laces of my sneakers and groaned an affirmative answer. "Damn, this stuff is heavy. Maybe we ought to leave the wine."

Ada snorted. "No way. If the wine stays, I stay."

I relented and took a deep breath.

"Okay, okay. I'm ready."

We trudged upward for a while, keeping on the dry patches of gravel, often ending up on rocky outcroppings that had come uncovered during countless rainstorms. Sometimes we had to sidestep a sudden gush of clear-running water babbling downhill on either side of the broken roadway.

After five minutes I stopped and unbuckled the backpack, removed it and found a broad tree that made another fine ladies' room doorway.

"I'll take the backpack now," Ada called to me. "You can carry the camera and my knife."

When I returned, I nodded. "Just for a while, until I catch my breath again."

But from that spot on, the pine trees grew taller, the chimney spouting smoke disappeared from view and the washed-out road got steeper. We stopped every few minutes to breathe deeply, enjoying the tingly effect of the pine-scented air on their lungs, and wishing for a place to sit down. Once there was noise in the underbrush alongside us that made me clench my Bowie and even unsheath it, accompanied by the warning of my pounding heart. But no wildlife other than chipmunks and birds appeared, and gradually, the little log cabin came once more into view. Even so, Ada slumped.

I put my knife away and insisted Ada share the backpack with me again. Ada seemed a tall, solid woman but in truth she was two-and-a-half inches shorter, with a narrower frame and lots less weight on her, than me. It was only her regal bearing that made her seem tall, I'd always thought, as I buckled on the backpack and turned over camera and knives.

We climbed more slowly now, sweat beginning to drip from under our headgear, and soon the noisy chatter of a brook made us halt our steps altogether.

Encouraged, we hurried the last few steps and were amazed to come into a large clearing, where water flowed across the path.

"Brook my butt," Ada moaned. "This thing's a river. Damn that Joe."

She dipped a hand in the water and mopped her face.

"Ooh, lovely. Obviously a perfect watering place for deer," she enthused.

"Or bear, or other main-course creatures," I suggested, noticing suddenly how my feet in the athletic shoes ached from the uneven surface of rocks, pebbles, logs and other debris beneath them. We stared upward, but realized that once again the hunting lodge where, hopefully, Danny waited, was now out of our view. Ada was mesmerized by the flowing stream as it widened and deepened.

"Do you think we can make it across? You are right it's much wilder and deeper than Joe Eagle Feather implied." I posited my behind onto a large log that lay along our side of the river to consider further options.

"Maybe we could roll this log into the water and climb across," she suggested.

"Ada the engineer," I quipped. "Won't work for me. You know I have no sense of balance at all." I eased closer to water's edge, sliding my toe into the liquid, snatching it back when I felt the river find the air holes in the sneakers, soaking my socks.

"Shoot! We have to do it, woman, there's nothing to do but go forward. We can't just sit here all day. Let's start across and call to Danny. He'll recognize your voice and come running to help us with this stupid backpack."

Ada roused herself, stretched and agreed. "I don't know what the devil two social security candidates are doing in a position like this, Lu."

"Speak for yourself, hon, I won't be eligible for a minimum of three years! Maybe longer if they keep changing regulations."

"I just meant, I apologize for getting you into this at our age. But, here goes. Let's make like Lewis and Clark, or whoever put this outlandish place on the map anyhow. Danny!" she called as we stepped into the water, laughing. The rising river immediately swirled up around their ankles, quickly numbing us with cold and soaking our jeans.

"Danny, it's Mom. Dan?" Her clear soprano carried in the silence of the wilderness. A faint echo came back at us.

For a flash of a second I thought it was the shock of cold water rising to my knees that made me twitch. But something else had startled me, too, a ping, a cracking sound that cut the air.

A sound I'd only ever heard in movies.

Then, another ping! Much closer.

As if in slow motion, Ada and I in all our brand new finery pitched flat on our stomachs into the rocky drink, arms reaching forward helplessly, the backpack pressing down on me with a vengeance, camera and knives spilling into the icy flow as the rifle shots whizzed past our heads.

It seemed like eons before we could get our footing and creep partway up on the opposite bank. By then the shooting had stopped, and Ada was coughing up water, too exhausted to call out Danny's name again.

Now we heard voices, movement coming toward us in the brush.

I squirmed closer to Ada. "Quick, Ada, the knives. Give me my knife."

With dismay Ada stared backward into the water swirling around her legs. "They're gone, Lu. The camera, too."

I tried to scramble to my feet, but couldn't get my footing with the pack holding me down. Despite the damp, my face flared with heat. "Never mind the damned camera, woman. We need our knives. Someone just tried to kill us." My voice had risen slightly above whisper level, and the voices that answered did so, too, with snips of attached laughter.

"Ma! Aunt Lu! What are you doing here? Are you okay?" At that exact moment we looked up to see the missing boy-turned-man skid down the hill, alarmed but half-chuckling, followed by a young woman in denim, her rifle pointed to the sky, but clearly ready to aim again.

"*Mama mia!*" I burst out. "It's Danny and bitchin' Annie Oakley!"

Twenty-three

Theo

Something haunted me about the Mendino family. They were close, they cared about each other, and yet, it was almost as if they didn't know each other. There were secrets in that household, even more than I'd already heard, and I believed if I could help them express their needs to one another, it would help them in their grief.

There was also desperation. Perhaps they could deal with that better if it were out in the open. And, who knew?—maybe the mutual knowledge could help solve the murder of their husband and father.

Around the time school let out, I finished up with my last big client of the day, a television company owner's wife planning their annual European circle tour, and asked Jeanine, the young receptionist, to cover the agency for the final hour. Then I followed an instinct and drove to St. Mary's Cemetery. The winding road off to the right took me into the newer, less planted area, and I cruised along slowly until I saw the mass of wilting flowers on a small patch of land where Raul's memorial stone would soon be lain. Poking among the flowers, removing the browning ones, was the doe-eyed slender boy of sixteen I'd first met a week ago.

I pulled up nearby and walked to the burial sites.

"Vittorio," I called, when I was still twenty yards away. "It's me, Mrs. Rutledge."

The young man looked up sharply, yanked his hand back from the half-dead flowers he'd been rearranging, and hung his head. When I came closer he nodded to me and apologized.

"I don't see you at first," he said. "It is very kind of you to come. I thought you had my mother with you, perhaps. She likes to come here and pray for Papa."

I shook my head. "But I did see her this morning, and, Vittorio, she told us all about it. Dr. Javitt and Lydia, and little Putito. Everything is going to be all right. You will take care of each other. Maybe now Lydia and the baby will come home, and you can all be together."

The boy's widened eyes closed briefly, and as he shook his head tear fell. "Lydia says she will never come back, as long..." He turned his head away with a jerk.

"I know," Theo said softly, risking a hand on the boy's slim shoulder. "But Lydia must understand there's no shame for her. And she needs you and your mother now."

His eyes turned back to me wide with amazement. "Mama told you about..."

"About Doctor Javitt, and what he did to Lydia, yes. No wonder your sister didn't want to stay around here if he wouldn't marry her."

Vittorio's eyes lit with a spark of venom. "Marry her? Him, marry someone from our family? Ha! Doctor Javitt is not like his aunt. Missus Ada is a good person, as good

270

as my mother or you, Missus Theo. But Lydia wouldn't marry *him* after what he did to her and poor Putito. The scum, the..." Anger flared his nostrils and pinched his brows together.

"You mean getting her pregnant."

The boy punched one fist into his other hand. "No. Worse!"

Theo shook him gently by the shoulder. "What are you saying, Vittorio? What did Doctor Javitt do to Lydia?"

"I don't know—something he shouldn't have." He kicked at the uneven clumps of cemetery lawn. "But I hear my poor Papa complain about it enough times. How he ruined Lydia, and how she couldn't work here anymore, then had no money to see a doctor for herself or the baby. But Papa made him, he—" The boy made a fist and cut the air with it. "He called him every week to remind him, 'You help to pay because he is your child, your own baby.' *Pobre Putito.*"

I steadied myself, leaning against the boy for support. I closed my eyes for a brief moment, praying for Raul and Lydia and the baby and whoever else had been hurt. I felt myself wobble. Life on the outside was more complicated than I'd ever imagined. Vittorio reached out a skinny arm and took my hand in his own to keep me upright. We both stared at the crumbling flowers.

"Your father was upset with Doctor Javitt? He talked to him many times on the telephone?" My stomach was knotted in fear. I thought of Ada, and how she'd feel knowing this about her nephew. And of Dorie, alone with the man on that stupid Florida tryst. And again of poor Lydia, ill, injured, her baby perhaps hurt, too. One selfish

man was using these women, had used them, put them all
in danger.

"He hurt her bad." The boy's voice cracked.

I suddenly understood. "You mean he tried to—-oh,
no." It couldn't be. Not that. Not Ada's own nephew.

The boy was nodding, gulping back tears. "*Si*. Doctor
Javitt, he tried to make her lose the baby when she ask
him for help. Whatever he did, I don't understand, it made
her sick. She had Putito, but now she can have no more
baby."

"Oh, I am so sorry. Poor Lydia."

Vittorio leaned against me now, silent sobs rocking his
chest. When he was finally still I took a few deep breaths
and suggested gently he do the same. With just a light
touch on his elbow I guided him to my car. Inside, I pulled
out my cell phone, explaining as I did the detective must
know what Vittorio had said. I would take Vittoriio home
and have Lieutenant Cascone meet us there.

"I think Doctor Dautrey probably drove your mother
home from her housecleaning jobs by now. We'll stay
with you both as long as you want. You'll get through
this, Vittorio. You have a lot of people to help your
family. You'll see."

He swallowed hard and nodded as we pulled out of the
cemetery, forcing a feeble little grin. "I know, Missus
Theo," he said. "All Missus Ada's friends. Mama says it.
You are all angels in funny hats and clothes."

I kept my eyes focused on the winding road. I
wondered if my vivid poncho would qualify as angel garb.

Twenty-four

Ada

"Danny! Thank God you're all right!" I was so relieved I let myself relax back into the water until it splashed on my forehead and I realized my new day-glo hat was in danger of shrinking. Besides, if I stayed half submerged a second longer, I'd pee my pants. I scrambled to my feet, as Danny came plunging into the stream to help me up.

"Mom, for crying out loud. Are you all right? How'd you get here? Jeeze!"

The girl with the gun stayed on dry land and watched Lucia make a fool of herself, trying to stand up with the backpack weighing her down. Lu kept slipping into deeper water. Danny noticed her plight, screamed "Whoa!" as he handed me over to the girl, then reached for Lucia, whose body was about to bob on down the rushing stream.

"I float real well," Lucia muttered, spitting out a mouthful of clean mountain water as Danny anchored her in his grasp. He lifted her to her feet, which continued to slip-slide on the muddy bank of the stream.

"Stay still, Aunt Lu," he ordered. He unhooked the pack from her shoulders with one hand, and guided her to shore with the other arm tight around her middle.

"You okay?" Dan asked. "Jan, this is my Aunt Lucia. And that's my mother. Wow, I never expected it was you two prowling up to the cabin on the camp road. You're wrecked, soaking wet. D'you have any clothes in the car?"

Lucia and I shook our heads. "But if you want a good meal," Ada said, "you'd better get that backpack and its contents dried out real quick. Aunt Lucia was planning to fix you a gourmet dinner."

Danny groaned. "Shoot, I hope it's not ruined. We've had nothing but canned soup and crackers for days. And they're about gone. But how did you find us? Who..."

The girl with the gun finally let the frown on her face ease into expectancy. "Joe, I'll bet. He's the only one knows we're here."

Shivering, I hugged myself. "He was worried about us coming, said maybe someone on the police and someone at the rehab was on Farquar's side. So he told us to come in the daylight, like we were two tourists checking out Chatanike."

Before Danny could start leading us up the trail, Lucia grabbed his arm. Water was still dripping from her barn coat and her face, but the green scarf tied around her hair was as jaunty as ever. "No, Danny, wait! Put that pack down and go see if you can find our knives and our camera."

"Your what?"

"Hunting knives. Mine's a Bowie, and it cost me over a hundred dollars! I think the current took it." Lucia prepared to head back toward the water but Danny ran in front of her.

"Janet," he called back, "get these ladies up to the cabin before they freeze out here. What the hell did you guys need knives for?"

"We wanted to look like tourists," I said in a half-whisper.

The girl Janet laughed for the first time. "You do," she said, grabbing me by the hand and pulling me up the hill. Lu followed, one eye on Danny, fishing in the stream.

He was a dozen-feet downstream when he yelled, "I've got it! What a dagger. It's so big it got wedged between a couple of boulders or it would have floated away. Can't find anything else, though."

I turned back with a look of remorse. "Mine was a lot smaller. Probably floating all the way to the Yukon."

"See, Ada," Lu said, catching up to console me despite the squish in our shoes as we trudged upward, "sometimes size does matter."

~ * ~

Within an hour we had composed a scene of domesticity even Chantal couldn't equal.

Danny had fed the fire until it roared in the big stone fireplace, and Janet had laid our clothes there to dry, and was turning them every twenty minutes. Thanks to her water repellent barn coat, Lu's upper clothes had stayed fairly dry, except for the hem of the sweatshirt. Her jeans and socks were soaked, but her running shoes were drying nicely after their unexpected bath. She wore an oversized pair of old man's trousers. "My dad's," Janet said. "He's dead."

Lu whispered to me it must have been the smell of the pants that killed the poor man. But outwardly she tried to be a good sport about it, padding around in dry socks of Janet's.

My own hunting boots had kept my socks dry, and the woolen jacket had surprisingly repelled most of the water. But my jeans were soaked, too, and Janet loaned me a long skirt of hers with a fringe of white fur I was afraid to ask her to identify. Janet also had mixed up some hot chocolate on the gas hot plate and we huddled close to the fire while Lu began sorting out the food she'd brought in for dinner. She held up the two soggy halves of the French loaf and Danny laughed.

"We've been making do on Campbell's and hardtack, so even that looks appetizing, Aunt Lu. We could dry it out by the fire and it'll be nice and crunchy." He came and retrieved the bread from Lu and wrapped it loosely in foil, setting it near the fireplace. Then he roamed over to the windows that looked down on the stream, and the battered roadway over which we'd come, as if it were a security check they performed every so often.

"All clear?" Janet asked. Danny nodded.

"Sorry," she told me, "but that's why I'm here, too. To make sure no one sneaks up on us. It's why I have the rifle, and why I nearly shot off your hat. I do apologize for that."

"I'm just glad you didn't aim for my kerchief. It was tied pretty tight around my head," Lu said from by the sink where she scrubbed her foot-long hunting knife and glanced around at empty cupboards and shelves. "I'm only grateful my Bowie didn't ride merrily down the stream with Ada's camera. It's obviously needed here."

"There's not much up here for cooking," Janet explained. "No utensils or pots or anything, except that old cast iron frying pan and a tea kettle. The folks only came here for weekend getaways, and they liked to cook on an outside wood fire. But we do have a single propane gas burner, and an iron pot over the fire where we can roast things."

Lu said not to worry. When it came to food she could make do.

"More like gourmet than make-do," I called across the open room.

Lucia cleaned the vegetables in the cold water that ran into a tiny camp sink, and started hacking away at them. Soon she had the chicken roasting, with vegetables around it, and a bit of red wine and peeled apple chunks ready to surround it as it came closer to being done.

Meanwhile I was giving my stepson the third degree. "I don't understand why you didn't go back to The Recovery Zone. And you, Miss Janet, letting him get away with it. Why aren't you at work today? Did you really have the flu?"

It was Janet's turn to laugh, a short bitter laugh. She wore a dark ponytail that left her pale, round face pure, plain and ascetic, but her dark eyes were sad, sadder than any I'd ever seen. The girl shrugged under scrutiny.

"No, ma'am, I'm here to keep Dan safe. Joe did give you an earful, didn't he?"

"And by the way," I snapped back, "Where's your car? He said you were at work yesterday. How did you get out here?"

Danny grinned. "We're trying to be careful, Mom. She hid it over in the campground, a mile or two back the way you came in, on the banks of the Chatanike. Then she hiked up through a shortcut she knows."

"My family's been coming here for ages," the girl said. "It was all my folks left Joe and me, this little place. It gets too cold in winter, but we spend May to September here when we can. It's pretty isolated, no phone or anything, I didn't want Dan to be here alone. Besides, I can shoot, and he can't. Hates guns."

Something flicked past my overburdened imagination, but without knowing why I felt pleased at the information. I sipped my cocoa while Danny tried to explain further.

"I'm sorry I got you both into all this, but when I got back to Fairbanks last week I called Joe for a ride back to the rehab, and he said not to come back there. He was thinking back to when Farquar got out, about a month, no, maybe six weeks ago, right, Jan?"

She nodded in agreement. "That's what he said. I wasn't working there yet. Joe recalls one of the guys on staff really pushed for Farquar to get out even though some of them thought he wasn't ready."

Danny set his empty cup down and his eyes pleaded for understanding as he faced me. "The same guy I mentioned to you about that time I had to fill out those admission papers, remember? I said Farquar kind of worked with this guy in his office, ran the computer systems for him and all? And how they were giving Judd the third degree that day we checked in? They were all like big buddies."

I remembered. "Stonefield, wasn't it? Or something like that?"

"Stoner," Janet said. "A weird dude. He's actually a physical therapist, but works as an OT here—that's occupational therapist. Nobody likes him. Not from around here, so he doesn't fit in. But it's more than that. I don't trust him."

Dan nodded. "So Joe's been worried about Stoner, didn't want him to know I was back, in case he was in with Farquar. And I never mentioned Farquar had murdered Raul."

Lu looked up from her work.

"We're not even sure of that anymore, Danny. The detective thinks there was a second person involved. Poor Raul's body had been moved after he died, and it's possible he died too early for it to be your friend."

"Farquar's not my friend," Danny corrected.

I agreed. "In any case, it seemed Farquar might have been the one to move the body after Raul was killed, just before I got home. That would explain the dried blood he had on his hands, remember, Lu?"

Janet shivered. I was relieved to notice the girl had normal human feelings. The cavalier way she'd shot the rifle at their approaching forms, I hadn't been so sure.

Lu nodded. "Seems he had stolen Raul's key to get in, so he had to have moved him to get into his pockets."

"So maybe Farquar did do it," Danny opined, "to see if he had to shoot him or not."

"If you'd seen him with a gun, Dan, you wouldn't think the man was used to handling one." Lu whipped three eggs into her chocolate cake mix. "To me it makes sense someone had already killed Raul when that crazy man came along. Besides, he didn't attack your mom until three hours or so after Raul died. Where was he all that time, with no car parked in the area?"

"Maybe trying to find a way to break into your Fort Knox until he thought of Raul having a key," Dan said with a grin.

Suddenly Janet picked up the rifle she'd left standing by the door and poked her head out. "Going to do a quick 360, Dan. Be right back."

I felt alarm prickle my scalp. "Did she see something suspicious, Danny? Should we help her?" I jumped up.

"Sit, Mom. You've been through a lot. No one knows this place like Janet. Except her brother. I'm not good at handling a gun. You remember, Mom, how Dad took me duck hunting one time, and was disgusted with me because when he made me shoot I purposely missed the bird?"

I nodded, and reached out to tousle Dan's hair. Always such a sensitive kid. How could I have suspected even for a second...

"Well, Janet grew up hunting. Fish and game were her family's mainstay in the summer and fall. Anyhow, it's her turn to check the perimeter. If anything's amiss out there, she'll take care of it."

"Like," Lu said, coming to join us by the fire now that her work area was spic and span, "by shooting their heads off?"

Her words were still hanging on the air when the rifle crack hit their ears. Again, crack!

Danny went running to the door and screamed at Lu and me to get down on the floor. We smooshed together behind the couch and held our collective breath while Dan hurried out, calling to Janet.

"It's okay, it's all right, Dan." Her voice was high pitched, just one note down from panic. "Come down here and help me, it's Joe! He's been hurt."

Lu and I followed Dan out and watched him race down the hill, where Janet was assisting the man we had talked with yesterday. Joe, his face bloodied and though a good six inches taller and a lot heavier than Dan, had slung his arm over the boy's shoulders and, with Janet helping on the other side, made it to the cabin doorway. He was about to sink to the ground when Ada and Lu lent their support from the front, Lu gripping his bloodied shirtfront, me wrapping my arms around his waist and tugging him in. We got him to the couch, where he sprawled nearly unconscious.

"Did you shoot him?" Lu asked.

"No!" Janet screeched. "He was like this when I saw him limping up the hill. I fired to alert Dan to help me."

Joe just groaned.

"Christ, what happened?" Danny was all over him, checking out his shirt, front and back, making certain there were no life threatening wounds, I assumed.

"Stoner. The bastard. Tried to get me to tell him where you were, saw me talking to your mom and figured I'd put her on your trail. Now he wants to take you hostage for real." He gestured his chin toward me. "Wants to make her pay up for real this time too, was what he said. Since Farquar bungled it, he says."

Janet had grabbed some paper towels, dampened them and was gently patting the scrapes and cuts on Joe's face. Lu brought him a glass of water.

"So he was in on it with Farquar!"

"Shit," Janet exclaimed. "You tell him anything, Joe? Could he have followed you?"

Joe squirmed under his sister's ministrations. "Hell, no." Breathing hard, he sipped from the cup of water Lu held out. "Naw, he couldn't have followed right away. I slashed his two front tires when he left me bleeding in the parking lot and ran back inside."

"Probably to call Harriman." Danny banged one fistful of knuckles into his other hand. "His cop buddy."

"That's right," Janet said. "I've seen them together more than once. That Harriman seems like a scuzzball to me."

Joe pressed forward, jarred by her words. "Yeah, you're right. I've noticed that—"

"Take it easy, Joe," I insisted. "I feel badly for getting you beaten up. Where do you hurt?"

"Everywhere, ma'am," Joe said, leaning back on the couch and groaning in pain. "I think it's my ribs. He kicked me in the ribs when I lost my footing. Shocked me to have him come at me like that just as I got out of my car. Oww."

I dug into the deep pockets of my drying lumber jacket and pulled out a pill box. "Here, Joe, I have some ibuprofen. Take three. It'll help."

Joe nodded, angled upward and swallowed the pills with more water. He leaned back down and shook his head. "It wasn't so bad until I started heading up the hill. Every step felt like fire in my chest."

"Just relax, hon," Janet said. "You're going to be okay." Her face was no longer a blank mask, held in objective judgment. She hurt because her brother hurt. Danny, too, seemed anguished. But for a different reason.

"Listen, Joe, you said 'they' when you were talking about Stoner maybe following you. You think Farquar is back up here?"

Joe shook his head. He closed his eyes and wriggled to get into a more comfortable position. "Meant him and Harriman. I've been wondering about him since he came around looking for you after that cop in Connecticut called. Harriman kept stressing not to talk to anyone else at the station, just him. Said he'd be the one, it was his case, and he'd even put overtime in to find you. Out of the goodness of his heart, it seemed."

"But that was nice of him," I half-whispered.

"Like hell. Sorry, ma'am. But he was no angel. I saw him twice having beers with Stoner off-duty. They were gleeful, like they had some big pot of gold waiting at the end of their rainbow."

"And Farquar the one on the front line," Danny said. "I wouldn't have thought he had the brains to do it alone." He chewed on his lip, then looked startled. " Jeeze, if a cop's in with Stoner, he can find out where your cabin is, Joe. They can get themselves up here and corner us. We ought to make a run for it."

"No, no way Stoner or Harriman know we even have this cabin. He'll be looking for Jan at her apartment and me at mine. And we don't keep anything around that could lead people here. Our dad was in enough trouble over his drinking and debts that we tried to separate ourselves from his trail." He groaned again and Lu adjusted his pillow.

Janet shook her head. "We can't move Joe. He hurts too much. I'm going to tape up his ribs and we'll see how he is then. Anybody got anything we can use?"

Danny ran to the kitchen drawers and started poking around in them. "Here," he yelled. "Duct tape."

"Ouch," Joe said. "That would hurt like hell to get off again."

"But if we're going to move you from here, Joe, without taping you won't be able to stand it." Danny stood poised with the roll of duct tape and Janet started unbuttoning her brother's shirt and tugging it off.

"Look," Lu said sympathetically, "it'll be all right. Dan can apply the duct tape right over your tee shirt. It'll stabilize your ribs, but not do a number on your skin."

"Great idea, Aunt Lu," Danny said. Joe agreed, and worked himself into a sitting position.

As Danny wound the tape, Joe muttered expressions of pain, but soon eased up and began glancing around the cabin. "What the hell...What's that great smell in here? Did you guys cook something? That doesn't smell like chicken noodle."

"But it is chicken something," Janet piped up, doing a patrol of the front windows once again. "Danny's aunt is roasting up a whole yummy meal over the fire. Just hope we can stay here long enough to enjoy it."

"You know," I clucked, "having the fire going may not be such a good idea. If someone's out in this area looking for you fellows, and they see smoke, they could trail you. Once they spot your car, Joe, we're cooked." I began following Janet around, as she checked the perimeter again, then decided to stay posted at the window to keep perpetual lookout. "If only we could get help, call the police or something…"

"But some of the police seem to be in with Farquar, Mom," Danny reminded me as he wound the last bit of duct tape around Joe's chest and fastened it, earning him a punch in his bicep from his counselor.

"Damn, that hurt!"

Lu stroked the poor man's brow. "Lie down and try to sleep, Joe. The ibuprofen should be taking effect shortly. And I've got to get working on our chicken dinner or we won't be eating anytime soon." Janet helped Lu slide the fireplace kettle out and add the apples and wine. The new scents filled the room, awakening appetites, and awakening something else, too.

I had been watching birds swoop from tall pine tree to tall pine tree when their musical chirping penetrated my brain. "That's it! For Zeus' sake, that's what I was trying to think of earlier. The cell phones. We're high up enough now that the cell phones ought to work. I know there are transmission towers, I've seen them on the way up here, not far from the Chatanike."

"You have cell phones?" Janet screeched. "Great. I know they work up here!" Her usually placid face danced with excitement. Danny hurried over to watch as I dialed.

"Who you calling, Mom? Not the police!"

"Don't be silly," I said. "I'm calling my friends in West Parkford. I want us to get out of this alive!"

Twenty-five

Meg

While Isabel unlocked the door to her little Cape Cod in the Elmtree section of town, I sagged forward against the steering wheel, my flushed face against my arms. The trip to Boston and back had knocked me out—the painful chat with Lydia Mendino, the anguish of knowing how Ada would feel when she heard the whole story. *And* worrying whether Dorie was safe right now.

I envied the Ecuadorian woman who had put in eight hours of vigorous housework like vacuuming, scrubbing, windows, even—all the things I hated—and still looked as if she could tackle dinner, clean-up, and run around the block. Of course, people grieving often overcompensated in their work to keep their sorrow at bay. I had witnessed it in grieving families enough times.

From the open doorway, Isabel forced a wan smile. "Come, Missus Doctor. I make tea."

I took a breath and felt new energy revive me. "Thank you." Tea would be good. With a drop of Arthur's Tanqueray gin, even better. But I could pretend.

I eased out of the car and headed for the house, then stopped in my weary tracks as two cars pulled up simultaneously behind me: one, Theo Rutledge's obscene Lexus, the other, Bernard Cascone's unmarked police car.

I stared blank-faced at the approaching group, arms bent outward at her sides, palms up. As the cars unloaded I began muttering. "But, how did you know? Did Lydia call you? How did you get here so quickly? I just picked up Isabel at her second cleaning job. I haven't even told *her* yet."

Theo reached me first and grabbed me by the arms. "My God, Meggie, you look awful. Have you even looked in a mirror lately? What do you mean, did we know? Know what?"

Vittorio approached and led the women into the house. I noticed his tear-stained face with a lump in my throat. This was going to be hard on everyone, I thought. Why does hard stuff have to be such a big part of our lives? Dealing with the dead had been so much easier than dealing with the living. Retirement wasn't supposed to work this way.

With effort I climbed up the steps and onto the concrete landing. Theo stepped in, the boy made room for me, and I felt Cascone supporting my back as I took the last stair up and inside the hallway. I turned to thank him.

"I'm glad you're here, Detective. Though how you knew Isabel and I have important things to tell you, I can't imagine."

"I'm all ears, Doctor Dautrey. But it was Mrs. Rutledge who got me here. Seems she found out some things today that require further checking."

"She? But I'm the one who's been to Boston and back to uncover the truth. Lydia Mendino finally talked. To me."

Cascone's eyes lit up even brighter. "Look," he said, "you know how this stuff works, Doctor. Technically this is all police business, and I should interview everyone privately. Hell." He closed the door behind him and cursed silently. "But screw it. This is an unusual case. Procedures seem pretty unnecessary and inadequate at this moment. So would you give Ms. Doyle a call and ask her over? I'm going to get my supervisor over, too. We'll be needing help to do all the checking, and it's nearly 5 o'clock. Places will be closing." He flipped open his cell and dialed, put in his request, and flipped the cover closed.

We had moved into the already crowded kitchen as we spoke, and now I stared at Cascone with bewilderment. "Places?" I muttered. "What places?"

Perhaps I was having one of my senior moments. It was like I had skipped a page in a good mystery and was suddenly lost, even though after today's revelation I'd have thought I was the one writing it!

Faltering, I stood there brushing my bossy salt and pepper hair away from my face. Damn, I needed a haircut, and a perm, and God knew what else.

The detective snatched up my hand. "Please, call Hannah for me. She deserves to be here. Besides, I'm anxious to know what she found out about Mrs. Javitt's search for the boy."

I slapped a hand across my mouth. "I'd forgotten. Yes, I'll call her right away." In the quieter living room I found the telephone on the desk and dialed, comforted by the clatter of tea-making in the kitchen.

Hannah, clearly irritated she was not already in the know, said she'd be right over. Meanwhile, Cascone and Vittorio invaded my quiet space in the living room and were tearing apart the small kneehole desk where Raul and Isabel apparently kept papers.

Theo dragged me into the kitchen. "Where have you been all day? Slaving away at the 'office' never left you looking this pooped."

I nearly burst into tears for an answer. I slipped off to the bathroom and splashed cold water on my face, combed my hair, wetting it down so it didn't, momentarily, stick out all over the place, and reapplied a bit of the City Rose lipstick Dorie had insisted I wear. I didn't bother with blush. No fooling anyone in this crowd that I had pink healthy cheeks.

Back in the kitchen Theo and Isabel had set up the scrubbed wooden table with mugs and plates of cookies. "Leftovers Missus Ada made us take after the funeral," Isabel explained when I eyed them. I hadn't eaten anything since breakfast, and not even a dried up old woman like me could survive without nourishment much longer.

"Go ahead, Missus Doctor, you have." I shook my head. My throat was parched.

"I'll have a glass of cold water first, if you don't mind."

"I'll get it for her, Isabel, you make the tea. You do look parched, Meg. What have you been doing?" Theo bustled around the kitchen.

"I went to Boston," I said, surprised no one realized I'd done so.

Isabel clanged the cover on the teapot and turned toward me with her jaw dropped open. Theo squatted onto the nearest available chair.

"You—what? To see Lydia?" she asked.

"Why, yes. For what other possible reason? You know I'm not a Red Sox fan."

Isabel came close, footsteps unsteady despite her sturdy dark oxfords. "How is she? Oh, Missus Doctor. Is she mad at me? Upset because I broke my word and told you..."

Now I remembered why I was here, and consoled Isabel by reaching out and clutching her hand. "No, oh, no, my dear. She's not angry with you. I got her to tell me—all about Judd Javitt—on her own. About the baby, and what he did, the awful man, and how Raul begged him..."

Hannah came through the door and into the kitchen at just the right moment. "Raul begged who? What's going on? Will somebody tell me, for God's sake?"

Bernie Cascone burst into the crowded kitchen with Vittorio at his heels. "We've got it..."

"Got what? You, too, Cascone," Hannah blurted. "Why are you leaving me out? I've been following you all over town. Left messages on your voice mail and beeped you twice."

"Sorry about that. I was over at St. Peter's checking on some evidence. Then Mrs. Rutledge called with her discovery, and said the Mendinos needed to talk to me."

291

Theo nodded. "But I didn't even know Meg had driven all the way to Boston to see Lydia about her medical situation."

Hannah's face froze. "Whoa!"

Cascone reached across me and touched Han's slender arm, bringing his crooked finger up under her chin and chucking it.

Her look dissolved, but she was trying hard to hang onto the anger.

"What the hell, am I supposed to be tending the damn home fires or something while the rest of you are out solving crimes?"

When she'd finished her outburst, Hannah peeked guiltily at Isabel and muttered an apology. "Not you, Isabel. I didn't mean—"

"I know, I know," Isabel said. "But now you sit, we all sit down and have tea. My legs cannot hold me up another minute, thinking about my poor Lydia and what she must be going through."

"She's all right, Mama," Vittorio said. "You heard what Missus Doctor said. She feels better now that everybody knows."

"And things are not so bad for her as she thought." I settled myself at the head of the table, started to move to a different seat, and found hands on every side holding me back. "Well, understandably, she had terrible psychological problems when Putito was born. Over him. His left arm, it's damaged, a little nerve damage. But nothing too serious. He'll have full use of it, with treatment. We'll get her a medical appointment down here with a specialist, and I'm thinking she'll want to move back nearer to you so she can work."

Wide-eyed, Hannah started to speak but pressed her fingers across her mouth to force herself to listen.

"Thank you so much," Isabel said. "I feel such, what do you call it, relief. You will tell us more. But for now, will you pour the tea, Missus?" She looked toward Theo, who began pouring the fragrant brew into the mugs.

Vittorio, squeezed in beside Theo, passed them around. At my left, Cascone got as close to Hannah as he could, She patted him on the hand as he gave her the plate of cookies and slung an arm across her chair. When Isabel settled on Meg's right on a tiny kitchen stool clearly used before for that purpose, I saw the woman of the tawny skin and jet black braids was finally not biting her upper lip any longer. And there was a sheen of moisture in her brilliant black eyes that mirrored something in addition to grief. Hope, maybe.

Something they would all share in the next few days if I was not mistaken.

First Isabel explained for the sake of those who hadn't known, how her daughter had fallen in love with Judson Javitt when she assisted him for months in the delivery and operating rooms at St. Peter's. Javitt lavished treats and dates on her, took her to conferences as his assistant, which meant she got paid and still had a whirlwind of a time mixing in a crowd she had only envied from afar. But soon Javitt got interested in other women, too, and began to let Lydia down, not so gently.

She explained her daughter's shame when she found she was pregnant, especially when Javitt refused to legalize their union. In fact, he dropped her like a hot potato. Vittorio echoed this information with memories of his own.

"Papa said Doctor Javitt didn't have to live as the daddy, but he had to help support her. We would take care of the baby ourselves, even adopt it, if Lydia didn't want to have a child at so young an age. But she wanted her baby. Right, Mama?"

Isabel nodded. "Raul wanted to protect his family. He says the doctor has enough money to pay the hospital and doctor bills at least. But after Raul spoke to him twice about it, Doctor Judd, he asked Lydia to go to his Florida house with him, stay a weekend and they would talk about it."

Hannah's eyes darted to mine, then to Theo's. I knew we were all thinking the same thing: Dorie.

"Instead," I said, trying to take the burden from Mrs. Mendino, "Judd convinced Lydia he would marry her if they could start fresh, no baby."

"No baby!" Vittorio murmured, pitching forward. "How do you erase a baby?"

Hannah looked to Theo, who said simply, "Judd is a doctor, Vittorio, they can do these things."

"But they are wrong things. Aren't they, Mama?"

Tears seeped from Isabel's dark eyes. "Thanks to God, it didn't work. When Lydia came home and told me, she was so sad she almost had a, what do you say, a nervous breakdown. She went to Boston to stay with a girlfriend from her nursing class, and went to see a counselor. Like you, Missus Theo. But when Putito was born with the bad arm, she got sicker. Couldn't do anything but cry."

"A common post-traumatic effect from what she'd gone through with Javitt, and seeing what the botched abortion may have done to the baby...." I explained.

Cascone had popped a few chocolate cookies into his mouth, but seemed to forget about them. Now he was jotting madly in his notepad. When I took a sip of my tea, Theo jumped in to explain more.

"Vittorio told me Raul was furious with Judd, and continued to try and get him to support Lydia through her ordeal, though I wasn't sure what the ordeal was until now. He sent a couple of small payments to Raul's account, since the Mendinos had wiped out their savings setting Lydia up in Boston, paying for tests, and doctors and the counselor."

"We found those records, too, didn't we, Vittorio?" Cascone let a small grin escape his work-focused face. "Thank you." He turned toward Isabel.

"*Si.* But the doctor wouldn't pay no more. Raul called him often at his office and sent him letters, putting copies of the bills inside. Then he got angry at Raul." Isabel stirred her tea. Her embarrassment among the group had dissolved, and she was holding my hand tightly as she spoke, as if grateful for the touch of another human being.

Cascone had to ask: "When was that, Isabel? That he got angry?"

"It was a Sunday, the week before..." Tears caught in her throat and her cup shook in her hand.

"It's okay," Theo said. "Take your time, Isabel."

Isabel drank, and Vittorio set down his mug and took over. "Papa went to the doctor's country club and waited for him to finish playing the golf. He told the doctor he had to pay or Papa would tell Missus Ada."

Isabel's face took on a pleading look. "The doctor banged a golf club on the ground and broke it in half. Raul got frightened, then. I told him, 'Leave it go, Raul.'"

"I'm sure there were witnesses. What happened next?" Cascone asked, chewing the end of his pencil absently.

Isabel smoothed her paper napkin out and stared at it. "Raul finally listened to me. Said he'd get another job to pay Lydia's medical bills. The girl felt awful. She already tried to hurt herself, she tried…"

Theo interrupted her. "We understand, Isabel. Just go on about what Doctor Javitt did, if you know."

"Oh, I know," she said, sighing deeply. "But Vittorio knows even better."

The boy stopped chewing cookies, drank and swallowed. He nodded vigorously, as if proud he could add to the unraveling plot. "The next day was Monday, he called here. I answered 'cause I just got home from school. Papa wasn't home yet. He told me to tell my father he would meet him at his aunt's house early the next day. Very early, because he had to catch a plane. He said everything would be okay. To tell my Papa that." Vittorio stared glumly at his raw-knuckled hands on the table. "I shouldn't have told Papa. I should have said, 'Go to hell, Doctor Javitt. I'll take care of my own sister.' I should have, Mama. I should have helped more!"

Isabel leaned away from me to comfort her child. The others sat stony-faced while Vittorio's words sank in.

"Motive," Hannah said.

"Opportunity," Cascone answered.

"So Danny had nothing to do with anything?" Theo asked, confused.

Hannah bit her lip. "My God. It all fits what I've been trying to tell you all for the last hour-and-a-half. Ada called me earlier. They're okay, Danny's still on the run from Farquar and company, but they're all together."

This time it was Cascone with the first response. "I figured it was you who had them call me, uh, Ms. Doyle. I've been back and forth on that end of things for the past hour. I've got warrants being worked up as we speak. And I'd like to leave in a couple of hours to deliver them myself. Maybe give the state troopers a hand in getting them to safety. The Fairbanks police are uncooperative, so far. Apparently because one of the wanted is an officer on the force."

I pushed my weary form back from the table. "I don't know what the hell you two are talking about but this is so sad and upsetting about Raul, and the possible circumstances of his, his passing." I covered my forehead with both hands and tried to breathe more deeply.

"Let them explain, Meg, dear," Theo said. "You'll be out of here soon. What you need is a hot bath, a bowl of soup and your recliner chair."

I nodded. "Please, Hannah, explain, and make it quick and make it clear for this old bean-brain."

Hannah pulled a face and poked me in the ribs. "It's good news, mostly, Meggie. Ada and Lu tracked Danny to his girlfriend's cabin in the Chatanike Forest preserve or some damn place. The girl's the sister of Joe, Danny's favorite counselor."

"It's this Joe who got Danny to hide out when he got back, apparently suspecting another worker at the Rehab of being in cahoots with Farquar." Cascone checked his watch and rose. "There could also be a dirty cop on the Fairbanks force, and I've put the wheels in motion to get the state police to overstep the locals, just in case. That's what I meant."

"But are Lu and Ada and Danny safe now?" Theo asked.

"We don't know." Hannah's face twisted into high tension mode, her brows knit tight. "When Ada called, Joe, the brother, had just gotten beaten up by this Stoner guy, who was in cahoots with Farquar. Joe had some broken ribs, and still drove out to the cabin to warn them, and to hide himself."

"Why the hell didn't Ada call sooner?" I asked, a frown furrowing her brow.

"Couldn't get any service on her cell, and no land phone in the cabin. It's pretty remote. But while Lu was fixing this fancy roast chicken dinner, Ada suddenly remembered they were up high enough now…"

"Chicken dinner!" Theo and I spat out in harmony. "Leave it to Lu."

Cascone knew the details, too. "The kid hadn't eaten much in several days. Guess Mrs. Catamonte came up to the cabin prepared. And this Joe, he's resting from his injuries a bit. Mrs. Javitt had some pain killers to share with him." There were small chuckles, and little surprise, around the table.

"They were going to eat, wait until dark and try to hike out to where the girl had her car hidden, leaving Joe's car as a decoy, in case Stoner located the cabin." Cascone himself guffawed. "Got to admit, it's a good plan. And they're staying in touch with me throughout. I've hooked them up with a Lieutenant in the State Police, who was to meet them when they come out of the park. We're hopeful they'll be all right."

Hannah sighed. "Or at least well-fed."

I had remained standing, and now I felt ready to collapse. I nodded at Isabel and Vittorio across the table. "Well, then, everything's working out in Alaska, as long as Farquar doesn't show up. Isabel, call Lydia tonight, dear. She's so anxious to talk with you about her plans."

Isabel nodded, smiling as widely as she could. "*Si,* maybe now my little girl will come home."

"Stay with them a while, Theo, okay?" I said softly. "And for God's sake, somebody keep me informed. I've got to go home and take a few aspirin myself."

Theo nodded understandingly. "That's fine, Meg. You go on. I'll stay. Wilson won't mind if dinner is late again tonight."

"Mama makes great *seviche,*" Vittorio said. "You could stay if you want. You, too, Missus Doctor."

From the doorway I nearly bent double as a laugh slipped out. "No, thanks, Vittorio. You have my share. I think I had some of that within the last decade, and that'll do for now." I paused, gathered my worried face into a grimace, then smiled. "Praise Allah," she said. "There's a silver lining, people. Ada is a great-aunt!"

A whoosh of exclamations followed me to the door.

Theo wasn't quite done. "What do we do about Dorie?" she asked.

Hannah growled. "I have a hundred calls into her. She doesn't answer. Don't know if it's my cell or hers, but I keep being disconnected as soon as it rings. I'm going by to feed Ramon. I'll try again from Ada's house."

As she passed Bernie, she let her fingers touch his neck just above his collar. She bent over and whispered close to his ear but loud enough to be heard. "Please call me later," she said. "Daddy is taking me out to eat, but I'll need to talk with you at some point."

He nodded, just as his supervisor Captain Handley came charging through the still opened door where my hand rested on the knob.

"Problems, Cascone? Sorry to be so long. I had a hold-up at a Seven-Eleven on the way over. What's going on? Should we get started?" The experienced cop surveyed the group with a frown. No one had the energy to answer.

Twenty-six

Dorie

I all but finished the painting that afternoon. Judd looked magnificent, his aristocratic features at their best around the relaxed smile he wore. I'd taken a few snapshots mid-afternoon to catch the beginnings of the westering light in his eyes and glinting in his blond hair, and started to pack up my things.

"I can finish it up at home very easily," I explained. "I have what I want, now."

"I don't," Judd said, stepping closer and preventing me from organizing my paints in the wooden box. "Leave it," he said. "Let's take a swim before it gets too late."

I wiped the sheen of sweat from my forehead and nodded. We changed into swimsuits and swam, though Judd had snuggling more than swimming in mind, and I felt myself longing to pull away and swim far out and back, cherishing the sense of freedom that moving through the water gives me.

Afterward I convinced Judd to run with me along the beach. We came back overheated and sipped Piña Coladas on the patio mesmerized by the orange-tipped waves ruffling the shore.

It was idyllic until I realized finishing up the portrait had erased any stalling excuses I'd had. If Judson were going to make any physical demands on me, this would be the moment. Sure enough, his hand reached across the slight distance between our chaises, and locked fingers with mine. I heard him sigh, watched him stir restlessly in his chaise. My sideways glance to his languorously stretched out body left no doubt about it, Judd wanted more of me—and soon.

When he'd held me close in the water, our nearly naked bodies touching from hip to shoulder, I felt my will collapsing. I'd never totally rejected the idea of going to bed with Judson Javitt. I just wasn't sure I could handle an affair for the physicality of it, minus the love and affection that ought to precede it. For my part, I felt a kind of caring rising up in me even now. But as to what Judd felt, I had no idea. Horny was the only adjective I could come up with.

I stalled him, made promises about later, and ran to the house to shower.

All through dinner, served by Judd's staff by the glass doors overlooking a moonlit beach, he romanced me. Brought me a gardenia from the garden for my hair, when I mentioned I loved their scent, slipped on my wrist an antique silver bracelet I'd admired it in his collection of family heirlooms in the glass case, and breathed pledges of devotion in my ear through every course.

I finally nodded a shaky yes, and once the lush Florida darkness had completely swallowed up the sun Judd had sent me up to prepare for bed while he dismissed the servants and locked up. I removed my scant bit of make up and slipped on my best nightgown, pulling over it the fawn silk robe I'd found on my bed when I'd arrived days ago. I was brushing out my hair when I decided to open the front window, and get some fresh air, perhaps the scent of jasmine, too, from the bushes below.

To my surprise, muffled male voices rose in pitch and intensity. A frisson of fear riddled my stomach. Was Judd being accosted? Or was the sound coming from across the road, the neighbor's yard, perhaps, and carrying on the breeze?

I flicked off the light switch and went to the front windows, pulled the blind a bit away from the window rather than separate the slats and risk being seen. There was a taxi waiting several yards down the street, and just below my window, the voices, now quieter, continued. Judd must have met someone he needed to speak with. Or argue with.

Tired from the day's work of trying to re-create what seemed to me the most handsome man in the world, I lay back on the satin coverlet and rested my head on the pillow. I'd close my eyes, eyes that burned from sun, paint fumes and weariness, and just lie comfortably until Judd returned.

I stretched, yawned, and curled onto my side, and instead, fell into a shallow sleep.

~ * ~

The sound of a shout, more of a scuffle, even, woke me. For a moment my eyes saw little until they grew accustomed to the dark. But the voices were more and more familiar. One was Judd's, raised in anger.

"Not a penny, you bastard," I heard him say. "Botched—you botched... (something)."

The other voice was harsh and unsophisticated, as unmodulated as Judd's was musical. I feared for Judd's safety, drew in a breath and leaned closer to the window screen. If he were being robbed, threatened, I ought to call 911.

Just then the second man backed away from the overhang of the front door, Judd's form moving after it, threatening.

"A deal" or "wheels," or something, the second man said. "Tomorrow," Judd clearly answered. The stranger moved away from the shadows and into the road toward the taxi, and the light slanting over the roof from the waterside moon fell over him, setting him in harsh chiaroscuro tones. I sucked in my breath and steadied myself against the sill.

The man was waving his arms, reminding me of the panicked way it seemed I'd seen him wave them before. But no, I must be wrong. *He* wasn't even from here. Didn't even know Judd. How could he? Their worlds could never have crossed.

It couldn't have been Farquar. My reaction must be traumatic stress post or whatever Theo had called it, an after effect on my part, nothing more. A shadow. A ghost.

There was another burst of angry words, but this time I couldn't hear as well, because my heart was pounding too loudly. I stepped back from the blinds, and flicked on the lights again. I stared in the mirror at my blanched features, my hair wild and pale in the light from the dresser lamp. My eyes underlit that way had a morbid glow, and the shadows of my nose and mouth danced across my face as I turned one way, then another.

I spun away from the dresser and hugged myself. It had to be my imagination going wild. My own grotesque image in the glass proved it: I was seeing things. Or had dreamt them. Hallucinations, maybe, or too much wine with dinner. I really had to watch that alcohol intake, knowing what it had done to Harry.

Wait until I tell the girls about this one. Theo had warned us about that stress thing, what it could do to you.

Which was exactly why I'd let myself come on this vacation.

"You need a break, Mom," even Liza had said it. "So what if he's a younger guy? He obviously likes you, what can you lose?"

I heard a car engine rev, move away, and footsteps on the stairs and in the hall outside my door. I took a deep breath and forced a smile. Maybe, after all, I was only pretending somewhere deep in my mind to see the, the *ghost* of Farquar, in order to get myself off the hook from sleeping with Judd. It hadn't been real. Of course not.

But this moment was.

The door opened, and the light-haired man with reddened cheeks and desire in his steel blue eyes came through. He was the paragon of my portrait, the most eligible bachelor in West Parkford, someone I'd never expected to have hold me in his arms. He seemed golden to me, an idealized image in oils, the object of my fantasies, not simply the flesh and blood Judson Javitt. He was Adonis.

Something, someone, whose beauty I'd re-created myself with brushstrokes on canvas.

Judd's lips were parted, full and expressive as a woman's. I'd heard something about the magic of his mouth.

"Sweetheart." As he came toward me I focused on that mouth and let the dizziness and confusion I sensed wash more and more away with every word he spoke. This was what was real. His hands around my neck, thumbs sliding up over my jawbone to caress my face, his scent of bay rum and spice.

"At last we can be alone. Celebrate the completion of the picture and this growing feeling we have for one another. Do you, do you care for me as much I care for you?"

It was what I'd yearned to hear.

His blue eyes pierced my soul. So different from Harry's dark and angry ones. The pale corn silk of his hair tumbled forward on his brow, and he tipped his head as he approached me, trembling.

Yes, I cared for him. I'd grown to care, to understand his loneliness and hurts, his desperation over the expanded costs of ministering to women and their babies. From childhood Judd grew up to be a man of privilege, but really, his plight was no better than mine. People judged him unfairly. He was human. He suffered. And I could console him.

I nodded, barely, and he slipped the robe from my shoulders.

Twenty-seven

Hannah

Before I headed home to pick up Dad for our dinner date I stopped by Ada's house to feed the bird. I was still muttering to myself about the fresh leads in the case, and couldn't wait to sit at my word processor to subtly incorporate some of those new facts about the infamous Dr. Javitt. But first I fed Ramon, cleaned out his cage, and sat nearby while he ate. Ada said he liked to be kept company, and Chantal didn't come in on Mondays, so he'd been alone all day.

"I don't know what the hell to make of it, bird. That Javitt is a sonofabitch. But would he have hurt Raul? I can't believe he'd go that far. Maybe, after all, it was an accident, Raul falling on his pruning shears, and Farquar showing up afterward coincidentally. But at whose instigation?"

After all, Raul had been told Javitt wanted to meet him. The good doctor was probably ticked at having been worked over to cover his mistakes with Lydia. Screwing up the poor girl with that botched abortion, and leaving her psychologically and apparently physically maimed as well. So much so that Lydia had tried to take her own life!

"And him a doctor."

Ramon spit out some hulls and perked up, jiggling from one foot to the other. "Doctor, Doctor, call the doctor."

A bitter laugh shot out of me. Ada had taught Ramon the strangest things. "You're incredible," I told the bird. He played with the sounds of "incredible" for a few seconds, then gave up and turned back to his birdseed.

I jumped, slapping a hand across my mouth as if the bird's busy beak had caught my lip.

"Call the *doctor*? No! Wait, Ramon. If Javitt's a killer, if there's even a chance, we've got to call *Dorie*, get her out of there. I'll try the house number this time. I've got to reach her."

I ran to Ada's desk, checked for the Palm Beach number in the rolodex and dialed. This time Judd Javitt's voicemail came on.

When the beep sounded, I spoke fast and low, hoping that technique would cover my anxiety over the call. "Hi, Judson," I said casually. "Hannah Doyle here. Need to talk with Dorie. Club plans, big emergency over our upcoming meeting. Do ask her to call me tonight. I'll be out with Dad, but I'll have the cell phone turned on. The plans are too precious. She'll love hearing about them, and we'll need her vote. No mistake, now. Please have her call *tonight.*" I repeated my cell phone number and hung up, then, fingers trembling, fished in my bag for a cigarette.

"Christ, that was hard, Ramon. I'm not much of an actress."

When the doorbell rang my nerves were so tattered I bobbled my lighted cigarette and burned two fingers. I thought of the last time I'd answered the muted, musical ring and it was Danny, backed by Cascone. It surely wouldn't be either of them, one in Alaska, one on the way up there.

I blew on my scorched fingers, took a drag of my Carleton, and, for a moment, stood behind the door wondering what to do. Whoever it was could see my Volvo parked in the driveway, knew I was there. But what if it was Farquar, still not having left town, still hoping to get in for Ada's bearer bonds or jewelry.

If I peeked out into the dusk through the sidelights of the door, whoever it was would see me. I'd be a visible target. I took another drag, paced around in a tight little circle, then heard the voice I'd most have chosen to hear.

"Hannah, it's me, Bernie Cascone. I smell you smoking. Let me in."

When I did, I fell into his arms before he even shoved the door closed behind himself. We clung to each other for a long minute.

"I'm worried, Bernie. Worried about Ada and Lu, yes, but worried speechless about Dorie. Javitt had a hand in this whole thing. I just know it. And she's with him! What the hell are we going to do?"

His voice was steady and low. I felt breath fill my lungs just hearing him start to speak.

"You're going to sit tight, try and reach Dorie, and advise her to take an early plane home. We don't want to alarm her, but that bastard *could* be behind this whole thing, considering what he did to Raul and Isabel's daughter."

"Dorie told Lu she'd seen scars on Lydia's wrists. Now we know the young woman was so distraught she tried to hurt herself."

He shook his head and muttered. "And that little baby damaged by what Javitt did. Damn! The doctor could be behind it all. Everything. I'm really sorry I have to leave for Fairbanks, Hannah. I don't trust the local police up there. I've got to go try and figure where Farquar is, what his connection is to Javitt, and who else is involved."

"I wish you weren't going." I tugged on the lapels of his windbreaker.

He tapped his breast pocket. "I've got the warrants. There's a flight out of Boston at nine. I'll be there by two a.m. their time, check things out. Make sure those Alaska State Troopers are as efficient as they sound."

"Okay," I said, "if that's how we have to do it. But what about Lucia and Ada in the meantime? Are they safe? Are we sure this Joe and his sister aren't going to hurt them or Danny? Are they on the up and up? Or in with Farquar, too, maybe?" The Carleton was down to where it was burning my fingers. I yanked open the front door and flung it outside, licked the two burned fingers from before. Then looked up to realize he was watching my every move.

"Burned myself when the doorbell rang," I said sheepishly, flicking my hair behind my ears like a teen-ager.

Cascone sighed, lifted my hand to his own mouth and kissed the blisters.

I shivered with surprise. "You probably wish I'd give those up. Smell lousy, taste worse, right?"

"Hannah, Hannah," Cascone murmured, pulling me close again. "The way you are, exactly that way, is how I like you."

He brushed my hair back from my face and little chills of remembered sensations traveled down deep into me.

Bernie grinned, settled his hands on my shoulders. "Now, yeah, I think your friends are safe. It doesn't sound like the kid or his girlfriend and her brother are into this whole scheme. But I'm lucky Handley is sending me off on this jaunt, new as I am here. I get up there in a hurry, I can make sure they stay safe. Okay?"

I reached up and put my arms around his neck, hugged him tight and quickly pushed him away. I couldn't bear to kiss him. "Thanks, Bernie. I know you can. Wish I could drive you up, but you'll probably go faster on your own."

"Lights on, sirens blaring," he said, grinning as he stepped backward, obviously understanding my reluctance to get closer at that moment.

Guys that have suffered, I decided, have more sensitivity to a woman's feelings. I sighed.

Bernie zipped up his windbreaker. "Now don't be worrying about me or anything up on the frozen tundra. Your department is getting Ms. Boulé out of that bastard's house and getting her home. Can you do it?"

I nodded, but without conviction. "But you'll stay in touch, right?"

He grinned at me, his cute overbite appealing, his eyes saying words he hadn't even attempted yet. Words that would scare the hell out of me if I knew them. Maybe.

He moved, opened the door. "Try and stop me. Now be sure and lock up when you leave."

I pressed the door closed behind him, head spinning at an image of closing another door behind another someone so long ago the memory came like a splash of cold water. Back when I was still trusting, naïve. Now I was wiser, and knew enough to be scared. Someone I cared about was walking, no, running, *flying*, into danger.

I wished I could forget what it was like eventually to discover my *someone* was never coming back.

Quietly I tiptoed over to Ramon's cage. His head was tucked under a wing, and he looked ready for a night's sleep.

"Goodnight, sweetheart," I said, hearing Bernie's car roar out of the driveway and picturing it tooling up I-84 to Logan Airport. I covered Ramon's cage and gathered my things, only to hear the bird echo, plain as day, "Goodnight, sweetheart, goodnight."

Twenty-eight

He called for a cab, then left the motel room without passing the office. The manager had been leaning on him for days to cover the bill, and all he needed was cops coming by before he had the wherewithal to blow this roach castle. Squinting against the early sun he lit a cigarette and leaned his long frame against the fence by the pool hall next door.

He hadn't told the rich guy where or when he'd meet him, just to be ready. Best to show up nice and early at his front door and throw him off guard. Personally escort him to his bank. Last night the bastard tried to scare him off, but last night was just a polite warning.

Chuckling harshly, he took a deep drag of his Marlboro and patted the bulge in his pants pocket. This time he held all the cards. And more comfortable with a blade than a shooter. He needed scratch and he needed a certain substance that made him happy. Mostly, he needed out of this dump and down to Key West. If it didn't work out down there, Cuba was right across the stream, and after that, freedom, and plenty of substances he could deal in.

Maybe a new gig, and not with a goddamned two-timer this time.

Those damn women in their fancy clothes had screwed him royally, too. Somebody had to pay. And it was going to be today or never.

Twenty-nine

Dorie

In the morning, confused and wobbly where I sat across from Judd Javitt, I poked at my fruit plate and coffee hardly daring to raise my eyes to Judd's. He had been gentle, sweet to me, yet somehow *passionless*, the night before. I'd wanted him to really care, to need me, to get carried away. But he was such a careful, cautious lover. He worried about protection, got almost clinical about the degree of my pleasure, and left my bed as soon as it was over. I tried not to express disappointment, filed it away as an educational experience and planned to leave today. Any fire I'd imagined between us seemed extinguished. If it had ever burned at all.

Especially because this morning Judd seemed distracted. He carried his coffee out to the patio and scanned the horizon. Then he came back in and went to the front door, stepped out and stared at nothing in particular.

"If you're looking for the newspaper, Martin left it here, by your plate." I tried to make my voice sound cheerful.

"Hmm? Oh, yeah." He wandered in, took a roll from the bread tray and munched on it, while he flipped through the pages of the Miami Herald.

I selected a chunk of papaya and told myself to savor it, realizing I wouldn't be having this exotic array of fruits on my breakfast plate again anytime soon. I picked at the kiwi, speared a slice of mango, and made myself chew with a remnant of a smile on my face. It was delicious, the watermelon best of all, that and the fresh figs that garnished the whole assortment. I nibbled, then sat back, my pretense slipping, my smile fading. As I sipped my coffee I noticed Judd had stopped reading and was staring into his own cup.

"I've started packing," I said, testing the waters.

"What?"

"I'd like to fly home today. First make arrangements to get the painting crated properly in a week or two when it's dry, and arrange for a flight later this afternoon."

"No, you're not going today."

I felt my spine stiffen. I looked up at him. For a crazy moment I thought the words, "Woman power" and of the collage I'd made for the lingerie shop.

"Are you?" He picked up his coffee and forced a smile over the cup's edge.

I nodded, and speared a piece of muskmelon more to balance the beautiful platter than out of desire for it. "My work here is done. You said yourself you had to get back to the hospital. Why don't we, uh, fly together?" His face was shifting expressions from indifference to some kind of agitation even as I watched. I felt the back of my neck prickle in tension.

"There's no reason for you to hurry home, Dorie. I could go up for a few days and fly back to be with you for the weekend. But not until tomorrow. I've got some business to wrap up today. And, we've just gotten close...haven't we?" His words turned hard, punched the air, making his question more an attack than a serious inquiry. His left eyebrow had cranked up and his mouth set into a straight line, like nothing I'd ever noticed when I painted him, or when I'd felt myself falling for him.

I took a breath. I'd explain, surely he'd understand. This wasn't Harry with his temper and his drunken fits. This was Judd, a reasonable, intelligent man who liked me, who had treated me as a gentleman would treat a lady, this was Ada's nephew, for God's sake.

Then why was I trembling?

Judd stood suddenly, closed the French doors and came around behind me. "You're shivering, darling. Is something wrong? What has changed you from my sweet, agreeable Dorie? Are you cold?"

I shook my head and tried not to shiver as he bent his face low to nuzzle my hair. For days I'd appreciated such sensitive gestures. Now I felt a frosty indifference to them, to him. Why? I wondered. Why doesn't it turn you on to have him tease you, be affectionate? It had, until last night. Now I actually felt squirmy under Judd Javitt's touch.

"I want to go home, Judd. I'm grateful for this respite; it's been wonderful. I hope you understand." Smiling up at him with all the graciousness I could muster, I eased away and slipped out of the chair. He smiled back, grabbed my shoulders to turn me toward him and gripped my chin with a thumb and forefinger, pinching it a shade too tightly.

Then he pulled his hand back so sharply it was like a blow, a rebuff. He waltzed away from me, trying, I sensed, for a casual mode but too tense in his facial expression, his rigidity of shoulders. "No problem at all, my dear. I have to go into town on an errand. I'll pick up your ticket for you." He stopped at the door and faced me, that flirty look he always kept for such moments not quite settling on his chiseled features.

"We'll have the whole day to ourselves, as Martin and his wife have this afternoon off. I've already told them to fix us a nice lunch on the patio, some lobster salad, one of her fabulous Key Lime pies. We can swim, relax, do whatever you like. Then I'll drive you to the airport. You'll be in your own bed tonight. How's that?"

A sense of relief flooded me. "Y-yes, yes, that would be lovely. We'll do that. I'll phone Liza while you're out and have a last chat with her. Maybe sun myself a little."

"Good idea, darling," Judd said, somehow squeezing the words between his teeth. "I noticed last night in bed you're still way too white." He turned and left me open-mouthed.

Violation washed over me, and embarrassment over my body, my body that was older than his, that was milky and soft, seeking its own gravity-induced levels. The creepy neck. The pale, puckery skin on the insides of my thighs.

I forgot to breathe until I heard his PT Cruiser convertible, his "Florida car," roar out of the driveway. Peering out the front windows I watched the yellow blur streak up the block and turn the corner, Judd's dark glasses glinting in the morning light, his carefully sprayed blonde hair barely lifting in the breeze. Maybe I was being ridiculous, but Judd Javitt was starting to give me the creeps.

Or maybe it was me.

I picked up my cell from the telephone table where I'd left it the night before during our romantic evening, saw I had voicemails, and noticed the beeping light on Judd's house telephone. Why hadn't he retrieved his calls?

Oh, well. Not my problem. I lay the phone back down.

For reasons I couldn't understand, or perhaps was afraid to, I did exactly what Judd had asked me to do; I extracted my swim suit from my suitcase and put it on, tucked the cell phone in my robe pocket, grabbed a clean beach towel, and headed out. Martin waved to me as I scuffed out to the patio. I was about to select a chaise in the sunny corner of the bricked terrace, when the glistening water of the Atlantic caught my eye. I carried my things down toward the beach. Martin came running after me.

"Would you like a chaise brought here, Miss?"

"Thanks, Martin, I think I'll just lounge on the sand today. Get the feel of it in my bones before I leave."

He nodded, obviously erasing his puzzled expression as quickly as he could. "Yes, ma'am."

I spread my towel out and sat on it, unable to take my eyes off the softly curling waves. The sun glinting on the water created floating diamonds of light, and the patio palms behind me swayed with a soft rustling. In the house a phone rang, was answered, taken care of. In the kitchen far off I could hear Martin and Corinne making lunch preparations over the hum of an appliance motor. It would be delicious, whatever it was.

I closed my eyes, breathed in the warmth of the sun. Odd, how the same place that had seemed so idyllic yesterday, so romantic and full of promise, now left me feeling unsettled. My eyes popped open. It seemed oddly important to keep them open. I stared out to sea, reminding myself to breathe deeply. Not so bad, Boulé, I thought to myself, it's still Palm Beach.

With sudden determination, I slipped off my sheer orchid cover-up, spread sun screen on face, neck, chest and arms, always the most vulnerable spots for someone as fair as myself, tugged the purple and aqua flowered suit down beneath my fifty-plus-year-old buttocks, and strolled toward the sea.

Damn Judson Javitt! Today the placid, nondescript waters of the pool or his sheltered little patio would not do. I needed the ocean, the briny splash of waves and crunch of crustaceans and errant pebbles under my feet. I needed to know I could still do it. And to wash every trace of him from my being.

Bending low, I adjusted my body temp to that of the water by anointing my wrists and temples. The ritual reminded me of being seventeen, feeling like I could conquer the world, both with my art and my love, and my ease at swimming. I took one last glance around at the empty beach, sucked in air and dove.

The christening of the tangy waters brought the refreshment I'd grown to expect and love since I was a child. A cleansing benediction. My senses snapped to life, my mind cleared, emotions calmed. I was making way too much of this whole business with Judd. I'd let it go. He'd been crude, thoughtless, but I'd let it go.

My long, powerful strokes transported me about fifty yards out, where I shifted to my back and studied the cloudless sky. Buoyed on the waves I felt purpose returning. For a while, I side-stroked north, imagining myself returning to Hartford like a huge, flying bird that slid through both water and ether with equal ease. Driven from within, whole, confident, swooping.

Woman power, indeed.

I giggled to myself, faced the deep water where I imagined or really saw—it didn't matter—a pair of Sunfish tacking into the breeze, their white sails stark against an indigo ocean. For a while they mated, scudding side-by-side in harmony. Then one slipped past the other, gained, and was soon barely visible in my sight line. Overcoming. Like I could, and will. Overcome this misguided alliance.

I might even admit Theo had been right.

I swam back toward the Javitt house on the shoreline, ducked under once to push my long hair back in one direction and scrambled up, facing the beach. I'd lie on the towel and relax on the sand. My last hours in the lap of luxury.

I realized I was all right now. I'd just been homesick, feeling a little pinned under Judd's strong masculine influence. He'd meant no harm. He'd been infatuated with me, but it hadn't worked out. Why he'd been so interested in me I couldn't imagine, especially as I was at least five years older. Now it was over, our brief history felt oddly mechanical, hollow, even bloodless. Okay, so I'd crossed a bridge, realized I couldn't ever enjoy sex without enduring love, and that was that. I owed him nothing. Nor he, me.

As I waded slowly into shore, the steady beat of waves rocked me deeper into the shifting sand. When the water was just below my knees, I bent forward, tossing my hair over one shoulder and gripping it in both hands to squeeze it dry. As I let it go, I sluiced the water from my arms and thighs, and lifted my head toward the house.

Sunspots made me squint. Movement on the patio. A man. Martin? No, the house man wore white. Judd, back so soon? But no, this man was taller, and when he turned in profile, looking up and down the beach, revealed a hooked nose. She thought of Cascone, dismissed the idea when she recalled the New Yorker's husky form. This fellow was tall and gangly, his nose a real beak.

He moved toward me now, thirty yards away up the beach, holding my gaze with his own.

I felt my knees go weak. I remembered the voices at the front door last night. Remembered Ada's house a week ago.

I could neither walk forward nor stay where I was. The shifting sands beneath my arches gave way. For one flash of an instant I thought of plunging back into the water, swimming frantically for—where? Suddenly he reached my stack of belongings tossed carelessly in the sand. He bent, lifted the towel, and held it up in two hands, grinning...

Perhaps Judd was there, too? They knew each other somehow? But no, that couldn't be. If it were so, then Judd, too, might be involved with Raul's death!

I swallowed hard. In the three or four seconds it took for my thoughts to register, I had moved far enough on the sand to no longer feel the lapping of waves at my feet. But the imprint of those waves on my body reminded me how strong I had felt in the water. How strong I could always be.

As long as I didn't waver.

I stepped forward and breathed deeply, eyes scanning the beach from left to right. No one was out, except, three or four houses up the row, the house boy arranging deck furniture in front of the Silverman's.

The approaching intruder met me half way and I snatched my towel from him, crushing it to myself and staring Farquar in the eye.

"What the hell do you want, you brute? If you don't get out of here quick, I'm screaming. And, as you know, I can scream loud enough to wake the dead." A picture of Raul lying in his coffin flashed in front of my eyes and I felt something crumbling inside. No, I thought, hang on, Dorie. "And when I'm done screaming I'll call the police."

"Whoa! Little lady's grown up. Hold on." He stood maybe a half-dozen feet away, and his thin lips curled in that sneering, nasty way he had. I pinned him with a look of disdain. His expression changed to doubt, panic almost, and he slumped backward, almost losing his footing on the soft sand.

"Don't do that, pink feather lady. You'll miss what I have to tell you. And I ain't got much time to do it."

I wrapped the towel around my suddenly chilled body and lifted my chin, hoping against hope I looked as self-assured as Ada, as unconcerned as Lu. Half as in-command as Hannah.

"Well?"

"That boyfriend of yours. You got to know. He's the one made me go up there to scare that gardener and rob his aunt. Said he'd pay damn good."

"You scared him pretty damn well, too, didn't you? You killed him!" My voice had risen. Good, anybody might hear me, see me out in the open, being talked to by a wild-eyed scruffy guy in black tee shirt and black jeans, a dark baseball cap.

Farquar's eyes grew wide. "No, naw, I didn't kill him! I found him that way, laying on his own clippers. I got into the house just in time, before the lady came home, and I thought, Christ, Javitt's set me up. I better get what I can out of her, as long as I'm into this, because he's obviously planning to give me nothin'."

I rocked, forced myself to stay standing. He'd said, "Javitt." Danny? No, not Danny...

His voice turned low and pleading. "Listen, lady, you got to help me or I'm calling in the cops myself on that boyfriend of yours. And when I do, I'll be long gone. The bastard's reneging on our deal. After getting me in all this trouble, he owes me."

He meant Judd, Dr. Judson Javitt. The man who'd slept in my bed...No!

I couldn't stop staring. His eyes narrowed, got mean-looking.

"All I need is money. Couple thousand to get the hell out of here," he croaked. With one arm, he shielded his face against the noonday sun, glancing up nervously as a plane flew over.

I let out a burst of laughter, and he gaped at me, shock in his eyes.

"You came to the wrong person, Mr. Farquar. I have no money. Nothing to give you, you creep. Zero. Zilch"

He reached for my arm but I twisted away and spat out my words between a clenched jaw. "And don't tell me Doctor Javitt had anything to do with that man's death, or holding us—his own aunt!—hostage. Now get out of here or I'm—"

"Heh-heh." Farquar's birdlike cackle was half-hearted. "Ain't no one here. The maid and her buddy just left. Saw them go. So listen. You don't think the doc's involved? How'd you like to know I met him down here almost a year ago? He's the one got me certain, uh, medications I needed. Had some good connections he did, and we worked out a deal, him, me and Stoner—yeah, ask Stoner—and that cop Javitt bought up in Fairbanks. To bring Miami coke up to the boonies."

I had to push the words out from a dry throat. "You're crazy, he wouldn't deal drugs. He helps people, delivers babies."

Farquar's face darkened. "Yeah? I heard he was broke. That's why he wanted out of helping the gardener's daughter. Why ya think he picked that rehab place for the kid? The old lady could've afforded any other posh place in the country."

My skin ran with goose bumps. We'd all wondered why Judd had insisted Danny go to Alaska for rehab. We'd trusted his answers: "Get him out of the mainstream drug lines." A wave of panic washed through me, weakening my knees. Judd into drugs? Working with this evil creep?

"Look," Farquar, said, when a horn sounded out front. "I got a cab waiting. The bastard was supposed to be here with the cash. If you don't want the big shot doc arrested, you better put it up now or your cushy gig here is over. For good. Decide quick, lady. I ain't planning to hurt you or nothin.' Just give me something so I can get the hell outta that stinkin' Super 8 and on the road."

I shook my head. Half unseeing in my panic, but suddenly sure of my movements, I spun around the long shadow he cast and reached for my cover-up, slung it around my shoulders and started to poke my arms through. At the same instant Gordon Farquar captured me up in his wiry arms and held me, wriggling, with one more plea pelting my ears.

"Don't make me hurt you. I'm desperate, see? I don't even have a watch to hock. Had to do that to get myself up to Connecticut in the first place when the Doc called me to come and scare the old gardener guy, which I'd have done, if he wasn't already dead. Now before I give you something to remember me by on that pretty face, give me *something*. Your watch, your ring, there, anything!"

This time I let my reflexes do the talking. I screamed at the top of my lungs, as loudly as I ever had in her life. He held tight. Without checking to see if anyone had heard, trying not to wonder if anything this wild man had said was true, I twisted from side to side to release his grip, and screamed again, then brought my knee to his groin at exactly the right instant.

This time he wailed, shoved me to the sand in recoil, and groped his way toward the house, doubled over. He stumbled, fell, rose again and ran a few steps more.

The heat settled on me, fusing my backside to the sand. My mind went dull as sunlight on tarpaper. I watched him cross the patio, run into the house, and then, from the sound of things, out the front door. In the few moments I sat there stunned, a car engine started up and moved away from the block. It hit me hard, that at any moment I might hear a different car engine coming closer.

Judd.

Judd involved with Farquar? No, no. It couldn't be. I had to sort this out, and fast. I fished for my cell phone in the robe pocket. It had fallen to the sand in the struggle. I snatched it up, blew on it, flicked it on. Good. Plenty of bars.

My fingers punched in the numbers, my heart slamming against my chest.

Should I call the police next? Judd would be home any minute. If he were connected to a murder, would he hesitate to kill me? Up the beach the Silverstein's houseboy was moving toward me at a slow trot, arms akimbo as if in question. Forcing a smile, I waved him away and focused on my call.

Hannah answered, her voice crisp and wide-awake. "Dorie, that you? I tried to get you three times yesterday,

twice already today. The house guy said you were not to
be disturbed. You all right?"

"Shut up, Han." I was about to describe what had just
happened. I was about to ask Hannah, from over a
thousand miles away, what to do. But a shadow loomed
over me, a chill rode up my back, and I knew without
even looking up, this time it was Judson Javitt standing
over me. I'd have to play my own cards. And play them
without falling apart.

I enunciated the words carefully, projected them
loudly. "I'm sick of your bird calls!" I screamed, and
tapped the off button, slid the phone back in my pocket.

"Wow. Where did that come from?" Judd crouched
down beside me. I saw my disarrayed hair and unsettled
features reflected in the sunglasses he still wore. "Never
heard your temper up before."

"I, oh, nothing you'd want to hear," I snapped.

"You've had a swim, sweetheart. How nice. Who were
you talking to? That Doyle woman? What's she pestering
you about? I forgot to tell you she called last night on the
house phone. Wanted you to call her, something about the
club you're all forming." He brushed my face with his
lips.

I nodded vacantly, scanning the horizon for at least one
of the Sunfish. They were both gone.

"You're all rosy-cheeked, honey. You must have had
quite a swim."

I swallowed hard. "I did. Swam up past Silverstein's."
At that moment I glanced up and saw the Silverstein's
houseboy returning homeward, still looking toward me

over his shoulder. I gave him a friendly wave and pretended he'd been hearing things.

Phantoms. Ghosts.

When I brushed my hair back from my face, I managed to press a smile where none had been.

Judd's grin was too enthusiastic. "About time you told her off. She's far too bossy a broad for my tastes."

I could hardly speak. I couldn't tell him about Farquar, couldn't ask if it were all true. I gulped hard. "She gets that way sometime. Bossy. As bad as Theo. Listen, Judd, I'm starved. Let's have lunch. Oh, and did you get my ticket?"

"Today's flights were all booked, sweetheart," he explained with exaggerated patience as they strolled up to the patio, circled the pool and went into the house. My heart sank. After I followed him in, Judd yanked closed the patio doors. "Keeps the air-conditioning in. It's going to be a scorcher today." Then before I could scoot away, he planted a firm, wet kiss on my mouth.

"Go ahead and shower, darling. I'll check on lunch." I heard him flick the lock on the back door.

Stomach reeling, I took the stairs by two's. In my room I slipped out of my suit, grabbed my robe and hurried to the bathroom. Once I turned the water on, I quietly closed the shower door and pulled my cell from the robe pocket. I stood there naked, dialing Hannah's number, my sunburned face a mask of shock and fear in the mirror. Hannah answered.

"Dorie? What the hell do you mean, shut up? Is something wrong? Again, you didn't answer when I called back."

"I shut it off," I said, and saw behind me in the steaming mirror, the bathroom door easing open, Judd eyeing me, his eyes blazing with the passion he seemed to have lacked the night before. Or maybe, he had been too distracted by his angry visit from—yes, it had been Farquar at the front door last night. Not a dream or traumatic anything.

"Right," I said to Hannah cryptically. "What do you think we are, eight super women, lounging around some motel waiting for a meeting agenda to pop up mysteriously? You buy the door prizes, woman. I haven't got the time!"

His voice was deep, accusing. "On the phone again?"

Before I let my trembling finger trip the disconnect, I spoke up loud and clear. "Just telling her off again, Judd, dear. You know how she can be!"

Apparently Judd was not going to let me out of his sight, today. And I didn't want to make an issue of it. I was beginning to think playing the dumb blonde might be the smartest move to make. Eventually, I'd finish that call or figure out all by myself exactly what to do.

This time, there was no one else to count on.

Thirty

Hannah

"Dorie! Watch out for him!" My scream was too late, the connection broken. I knew without dialing the phone would be off. And Dorie was in trouble, serious trouble, or she wouldn't have told me to shut up, wouldn't have said the things she did. Sure, Dorie got her words mixed up sometimes, but never insulted, never cut anyone. And she'd made it clear her trouble was at the hands of Doctor Judson Javitt. I dialed anyway, as I ran from the living room of our condo to my father's darkroom.

"Daddy. I need your help. Let me in, please!"

But when he came out, lifting the special eye protectors he wore while developing, and I explained the dilemma, there wasn't much Daddy could think of to do.

"Let's call the Palm Beach Police," he said with a shrug.

"Do it," Hannah said. "Meanwhile, I'll call Ada on my phone, get the address of the house down there. Or Sol Sherman. He'll know. And I'll try Cascone, if he has his phone on in Fairbanks."

Dad called the police while I tried to connect with Ada. The last I'd heard they were leaving the hunting lodge and heading, under cover of darkness, to Janet Eagle Feather's tiny Subaru parked in a State Campground two or three miles away. If Ada and Lu could make it, and Janet's brother was not in too serious a condition, they should be safe by now, but exactly where, I had no idea. If I couldn't reach Ada or Cascone, the Alaska State Troopers might know.

I tried not to obsess over my father's frantic dialing back to Palm Beach after getting the Palm Beach County police emergency number from Information Service. I dialed Bernie when Ada's number wouldn't connect, reached his voicemail and left an anxious message.

"Bernie, damn you, why aren't you answering? Dorie's in trouble. I don't know exactly what, but she's letting me know through quick, interrupted calls she feels endangered. And she's with Judson Javitt. What shall I do? Dad is trying to reach the County Police. Should we do something else? Christ, Bernie, I wish I were down there, so I could go to her." I gulped and pushed the last of my frantic words out.

"Bernie, I need you." I'm scared! I wanted to say, but I'd never admitted that in my life, except as it involved aircraft. After all I had a reputation to live up to. I pressed the off button and winced. I hadn't told anyone I needed them in thirty years. Not me. Not Wonder Woman who raised two kids alone, without a man in her life for most of it. Not the quick-witted, invincible Hannah Doyle. In fact I'd rarely even admitted to myself I was scared. Maybe never.

My family flashed through my mind—eager, overeducated Tim up in Boston trying to get the right job, Kevin and Penny with their precious baby Dylan about to move halfway around the world. How I wanted to hold that baby, hug my sons. What made me think of them?

Then I knew. Dorie, and Dorie's daughter Liza. My God, poor Liza. Could she do anything to help her mother? But she was miles and miles away in Gainesville, wasn't she? Probably without a car, too.

The first itch of a nervous thought zigged into my mind and zagged out again. "Daddy, should I—"

He held up a stop sign hand and I paused, listening. Grateful for a moment of having to decide nothing. My stomach curled around my fear.

"No, Officer, I'm not the person who spoke with the woman. Here, I'll put her on." Dad eyed me over his glasses and passed the phone. "He's doubting, Hannah. Says he'd need to hear exactly what you know."

I gave the officer in Palm Beach County a quick run through, trying not to sound hysterical. I explained Judson could be a threat, because apparently he'd been blackmailed, and the man forcing payments from him was murdered. I invited the officer to telephone the West Parkford Police himself and ask about it. And gave him the number. I mentioned Cascone, explained he had gone north to search for the other suspect in the case, the one who'd accosted and held four women hostage.

By now the Palm Beach cop admitted he'd found the Javitt address in the phone book. "Nice neighborhood," he said, "just up the road from the Kennedys' and Kresges'. I doubt we can do much of anything. These aren't your everyday perpetrators, ma'am. We like to treat our residents with respectful dignity."

I nearly choked. "The murderers, too?" I cracked.

There was a grumble of resentment on the other end. "Look, we'll pay a courtesy call on the doctor, ma'am. See if everything there seems to be okay."

"No," I said. "That would be the worst possible thing to do. Then the suspect, er, Dr. Javitt, would know the woman in his home has tried to call for help, and he might hurt her just as he probably hurt the poor gardener up here."

We tossed it back and forth for several minutes, until I agreed they should pay a call, but be sure to interview Dorie privately and take her into protective custody if nothing more. They said they could do that.

I shook my head at the infernal resistance of lawmen, and followed up by calling Cascone's supervisor, Captain Handley. While I waited for his return call, I punched in Dorie's cell again, and again reached her voice mail. I groaned. Waiting is not my strong suit.

For thirty minutes I prayed for callbacks from Cascone, Ada, Dorie, or Handley. Somebody to tell me what to do, or convince me everything would be okay. I paced, almost wearing holes in my socks, while Dad made useless efforts at changing the subject. He made us coffee and I drank two cups, ran on my treadmill for ten minutes and sat by the phone jiggling my leg up and down for ten more.

Then I knew I couldn't wait a second longer. When my fears for Dorie and my impatience had mounted beyond my own need for safety, I yelped aloud, rose from my seat, snatched the phone and called Theo. "Don't ask questions, Thee. All I know is Dorie's in danger. Get me a seat on the first plane to Palm Beach."

In five minutes Theo had e-mailed me an e-ticket for the 5:15, and sent prayers to guide me.

My eye flicked over my watch and caught Dad's worried glance. On one long breath I nodded, printed out my ticket and shoved it in my pocket. Hyperventilating, I steadied myself as I reached for my knapsack on the closet shelf.

"Daddy, get the car, would you? I need you to drive me to Bradley and I want you to break every speed limit on the way."

"But—"

"I'm flying to Florida."

He drew in a long breath, too. "Hannah."

"The car, Daddy." I grabbed my cell phone, tossed it into the knapsack and preceded him out the door. "And hurry."

I knew exactly what my father was thinking as we drove. He was keeping quiet because he expected something to change before we reached I-91. It didn't. Then when we'd driven up the ramp to the departure gates, he'd expected me to say, "Turn back." I half expected to, myself.

But I didn't.

Still, as I got out of the car my gaze held his for a long second. "I'm scared, Dad. More scared than I've ever been in my life. I've got to go."

He nodded. His voice was husky with emotion when he spoke. "I'll go home and call Ada again. Maybe she knows a neighbor down there who could check on Dorie."

I nodded, too choked up to answer. As my father shifted into drive and looked straight ahead, I slapped on my green beret, taken for good luck, and raced across the airport lobby to my gate.

Even then, I knew he'd expect me to turn and run back to him at the curb outside. Was probably going to idle there for five minutes, just to be sure. But I couldn't allow myself the luxury of self-preservation. My friend was in trouble. Whatever it took, I had to go, even if I had to throw up all the way to Palm Beach to do it.

~ * ~

The endless path across the non-static carpets, the shiny marble and the cool, semi-darkened interior of Bradley International seemed impossible to cross. Not even memories of my special evening with Cascone on these premises could help. Though I did wonder at the irony of finally having someone exciting in my love life and yet taking the plunge to fly, after 30 years of abstinence. Both kinds. The soles of my shoes bit into even the glossy surface of acres of terminal, and my eyes strained to read the jumping digital data on the overhead screens. More than once I heard myself speak aloud.

"I can't do this."

"It's not my fault."

"No, no, I won't. I can't." But I kept walking, kept staring down the long straight corridor, hardly breathing through the security checks, then hit the Woman's Room beside the gate to lose my lunch.

336

It'll be better, I thought, now that's over with. But it wasn't, and when I eased into the boarding line I found myself walking in tight little circles, circles that might somehow expand and take me magically away from the line, from the gate, from the airport.

From flying.

What nearly startled me into doing it was Ada calling when I was number five in line. I jerked backward, almost ready to run, when Ada said they were all okay, in some safe house in a town called North Pole, and Cascone was even now delivering warrants and such to get the Fairbanks Police to cooperate with the Troopers who had helped bring Ada and her gang in at Bernie's request.

I held my breath, trying to ignore the waves of nausea that rode my gut.

"For security reasons, they wouldn't even let poor Joe go to the hospital, but had a doctor come here and treat him. Said he was already taped up fine. Lu and Danny did a great job. They can wait until tomorrow to do x-rays. Gave him some heavy duty drugs, and, since I'm out of Advil, he's sharing them sparingly with Lu, who sprained her ankle in her Reeboks on our jaunt over the river and into the campground."

Ada complained the appointments in the safe house were barely mediocre. She had to share a room with both Lu and Janet, but at least Danny was safe, and Joe, and, hopefully, Cascone, too, who was still down at the police headquarters.

"Now," she said, taking a breath, "what are you wound so tight about?"

In my tempest, I'd let a slew of passengers step in front of me. Now I saw them post the "Last Call" sign and I got dizzy. I ordered Ada to give me the Palm Beach address, scribbled it on the palm of my hand and took a half-dozen deep breaths as the line in front of me jumped ahead. Quickly I explained why I needed the address. I tried to let Ada down easy, but had to fill her in on what Isabel and Vittorio had said about Judd's desertion of Lydia, and how Raul had begged him for money to take care of the baby's special needs, and how Judd had refused. I could hear Ada's lungs expel air.

"My own nephew! No...oh, Hannah..."

Suddenly the line had disappeared, and I was facing the uniformed official at the doorway to the gate. I wrested my ticket from my sweaty left paw to my right, trying to ignore the quaking of my fingers. I kept talking to distract myself, tried to smile as I let the ticket go.

"I know, it's too horrible for words. But we're thinking, and Cascone might tell you more about it when he gets back to your safe-house, that Judd could...could even be behind Raul's...death." I'd hesitated to say murder. "Now, if this doesn't tell you how worried I am about Dorine, let me also explain that as we speak I'm boarding a Delta flight for Palm Beach."

Ada gasped, asked me to repeat myself. I did. "Yes, a flight."

The gatekeeper handed me back my boarding pass and I just plain stalled, stony-faced and paralyzed, on the threshold of the ramp until someone bumped against me and made me move down the gangway into the plane. It was huge, it was silvery, with bright red letters somewhere. I gripped the framework of the entry.

Ada's voice kept buzzing in my ear. "Then, you're really worried. To do that, to get yourself on a plane. Hannah, I feel so responsible. I practically threw them together."

"Not your fault, Ada, no one could possibly blame—"

"But what about the local police? Have you called them?"

"Yeah, they balked," I told her. "They'll make a cursory check, but that could be more dangerous than not checking." I stared blankly as the flight attendant helped me into the cabin, probably thinking I was drunk I shook so, and directed me toward my seat. Row 19-B. B for bastard Judson, for making me do this. B for Battle, the one I'd joined now, never mind how I'd make out. Just move toward your row. B for Bernie, oh, Bernie, help!

Ada's voice squawked on. "Let me call Judson, Hannah. I'm sure there's been some mistake. I'll tell him to put Dorie on a plane and—"

"No, don't!" I heard myself shouting. "I mean, I hate to say it, Ada, but what if Judd has gone bonkers over this whole thing with Lydia Mendino? What if somehow he takes it out on Dorie? She's so helpless, Ada. He'll mess with her. He'll…"

I stopped mid-sentence when I pictured again what might really be happening in Palm Beach. At the same moment I recognized the numbers "1-9" overhead, and sank into my seat.

Ada was silent, as if filling her lungs, praying, pinching herself perhaps. Finally she asked, "What about the West

Parkford Police? Couldn't they send someone? Isn't it dangerous? I mean, I can't believe Judd is involved, but in case that Farquar man is, Dorie *could* be in danger."

It was then and only then I hit the mental jackpot. "Say that again, Ada, slowly. Something just clicked in my brain about that first shred of conversation I had with Dorie."

Ada repeated her concern over Farquar, and I yipped.

"That's it. Oh, my God. Farquar *is* involved! Jesus, I wish this plane were ready to take off." I explained what Dorie had said about birdcalls. "But I never made any bird calls. It's not my thing. You know that. And I don't think it was about Ramon, either. No, it was Farquar who had that cackling, squawking laugh someone commented sounded more birdlike than even your macaw."

"Oh, Zeus," Ada said, her voice almost too choked to continue. "You think—you mean Farquar could be there, too? In Palm Beach, threatening Dorie? Not up here in Alaska after all?"

"The birdman himself."

"Oh, Hannah, be careful. Make sure you don't go there without police help. Maybe he's holding them both hostage."

I was pretty sure my friend was wrong: Farquar might be down there and certainly involved, but I guessed Judd was the one doing all the holding. "Look, Ada, they're ready to take off. Talk to Daddy, he has an idea for you about neighbors who might look in on Dorie. But, I'm, gulp, going now. They just told us to put our phones away."

"But Hannah, the danger—"

"Don't you worry, I brought my hairspray, you know the one, and I wore my green hat for luck. Just make a mitzvah for me, and tell Cascone everything." Since I despised goodbyes, I flipped the cover of the phone down, turned it to off, slipped it in my backpack and slid the whole package under the seat in front of me. As I fastened the seatbelt and located the white waxed bags in the seat pocket in front of me, I pretended the palpitations of my heart were the fuel that was going to get me all the way to Palm Beach.

~ * ~

I managed to keep down most of my pretzels and red wine until we landed in balmy, humid, Florida. Then I spent several anguished minutes in the rest room staring at my canary yellow face, alternately chewing antacid tablets, and sneaking Carletons. I'd done it, lived through it. Flown.

But now I felt blank and empty, with no idea of what to do or where to go. Splashing tepid water on my face over and over helped.

After my head cleared a bit I got to thinking of what Dorie had said about us being super women. Hannah was sure it was a coded message of some sort. What had she said, something about the eight of us? But there weren't eight. There were only six, Lu and Ada, Meg and Theo, Dorie and herself. And oh, yes, they had invited Isabel Mendino. That was seven. Seven super women in a motel. No, wait—motels were Super 8's, it was a brand, wasn't it?

"Christ," I said, trying to make it a mental prayer as I stared at my blanched face in the restroom mirror. Now I knew how we might track down Farquar. Dorie might be a bungler with words, but this time she'd been brilliant.

I rushed out of the airport. By then the taxicab queue was empty, and I had no trouble catching a quick ride. From my cell I phoned the young cop who had pacified me. To my surprise he took the call.

"Did just as you asked, ma'am. Doctor Javitt says there's no problem there. I even saw the lady sitting at the dining table, came up pretty close to her and she seemed fine. Said herself there must have been some mistake, she and the doc were having an early dinner and going for a boat ride out of Meecham's Marina. Don't know why she mentioned that, except she seemed pretty excited. You know, happy."

I wanted to say, "You idiot—obviously it was a plea for help, a clue!!" but curbed my enthusiasm for pejoratives and casually asked the young cop where Meecham's was. He mentioned the street but not the number. This time I wasn't taking no for an answer. "Meet me there, Officer. I'm instructing my cab to take me there right now." I spat out the name of the place to the cabby, who did a quick U-turn and headed north.

The flustered young man on the other end was making serious objections, which I ignored. "It's not even our jurisdiction, ma'am. Not our county. I can't..."

"Did I mention I'm a journalist with a respected New England paper, officer? If anything happens to Ms. Boulé, I will hold you personally responsible, and make sure my story gets in all the syndicates. And earns a Pulitzer Prize. If they find me dead, too, this cabby here will be a rich man, because he'll have the goods on you and your potentially slack-assed department. Now are you going to meet us at the marina or not?"

The officer swallowed so hard I could almost hear his Adam's apple jiggle.

Finally it squeaked out of him, "Yes, ma'am. The doctor's boat is called King's Reward. It's parked on the Front St. side. I know because I already checked it out on my way back in to the station."

"Thanks, Officer. I may have something good to say about you in my story after all. And now, one more very large thing." She told him about Farquar, asked if there were any Super 8 Motels in the area.

"Well, there's one over in West Palm. Not a great neighborhood."

"A fleabag, huh? Sounds like exactly where our guy would be. You'd better get someone on it, right away." I gave him a description, explained there was a live warrant out for the guy's arrest and the writing cop would be on his way down tomorrow. "Find him and you'll get the goods on Javitt, Officer, I'm sure of it."

All the way down in the plane, when I had for brief moments been able to think of something other than my flip-flopping stomach, I thought about how Farquar and/or Judd might hurt Dorie. If they wanted to kill her for some reason, like maybe Dorie had found the two of them plotting together, Judd would make sure it wasn't at the house. Too hard to hide. And the house belonged equally to Ada, who could get in or out anytime she chose.

They wouldn't try to drown her at the beach, either, because Dorie was an excellent swimmer. Had been on the swim team in college, was a torpedo in the water. No way.

But a boat, now, that had a certain ring to it. You could easily fall and hit your head in a boat. And the Intercoastal Waterway was fed from marshy swamps and lakes. And in such waters, one often found various forms of pestilence and predators, such as 'gators. Weren't they the state animal or something? Big, ugly alligators who maintained a high protein diet, and just loved pretty woman falling overboard into their domain.

They could eat the evidence long before anyone knew Dorie were missing.

Maybe I watched too much Miami CSI shows, but my stomach hopscotched again, and I dry-heaved into my hanky. My feet tapped symbolic SOS messages on the floor of the cab, and I eased myself from side-to-side trying not to picture what might happen. That was one dunk not even my ditzy, Aquarian friend would enjoy.

The driver made a cut left and took off on a long road between acres of saw palmetto, a short cut, he called it. While we traversed it in the darkening evening, Cascone called back. He hadn't talked to Ada yet.

"They already picked up this Stoner guy, and relieved the cop Harriman of his duties temporarily. He admits Judd Javitt quizzed him once, made him promise to look out for the kid, but I think it's more than that, Han. I think they were in on it. Stoner's going to let the cat out pretty quick, I feel it in my bones. Especially if we pick up Farquar. No sign of him, yet, though. Now how are you? And where are you?"

"Probably a couple of miles from Gordon Farquar," I said. When I told him I'd flown to Florida, he whistled long and low over the connection. "Christ, Hannah, you flew? Damn it, you turn around this second. I don't want you anywhere near Farquar *or* Javitt. If Dorie's worried for herself, it's got to be serious, probably involving him and Farquar both. I'm begging you, go to a hotel and let the police handle it."

I sighed. "Thanks for caring, Bernie, but you don't know me too well yet. This is my shtick. Yeah, I was scared to fly. I would have asked you to fly down instead if you'd been there. But, hell, I've worked on police stuff since I was a kid. I followed my older brother the rookie policeman around like a shadow and became the only girl in the police cadets when I was fourteen."

He cut in with a snort of a laugh. "Solve a lot of cases, did you, sweetheart?"

I held my own laugh back. "Naw. I enjoyed the poker games we got into with the cops after our ride-arounds even more than seeing them break up fights or put shoplifters in a cell. I've been a whiz at Five Card Stud ever since." Finally, I did laugh, remembering. But my eyes were moist with tears.

"Hannah, you're cute. And I can't wait to whip you at Five-Card Stud. Knowing you has been a real gift, and I sure want to know you even more. I'm not throwing that away anytime soon. But you've got to go to a hotel."

"Get out of town, Cascone. I can do this. I'm not letting anything or anyone get thrown away if I can help it. Reinforcements are on the way. Now go get that Stoner, tell him we're about to nab his buddy, and you keep my friends up there safe. I'll buzz you when we're done here."

I clicked off before Bernie could answer. The moisture in my eyes had mounted, and I wanted perfect vision for what I was about to encounter. Besides, I was sick of mushy feelings hampering my judgment. That'd happened enough times over the last thirty years, and I was done with it. I couldn't work with those grieving children at the center if I gave in to every emotion. For God's sake, sometimes it made me a prisoner of my fears. A stupid hostage!

The taxi driver pulled up at a marina where the tall masts of day runners were lighted and gay against the backdrop of the darkened bay. As I opened the car door, live jazz, the tinkling of glasses and laughter carried on the evening's tropical breezes. Wrapped around a small central building was Meecham's Marina, where big hulking yachts and a few sleek day models glinted brightly. I tipped the driver generously and asked him to cruise away nice and quiet. He did, and in a hurry.

There were small groups of celebrators on the boats, and some standing around on the decks of the marina, but none that even resembled Dorie and her doctor friend, where the horseshoe bar skirted the docks and only a few vacant seats remained. Out on the boats lights moved to the rocking of the gentle waters, and voices echoed from several long arms of walkways.

I slid cautiously up to the hospitality building, stepped inside and quickly out again, trying to look as if I had just emerged from there. I eased way out toward the water, staying in the shadows when I could and trying not to shake. I'd wait for the cops if I could. But, first, it would do my heart good to hear Dorie's voice, to figure out where the boat was, and if they were in it, just who "they" included.

Two guys in brand-boasting tee shirts were standing at the beginning of one of the walkways ho-hoing it over a couple of beers I ambled over and tried to look "cute," as Bernie had called it, green beret tilting flirtatiously, I hoped, on my streaky hair.

"Which boat is King's Ransom, d'you know?" I quizzed. "Damn boyfriend said to meet him there."

"Really?" one guy boomed. They looked impressed, but chuckled.

"What? You never heard of it?"

The quieter fellow took off his yachting cap and tipped it. "Yes, ma'am, and it's on the walkway at the farthest end." He gestured with a nod to the left. "Only the big boys get to park there. Your boyfriend must be some dude."

I gave him a coy giggle, said, "You could say that. Thanks," and wandered off on wobbly steps. When I got to the last bit of decking to the left, the big boats loomed, fifty- and sixty-footers, one or two awash in light as their owners and guests partied. A kid of about twelve came off one boat and headed toward the marina building. I poked him and asked if the King's Ransom was docked.

"Naw," he said. "I don't think so." He shielded his eyes with his hand and stared out to the far end of the dock, the end closest to the waterway. "Oh, yeah," he said, "there she is. No lights, though. The people aren't on it tonight. I think they live around here."

"Thanks." I moved slowly in the direction he'd pointed. I would have kept going, too, but suddenly there were footsteps and hushed voices behind me. An argument in pianissimo. A familiar voice.

I pressed my back against the hull of a darkened boat and tried to disappear into the shadows. They'd have to pass right by me—there was no place to hide, and no place to run.

Thirty-one

The man in dark clothes had lost his lock-picking tools since breaking into that doc's house up in Connecticut, where he'd spent that first nervous night. He fiddled now with the ring of keys and dared them not to work. His curse words were his version of a prayer.

When the smallest key unlocked the cabin door, he breathed a sigh of relief.

"Finally!" After trying a dozen different boats in three marinas, he'd found it. "And now it's so dark I'll have a hell of a time getting it out of this damned docking." He fumbled around and found a light switch, flicked it on and stood mesmerized by the sheen and beauty of every appointment in the rich man's cabin. He snapped himself out of the stupor: no time for that. Had to figure out the gadgets and gizmos all around him. But everything distracted him, the bar shelf, loaded, the gold-edged trim and beautiful woodwork—it was like a movie.

Concentrate. There had to be an ignition place, that much he knew. And he'd have to untie the boat from the pier. Other than that he'd be guessing. Mainly figure out how to put it in reverse, then throttle it forward and blow this damn hoity-toity boat dock. There might even be a map, a chart he knew they called it, for getting to Key West.

He reached for his cigarettes, remembered he was out, and swore again. That's when he heard footsteps on the dock, over and above the party sounds from the other rigs. Quickly he flicked off the light and stood there motionless, trying to pick out the noises.

"It's that sonofabitch doctor and the woman," he muttered. "Heading right here!"

That's when the noises got louder, the bastard and not one but two women, yelling, a scuffle on the pier. He backed into the shadows, ears tuned for clues to what was happening

Jesus, he'd better get the hell out fast. Key West was going to have to wait.

The man ran his fingers over the smooth mahogany dashboard for a final time and slipped out of the cabin, stood motionless on the deck, ready to drop to the pier a foot or so below. Inadvertently his hand ran across the bulge in his pocket, and suddenly he grinned.

Hold on, he told himself. Maybe I could get the doc himself him to run this damn rig out to the ocean before I take care of them both.

He didn't hear the whine of the cop car's siren until he yanked his shiny new blade from his pocket with shaking hands and hollered to the group below. Then its whine and blip were in his ears, and people were shouting.

Shit. Just like that day in Connecticut with those damn broads. Exit time, Farquar. Now.

Thirty-two

Hannah

"But I don't want to go for a moonlit ride. Told you, I want to leave. I've really had it."

I couldn't make out the rest of the words, but I knew the woman speaking and coming toward me was Dorie. When a male voice answered, cajoling, persuading, I couldn't help but step out—and pop up right into in front of my dear sweet Dorie, whose arm was seriously gripped by the supposedly healing hands of the one and only Doctor Judson Javitt!

I started talking fast.

"I got jealous of you guys down here in the sunshine and thought I'd join you."

Judd's eyes darted left and right, his chin sticking out in defiance.

"Hannah?" It was nothing more than a squeak. Dorie suddenly slumped, as if at the end of her resistance.

Javitt shoved her forward. "I don't think so, Ms. Doyle, you've been a pain in the ass the last few days. How come? Miss your little girlfriend that much? Or maybe you were jealous of all the time she's spending with me. That it? Want a little piece, huh, Ms. Doyle?"

I felt gall rise in my throat. "Not! Not like you think!" I hollered, trying to bar his path with one arm stiff against the darkened boat, and the other grasping Dorie's free arm. Like a drunken chicken, Dorie flopped to one side, then the other as we tugged on her. She wore heels, and they kept getting stuck between the dock boards, helpful in delaying the couple's progress. Someone from another boat on the opposite side called out, asking what was going on. Someone else invited us up for drinks. Judd waved them off.

I ignored the hot flash assaulting my body and face, and snatched at any possibly helpful ideas in my mental purse.

"So, where are you going at this hour, you two? Why don't you hang around? We'll get a drink somewhere. There's someone I want you to meet." I managed to keep chattering for two full minutes, tugging Dorie back toward me every time he tried to pull her further down the gangplank, until the blip of the patrol car sounded and its tires spat gravel in the parking lot.

Suddenly Judd's expression changed from tolerance to panic. He let go of Dorine so abruptly she nearly fell into the water, but I managed to grab her around the waist, and pulled her close just as the two cops emerged, guns drawn, calling for everyone to halt. Judd paused, scooted back to grab Dorie's arm away from me and laughed in their faces.

Before he could move down the dock again, Dorie put out her nicely pointed high heel shoe into his path, and he flew, face first, onto the dock. She drove the heel of the shoe into his back, with only the slightest restraint.

"Good job, Dorie! You got him." Breathless, I told the approaching officers who Judd was: the man most likely responsible for the death of Raul Mendino. "I'll get Detective Cascone or his boss on the line, and you'll have enough to hold this cretin," I told them.

"We'll have to have that warrant if we're gonna hold him more than seventy-two hours," the young officer explained to me, as they slipped handcuffs on the fallen Judd and wrestled him to his feet.

I assured them they'd have it.

The good doctor bitched and moaned I didn't know what I was talking about, and he'd done nothing wrong.

Dorine sprang to life. "If nothing else he's held me hostage for the last 10 hours. And I'll iron the charges, or whatever you call it."

The young officer smiled, and yanked Judd further away.

Dorie and I exchanged nods etched with small grins.

"I still don't understand. How did you know he was involved with Raul's death?" Dorie said, leaning against the ladder down to a ghostly white yacht.

I wrapped an arm around my friend and boosted her upright. "Long story, hon. But mostly with your help."

Dorie gaped back, still shaking. "But the other one was here, he threatened me…"

I started to respond but as the police prepared to lead Judd away, the officer I'd talked to paused. "Oh. We didn't find that other guy you told us about, ma'am, but the desk clerk verified someone with that description had been there until this morning. Skipped out on his rent."

Suddenly, Dorine went into motion.

She sucked in a huge breath and bolted upright. She whipped along after the handcuffed Javitt, his blond hair tossed in the offshore breezes, his wry smile barely diminished, blue eyes faded in the glare of boat lights on every side.

"Wait," she said. "Don't put him in the car yet. I need something."

Without another word she shoved her hand into Judd's pants pocket and wrenched out a set of keys even as he tried to tear himself away. "For the house, and the car!" She held them up triumphantly with a wink toward me, then blanched.

"My god. Wait. The *other* keys. Judd said his extra set of keys was missing, including the keys to the boat. He blamed me. But I never...It must have been—Officer?" She kind of shrieked the last words, pointing toward the end of the dock, where something had rattled, and an engine had whined in warm-up, then clunked off. Twice. They all turned toward the water, seeing nothing. Then one of the officers flipped on a flashlight, and they all saw it—movement on the ladder Dorie had just vacated, a dark figure clattering down the side of a boat. The King's Ransom!

Flipping off her shoes in one quick motion, Dorie streaked back toward the end of the dock like a whirling dervish in her filmy white dress, and crashed into the dark form, who'd leapt from the boat and was about to escape by jumping into the water! There was a male groan, a female shriek. Both bodies rolled right to the edge of the dock.

I beat the officer there, and threw myself on top of Dorine to keep her from slipping off the edge.

"It's him! It's Farquar!" I screamed, trying for a hold on his shirt as the man regained his footing and scrambled away. The policeman grabbed for him, lost him, and Farquar's awkward footsteps thumped against the dock

Suddenly Judd's voice cut the air like a bullet. "You! On my boat! You moron! I told you to get lost."

I watched Judd try to wrench away from his captor, spitting expletives, but the husky officer hung on.

Farquar cawed back. "You got the bastard! Good!" he screeched as he spotted Javitt in cuffs. It was just the delay the younger officer needed to tackle the ungainly man in black and pin him to a piling and for a shiny blade to go rattling to the dock.

"Stop! Don't resist," the policeman warned. "You're under arrest."

Farquar sneered. "Fine, as long as he is, too. The bastard. All I needed was five more minutes and I would have figured out how to operate the damn boat. I'd have been in Key West by morning."

I helped Dorie to her feet and we limped into the circle of light together, pointing at the knife behind us.

"See, Doctor Dread," Dorie snapped, poking a forefinger nearly into Javitt's chest. "I wasn't the one who had your keys. He's the one. Probably stole them this morning from the house while you were out trying to track him down and run him over, knowing you!"

Gordon Farquar squawked again while the officer frisked him. "I know about a gun you'd be interested in, too, officer. One I dropped, in Connecticut where these broads come from. You'll see—registered to him, I bet. He left it where he killed that gardener so I'd be blamed!"

"He means the nine-millimeter he held us hostage with," I said in excitement.

The policeman shone his searchlight along the dock, and picked out the metal gleam near the ladder. They bagged it, more evidence on Farquar's neck, while Judd Javitt laughed maniacally.

Farquar snarled at him and spat into the water. "Damn you," he said suddenly in my direction, "you had to come snooping, asking that kid if anyone was on the boat. I was about to start it up, but heard you and had to wait. It took me all afternoon to find the freakin' boat, and just when I might have got away, you show up! I never liked you, lady, not one bit."

I couldn't resist mimicking his squawking voice. "Well, I never liked you either, you, you sofa shooter, you!"

As the small sideshow made its way into the parking lot lights, another Palm Beach County cruiser arrived on the scene, then two more from Dade, and countless cops assembled around the two cursing prisoners.

Judd was loudest. "You ass, Farquar. Why the hell didn't you stay the hell away from me? Just like you couldn't stay away from my house in Connecticut once I'd left. Nearly got us screwed then. They never would have figured it if you hadn't…"

Dorie gave Judd a look to kill. "Oh, yeah, we would have and we did. Why do you think she's here? So it *was* him in your house the night you changed your mind about having me stay. You bum!" She wrapped her fingers tight around Hannah's arm. "I only regret how hurt Ada's going to be when she hears what you've done," she hissed at Judd.

"You haven't heard but half the story yet, Dorine," I said. "You haven't been the only one to fall for the smooth talk."

Dorie squared her shoulders and huffed a little.

Farquar stuck his chin in at a very helpful moment. "Well, I been listening, too. And when they hear what I got to say, you're gonna fry, buddy boy. You with all your big deals. Setting up the drug route to Fairbanks. Telling me to stay in your fancy house, then "forgetting" to give me the key. Setting me up to rob your aunt and scare off the stupid gardener. The gardener you'd already killed!" Farquar had stuck his chin out at Judd.

Judd's face blanched. "I never meant to kill him, I was going to offer him a final payment, but he jerked away from me and fell."

"Duh! After you hit him over the head with your gun!" I declared.

"And you figured you could pin it on me!" Farquar sneered.

"And find what, wedded bliss with me, sharing your aunt's trust fund?" Dorie spat out. I had to hold her back from slapping Judd.

He finally stopped denying everything and tried to ignore us all with a look of long-suffering. The officer gripping Farquar's arms led him away. Farquar watched his own feet make bumbling tracks on the sandy path, still whining.

Judd Javitt tossed a look at us, Dorie and me, hugging each other close now. "I'll be out by morning," he snapped. "And you two bitches had better be out of my house by then."

At the last minute he said something about a lawyer and I laughed.

"Seems it wasn't too long ago you were berating 'lizard lawyers' for all they did to your medical practice," I said.

"You can be sure you won't see the inside of that house again, Judson Javitt." Dorie's face had turned nearly purple. "Your aunt will see to that." We glared as Judd got squished into the back seat of the police cruiser, then turned toward each other and breathed. When we gave each other a thumb's up sign, we were suddenly grinning from ear-to-ear.

"Not to interrupt the party, ma'ams, we're going to need a statement from both of you," the young officer said.

"You got it!" we answered in unison and said we'd be down first thing in the morning. "By then you'll hear from the West Parkford Police and the Alaska State Troopers. They ought to help wrap it up. Meanwhile, you know where we'll be."

The young officer nodded, mouth hanging open. "Yes, ma'am."

"C'mon, Han," Dorie said, brushing dock debris from her long, swirling skirt. "I've had enough of these two.

Let's make sure the boat is all locked up for Ada's sake. It's hers, too. Then I'll drive you home in Judd's PT Cruiser. Don't want to leave it here all night, now, do we? Besides, you've got to be hungry, and tired."

"Starved," I said. "You know that damned airplane food."

Dorie staggered, bumped into a cop, and leaned against him for support. "Oops, sorry, officer." She turned back to me gasping. "Oh, migod! You *flew* here?"

"Naw, I came on a broom." I laughed so hard my beret tumbled off and I caught it midair. "Honestly, Dorine, you never change."

But in the flashing awareness of the moment, I knew she had. I also realized Dorie wasn't the only one who had.

~ * ~

Later we got on the phone together with Ada, who apologized over and over for what her nephew, step-nephew to be exact, had done to Dorie. In turn, we expressed our regrets and tried to convince her to let it go.

"Stop apologizing, he's not your blood, not your responsibility in any case," Dorie said.

"I should have listened to Theo. The man was a born womanizer. You said yourself he inherited it from B.J. along with his genes for good looks."

"I just pray my Danny isn't like that, so selfish and cruel. It's just too awful to imagine."

I cut in. "How's he looking to you right now, Ada?"

"Well, right now he and Janet are doing all the cooking, like a pair of lovebirds, arms around each other and stars in their eyes. Lu is sitting here on a stool at the breakfast bar, her ankle all bound up, and she's giving them every bit of instruction she can think of. And that's just for making scrambled eggs!"

"Ohh," Dorie squealed, "how can they stand it?"

"I think they figure they owe her, for that fabulous chicken dinner she made us in the wilderness, chicken on an open fire and a chocolate cake in a frying pan. Can you believe it? I swear, we have to make that woman open a gourmet restaurant. She'd be a hit in our little old town."

I figured it was time to do some serious cheering up. "Speaking of gourmet restaurants in our town, are you two going to be back for our inaugural meeting?"

Ada hiccupped over latent tears in her throat. "Yes, darlings. We fly out with Lieutenant Cascone tomorrow. He'll have Mr. Aldo Stoner chained to him all the way, so he said to tell you he won't be able to telephone until he gets some privacy. But he'll be ecstatic you're okay."

"Me, too," I admitted. "About him."

"It may be pretty uncomfortable for the poor detective flying back to Bradley, being hooked to that scumbag who beat up poor Joe and chased us all out of Janet and Joe's house."

"I'll console him when I see him," I laughed.

"I'll bet you will. But he'll have Lu and me to watch over things in the meantime, so how could anything go wrong?"

Dorie and I giggled in harmony.

"And, girls? I'm not planning on lifting one little finger to help that scoundrel Judson. He can sink or swim on his own now, since that's how he got where he is."

"Good for you, hon," Dorie said, "you've borne enough of the burden of that man's hedomystic nature. Is that the word I mean, Hannah?"

I squelched a chuckle. "No matter." I took the phone. "Judd said he'd be acquiring legal counsel, and didn't seem at all concerned."

"Well, then, good," came Ada's weary response that ended the call. "I won't be either."

~ * ~

In the morning, after the police had taken our separate and condemning statements regarding the exploits of Dr. Judson Javitt and Mr. Gordon Farquar, and told us the warrant from the West Parkford Police had arrived, Dorie and I took a dip in the pool. As we relaxed on the patio later we tried to stop reliving the horror of the night before.

Just before lunch Rachel Silverstein from up the road came by with flowers from her garden. Martin led her out onto the patio where Dorie and I introduced ourselves, admiring her purple sundress imprinted with huge tropical flowers in pinks and reds.

"How terribly bizarre this whole thing was," Rachel said. "Miguel, my houseboy, said you screamed apparently for help, Miss Boulé, but he saw Dr. Javitt come home and thought—Well, we never dreamed Judson was involved in something illicit. Ada is a friend from the many times she's been down here. And I had Judd to dinner frequently during the season. Eligible bachelors are always in demand. And he was so—"

"Smooth," Dorie interrupted.

Rachel nodded enthusiastically. "Exactly so. The bastard." She shook her head in shock and pressed the bouquet forward. "I can hardly believe it! I'm so sorry for you."

Dorie accepted the flowers and the concern. "Dr. Javitt had me fooled, too."

"But to have killed someone!" Rachel perched on a lawn chair and pulled down her sunglasses from top of head to eyes.

"Well, that's not proven yet," I said, surprised at my own sense of fairness. "It may turn out to have been manslaughter. But the doctor sure revealed his ulterior motives all around. We appreciate your coming by. Can we give you something cold?"

Rachel laughed. "No, dears, thank you. I'm off in a few minutes for my Garden Club meeting. A group of us are starting a new branch for us, let's say, perennials, who've been around a bit longer."

Their combined squeal stopped her from rising from her chair.

"Really? But that's just what we're doing up in Connecticut!" Dorie yelped.

"Tell me about it!"

"Having our first meeting on Monday," Hannah explained. "We still don't know what direction it will take. Ada is our Queen Mum, and she's got lots of plans. Not connected to the garden club, but more to our stage in life."

Dorie interrupted. "Some of us are kind of like flowers who might be in the wilting stage, except when we're in a bouquet, we kind of hold each other up."

Rachel Silverstein bloomed with smiles. "You are just going to have such fun. What do you call your group?"

"Women on Fire," we said in unison. "With no rules except to live and be fully alive."

"Ada will be perfect as your queen. And you two, so attractive and—-young! You'll add a spark, I'm sure. Down here, most of us way over-qualify to be members of the Garden Crones, but we have younger gals begging to join!"

Dorie and I had the first good laugh of our first private, all-girl vacation. Long after Rachel left, we talked about planning a slumber party here in Palm once the group got established. We might even share a meeting with Rachel's gang.

Liza arrived, in her boss' borrowed car, hoping to reassure herself her mother was okay after her traumatic experience. Dorie surprised her daughter with her new bounce-back-ability. We all swam, and went out for seafood, and had our own slumber party. The next morning, when Liza left to drive back to Gainesville, she dropped us at the airport where we rented a car to drive home in. But not before Liza told her mother some interesting news.

"My boss says someone called last week and made a huge donation to the alumna fund, and insisted they take a look at me for the summer program," she confessed. "I would have felt badly to get the job that way, except Professor Ernst says he had earmarked me for the spot already, and almost changed his mind after that manipulative call. Until I convinced him my family and friends had nothing to do with it."

"Can you believe it?" Dorie asked. "That bum Judson invested money to get me to come down here!"

"With probably no intention of ever really sending the check," scoffed I.

"But what on earth did he want with me, anyhow?"

"Probably your trust fund, Dor, as you said last night. Although—" and I emphasized the point, "you are an attractive woman."

"Yeah, sure," Dorie finally laughed. "One he figured he didn't have to worry about getting pregnant."

Before we left town we called the Alaska contingent and told them the rest of the news, Liza'a contribution, and the next door neighbor's. We could almost see Ada shaking her head and trying to understand her nephew's offenses, to make sense of it all.

Ada congratulated me on flying when life or limb depended on it.

"Yes, but we're about to leave—by car," I said. "I'm not exactly converted to round-trip flying yet."

Then, on the other end, Lu snatched the phone away. "Listen, I heard what you were talking about earlier, about me giving those kids so much advice and instruction."

Danny Javitt shouted out so they could hear him all the way to Florida: "Yeah, she sure can hand out advice, but we only take about half of it."

"Ha!" Lu exclaimed, "that's why I give 'em twice as much as they really need!"

~ * ~

We pulled into Hartford at about 1 a.m. two days later, and Arthur and Megan Dautrey were there to pick us up at the car rental depot at Bradley Airport. Arthur

364

had condemned the violets to their own resources, mitewise, and the couple had a new, special glow about them.

I told them so, and Meg blushed.

"You two, on the other hand, look exhausted," Arthur said, inspecting us as we unloaded our luggage.

"Well, duh, Arthur, they've been on a manhunt, and a police chase, and another hostage-taking from what I hear. What do you expect? I'd say they look pretty darn good. They even have a little tan."

"You should have flown," Arthur said.

Dorie and I exchanged sleepy glances and crawled in the back of Arthur's serviceable old Buick. Nobody even considered answering.

But the usually taciturn Meg could hardly contain herself. "Wait'll you hear," she said as we all belted up for the ride down I-91, "Theo's planning a special grace before the start of our first Women on Fire meeting. She says we ought to have it, because we've all come through so much. What do you think about that?"

"Dunno," I muttered sleepily as Dorie curled up beside me. All I could think of was in the morning Cascone would be off-duty and was meeting me for breakfast. And who knew what else? In the darkness I grinned to myself. "What do you think, Meggie?"

Meg cleared her throat and coughed. "Well, I think, it's scientifically impossible to have gone through what we have, and not have another body on the table by now. For that alone, we ought to say something."

Arthur chuckled. "Yes, dear. A kind of heavenly 'Cheers!'"

Thirty-three

Women on Fire

Ada Dornan Harris Javitt gaveled to order the first official meeting of the newest West Parkford women's group, Women on Fire, in the Bee's Knees Restaurant at 12:31 p.m. on Monday, the 29th of April. Her royal blue dress was a fashion statement, sleek and fitted to her well-kept form, with a daring side slit, and shirring at the bust that flattered. On her smooth, Fifth Avenue-styled, silvery hair the day-glo wool hunter's cap, earflaps tied on top to hold a single peach-colored rose at a jaunty angle, completed her outfit with a devil-may-care nonchalance. It set the perfect tone, even for the coming month of May.

"Ladies, I can't tell you how much I appreciate your help in getting through the past weeks," she began. "Isabel Mendino thanks you, too, and promises to come to a meeting soon. She's already picked out a lovely fedora to be her totem, one ironically identical to the style the women of her village wear. She feels she'll be ready for its debut in another month or so."

Theo nodded and smiled at the assembled group, at Lu in a mauve challis pants suit and the high-heeled Manolo

Blahniks, and Meg in a new blouse printed with vivid pink and burgundy African violets over her black slacks. More importantly, the group heartily approved Meg's burgundy colored pillbox, perched above her recently curled hair.

"Pillbox! Perfect for a doctor," Lucia had whooped.

Hannah hadn't acquired anything new beyond her green beret, but had fastened to that very chapeau a huge golden medal Bernie had given her, imprinted with the words "My Hero." She also had news. "In another two weeks or so I should be back from my California trip to see my baby grandson, ladies, and ready for a second meeting."

"California?" Ada squealed. "Tell us all about it."

When the server approached, grinning at their attire, they ordered glasses of wine in various shades and yap-yapped at the intrepid Hannah, hat cocked at a typically rakish angle, demanding answers.

"Well, I'm not taking the train after all." A groan lumbered its way around the group. "Actually, I'm flying." There were hoots and yips of joy. "With one Detective Bernard Cascone holding me up in case I pass out or turn the color of my favorite hat."

Dorie couldn't restrain herself from flapping her pink boa. "Oh, Han, that's perfect. You two are an item, then."

"Didn't say any such thing," Hannah retorted.

"Didn't have to," Meg cajoled.

Hannah's cheeks turned pink, and she puffed out air. "Fact is, the detective is taking his daughter Sara to visit UCLA and Southern Cal, and since the timing works out, we'll travel together. That's all. All I wish to say at this time."

"Still, you've come so far, honey," Ada said, a tremulous smile on her lips.

"You have, too, Ada. You are indomitable. We know it hasn't been easy getting over the fact of Judd's involvement in this whole mess." Lu straightened her place setting and firmed her mouth into a motherly smile of approval.

"At least they're not calling it murder, if you don't mind my saying it," Meg answered. "Apparently, if Judd is to be believed, he just wanted to scare Raul off, to get him to stop harassing him for money to support the baby and Lydia, both badly hurt by his botched abortion effort and all that. Though even that motive showed a definite lack of character in the man." She shuddered and tapped the tabletop to make her point.

Ada inhaled and gritted her teeth. "Yes, it was too cruel of Judson to want to scare Raul with the gun, then to hit him over the head with it that way, and then the poor gardener falling on his own shears. Judd must have been frightened to death himself when that happened. Angry as I am at him, I can't help but feel for him, too. I know it's crazy."

"Not at all, dear. It's the kind of woman you are," Lu consoled.

"Evidently Raul was ready with those shears in case Judson was out to hurt him, which he apparently was. The worst part is Raul himself was the one hurt—only because he was trying so hard to help his family." Theo's eyes had filled, but she lifted her chin, settled her colorful poncho more firmly around her dark silk suit. "Sorry, Ada. And imagine, setting up Farquar to take the blame, by leaving the gun for Farquar to find."

Lucia chimed in. "Who didn't hesitate to use it. And having that creepy Mr. Stoner in on it, getting Dan to call home at a certain time as if you'd asked him to, Ada."

Ada groaned lightly, tapping the scar on her temple. "No matter how you slice it, Judd was behind the whole scenario.

Hannah jumped back in. "It was he who got Farquar involved, even egging him on to rob you by telling him about your safe and your bearer bonds. He'd already met with Farquar in Florida and set things up months ago! Only Farquar, in a drugged haze back then, had forgotten where Judd said the safe was."

"And he did hide out in Judd's house after he ran away from us, taking a cab to the airport in the middle of the night when no one would see him," Dorie explained. "When I drove Judd home that evening, I...I thought I saw Farquar behind the curtains, but I assumed it was my too-vivid imagination working overtime."

Ada breathed, shook her head and went on. "Dorine, don't ever let us tell you again you have too vivid an imagination. You are just exactly perfect, as you are, and we cherish you. It's Judson, all Judson to blame. Or maybe me for coddling him all these years. I'm disturbed, but not so surprised after all. Judd's always been a terribly self-centered man. Wanting his way. Furious whenever I spent a penny, as if he had it coming to him!"

"Which I'm sure he expected," Dorie said softly. "Those last hours when he kept me at the house and I wanted to leave, he kept asking me questions about the trust fund you so generously set up for me and Liza. Wanted to get his hands on that, plus I'm sure he thought I'd be one girlfriend who wouldn't get pregnant. He complained he'd been burned by that happening before."

"*He'd* been burned!" Hannah yipped.

"More like, poor Lydia," Meg recalled.

Theo nodded slowly, a light dawning on her stern, controlled features. "Judd may not have planned to murder Raul, but after what we heard about him conspiring with that police lieutenant and the two men at the rehab, setting up a drug delivery route from Miami, I'd say he had something pretty sinister in mind for a long, long time. They say even the Feds are involved now, because of that drug scheme of his. Sorry again, Ada."

Ada nodded her head, the hunting cap now perched more daringly. "No, Theo, you're absolutely right. Now I think of it, how he insisted on that facility in Alaska, it proves he possibly already knew Farquar, and was assembling some plan, at least to get Danny in trouble with drugs, maybe even to get him out of the way. Kill him, even. Oh!" Her stoic face crumbled, and Hannah, beside her, wrapped an arm around her friend.

Lucia looked up startled from the other side, having expected to reach over and take on that task herself. She smiled a secret smile and Dorie received it knowingly across the table. So all the group's mothering wouldn't be left to Lu anymore. She was gratified.

"Or even to have Farquar rob you all along. Bernie says that man's singing at high pitch, now. It'll all come out at the trial." Hannah eased back in her chair.

Dorie shook her head. "That awful Farquar! I can't believe I faced him down and stood my ground with Judd, too. Ask Hannah. I even stole Judd's key to get us back into the mansion when they were about to take him away. Do you ladies realize that's the boldest thing I ever did in my life?"

Hannah put up a hand to interrupt. "That and tackling Farquar when he made a run for it! You should have seen her."

The group applauded with new energy.

Ada straightened. "We're proud of you, Dorie, and proud of Hannah for taking off after you."

"In a plane, no less!" Theo exclaimed. "I'd say several of us have conquered some demons in launching this little group. I'm so happy to be included."

Ada agreed. "Everyone went above and beyond the call. And, people, you should have seen Lu in Alaska. What she can do with a Bowie knife! But thank goodness it's all over, at last."

"No, hon," Lu said, "it's just beginning: our own Women on Fire group."

Ada nodded. "Well, the sofa has been repaired, the bad part's over, at least for us. Although for poor Isabel it never will be."

She pressed her knuckles to her eyes, and nearby, her friends patted their queen's back.

Ada straightened, and offered a small smile of resignation. "Judson will have to pay for what he did, and all those others, too. Do you think they would have killed Danny, Hannah?"

Hannah shrugged. "They probably would have tried to extort money from you first. Got him back on drugs, if they could. I doubt Farquar was in on that part, but once he found Raul dead, he figured he'd been set up. That's why he was so adamant to find your treasures, while he held us all captive. I don't think he ever planned to go back to Alaska. Cascone says so far the gun is untraceable, but I'm thinking they'll eventually trace it to Judson, as well. Speaking of Judson, I'm guessing he's the one who called Danny after you did, Ada, and told him Raul had been killed. Funny thing is, he shouldn't have known by then, because you hadn't told him."

Lu posited an idea. "Right, Danny told us in Alaska Judd called him a half-hour after Ada did, and told him about Raul. Tried to implicate him in some way."

"And pretended to me he knew nothing about Raul until I called him from your house at supper time." Dorie pouted for a few moments.

Lucia nodded. "So, after we chased him out, Farquar returned to Judd's house through the woods, discarding the clothing Judd had left for him in his backyard to use as a disguise. Whew!" She blew out a long breath. "I'm just beginning to understand the whole thing."

Dorie seemed puzzled. "I've always wondered how Judd could have been involved in Raul's death if he was on a plane for Palm Beach at 8 a.m."

"He wasn't on that plane as he claimed," Hannah explained, shaking her head until her streaky blond hair made feathery flashes in the dim interior. "Cascone checked that out with an airline employee friend of his." Something mischievous sparkled in her smile. "Of ours, I mean. Judd missed his flight, took a later one for Atlanta and made a different connection there. He never dreamed he'd be a suspect once Farquar got involved. Probably figured he'd have to track him down for his part of Ada's loot."

"And thought Farquar would keep quiet, for some reason," Lu retorted.

Hannah nodded. "Bernie says Judd was blackmailing Farquar, with Stoner's help, for stealing a share of their drugs up in Fairbanks. That's why he figured Farquar would keep quiet, never dreamed he'd break in to Judd's and spend a night there."

Ada grimaced. "And to think that nasty Fairbanks policeman, Harriman, got the department to look the other way! Judd was already planning to get Danny out of the picture. He went to great lengths, from Florida to Alaska. Scum leads to scum, I guess."

Lu fingered her still slightly puffy nose. "That particular scum Farquar will pay for what he did to us that day in your house, too, Ada. He may not be charged with murder, but Tony says he'll get at least 15 years for holding us hostage and physically and mentally abusing us."

"And destroying my living room and trying to get hold of my precious bearer bonds!" Ada sighed.

The server carried over an array of filled wine glasses, red, white and pink, and delivered them to the women around the table. Ada was the first to hold her glass high.

"Theo has a blessing for our gathering, but first, I'd like to say I for one am glad this hostage and murder business are over. I trust the justice system will see everybody punished or rewarded appropriately. And I personally am setting up another trust fund, one for Isabel and her family, with money I've sidetracked from Judd's original account."

There was a murmur of approval. Ada took a deep breath at last. "The best news is Danny will be released in July, and Janet's moving east with him. They're going to stay with me, until they decide where they're going to school. She wants a full degree in recreational therapy, and Danny's always dreamt of designing homes, happy homes, for happy families, the kind he never had."

"Till now," Hannah finished. "Here's to families, and…" she paused while she lifted her beret and waved it in the air. "And to freedom, the freedom to be ourselves. And to fly if we want to, and to…" Hannah blushed the tiniest bit as she clutched her hat to her chest and sat down in a rush. She finished on a softer note, and there wasn't a dry eye in the house. "To taking a chance on love."

"Amen," said Theo.

"And to our young, Danny and Janet, and all our kids and grandkids!" Dorie declared.

"And to us," Megan Dautrey added, the tiniest tremor in her voice. "The survivors."

"And even to our elders," Lu snuck in, then limped up to the head of the table and held her glass aloft, fanning away a bright flush with the other hand. "Nonna insists I come right over after lunch as something weird is going on at the Golden Age. Since I told her about Raul's murder and our part in solving it, she's convinced we can help. Naturally."

"Naturally," Ada crooned, lifting her glass high to meet Lu's. "To Nonna, too. And to all Women on Fire everywhere. May they blaze brightly but eat plenty of tofu forevermore!"

Laughter and "Here-here!" echoed around the table until the menus were passed, the choices exclaimed over, and the question plaintively asked more than once, "Is there something good and very chocolate for dessert? I'm saving room for that."

"Saving room? To heck with that. Life's too short. Today I'm starting with dessert!"

Meet

Eleanor S. Sullo

Eleanor Sullo writes a food and spirituality column and gardens voraciously all-year-round. Between traveling and writing, she directs programs for families and adults and spends enough time with strong women to feel their inspiration and support, along with that of her terrific husband and extended family who all live on a self-sufficient family farm in rural Connecticut. Her ongoing commitment to help others face life's trials and grow has evolved from her training as teacher and spiritual guide. As with the besieged characters in **The Moonrakers**, and in **Menopause Murders**, so often love is the answer, says Ms. Sullo, while faith and trust, and a sense of humor, put the frosting on the cake